Tom Clancy's Op-Centre
Acts of War

D1352538

CREATED BY
TOM CLANCY & STEVE PIECZENIK
WRITTEN BY JEFF ROVIN

BY TOM CLANCY

BY STEVE PIECZENIK

TOM CLANCY'S

Op-Centre

ACTS
OF WAR

CREATED BY

Tom Clancy
AND
Steve Pieczenik

Written by

JEFF ROVIN

HarperCollins*Publishers*

This novel is entirely a work of fiction.
The names, characters and incidents portrayed in it are
the work of the author's imagination. Any resemblance to
actual persons, living or dead, events or localities is
entirely coincidental.

HarperCollins*Publishers*
77–85 Fulham Palace Road
Hammersmith, London, W6 8JB

www.harpercollins.co.uk

Special overseas edition 1997
This paperback edition 2004
2

First published in the USA by
Berkley Books 1997

A catalogue record for this book
is available from the British Library

ISBN 978 0 00 786999 2

Set in Times

Printed and bound in Great Britain by
Clays Ltd, St Ives plc

Acknowledgments

We would like to thank Jeff Rovin for his creative ideas and his invaluable contributions to the preparation of the manuscript. We would also like to acknowledge the assistance of Martin H. Greenberg, Larry Segriff, Robert Youdelman, Esq., Tom Mallon, Esq., and the wonderful people at The Putnam Berkley Group, including Phyllis Grann, David Shanks, and Elizabeth Beier. As always, we would like to thank Robert Gottlieb of The William Morris Agency, our agent and friend, without whom this book would never have been conceived. But most important, it is for you, our readers, to determine how successful our collective endeavor has been.

—Tom Clancy and Steve Pieczenik

Middle

East

TOM CLANCY'S

Op-Centre

ACTS
OF WAR

ONE

Monday, 11:00 a.m., Qamishli, Syria

Ibrahim al-Rashid raised his sunglasses. He peered through the dirty window of the 1963 Ford Galaxy.

The young Syrian kept his eyes open, and enjoyed the jolt of sunlight as it bounced off the golden desert. He enjoyed the pain just as he enjoyed the heat on his face, the hot air in his lungs, the warm perspiration on his back. He enjoyed the discomfort as the Prophets must have enjoyed it, the men who came to the desert to be hammered on the anvil of God, made ready for His great purpose.

Anyway, he thought, enjoy it or not, most of Syria is a furnace in the summer. The car's struggling fan did little to relieve the heat, and the presence of three other men raised it even higher.

Ibrahim's elder brother Mahmoud was beside him in the driver's seat. Though Mahmoud was sweating heavily, he was uncharacteristically calm, even when the newer, faster Peugeots and Fiats passed them on the divided highway. Mahmoud didn't want to get into a fight, not now. But when it was time to fight, there was no one bolder. Even when they were children, Mahmoud had always been ready to take on larger boys in greater numbers. Behind them, in the back seat, Yousef and Ali played cards for a piastre a hand. Each loss was accompanied by a mild oath. Neither man suffered defeat graciously, which was why they were here.

The restored eight cylinder engine moved them smoothly along the modern Route 7. The Galaxy was ten years older than Ibrahim and had been rebuilt many times, most recently by himself. But the trunk was spacious enough to hold what they needed, the chassis was solid, and the car was strong. Like this nation of Arabs, Kurds, Armenians, Circassians, and many others, the Galaxy had been cobbled together from many parts, some old and some new. But still it moved forward.

Ibrahim looked out at the blanched landscape. It wasn't like the desert in the south, all sand and dust clouds, shimmering mirages and graceful twisters, the black tents of Bedouins and occasional oases. It was an endless stretch of dried and broken dirt, of barren hills and hundreds of tells—mounds of ruins that marked the cites of ancient settlements. There were a few modern additions to the landscape, such as abandoned vehicles and petrol stations as well as sheds where people sold stale food and hot drink. The Syrian desert had always been a lure for adventurers and poets, caravans and archaeologists who embraced and then romanticized its dangers. But this region located between the great Tigris and Euphrates had once been *alive*. Not like it was now. Not like it was before the Turks began to strangle the water supply.

Ibrahim thought back to this morning, to words his father had said to them all before they set out.

"Water is life. Control one and you control the other."

Ibrahim knew the history and geography of the region and its water. He had put in two tours of duty in the Air Force. Since his discharge, he'd listened to the old hands talk about drought and famine as he repaired tractors and other machinery on a large farm.

Formerly known as Mesopotamia, Greek for "the land between the rivers," the Syrian land was now called al-Gezira, "the island." An island without water.

The Tigris River was once one of the most important transportation routes in the world. It originates in eastern Turkey and flows nearly 1,150 miles southeast through Iraq, where it meets the Euphrates at Basra. The equally mighty Euphrates is formed by the confluence of the Kara and Murad Rivers in Eastern Turkey. It flows mostly southward and then southeast for almost 1,700 miles, surging through great canyons and jagged gorges along its upper course, and a vast flood plain in Syria and Iraq. Where they meet, the Tigris and the Euphrates form the river channel Shatt al Arab, which flows southeast into the Persian Gulf and is part of the border between Iraq and Iran. The two countries have long fought over navigation rights to the 120 mile waterway.

The Tigris and Euphrates in the east and the great Nile River in the west once defined the Fertile Crescent, the cradle of a number of early civilizations stretching back as far as 5000 B.C.

The Cradle of Civilization, Ibrahim thought. His homeland. One third of his great nation, now lifeless and rotting.

Over the centuries, warships came down the Euphrates and tribes were forced to move west. The waterwheels and irrigation canals in the east were neglected as the western part of the country grew—the line of great cities stretching from Aleppo in the north down through Hama, Homs, and eternal Damascus. The Euphrates was abandoned, and then it was murdered. Its once-bright waters were turned brown with industrial and human waste, most of it from Turkey, and not even the melting mountain snows or heavy rains could cleanse it. In the 1980s, Turkey began a massive reclamation project by constructing a series of dams along the upper course of the Euphrates. This effort helped to clean the river and keep Turkey fertile. But it caused the north of Syria and especially al-Gezira to fall further into drought and starvation.

And Syria did nothing to prevent it, Ibrahim thought bitterly. There was Israel to fight in the southwest and Iraq to watch in the southeast. The Syrian government did not want its entire northern border, over four hundred miles, jeopardized by tension with the Turks.

More recently, however, there had been other voices. They had grown increasingly loud in 1996, after repeated, vicious attacks against the Kurds. Thousands of Kurds died in clashes with the Turks in the Hakkari Province near the border with Iraq. Thousands more died when Sadam Hussein used poison gas on Kurds at Halabja. The bloodshed was made worse by infighting among the various Kurdish sects—battles over land, over tradition, over the degree of interaction that would be tolerated with non-Kurds.

Finally, a truce was called by the ailing Mullah Mustafa Mirza, leader of the small but powerful Mirza clan in Iraq. He asked for unity. And the charismatic Walid al-Nasri, leader of the PKK, the Kurdistan Workers Party, agreed to help provide it.

Over the past few months, Ibrahim had spent all of his free time in Haseke, a quiet city to the southwest, working with the local patriots in the PKK of which his brother was an officer. As he made sure printing presses and cars were working as they were supposed to, Ibrahim had listened eagerly to Mahmoud's views about establishing a homeland. As he helped carry guns and bomb-making material under the cover of night, Ibrahim had listened to their bitter debates about unification with other Kurdish factions. As he relaxed after helping to train small groups of fighting men, he'd listened as arrangements were made to meet with Iraqi and Turkish Kurds, to plan for a homeland, to select a leader.

Ibrahim put his sunglasses back on. The world became dark again.

Today, the only reason most people cross al-Gezira is to travel to Turkey. That was true for Ibrahim, though he wasn't most people. Most people came with cameras to photograph the bazaars or the World War I trenches or the mosques. They came with maps and picks for archaeological digs, or with American jeans or Japanese electronics to sell on the black market.

Ibrahim and his team came with something else. A purpose. To return the waters to al-Gezira.

TWO

Monday, 1:22 p.m., Sanliurfa, Turkey

Attorney Lowell Coffey II stood on the shaded side of a nondescript, six-wheel white trailer and touched the hem of his red neckerchief. He dabbed away the sweat that was dripping into his eyes. He silently cursed the hum of the battery-powered engine that told him the air-conditioning was running inside the van. Then he stared across barren terrain, which was dotted with dry hills. Three hundred yards away was a deserted asphalt road that rippled beneath the afternoon heat. Beyond that, separated by three barren miles and more than five thousand years, was the city of Sanliurfa.

Thirty-three-year-old biophysicist Dr. Phil Katzen stood to the attorney's right. The long-haired scientist shielded his eyes as he looked toward the dusty outline of the ancient metropolis.

"Did you know, Lowell," Katzen said, "that ten thousand years ago, right where we're standing, is where beasts of burden were first domesticated? They were aurochs—wild ox. They tilled the soil right under our feet."

"That's great," Coffey said. "And you can probably

tell me what the soil composition was then too. Right?''

"No.'' Katzen smiled. "Only now. All of the nations in this region have to keep records like that to see how long the farmlands'll hold out. I've got the soil file on diskette. As soon as Mike and Mary Rose are finished, I'll load it up if you want to read it.''

"No, thanks,'' Coffey said. "I have enough trouble retaining all the goddamn information I'm supposed to learn. I'm getting old, y'know.''

"You're thirty-nine,'' Katzen said.

"Not much longer,'' Coffey said. "I was born forty years ago tomorrow.''

Katzen grinned. "Well, happy birthday, counselor.''

"Thanks,'' Coffey said, "but it won't be. Like I said, I'm getting old, Phil.''

"Don't knock it,'' Katzen said. He pointed toward Sanliurfa. "When that place was young, forty *was* old. Back then most people lived to be about twenty. And not a healthy twenty at that. They were plagued by rotten teeth, broken bones, bad eyesight, athlete's foot, you-name-it. Hell, today the voting age in Turkey is twenty-one. Do you realize that ancient leaders in places like Uludere, Sirnak, and Batman couldn't even have voted for themselves?''

Coffey looked at him. "There's a place called Batman?''

"Right on the Tigris,'' Katzen said. "See? There's always something new to learn. I spent a couple hours this morning learning about the ROC. Helluva machine Matt and Mary Rose designed. Knowledge keeps you young, Lowell.''

"Learning about Batman and the ROC aren't exactly things to live for,'' Coffey said. "And as far as your ancient Turks are concerned, with all the planting and

7

sowing and irrigating and rock-hauling those people did, forty years old probably felt like eighty.''

"True enough."

"And their life's work was probably the same job they'd been doing since they were ten," Coffey said. "Nowadays we're supposed to live longer and evolve, professionally.''

"You trying to say you haven't?" Katzen asked.

"I've evolved like the dodo," Coffey said. "Stasis and then extinction. By this time in my life I always thought I'd be an international heavy hitter, working for the President and negotiating trade and peace accords.''

"Ease up, Lowell," Katzen said. "You're in the arena.''

"Yeah," Coffey replied. "The nosebleed seats. I'm working for a low-profile government agency nobody's ever heard of—''

"Low-profile doesn't mean lack of distinction," Katzen pointed out.

"It does in my end of the arena," Coffey replied. "I work in a basement at Andrews Air Force Base—not even Washington, D.C., for God's sake—brokering necessary but unexciting deals with grudgingly hospitable nations like Turkey so that we can all spy on even less hospitable nations like Syria. On top of that, I'm roasting in the freakin' desert, sweat running down my legs into my goddamn socks, instead of arguing First Amendment cases in front of the Supreme Court.''

"You're also starting to whine," Katzen said.

"Guilty," Coffey said. "Birthday boy's prerogative."

Katzen pushed up the back of Coffey's felted wool Australian Outback hat so it covered his eyes. "Lighten up. Not every useful job has to be a sexy one.''

"It isn't that," Coffey replied. "Well, maybe just a little it is." He removed the Outback hat, used his index finger to wipe sweat from around the band, then settled the hat back on his dirty blond hair. "I guess what I'm really saying is that I was a law prodigy, Phil. The Mozart of jurisprudence. I was reading my dad's statute law books when I was twelve. When all my friends wanted to be astronauts or baseball players, I was thinking it'd be cool to be a bail bondsman. I *could've* done most of this stuff when I was fourteen or fifteen."

"Your suits would've been way too large," Katzen deadpanned.

Coffey frowned. "You know what I'm saying."

"You're saying you haven't lived up to your potential," Katzen said. "Well, ditto, ditto, and welcome to the real world."

"Being one disappointment among many doesn't make it sit any better, Phil," Coffey replied.

Katzen shook his head. "All I can say is, I wish I'd had you at my side when I was with Greenpeace."

"Sorry," Coffey said. "I don't hurl my body off ship decks to protect baby harp seals or stop six-foot-six hunters from setting out raw meat to draw out black bears."

"I did both of those once," Katzen said. "I got my nose broke doing one and scared the hell out of the harp seal doing the other. The point is, I had these pro bono slackers who didn't know a porpoise from a dolphin. What's worse was they didn't give a shit. I was in your office when you negotiated our little visit with the Turkish ambassador. You gave it everything and you created a handsome piece of work."

"I was dealing with a country that's got forty billion dollars of external debt, most of it to our country," Coffey said. "Getting them to see our point of view doesn't exactly put me in the genius class."

"Bull," Katzen said. "The Islamic Development

Bank holds a lot of Turkish chits as well, and they exert a lot of pro-fundamentalist pressure on these people."

"Islamic law can't be imposed on the Turks," Coffey replied, "not even by a fiercely fundamentalist leader like the one they've got now. It says so in their Constitution."

"Constitutions can be amended," Katzen said. "Look at Iran."

"The secular population in Turkey is much higher," Coffey said. "If the Fundamentalists ever tried to take over here, there'd be civil war."

"Who can say there won't be?" Katzen asked. "Anyway, none of that is the point. You sprinted through NATO regulations, Turkish law, and U.S. policy to get us in here. No one else I know could've done that."

"So I had to cajole a little," Coffey said. "Even so, the Turkish deal was probably the high point of my year. When we return to Washington it'll be business as usual. I'll go to see Senator Fox with Paul Hood and Martha Mackall. I'll nod when Paul assures the senator that everything we did in Turkey was legal, that the soil studies you did in the east will be shared with Ankara and were the 'real' reason we were here, and I'll guarantee that if the Regional Op-Center program receives further funding we will continue to operate legally. Then I'll go back to my office and figure out how to use the ROC in ways not covered by international law." Coffey shook his head. "I know that's how things have to be done, but it's not dignified."

"At least *we* try to be," Katzen pointed out.

"*You* try to be," Coffey said. "You spend your career looking into nuclear accidents and oil fires and pollution. You make a difference, or at least you challenge yourself. I went into law to wrestle with real global issues, not to find legal loopholes for spies in Third World sweatboxes."

Katzen sighed. "You're *schvitzing*."

"What?"

"You're sweating. You're cranky. You're a day shy of forty. And you're being way too hard on yourself."

"No, too lenient." Coffey walked toward the cooler nestled in the shade of one of the three nearby tents. He saw the unopened paperback copy of *Lord Jim,* which he'd brought along to read. It had seemed an appropriate selection when he was standing in the air-conditioned Washington, D.C., bookstore. Now he wished he'd picked up *Dr. Zhivago* or *Call of the Wild.* "I think I'm having an epiphany," Coffey said, "like all those patriarchs who used to go into the desert."

"This isn't desert," Katzen said. "It's what we call nonarable pastureland."

"Thanks," Coffey said. "I'll file that next to Batman, Turkey, as something to remember."

"Jeez," Katzen said, "you really are cranky. I don't think being forty is what's doing this. I think the heat's dried up your brains."

"Could be," Coffey said. "Maybe that's why everyone's always been at war in this part of the world. You ever hear about the Eskimos fighting over ice floes or penguin eggs?"

"I've visited the Inuit on the Bering Coast," Katzen said. "They don't fight with each other because they have a different outlook on life. Religion is comprised of two elements: faith and culture. The Inuit have faith without fanaticism, and to them it's a very private matter. The culture is the public part. They share wisdom, tradition, and fables instead of insisting that their way is the only way. The same is true of many tropical and

11

sub-tropical peoples in Africa, South America, and the Far East. It has nothing to do with the climate.''

"I don't believe that about the climate," Coffey said. "At least, not entirely." He removed a can of Tab from the melting ice in the cooler and popped it. As he poured the soda into his mouth, he squinted back at the long, gleaming van. For a moment, the despair left him. That seemingly nondescript vehicle *was* beautiful and sexy. He was proud to be associated with it, at least. The attorney stopped drinking and caught his breath. "I mean," he said, panting after the long, unbroken swallow, "look at cities or prisons where there are riots. Or compounds like Jonestown and Waco where people turn into cult-kooks. It never happens during a cold spell or a blizzard. It's always when it's hot. Look at the Biblical scholars who went out into the desert. Went out men, stayed in the heat, came back prophets. Heat lights our fuses."

"You don't think that God could have had anything to do with Moses and Jesus?" Katzen asked solemnly.

Coffey raised the can to his lips. "Touché," he said before he drank again.

Katzen turned to the young black woman standing to his right. She was dressed in khaki shorts, a sweat-stained khaki blouse, and a white headband. The uniform was "sterile." Nowhere did she display the winged-lightning shield of the rapid-deployment Striker force to which she belonged. Nor was there any other sign of military affiliation. Like the van itself, whose side-mounted mirror looked just like a mirror and not a parabolic dish, whose walls were intentionally dented and artificially rusted and didn't show a hint of the reinforced steel underneath, the woman looked like she was a seasoned archaeological field worker.

"What do you think, Sondra?" Katzen asked.

"With all due respect," said the young black woman, "I think you're both wrong. I think peace and war and sanity are all questions of leadership. Look at that old city out there." She spoke with quiet reverence. "Thirty centuries ago the prophet Abraham was born—*right* there. That was where he lived when God told him to move his family to Canaan. That man was touched by the Holy Spirit. He founded a people, a nation, a morality. I'm sure he was as warm as we are, especially when God told him to put a dagger into the bosom of his son. I'm sure his sweat as well as his tears fell onto the frightened face of Isaac." She looked from Katzen to Coffey. "His leadership was based on faith and love, and he is revered by Jews and Muslims alike."

"Nicely put, Private DeVonne," Katzen said.

"Very nicely put," Coffey agreed, "but it doesn't contradict my point. We're not all made of the same obedient, determined stuff as Abraham. And for some of us, the heat makes our natural irritability worse." He took another long drink from his sweating can of Tab. "There's another thing too. After twenty-seven hours and fifteen minutes of camping here, I hate the living hell out of this place. I like air conditioning and cold water from a glass instead of hot water from a plastic bottle. And bathrooms. Those are good too."

Katzen smiled. "Maybe you'll appreciate them a whole lot more when you get back."

"I appreciated them before I left. Frankly, I still don't understand why we couldn't have tested this prototype in the U.S. We have enemies at home. I could have gotten clearance from any number of judges to spy on suspected terrorists, paramilitary camps, Mafiosi, you-name-it."

"You know the answer as well as I do," Katzen said.

"Sure," Coffey said. He drained the can of soda,

dropped it in the plastic trash bag, and walked back to the van. "If we don't help the moderate True Path Party, the Islamic fundamentalists and their Welfare Party will continue to make gains here. And then you've got the Social Democratic Populist Party, the Democratic Left Party, the Democratic Center Party, the Reform Democratic Party, the Prosperity Party, the Refah Party, the Socialist Unity Party, the Correct Way Party, and the Great Anatolia Party, all of which have to be dealt with and all of whom want their piece of the very small Turkish pie. Not to mention the Kurds, who want freedom from the Turks, Iraqis, and Syrians." Coffey used his index fingers to wipe sweat from his eyes. "If the Welfare Party does happen to take control of Turkey and its military, Greece will be threatened. Disputes in the Aegean Sea will come to a head and NATO will be torn apart. Europe and the Middle East will be endangered and everyone will turn to the U.S. for help. We'll gladly provide it, of course, but only in the form of shuttle diplomacy. We can't afford to take sides in a war like that."

"Excellent summation, counselor."

"Except for one thing," Coffey continued. "For my money, they can all take a flying leap. This isn't like when you took a leave of absence to save the spotted owl from loggers."

"Stop," Katzen said. "You're embarrassing me. I'm not all that virtuous."

"I'm not talking about virtue," Coffey said. "I'm talking about being committed to something worthwhile. You went to Oregon, did your on-site protest, testified at the state legislature, and got the problem solved. This situation is fifty centuries years old. Ethnic factions have always fought one another here and they always will.

We can't stop them, and it's a waste of valuable resources even trying."

"I disagree," Katzen replied. "We *can* mitigate the situation. And who knows? Maybe the next five thousand years *will* be better."

"Or maybe the U.S. will get sucked into a religious war that'll tear us apart," Coffey replied. "I'm an isolationist at heart, Phil. That's one thing Senator Fox and I have in common. We've got the best country in the history of the world, and those who don't want to join us in the democratic melting pot can shoot, bomb, gas, nuke, and martyr each other until they're all in Paradise. I really don't care."

Katzen scowled. "That's one point of view, I suppose."

"Damn right," Coffey replied. "And I'm not apologizing for it. But there is one thing you can tell me."

"What?" Katzen asked.

Coffey's mouth twisted. "What *is* the difference between a porpoise and a dolphin?"

Before he could answer, the door of the van opened and Mike Rodgers stepped out. Coffey savored the blast of air-conditioning before the ramrod-straight general shut the door. He was dressed in jeans and a tight gray Gettysburg Campaign souvenir T-shirt. His light brown eyes seemed almost golden in the bright sun.

Mike Rodgers rarely smiled, but Coffey noticed the hint of a grin tugging at the side of his mouth.

"So?" Coffey asked.

"It's running," Rodgers said. "We were able to uplink to all five of the selected National Reconnaissance Office satellites. We have video, audio, and thermal views of the target region as well as complete electronic surveillance. Mary Rose is talking to Matt Stoll right now, making sure all of the data is getting

15

through." Rodgers's reluctant smile bloomed. "The battery-powered son of a gun works."

Katzen offered him his hand. "Congratulations, General. Matt must be ecstatic."

"Yeah, he's a pretty happy fella," Rodgers said. "After everything we went through to put the ROC together, I'm pretty happy myself."

Coffey toasted General Rodgers with a swig from the water bottle. "Forget everything I said, Phil. If Mike Rodgers is pleased, then we really must've batted one out of the park."

"Grand slam," Rodgers said, "That's the good news. The bad news is that the chopper which is supposed to take you and Phil to Lake Van's been delayed."

"For how long?" Katzen asked.

"Permanently," said Rodgers. "Seems someone in the Motherland Party objects to the excursion. They don't buy our ecology cover story, that we're out here to study the rising alkaline levels of Turkish waterways and its percolation effect on the soil."

"Aw, jeez," Katzen said. "What the hell do they think we want to do out there?"

"You ready for this?" Rodgers asked. "They believe we've found Noah's Ark and that we plan to take it to the U.S. They want the Council of Ministers to cancel our permits."

Katzen angrily jabbed the toe of his boot at the parched ground. "I really did want to have a look at that lake. It's got just one species of fish, the *darek*, which evolved to survive in the soda-rich water. We can learn a lot about adaptation from it."

"Sorry," Rodgers said. "We're going to have to do some adapting of our own." He looked over at Coffey. "What do you know about this Motherland Party, Lowell? Do they have enough power to screw up our shakedown session?''

Coffey dragged the kerchief along his strong jaw and then across the back of his neck. "Probably not," he said, "though you might want to check with Martha. They're pretty strong and considerably right-of-center. But any debate they start will go back and forth between the Prime Minister and the Motherlanders for two or three days before it's brought to the Grand National Assembly for a vote. I don't know about Phil's excursion, but I think that'll give us the time to do what we came here for."

Rodgers nodded. He turned to Sondra. "Private DeVonne, the Deputy Prime Minister also told me that leaflets are being passed out in the streets, informing citizens about our plan to rob Turkey of its heritage. The government is sending an intelligence agent, Colonel Nejat Seden, to help us deal with any incidents. Until then, please inform Private Pupshaw that some of the people who'll be heading to the watermelon festival in Diyarbakir may be carrying a grudge as well as fruit. Tell him to stay cool.''

"Yes, sir."

Sondra saluted and jogged toward the burly Pupshaw, who was stationed on the other side of the tents. He was watching the road where it disappeared behind a row of hills.

Katzen frowned. "This is great. Not only could I miss out on the chance to study the *darek,* but we've got a hundred million dollars worth of sophisticated electronics in there. And until this Colonel Seden gets here, all we've got to protect it are two Strikers with radios on their hips and M21s, which, if they use 'em, we'll get clobbered for because we're supposed to be unarmed.''

17

"I thought you admired my diplomatic finesse," Coffey said.

"I do."

"Well, that was the best deal we could get," Coffey said. "You worked with Greenpeace. When the French secret service sunk your flagship *Rainbow Warrior* in Auckland Harbor in 1985, you didn't go out and kill Parisians."

"I wanted to," Katzen admitted. "Boy, how I wanted to."

"But you didn't. We're employees of a foreign power conducting surveillance on behalf of a minority government so that their military can keep an eye on Islamic fanatics. We don't exactly have a moral imperative to gun down locals. If we're attacked, we lock the van door, get inside, and radio the local *polisi*. They rush out here in their swift Renaults and deal with the situation."

"Unless they're Motherland sympathizers," Katzen said.

"No," Coffey replied, "the police here are pretty fair. They may not like you, but they believe in the law and they'll uphold it."

"Anyway," Rodgers said, "the DPM doesn't expect us to have that kind of trouble. At worst there'll be tossed watermelon, eggs, manure, that sort of thing."

"Terrific," Katzen said. "At least in Washington they only sling mud."

"If it ever rained here," Coffey said, "we'd get that too."

Rodgers held out his hand and Coffey passed him the water. After taking a long swallow the general said, "Cheer up. As Tennessee Williams once said, 'Don't look forward to the day you stop suffering, because when it comes you'll *know* you're dead.'"

18

THREE

Monday, 6:48 a.m.,
Chevy Chase, Maryland

Paul Hood sat sipping black coffee in the den of his comfortable suburban home. He'd opened the ivory-colored drapes, had cracked the sliding glass door an inch, and was looking across the backyard. Hood had traveled the world and was intimately familiar with many parts of it. But there was nothing that thrilled him as much as the dirty-white picket fence that marked his small part of it.

The grass was glistening-green, and a warm breeze carried the smell of roses from his wife's tiny garden. Eastern bluebirds and yellow warblers were lively with song, and squirrels were acting like furry little Strikers as they moved, stopped, reconnoitered, then moved again. The rustic tranquility was broken now and then by what the jazz-loving Hood called the morning door jam: the slap of a screen door, the groan of a garage door, or the slam of a car door.

To Hood's right was a dark oak bookcase filled with Sharon's well-used volumes on gardening and cooking. The shelves were also packed with the encyclopedias, atlases, and dictionaries Harleigh and Alexander didn't consult anymore since all that material was on CD-ROM. Then there was a small corner section for Hood's own favorite novels. *Ben-Hur. From Here to Eternity. The War of the Worlds. Tender Is the Night.* Works by Ayn Rand, Ray Bradbury, and Robert Louis Stevenson. Old Lone Ranger novels by Fran Striker that Hood had read as a kid and went back to every now and then. To Hood's left were shelves filled with mementoes of his tenure as the mayor of Los Angeles. Plaques, mugs, keys to other cities, and photographs with domestic and foreign dignitaries.

The coffee and fresh air were equally invigorating. His lightly starched shirt was comfortable. And his new shoes felt rich, even though they weren't. He remembered when his father couldn't afford to buy him new shoes. It was thirty-five years ago, when Paul was nine and President Kennedy had been assassinated. His father, Frank "Battleship" Hood, a Navy man during the Second World War, had quit one accounting job to take another. The Hoods had sold their house and were about to move from Long Island to Los Angeles when the new firm put a sudden freeze on hiring. The firm was very, very sorry but they didn't know what was going to happen to the company, to the economy, to the country. His father didn't work for thirteen months after that, and they had to move into a small apartment. An apartment small enough so he could hear his mother consoling his father when he cried at night.

Now here he was. Relatively affluent and the director of Op-Center. In less than a year, Hood and his core team had turned the agency, formally known as the National Crisis Management Center, from a liaison office between the CIA, the White House, and the other big boys to a crisis-management team in its own right. Hood had an often fractious relationship with some of his closest people, most notably Deputy Director Mike Rodgers, Intelligence Officer Bob Herbert, and Political and Economics Officer Martha Mackall. But he welcomed the differences of opinion. Besides, if he couldn't manage personality clashes in his office, he couldn't handle political and military clashes thousands of miles away. The desk-side skirmishes kept him alert and in shape for the bigger, more important battles.

Hood drank his coffee slowly. Virtually every morning he sat comfortably alone on this sofa. He surveyed his life and invited contentment to lap him like an island. But it rarely did. Not on all sides, anyway. There was a hole, much larger in the month since he'd returned from Germany. A void which had been filled unexpectedly with passion. Passion for his one-time love Nancy, whom he'd met in Hamburg after twenty years. Passion that burned on the beach of his little island and disturbed his rest at night and fought for attention during the day.

But it was passion that he had not and could not act upon. Not unless he wanted to destroy the people for whom this home and this life *were* contentment. The children to whom he was a constant and reliable source of strength and emotional security. The wife who respected and trusted him and said she loved him. Well, she probably did. She probably loved him in the same buddy-sisterly-shared-goals way that he loved her. Which wasn't bad, even though it wasn't what he felt for Nancy.

Hood drained his mug, regretting that the last mouthful never tasted as glorious as the first. Not in coffee, not in life. He rose, put the mug in the dishwasher, grabbed his trench coat from the closet, and walked into the balmy morning.

Hood drove southeast through Washington, D.C., to

Op-Center's headquarters at Andrews Air Force Base. He negotiated traffic that was already thick with trucks, Mercedes, and fleets of overnight courier vans rushing to make morning deliveries. He wondered how many people were thinking like he was, how many were cursing the traffic, and how many were just enjoying the drive, the morning, and some upbeat music.

He plugged in a tape of Spanish gypsy music, a love he'd acquired from his Cuban-born grandfather. The car filled with Romany lyrics whose words he didn't understand but whose passion he did. And as the music washed over him, Hood tried once again to fill the gaps in his contentment.

FOUR

Monday, 7:18 a.m.,
Washington, D.C.

Matthew Stoll disdained the traditional labels for "his kind." He loathed them almost as much as he hated chronic optimists, unreasonably high prices for software, and curry. As he'd been telling all his friends and co-workers since his days as an MIT wunderkind—a term he *didn't* mind—he was not a computer nerd, a techno-weenie, or an egghead.

"I think of myself as a techsplorer," he'd told Paul Hood and Mike Rodgers when he first interviewed for the job of Operations Support Officer.

"Excuse me?" Hood had said.

"I explore technology," the cherubic Stoll had replied. "I'm like Meriwether Lewis, except I'll need more than his twenty-five-hundred-dollar Congressional appropriation to open up vast new technological lands. I also hope to live past the age of thirty-five, though you never know."

Hood had later confided to Stoll that he'd found the neologism corny, though the scientist hadn't been offended. He'd known from their first meeting that "Saint

Paul'' had neither a vaulting imagination nor a sharp sense of humor. Hood was a deft, temperate, and remarkably intuitive manager. But General Rodgers was a big-time history buff, and he'd been won over by the Meriwether Lewis reference. And as Hood and Rodgers had both admitted, there was no ignoring Stoll's credentials. He'd not only finished at the top of his class at MIT, he'd finished at the top of MIT's classes for the previous two decades. Corporate America had wooed Stoll energetically and won him for a time, but he grew tired of developing new easy-to-program VCRs or sophisticated heart monitors for exercise machines. He yearned to work with state-of-the-art computers and satellites, and he wanted the kind of research and development budgets that private enterprise just couldn't provide.

He also had wanted to work with his best friend and former classmate, Stephen Viens, who headed the government's National Reconnaissance Office. Viens was the man who had arranged the Op-Center introduction for him. He also gave Stoll and his coworkers first-dibs access to NRO resources to the detriment and annoyance of his colleagues at the CIA, FBI, and Department of Defense. But they could never prove that Op-Center was getting a lion's share of satellite time. If they could, bureaucratic backlash would be severe.

Viens was on-line with Stoll at Op-Center and Mary Rose Mohalley in Turkey to make certain the data coming from the Regional Op-Center was accurate. The visual images being channeled from the spy satellites weren't as detailed as those at the NRO: The mobile equipment provided just under half of the more than one thousand lines of resolution of the NRO monitors. But they were coming in fast and accurate, and intercepts of cell-phone conversations and faxes were equal to those that were being received by both the NRO and Op-Center.

After running the last of the tests, Stoll thanked Mary Rose and told her she was free to solo. The young woman thanked him, thanked Viens, and got off the secure downlink. Viens remained on his line.

Stoll took a bite of sesame bagel and washed it down with a swallow of herbal tea. "God, I love Monday mornings," Stoll said. "Back in the harness of discovery."

"That was pretty," Viens admitted.

Stoll said through cream cheese, "We build five or six of these things, pack 'em inside planes and boats, and there isn't a corner of the world we can't watch."

"You do that and you'll put me out of business faster than the Senate Intelligence Committee," Viens cracked.

Stoll looked at his friend's face on the monitor. The screen was the center one of three built into the wall beside Stoll's desk. "That's just a frosh dingbat's witch-hunt," Stoll said. "Nobody's going to put you out of business,"

"You don't know this Senator Landwehr," Viens replied. "He's like a little dog with a very large bone. He's made it his personal crusade to put an end to forward funding."

Forward funding, Stoll thought. Of all the government sleights of hand, Stoll had to admit that that was the sneakiest. When money was earmarked for a specific purpose and those projects were back-burnered or altered, the funds were supposed to be given back. Three years before, two billion dollars had been given to the NRO to design, build, and launch a new series of spy satellites. Those projects were later canceled. But instead of being returned, all of the money was slipped into various other NRO accounts and disappeared. Op-

Center, the CIA, and other government agencies also lied about their finances. They created small, so-called "black budgets," which were hidden in false line items of the budget and were thus concealed from public scrutiny. Those monies were used to finance relatively modest secret intelligence and military operations. They were also used to help finance Congressional campaigns, which was why Congress allowed them to exist. But the NRO had gone too far.

When the NRO's forward funding was discovered by Frederick Landwehr, a freshman senator who used to be an accountant, he immediately brought it to the attention of the Chairman of the Senate Intelligence Committee. Congress acted swiftly to reclaim what was left of the money—with interest. And the interest included the heads of the responsible parties. Although Viens hadn't been involved in the parceling out of the money, he'd accepted budget increases for his satellite reconnaissance division knowing exactly where it came from.

"The press has to give space to a new face with a new cause," Stoll said, "I still think that when the headlines shrink, everything'll be sorted out quietly."

"Deputy Secretary of Defense Hawkins doesn't share your atypical optimism," Viens said.

"What are you talking about?" Stoll asked. "I saw the Hawk on the news last night. Every coif with a mike who accused him of mismanagement got his or her nose bit off."

"Meanwhile, the Deputy Secretary is already looking for a job in the private sector."

"What?" Stoll said.

"And it's only been two weeks since the forward funding was uncovered. There are going to be a lot more defections." Viens raised his eyebrows forlornly. "It really sucks, Matt. I finally get my Conrad and I can't even enjoy it."

The Conrads were an unofficial award given at a private dinner every year by the foremost figures in American intelligence. The dagger-like trophy was named after Joseph Conrad, whose 1907 novel, *The Secret Agent,* was one of the first great espionage tales. Viens had coveted the award for years, and had finally won it.

Stoll said, "I think you're going to weather this thing. There won't be a real investigation. Too many secrets'll be made public. There'll be some wrist-slapping, the money will be found and returned to the treasury, and they'll watch your budget more closely for the next couple of years. Just like a personal audit."

"Matt," Viens said, "there's something else."

"There always is. Action followed by an equal and opposite reaction. What else are they planning?"

"I hear they're going to subpoena our diskettes."

That got Stoll's attention. His round, beefy shoulders rose slowly. The diskettes were time- and destination-coded. They would show that Op-Center was getting a disproportionate amount of satellite time.

"How solid's your info?" Stoll asked.

"Very," Viens said.

There was a sudden gurgling in Stoll's belly. "You, uh—didn't get that yourself, did you?"

Stoll was asking Viens whether he'd ordered surveillance on Landwehr. He prayed that his friend had not.

"Please, Matt," Viens said.

"Just making sure. Pressure can do funny things to sane people."

"Not me," Viens said. "Thing is, I won't be able to do much for you during the rest of the shakedown. I've got to give the other bureaus whatever time they need."

"I understand," Stoll said. "Don't sweat it."

Viens smiled halfheartedly. "My psych profile says I never sweat anything," he said. "Worst that happens is I follow the Hawk into the private sector."

"Bull-do. You'd be as miserable as I was. Look," Stoll said, "let's not go counting Mother Carey's chickens before the storm hits. If the Hawk flies the coop, maybe that'll take some of the pressure off."

"That's a slim maybe."

"But it's a possibility," Stoll said. He glanced at the clock in the lower right corner of the screen. "I'm supposed to see the boss at seven-thirty to let him know how the ROC is working. Why don't we have dinner tonight? On Op-Center."

"I promised the missus we'd go out."

"Fine," Stoll said. "I'll pick you both up. What time?"

"How's seven?" Viens asked.

"Perfect," said Stoll.

"My wife was expecting candles and hand-holding. She'll kill me."

"It'll save Landwehr the trouble," Stoll pointed out. "See you at seven."

Stoll clicked off feeling miserable. Sure, Viens had given him access to the NRO, but Op-Center had had the crises to justify that access. And what did it matter whether Op-Center or the Secret Service or the NYPD needed assistance? They were all on the same team.

Stoll phoned Hood's executive assistant, "Bugs" Benet, who said the chief had just arrived. Finishing his tea and engulfing the second half of his bagel, the portly young chief technical officer strode from his office.

FIVE

Monday, 2:30 p.m., Qamishli, Syria

Ibrahim was asleep when the car eased to a stop. He awoke suddenly.

"Imshee . . . imshee—!" he cried as he looked around. Yousef and Ali were still playing cards in the backseat. Ibrahim's eyes settled on the round, dark face of his brother, which was sleek with sweat. Mahmoud was looking in the rearview mirror.

"Good afternoon," Mahmoud said dryly.

Ibrahim removed his sunglasses and rubbed his eyes. "Mahmoud," he said with obvious relief.

"Yes," his brother said with a half-smile. "It's Mahmoud. Who was it that you wished would leave you alone?"

Ibrahim put his sunglasses on the dashboard. "I don't know. A man. I couldn't see his face. We were in a market and he wanted me to go somewhere."

"Probably to see a new automobile or an airplane or some other device," Mahmoud said. " 'Friend Ibrahim, I am the djinn of dreams and I will take you anywhere you want to go. Tell me. Would you like to meet a

29

beautiful young woman who will be your wife?' 'Oh, thank you, djinn. You are most generous. But if you have a motorboat or a computer, I would very much enjoy making their acquaintance.' "

Ibrahim scowled. "Where is it written that one cannot enjoy speed and power and machines?"

"Nowhere, my brother," Mahmoud replied. He turned from his brother and looked up at the rearview mirror.

"I like women," Ibrahim said. "But women like children and I do not. So we are stalemated. Do you understand?"

"I do," said Mahmoud. "But you miss the point. I have a wife. I see her one night a week for an evening of fire. I kiss the sleeping children before I leave in the morning, then go off to do my work with Walid. I am content."

"That is you," Ibrahim said. "When it is time, I want to be more of a husband, more of a father than that."

"If you find a woman who wants that or needs it," said Mahmoud, "I will be very happy for you."

"Shukran," Ibrahim said. "Thank you." He yawned and vigorously dug his palms into his eyes.

"Afwan," replied Mahmoud. "You're welcome." He squinted into the rearview mirror for a moment and then opened the door. "Now, Ibrahim, if you've washed away the dust of sleep, our brothers are arriving."

Ibrahim looked ahead as two cars passed them and pulled off the road. Both were large, old cars, a Cadillac and a Dodge. Beyond the two vehicles, less than a quarter of a mile distant, were the first low-lying stone buildings of Qamishli. They were misty gray shapes rippled in the radiant heat of the burning afternoon.

Ibrahim, Mahmoud, and their two companions emerged from their car. As they walked ahead, a 707 came in low headed for a landing at the nearby airport. The noise of the engines rumbled loud and long across the flat wasteland.

As Ibrahim and his party approached, three men emerged from the Cadillac, four from the Dodge. All but one were clean-shaven and dressed in jeans and button-down shirts. The exception was Walid al-Nasri. Because the Prophet had worn a beard and a loose-fitting *abaya*, so did he. The seven men had come up from Raqqa, in the southwest corner of al-Gezira on the Euphrates. It was partly the desperate plight of their once-fertile city that had driven Walid to become active in the movement. And it was the strength and conviction of their newly chosen leader, Commander Kayahan Siriner, that kept Walid and the others active.

The seven Kurds welcomed the others with heartfelt hugs and smiles and the traditional greeting of *Al-salaam aleikum*, "Peace be upon you." Ibrahim and the others replied with a respectful *Wa aleikum al-salaam*, "And upon you be peace." They gave their confederates equally warm embraces. But the warmth quickly gave way to the business at hand.

The man in the robe spoke to Mahmoud. "Do you have everything?"

"We do, Walid."

Walid squinted at the Ford. As he did, Ibrahim regarded the revered leader of their band. His features were extremely dark, and the thick beard hid most of the lower half of his long face. The salt-and-pepper expanse was broken only by a long, diagonal scar that ran from the left corner of his mouth to just behind his chin. It was a memento of the June 1982 Israeli invasion of Lebanon, when his was one of over eighty Syrian planes shot down in the Bekaa Valley. Ibrahim felt humbled to

31

be with him and deeply honored to be serving under him.

"The trunk of your automobile," Walid said. "It appears light."

"Aywa," Mahmoud said. "Yes. We put many of the weapons under the front and back seats. We did not want to be back-heavy."

"Why?"

"American satellites," Mahmoud said. "Our man at the palace in Damascus says that the satellites can see everywhere and everything in the Middle East. Even footprints. We have crossed sand in many places, and these satellites are able to measure the depth of tire tracks."

"They dare to be like unto the Mighty One, the Merciful," Walid said. He turned his face toward the skies. It was a face eroded by the hot sun and years of stress. "Allah's eyes are the only ones that matter!" he cried. "But we are told to keep vigil against our enemies," he said to Mahmoud. "You've acted wisely."

"Thank you," Mahmoud replied. "Also, the sentries on our own border might have noticed the weight. I didn't want them to move against them."

Walid regarded Mahmoud and his companions. "Of course not. We are peaceful, as the Koran teaches. Murder is forbidden." Walid raised his hands toward the heavens. "But killing in self-defense is not murder. If an oppressor lays violent hands upon us, are we not obliged to cut them off? If he writes ill of us, do we not sever the tips of his fingers?"

"If it is the will of God," said Mahmoud.

"It is the will of God," Walid confirmed. "We are His hand. Does the hand of God shy from an enemy, however great his numbers?"

32

"La," replied Mahmoud and the others, shaking their heads. "No."

"Is it not inscribed in the Celestial Plate, and thus inerrant? 'There was a sign for you in the two armies which met on the battlefield. One was fighting for the cause of God; the other was a host of unbelievers. The faithful saw with their very eyes that they were twice their own number. But God strengthens with His aid whom He will.' Is God not offended by our treatment at the hands of the Turks?" Walid asked, his voice rising. "Are we not the chosen instruments of God?"

"Aywa," replied Mahmoud and the others.

Ibrahim's response was quieter than that of his companions. He was no less devout than Walid or Mahmoud. But he believed, as did most, that the Koran advocated justice and not retribution. It was a matter of some debate between Ibrahim and his family, just as it was throughout Islam. Yet the Koran also taught devotion and fealty. When attacks against the Kurds had begun to intensify and Mahmoud had asked him to join the group, Ibrahim could not have refused.

Walid lowered his hands. He regarded Mahmoud's team. "Are you ready to move on?"

"We are," said Mahmoud.

"Then let us first pray," said Walid. Acting the role of the *muezzin,* the caller to worship, he shut his eyes and recited the *Adhan,* the summons to prayer. *"Allah u Akbar.* God is greater. God is greater. I witness that there is no god but God. I witness that Mohammad is the Prophet of God. Rise to prayer. Rise to felicity. God is greater. God is greater. There is no god but God."

As Walid spoke, the men removed their prayer rugs from the cars and placed them on the ground. The *qibla,* the direction of prayer, was chosen carefully. The men faced south, toward western Saudi Arabia and the holy

33

city of Mecca. Bowing low, they offered their mid-afternoon prayers. This was the third of their five daily devotions, which were given at dawn, noon, mid-afternoon, dusk, and after dark.

The prayers consisted of several minutes of private recitations from the Koran as well as personal meditations. When they were finished, the men returned to their cars. A short time later they were driving northeast toward the small, old city. As they did, Ibrahim reflected that they were one more caravan among the countless caravans that had passed this way since the beginning of civilization. Each had had its own means of travel, its own personality, its own goals. That thought gave Ibrahim a precious sense of continuity, but also of insignificance. For each set of footprints lasted no more than a moment in the impermanent sands of al-Gezira.

Qamishli passed quickly. Ibrahim paid no attention to the ancient minarets and the cluttered market. He ignored the Turks and Syrians who mingled freely in this border city. His mind was on the job and on his faith, not as separate things but as one. He reflected on how the Koran speaks of Judgment Day, the final fulfillment of both God's threat and His promise. He thought about how those who live according to the holy words and commandments will join the other faithful and the alluring, virginal *houri* in Paradise. And those who do not will spend eternity in Hell. It was that faith, intensely held, that told Ibrahim that he needed to do what he would be called upon to do.

After they passed through the village, the cars moved on toward the Turkish border. Ibrahim rolled down his window.

The border crossing consisted of two sentry posts, one behind the other. One was Syrian, the other Turkish.

There was a gate arm beside each booth and thirty yards of roadway between them. The road was weed-strewn on the Syrian side, clean on the Turkish side.

Walid's car was in the front of the caravan, Ibrahim's in the rear. Walid presented the visas and passports for his car. After the clerk examined them, he signaled an armed guard beside him to raise the gate arm.

Ibrahim began to feel the weight of destiny on his shoulders. He had a specific goal, the one Walid had selected for them. But he also had a personal mission. He was a Kurd, one of the traditionally nomadic peoples of the plateau and mountain regions of eastern Turkey, northern Syria, northeastern Iraq, and northwestern Iran.

Since the middle 1980s, the many guerrilla factions of the Kurds living and operating in Turkey had fought repression by the Turks, who feared that Kurdish autonomy would lead to a new and hostile Kurdistan comprised of portions of Turkey, Iraq, and Iran. This was not a religious issue, but a cultural, linguistic, and political one.

The undeclared war had claimed twenty thousand lives by 1996. Ibrahim did not become involved until then, when water became even scarcer in the region due to Turkish operations and his cattle began to die of thirst. Although Ibrahim had served in the Syrian Air Force as a mechanic, he had never been a militant. He believed in the Koran's teachings of peace and harmony. But he also felt that Turkey was strangling his people, and the genocide could not go unavenged.

In the two years that Ibrahim had been part of the eleven-man band, the work had taken on an importance all its own. Acts of terrorism and sabotage in Turkey were no longer just a matter of vengeance to him. As Walid had said, Allah would decide whether there was ever to be a new Kurdistan. In the meantime, the rebel actions were a way of reminding the Turks that the Kurds were determined to be free with or without a homeland.

Typically, two, three, or four of the men would sneak into the country at night, elude the border patrols, and disable a power station or pipeline or snipe at soldiers. But today's objective was different. Two months before, Turkish troops had taken advantage of a spring thaw and a unilateral cease-fire with Turkish Kurds to begin a massive offensive against the rebels. Over one hundred Kurdish freedom fighters had been killed in three days of relentless combat. The attack had been designed to quiet the western regions before Turkey turned its attention to the east. There, territorial disputes with Greece as well as tension between Christian Athens and Islamic Ankara were becoming more and more intense.

Walid and Kenan Demirel, a leader of the Turkish Kurds, had decided that the latest aggression could not go unpunished. Nor would the strike be small, worked by a team that snuck over the border. They would enter the country boldly and show the enemy that acts of oppression and betrayal would not be tolerated.

The caravan passed a black wooden stake stuck in the side of the road. They were in Turkey now. When they reached the Turkish gate, an armed guard poked the barrel of an M1A1 submachine gun through a small opening cut in the glass. His companion emerged and walked over to Walid's car. He wore a 9mm Capinda Tabanca in a crisp new holster.

The agent bent and looked into the car. "Your passports, please."

"Certainly," Walid said. He slid the bundle of small orange documents from a pocket in the visor. He smiled as he handed the documents to the official.

The small, mustachioed Turk compared the photographs to the faces in the car. He went about his work slowly and carefully. "What business have you in Turkey?" he asked.

"We are attending a funeral," Walid replied. He gestured to the cars behind him. "All of us."

"Where?"

"In Harran," Walid told him.

The guard looked back at the other cars. After a moment he asked, "The deceased had only male friends?"

"Our wives are with our children," Walid said.

"They do not mourn him?"

"We sold barley to this man," Walid replied. "Our wives and children did not know him."

"What is his name?" the guard asked.

"Tansu Ozal," Walid replied. "He died on Saturday in a car accident. He drove his car into a deep ditch."

The guard idly pulled at the hem of his green military jacket, regarded Walid for a moment, then returned to his booth. The other sentry continued to point his submachine gun at the car.

Ibrahim had listened to the conversation across the quiet stretch of road. He knew that Walid had told the truth, that this Tansu Ozal had died as he'd said. What Walid hadn't mentioned was that the man was a Kurd who had betrayed his people. He'd guided the Turks to a weapons cache under an old Roman bridge in Koprulu Kanyon. Kenan's people had killed him for his treason.

Ibrahim used a finger to wipe sweat from his eyes. He continued to perspire, as much from nerves now as from the heat. Like his own documents, Walid's papers were obtained using a false birth certificate. Walid's name, though not his likeness, was known to the Turks. Had the border guard known who he was, the Syrian would have been arrested at once.

37

The Turkish agent made a telephone call and read from each of the passports in turn. Ibrahim hated him. He was a minor official who acted as though he protected the Dome of the Rock. These Turks had no sense of priority.

Ibrahim turned his attention to the armed guard. From their planning sessions, Ibrahim knew that if anyone in the car were wanted by the authorities or seemed suspicious, the guard would shoot the tires out of hand. If any of the Syrians drew a weapon, the guard would shoot to kill. Before returning fire, his companion would step on a button to alert the patrol station five miles up the road. A helicopter gunship was at the ready and would be dispatched at once.

The Syrian border guards would not act unless fired upon. They had no jurisdiction in Turkey.

Ibrahim was slumped low in his seat, his eyes on the Cadillac. To his right, between the door and the seat, was a canister of tear gas. When Walid gave the signal, he would be ready.

The small Turkish guard shut the door of the booth and returned to the car. He bent slightly and displayed the passports like a cardplayer showing a winning hand. "You have been cleared for a twenty-four-hour visit. When you are finished you will return through this checkpoint."

"Yes," Walid said. "Thank you."

The guard stood and returned the passports. He held up his hand toward the second car. Then he returned to the booth, raised the gate, and allowed Walid's car to pass. When the Cadillac had gone through, the gate was lowered.

The Dodge drove up to the gate. Walid stopped the Cadillac just beyond the gate.

"Move on!" the guard shouted to him. "They will catch up to you."

Walid stuck his left hand out the window and raised it. He moved it from side to side. "Okay," he said, and let the hand drop over the side of the car door.

At that instant, Ibrahim and the passengers in the front two cars leaned out the windows, popped the tops on the palm-sized cylinders, and threw them at the booth. While the small guard reached for his pistol, the other opened fire through the thick, orange smoke. As he did, Walid threw his car into reverse, crashed through the gate, and rammed the booth. The outpost shook and the shooting stopped, but only for a moment. A moment later the driver of the middle car thrust a Makarov pistol out the window. He began firing and shouting oaths at the Turks.

Through the rising tear gas, Ibrahim saw the guard outside the booth go down. The guard in the booth began firing again, though the booth was lopsided and filling with tear gas. Walid drove forward a few feet, jerked into reverse, and hit the booth again. This time it went over.

Two men had emerged from the second car. They were wearing gas masks. They disappeared into the spreading orange cloud, and Ibrahim heard several more shots. Then everything was quiet.

Ibrahim looked back at the Syrian guards. They'd taken refuge behind their own weapons in their own booth, but they didn't fire.

After making sure that both of the Turks were dead, and after thanking Allah for their victory, Walid returned to his car. He motioned the caravan onward.

Speeding into Turkey, Ibrahim experienced a new sensation. A feeling of burning anticipation in his belly now that events had irrevocably been set into motion.

"Praise Allah," he said softly, involuntarily. Then his voice rose in his throat and he cried, *"Praise Mohammad, peace be upon Him!"*

Mahmoud said nothing. Sweat flowed from his temples along his swarthy cheeks to his tight mouth. In the back seat their companions were silent.

Ibrahim watched Walid's car. After two minutes the Cadillac swerved off the road onto the golden desert. The Dodge and Ford followed, spitting up sand as they plowed westward. After less than a hundred yards the cars became bogged down in the sands. The men got out.

While Ibrahim and Mahmoud removed the seats from the car and pulled the false floor from the trunk, the other men went to work swiftly and purposefully.

SIX

Monday, 2:47 p.m., Mardin, Turkey

The Hughes 500D is an extremely quiet helicopter due to sound baffles in the Allison 250-C20B engine. The small T-tail construction provides great stability at all speeds, as well as enormous maneuverability. It holds a pilot and two passengers in the forward bench as well as two to four passengers in the aft. With the addition of a side-mounted 20mm cannon and a .50-caliber machine gun, it makes an ideal vehicle for border patrol.

When the alarm from the guard north of Qamishli sounded at the Mardin Air Force outpost, the pilot and copilot were having a late lunch. They had already been out once on their hour-long late-morning patrol. They weren't scheduled to go out again until four o'clock. But the two men welcomed the signal. Since the government had begun coming down hard on the Kurds, things had been quiet. So quiet that the fliers feared they might become rusty. With an exchange of smiles and a thumbs-up, they were airborne within five minutes.

The two men flew low, passing isolated villages and remote ranches and farms on their way to the border outpost. Unable to raise the two sentries by radio, the fliers were on high alert as they closed in on the border. The pilot guided his craft swiftly over the dry earth. He always kept the helicopter in front of the sun to present a difficult target to anyone on the ground.

The two fliers saw the wreckage of the automobile moments before they saw the destroyed guardhouse. Circling the area from just north of the border to north of the cars, they radioed headquarters that they saw the two dead border guards, as well as three dead drivers.

"The vehicles appear to have been shot at," the pilot said into his helmet microphone. He peered for a moment through his amber-tinted visor. "Two of the drivers are not moving and one of them is moving only slightly."

"I'll send a medical team by air," said the dispatcher.

"It appears as though the cars ran the gate, struck the booth, and were shot by the guard," the pilot said. "The survivor may not be alive for long," he added. "I want to go down and question him before he dies."

There was a short consultation on the other end. "Captain Galata says you are to proceed at your own discretion," the dispatcher told him. "What about the Syrian border guards?"

"Both men are inside the booth," said the pilot. "They appear to be unharmed. Do you want us to try and raise them?"

"Negative," said the dispatcher. "They'll be contacted through government channels."

The pilot wasn't surprised. If the dead and dying were Syrians, then the Syrian border guards would not say anything to the Turks. If they were Turks, the Syrians would not be believed. Just getting the pilots across the border to talk to them would require high-level approvals. The entire process would be a long and practically useless exercise.

The pilot dropped the 500D to forty feet. He circled again. The rotor whipped the loose sands and obscured their view. He told the copilot they were going to have to land.

The chopper settled down nearly fifty yards from the three cars. Both men retrieved old Model 1968 submachine guns from the wall rack just inside the cabin. They put on goggles to protect themselves from sands swirled by the rotor blades. The copilot exited first. He shut his door and came around to the pilot's side. Then the pilot got out. He left the rotor on in case they had to get away quickly. He closed his door. The men walked one behind the other toward the first car, a Cadillac, where the driver was still alive.

The man was leaning through the partly open window. His arm was hanging along the door, blood dribbling from under the sleeve of his robe, down to his fingers, and onto the sand. He looked up with obvious effort.

"Help . . . me."

The copilot raised his weapon. He looked to the left and to the right. The pilot walked in front of him, his weapon pointed up.

The pilot turned. "Cover me," he said as they neared the car.

The copilot stopped, tucked the stock of his weapon against his shoulder, and aimed the gun at the driver. The pilot continued to walk ahead, slowing as he neared the vehicle. He peered into the back and then walked sideways, moving around the car and bending to make sure no one was hiding beneath it. He checked the blown tires and then returned to the driver's side.

The bearded man looked up at him.

"Who are you?" the pilot asked.

The man tried to speak. His voice was a whisper.

The pilot leaned closer. "Say it again."

The driver swallowed. He raised his bloody hand. And then with one swift and fluid motion he reached behind the pilot's neck and pulled his forehead hard into the top edge of the open window.

The pilot was blocking the copilot's fire. As he shifted to shoot, a man rose from the sand behind him. He had been lying beneath it, his gun at his side; the Turk never saw the burst of gunfire that ended his life. As soon as he went down, Walid released the pilot. The Turk staggered back and fell. Sand was still falling from Mahmoud's shirt and trousers as he shot the pilot.

Ibrahim rose from the sand on the other side of the car. He had been waiting there in case the helicopter had landed on that side. The other Syrians climbed from the trunks of the three cars.

Walid opened the door and got out. He untied the leather thong around his upper arm and removed the packet of goat's blood that was under his sleeve. He threw it into the car, then retrieved the pistol that had been under his right thigh. He tucked it into his belt.

Walid jogged toward the helicopter. "We lost no one," he shouted proudly. "The extra men we brought— not needed. You planned well, Mahmoud."

"'Al-fi shukr," Mahmoud replied as he vigorously brushed sand from his hair. "Thank you very much."

Ibrahim ran after Walid. Except for the former Syrian Air Force pilot, Ibrahim was the only one with any knowledge of helicopters.

"I feared—" said Ibrahim, angrily spitting sand. "I feared the rotors might uncover us."

"Then I would have shot the Turks," Walid said as he opened the pilot's-side door. Before he got in, he put his hand over the switch to turn off the radio.

Ibrahim went around to the copilot's door. As the other men came running over, he prepared to close down the helicopter's tracking beacon. When Walid nodded, he and Ibrahim shut the switches simultaneously. At Mardin, the Turks would assume the helicopter had suddenly lost power and gone down. Rescue efforts would be centered on the flight path.

"The Turks are not what bothers me," Ibrahim said. "We planned every detail of this operation. I repaired helicopters and you flew them. Yet neither one of us anticipated that."

"There is always the unexpected," Walid pointed out as he climbed into the cockpit.

"That's true," Ibrahim said. "But this was our area of expertise."

"Which is *why* we overlooked it," Walid snapped. "This was a warning. We are told, 'Nor do We punish a nation until We have sent forth an apostle to forewarn them.' We have been forewarned."

Ibrahim reflected on Walid's words as the other men ran over. Three of them embraced the others and wished them well. Then they returned to the cars to drive them back to Syria. With a helicopter gunship at their back, the Syrian guards would let them through without any questions. Nor would they help investigators from Damascus or Ankara, for fear of reprisals.

"Now we don't look back," Walid said to the three men in the helicopter. "We look ahead. Backup aircraft will be here in less than ten minutes." Walid glanced over his shoulder. "Are you ready?"

Mahmoud had waited for the other man, Hasan, their radio operator, to get in. Extra containers of fuel were loaded from the car, along with a backpack, which was handled gingerly. It was studded from the inside out with nails. When Ibrahim had settled into his seat with the

45

backpack nestled between his feet, Mahmoud climbed aboard.

"We're ready," Mahmoud said, shutting the door.

Without a word Walid checked his instruments and throttled up, and the helicopter was airborne.

Ibrahim watched the desert sink away. The road became lace, patches of asphalt covered with patterns of sand, and the carnage below became even more impersonal. He turned his face to the sun. It burned through the windshield, dwarfing the efforts of the air-conditioner to keep them cool.

As we will burn through the Turks for attempting to keep our own fires from burning, Ibrahim thought.

Walid was right. They'd made a miscalculation; just one. And they'd still managed to achieve their goal. Now they must look ahead to the next, much bigger target. To an adventure that would be celebrated throughout the Kurdish world. To an act which would force the world to pay long-overdue attention to their plight.

To the beginning of the end of the world order as it stood.

SEVEN

Monday, 7:56 a.m., Washington, D.C.

"I'm unhappy about it too, Matt," Paul Hood said as he finished his first Op-Center cup of coffee. "Stephen Viens has been a good friend of ours and I'd like to help him."

"Then let's," Stoll said. He sat on the couch to the left of the door, nervously moving his knee up and down. "Cripes, we're secret agents. Let's abduct the guy and give him a new identity."

Hood frowned. "I'm open to *serious* suggestions."

Stoll continued to look at Hood instead of at Political and Economics Officer Martha Mackall. She sat to his left on the couch. Her arms were crossed and she wore an unsympathetic expression.

"Awright, I don't know what we can do," Stoll admitted. "But the bloodhounds on the Hill won't get to work for another ninety minutes or so. We can do something by then. Maybe we can put together a list of the missions Stephen's assisted us on. Or we can bring in people whose lives he's saved. Jesus, that's got to count for something."

"Not unless those lives add up to a hell of a lot of votes," Hood said.

Martha crossed her long legs. "Matt, I appreciate your loyalty. But forward funding is a super-hot topic these days. Stephen Viens got caught taking money from one project and putting it into another."

"Because he knew that project was needed for national security," Stoll said. "It's not like the guy got rich off what he was doing."

"Irrelevant," said Martha. "He broke the rules."

"They were stupid rules."

"Also irrelevant," she said. "Frankly, the best we can hope for is that no one on the committee decides to investigate Op-Center because we've had improper access to NRO assets."

"Preferred access," Hood corrected her.

"Right," said Martha. "Let's see if Larry Rachlin calls it that when his CIA guys testify that we got ten times as much satellite time as they did. And what do you think'll happen if the Congressional Intelligence Oversight Committee decides to go through our finances? We didn't always rebate the NRO for that time because it wasn't in *our* budget."

"We've logged all of that debt and put it into next year's budget," Hood said.

"Congress'll still say we're living beyond our means," Martha told him. "They'll come looking to see how and why."

"There!" Stoll said, clapping his hands together. "That threat is all the more reason to line up behind Stephen from the get-go. One bureau is a target. Two is a unified front. It's power. If we go to bat for the NRO, Congress may think again about taking us on. Especially if there's the hint of a threat that national security is going to suffer."

Martha looked at Hood. "Frankly, Paul, some of those representatives would love to roll up their sleeves and overhaul all of national security. You know what I've been hearing from my friends in Congress ever since Mike Rodgers saved Japan from that North Korean nuke? Some have been saying, 'Why should we pay to protect Japan from terrorism?' The rest've been saying, 'Nice job, but how come you didn't know about the plot before it got so far?' Same with the tunnel bombing in New York. We found the perpetrator, but what the bottom-liners on the Hill wanted to know is why didn't our intelligence resources know it was going to happen and stop it. No, Matt. We're too close to sinking ourselves to start rocking the boat."

"I'm not asking you to rock anything," Stoll said. "Just throw the guy a life preserver."

"We may need it ourselves," Martha replied.

Stoll raised his hands as if he were going to protest, then let them drop. "So is this the best we can do for a good and loyal friend? Leave him twisting in the wind? Hell, Paul, is that what would happen to me or Martha or any from Op-Center who got into trouble?"

"You should know me better than that," Hood said.

"Anyway, that's different," Martha said.

"Why?" Stoll asked. "Because we get a paycheck from this place instead of from another place?"

"No," Martha replied coolly. "Because the people running Op-Center would have to approve whatever you did that got you in trouble. If we okayed it and it was wrong, then we'd take the heat with you. We'd deserve to."

Stoll looked from Martha back to Hood. "Excuse me, Paul, but Martha's here because Lowell's out of town. You wanted a legal opinion and she's given you one. Now I'm asking for a moral judgment."

"Are you saying that obeying the law is immoral?" Martha demanded, her large brown eyes flashing.

"Not at all," Stoll said. "I pick my words pretty carefully. What I said was that you gave a legal opinion."

"My moral opinion would be the same," Martha huffed. "That man did wrong. We didn't. If we go to the mat for him, some headline-grabber's going to take a magnifying glass to our operation next. Why should we risk that?"

Stoll said, "Because it's the right thing to do. I thought we're all supposed to be brothers and sisters here in the intelligence community. And I don't really think it will raise any red flags if Paul or especially you, as a black woman—"

"African-American," she said firmly.

"—were to go to the Congressional investigators and tell them that Viens's good deeds outweigh the bad call he made with the forward funding. Christ, it's not like he pocketed any of the money himself. It all went into the NRO coffers."

"Unfortunately for him," said Martha, "the national debt rose a little because of what he did. And the taxpayer got hit for the interest. I figure Jane Citizen is in the hole for about eighty million dollars because of his creative bookkeeping."

"He used the money to do his job better," Stoll said through his teeth. "He served Jane Citizen."

Hood looked at the empty mug as he gently tapped its side. His wife only allowed matched coffee cups in the house. This mug was his, an old L.A. Rams mug given to him by quarterback Roman Gabriel during an Old-Timers Day tribute at Los Angeles City Hall.

Op-Center was his too. His to look after and protect. His to make work. Stephen Viens had helped make that happen. He'd helped Op-Center save lives and protect nations. Now Viens needed help.

The question was, did Hood have the right to risk the futures of people who reported directly to him, people who might be hurt by backlash and cutbacks, to help someone who didn't?

As though reading his boss's mind, Stoll said mournfully, "I guess Op-Center policy is to look out for people who have to give us their loyalty instead of one who gave it freely."

Hood said, "This issue isn't as absolute as either of you make it, and you both know it."

Martha wiggled her foot. That was an indication that she was pissed off but wasn't going to get into a spitting contest. Martha got pissed off a lot at Hood and others in government who did anything that might jeopardize her own career. Still, ambition didn't necessarily make her wrong.

"Who's our best friend on the committee investigating this?" Hood asked Martha.

"That depends," she said, still irritated. "Do you consider Senator Fox our friend?"

Senator Barbara Fox had led the charge to gut the budget for Op-Center. She'd done an about-face when Hood, on business in Germany, had found the man who had murdered the senator's daughter decades before.

"For the moment Senator Fox is our friend," Hood said. "But like Matt said, one is a target while two is power. If we have to go in there swinging, who else've we got?"

"No one," Martha said. "Five of the other eight committee members are up for re-election, and Chairman Landwehr is on a crusade. They'll do whatever it takes to look good. Meaning protect the taxpayer by punishing the squanderer. The two senators who aren't up for re-election are Boyd and Griffith. And they're tight with Larry Rachlin."

Hood frowned. CIA Director Rachlin was not a friend of Op-Center. He perceived the crisis management group as having stolen a great deal of his overseas thunder— and with only seventy-eight full-time employees. Barbara Fox was the only one they could even hope to count on. And there was no telling which way she'd go if the other members of the SIC and the press leaned on her. It might toughen her or cause her to back-paddle.

"You've both made strong cases," Hood said, "but there's one thing we can't ignore. We're in this whether we want to be or not. It makes sense to me that we take the offensive."

Matt brightened. Martha shook her foot and drummed her fingers on the armrest.

"Martha, how well do you know Senator Landwehr?"

"Not very. We've bumped into one another at a couple of dinners, a few parties. He's quiet, conservative, like it says in the papers. Why?"

"If there are any subpoenas," Hood said, "they'll probably go to me, to Mike Rodgers, and to Matt. But if you get in there first, we can spin this our way."

"Me?" she said. "As in 'They won't dare to attack a black woman?' "

"No," Hood replied. "You're the only one of us who was in the loop but didn't deal directly with the NRO. You don't have friends there. That makes you qualified in the eyes of the committee. Equally as important, it makes you the least-biased high-ranking official in the eyes of the public."

Martha's foot stopped wiggling and her fingers stopped tapping. Hood knew she was interested. She was a woman in her late forties who didn't want to stay at

Op-Center forever. Voluntary, impassioned testimony would give her valuable national exposure. That would be her motivation for taking the stand. Hood's was that while their cause was just, Congressional hearings were also high drama. If the exits, entrances, and players were carefully selected and stage-managed, defeat could be made into triumph.

"What would I be saying up there?" Martha asked.

"The truth," Hood said, "which is what makes this very sweet. You would tell the committee that yes, we've occasionally and for very short periods monopolized the NRO for national security. You'd tell them that Stephen Viens is a hero who helped us protect human rights and lives. Senator Landwehr won't be able to attack us for telling the truth. If we get him and Senator Fox behind us, and portray Viens as a patriot, that robs the committee of some of its power to grandstand. Then it'll just be a matter of the NRO giving the money back, which is pretty boring stuff. Not even CNN will give it much coverage."

Martha sat still for a moment, then said, "I'll think about it."

Hood wanted to say, *"You'll do it."* But Martha was a thorny woman who also had to be handled with care. He said, "Can you let me know by this afternoon?"

She nodded, then left.

Stoll regarded Hood. "Thanks, Chief. I really mean that."

Hood drained the last cold drop from his mug. "Your friend screwed up over there, Matt. But if you can't go to bat for a good man who's been a loyal ally, then what the hell good are you?"

Stoll made a zero with his thumb and index finger, thanked Hood again, then left.

Alone again, Hood pressed his palms into his eyes.

He had been a big-city mayor and a banker. When his father was his age, forty-three, he was a CPA struggling to keep his own small accounting firm afloat. How did Frank Hood's son come to this place in life where careers could live or die, where *people* could live or die, based on decisions he made here?

He knew the answer, of course. He loved government and he believed in the system. And he did it because he believed that he could make these decisions compassionately and intelligently.

But Lord, he thought, it's difficult.

With that, the self-pity ended. Rising with his mug, Hood left the office to start on his next cup of coffee.

EIGHT

Monday, 3:53 p.m.,
Sanliurfa, Turkey

Mary Rose Mohalley finished running the last of the local systems checks. The software for the ALQ-157 infrared jammer was on-line and functioning. So was the hardware of the three-foot-by-two-foot-by-two-foot X-poser, which was designed to detect the residue of nitroglycerin, C-4, Semtex, TNT, and other explosives. Then she checked to make sure the ROC's batteries and solar panels were working at full capacity. They were. Two dozen batteries were dedicated to the ROC's internal systems. Another four batteries were devoted to powering the van's engine when, unlike now, gasoline wasn't readily available. The latter four batteries consisted of a pair of low-rate-energy storage batteries and two high-rate-energy flywheel batteries. Together the four batteries provided a total of eight hundred extra miles of travel capacity without recharging. All of the nickel metal-hydride batteries were stored in two fifty-eight-by-fourteen-inch compartments that were built into the raised floor. The solar panels that powered the van's air-conditioning and water were also working perfectly.

The twenty-nine-year-old got up. She had intended to go out and stretch, maybe catch a few minutes of sun, when Mike Rodgers spoke.

"Mary Rose, would you mind getting Matt's OLM program up and running before you do anything else?"

The young woman's shoes squeaked as she stopped suddenly on the smooth, black rubberized floor covering. Rodgers hadn't turned around or he would have seen her shoulders slump.

"No, I wouldn't mind at all," Mary Rose replied lightly. She plopped back down. Back at Op-Center, psychologist Liz Gordon had warned her that the only rays she'd get working with Mike Rodgers were whatever low-level radiation leaked from her computer monitor.

After giving his associate her assignment, Rodgers arched his back and stretched in silence. Then he continued going through his own checklist.

There it was, Mary Rose grumbled to herself. General Rodgers just took his break.

She looked at the screen and began moving the mouse around. The OLM was Matt Stoll's On-Line Mole. Though they had both been eager to try it, the OLM was part of the second wave of software installations. It was scheduled to be up and running by four p.m. However, with General Rodgers, a request was as imperative as a command.

The young woman rubbed her tired eyes, but that didn't make them feel any better. She was still jet-lagged from the flight over, and the fatigue went deep. Thanks to her doctorate in advanced computer applications, she had the luxury of using tireless machines to help her exhausted human brain. But she wondered how many bad deals American statesmen had made in this part of the world because they were just too tired to think clearly.

Then again, General Rodgers doesn't seem to feel it, she told herself. If anything, he appeared invigorated. He sat with his back to her, facing a wall of monitors that displayed satellite views of the region as well as information that ranged from levels of microwave radiation to local smog and allergen levels. Large rises in microwave levels indicated an increase in cellular communications, which was often a forerunner to military activity in a region. A higher smog or pollen count told them what kind of efficiency levels they could expect from soldiers. Mary Rose had been astonished to learn from Op-Center's chief medical officer, Jerry Wheeler, that antihistamines weren't deeply stockpiled by many of the world's armies. However sophisticated a nation's weapons were, they'd be useless in the hands of itchy-eyed warriors.

No, General Rodgers didn't feel the exhaustion. Mary Rose could tell that he was happily immersed in studying his data. That was why they hadn't had a break since their early, fifteen-minute lunch. He was lost in this first glimpse at wars of the near future. Wars that wouldn't be fought between great armies, but by small bands against small bands, and by satellites against computers and communications centers. Enemies of tomorrow would not be battalions, but groups of terrorists who used chemical and biological weapons against civilian targets, killing and vanishing. Then it would be up to teams like the ROC crew to plan a swift and surgical response. Find a way to get as close to the enemy brain as possible and lobotomize it, using an elite unit like Op-Center's Striker or a missile hit or a booby-trapped car or telephone or electric shaver. Hope that with the head gone, the hands and feet would no longer function.

Unlike many "old soldiers" who longed for the old ways, Mary Rose knew that the forty-something Rodgers relished this new challenge. He enjoyed new ideas and new ways almost as much as he enjoyed his bottomless supply of old aphorisms. As he'd told her with boyish enthusiasm when they'd settled into their seats early this morning, "Samuel Johnson once said, 'The world is not yet exhausted; let me see something tomorrow which I never saw before.' I'm looking forward to this, Mary Rose."

Getting Matt's OLM up and running took just over fifteen minutes. When she'd loaded it and run the diagnostics, Rodgers asked her to break into the Turkish Security Forces computer file. He wanted to learn more about Colonel Nejat Seden, the man who was being sent to work with them. He said that Seden was undoubtedly being sent to *watch* them as well, though Rodgers had expected that. That was how what he called the "watch out" worked. It was the nitrogen cycle of spying. Rodgers himself was watching the Turks as well as the Syrians; the Israelis were probably watching them both, while the CIA watched the Israelis. Rodgers said it was only fitting that the Turks would watch *them*.

But Mary Rose suspected that more than politics was behind his request. The general also liked to know the caliber of the individual with whom he'd be spending his time. Sitting beside him on the C-141A that had brought them to Turkey, she'd discovered one quality above all about General Mike Rodgers. He didn't enjoy being surrounded by people, even enemies, who weren't as committed to their jobs as he was to his.

Mary Rose wriggled uncomfortably in her seat as she typed commands into the computer. Because chairs with wheels made a familiar and distinctive sound, the seats in the ROC were bolted to the floor. As Op-Center's

Yale-educated Chief Engineer Harlan Bellock had said during the design phase, "Casters would be a tip-off to snoops. It would be very odd to hear the sounds of office furniture coming from an archaeologist's van, you know."

Mary Rose understood. But that didn't make the aluminum chairs any more comfortable. She also felt sunlight-deprived in here, just as she did when she worked in her Op-Center cubicle. All of the windows in the back had been deeply darkened, and lead-lined walls separated the front section of the van from the rear, with only a narrow, doorless opening in the center. Stoll had insisted on that precaution because many modern spies were equipped with "detection kits" or "DeteKs." These portable receivers literally read the electromagnetic radiation that was emitted by the computer monitor and permitted the spies to monitor the screens from outside and from a distance.

Maybe I should have been a Striker, she thought. Drill, play sports, shoot, rockclimb, and swim at the FBI Academy in Quantico, Virginia. Get some rays. Kick some derriere. But she had to admit she got a lot of sun on her days off, and she loved computers and cutting-edge technology. *So stop complaining and do your programming, young lady.*

The woman's long, fine brown hair was pulled back with a bow to keep it from tumbling onto the keyboard as she worked. Her hazel eyes were alert, her mouth tight as she modemed OLM to TSF headquarters in Ankara. There, like a perfect little spy, the OLM made room for itself by downloading a legitimate program to the ROC computer for storage.

"Attaboy," she said, her shoulders and thin lips relaxing slightly.

Rodgers chuckled. "It sounds as if you're coaxing one of your father's trotters and pacers."

Her father, William R. Mohalley, was a magazine publisher who owned several of the finest race horses on Long Island. He had always hoped that his only child would ride for him. But when Mary Rose reached a height of five feet seven at age sixteen, and kept on growing to five ten, that became unlikely. And she was just as happy. Horses were one of Mary Rose's passions. She had never wanted it to become work.

"I do feel like I'm racing," Mary Rose replied. "Matt and his German partners packed a lot of speed into this rig."

Assuming the borrowed file name, the On-Line Mole slipped into the system. Once there, OLM found the information it wanted, copied and downloaded it, then shed its assumed skin and left. As it departed, the program it had temporarily replaced was returned: one bit of OLM would leave as one bit of the original program returned, so that no change in available memory was ever registered. The entire procedure took less than two minutes. If, during the course of the operation, someone went looking for the file OLM had temporarily "become," OLM would quickly restore the program and either impersonate a different file or put the downloading process on hold. The OLM was much more sophisticated than the "Brute Force" attack programs used by most hackers. Instead of randomly flinging passwords at a computer, which could take hours or days, the OLM went right to the "recycle bins" or "trash cans" to find discarded codes. Unobserved in the computer's dumpster, the OLM quickly sought and usually found recurring sets of sequential numbers that gave it a key to valid programs.

Nine percent of the time, nothing useful was located.

When that happened, the OLM switched quickly to its "feed mode." Many people used birth dates or the names of favorite movies as codes, just as they did on personal license plates. The OLM rapidly fed in sequences including post-1970 years, which was when most computer-users were born; thousands of first names, including Elvis; and movie or TV titles and characters such as *2001, Star Trek,* and 007. Nearly eight percent of the time, OLM found the correct sequence within five minutes. It resorted to "Brute Force" only when faced with the elusive one percent.

Mary Rose beamed as Colonel Seden's dossier appeared, pulled from the recycle bin. "Got it, General," she said.

Mike Rodgers slid to the left. It was a tight squeeze getting out of the chair, and there wasn't enough room for him to stand upright once he was on his feet. Rodgers stood, his head bent low as he leaned over Mary Rose's seat. His chin touched her hair and he withdrew quickly. She was sorry that he did. For a moment, Rodgers had been just a man and she'd been just a woman. It had been a surprising, very exciting moment. Mary Rose turned her attention to the dossier.

According to the file, forty-one-year-old Colonel Seden was a rising star in the Turkish Security Forces. He had joined the paramilitary gendarmerie Jandarma when he was seventeen, two years older than many new recruits. After overhearing three Kurds in a cafe plotting to poison a large shipment of tobacco headed for Europe, Seden had followed them to their apartment and single-handedly arrested them. He'd been offered a post in the TSF two weeks later. There was an eyes-only note in the dossier from Seden's commanding officer at the TSF. General Suleyman feared that the "takedown" of the Kurds had been too fortuitous. There was Kurdish blood on Seden's mother's side, and the general worried that the Kurds had willingly sacrificed themselves so that Seden could infiltrate the security force. However, nothing in the colonel's subsequent record indicated anything but complete devotion to the TSF and to the government.

"Of course his record would be impeccable," Rodgers muttered when he reached that section of the file. "You don't slip a mole in and immediately set him spying. You wait."

"For what?" Mary Rose asked.

"For one of two things," he replied. "For a crisis, when you absolutely need data. Otherwise you wait for the person to work his or her way up to the highest levels of security clearance. At those levels, a mole can bring in other moles. The Germans did a lot of that during World War II. They would attempt to locate just one sympathizer in some area of the British aristocracy. That person would then recommend chauffeurs or domestics to lords or officers or members of the government. Those workers were all German plants, of course, who would then spy on their employers and pass information on to milkmen, postal workers, and others who had been bought by the Germans."

"Gee, they never taught me that in my computer and fiber-optics classes," Mary Rose remarked.

"It isn't even taught in most of the history classes," the general lamented. "Too many professors are afraid of insulting the German-Americans or the British-Americans or any other hyphenate group which might be wounded, every inch of it, if you insult a fraction."

Mary Rose nodded. "So does this mean Seden is absolutely tied to the Kurdish underground?"

"Not at all," said Rodgers. "According to the Turks, only about a third of the people who have some Kurdish blood sympathize with their cause. The rest are loyal to their host country. It does mean we show him as little as possible.''

They continued to scan the dossier as they spoke. Seden was unmarried. He had a widowed mother who lived in an apartment in Ankara and an unmarried sister who lived with her. His father was a riveter who had died in a construction accident when the boy was nine. The colonel had attended secular school in Istanbul, where he'd studied hard and at the same time excelled at weight lifting. He'd been part of the Turkish weight-lifting team in the summer Olympics in 1992. He'd then quit school in order to join the Jandarma.

"No dependents," Rodgers said. ''Well, these days that doesn't mean much. Marriages of convenience between spies is the new thing. Investigators always look for lone wolves.''

Mary Rose closed the file. ''So where does that leave us with Colonel Seden?''

''Informed,'' Rodgers smiled.

''That's all?'' Mary Rose asked.

''That's all. You never know when information will come in handy.'' Rodgers's smile broadened. ''Why don't you take a break now. We'll continue after Colonel Seden has—''

Rodgers stopped as one of his computer alarms began pinging softly but insistently. It sounded twice for a second, was silent for a second, sounded once, and then was silent for another second. After that it repeated the pattern.

''That's the ABA warning,'' Mary Rose said. She bent her head sharpy as she stood and leaned behind Rodgers.

The ABA, Air Border Alarm, was an advanced radar-and-satellite system that constantly monitored air traffic within a nation or province. Detailed relief maps could be brought up to tell the ROC how high and how fast the craft was flying. At the same time, heat tracking from space told the ROC how fast the ship was moving. Reconnaissance craft were typically slower-moving and flew higher than attack craft. The ABA also used a digitized template of a nation or province to ascertain when an aircraft was within a mile of crossing the border. That was the reason it had sounded now.

A low-flying, fast-moving ship headed to the border was presumed to be hostile. The alarm sounded when such an aircraft was spotted.

"It's heading almost due west," Rodgers said. "The speed and height indicate that it's a chopper." There was concern in his voice, but also excitement. The ROC was doing its job flawlessly.

Mary Rose crouched beside a console to Rodgers's left. "Are you surprised to find one traveling alone?"

"Border patrols travel solo," Rodgers said. "But this one is going too fast for just a look-see. It's got a destination."

Mary Rose punched an auto-tune button on the console. At once, an antenna hidden in the van's dark, domed sunroof turned toward the ABA's target. It began listening to communications to and from the target vessel. The computer was programmed with hundreds of languages and dialects. After digitally cleaning away static and other imperfections, the monitor displayed a simultaneous translation of any electronic transmission it received.

''. . . find out there?''

There was silence from the chopper.

''Repeat, Mardin One. What did you find at the crossing?''

There was still no answer.

"The chopper is from the Turkish air base at Mardin," Rodgers said. He punched a few keys and brought up data on the facility. "What've they got there? Two choppers, both Hughes 500Ds, and a Piper Cub." He glanced at the ABA speed indicator. "This one's traveling at one hundred and thirty-four MPH. That sounds about right for the 500D."

"So what have we got?" Mary Rose asked. "A lost pilot?"

"I don't think so," Rodgers said. "It looks like a crew was sent out to reconnoiter and hasn't reported in. He wouldn't be flying at his maximum speed if he were lost. And it sure doesn't look like he's defecting because the chopper's headed further into Turkey."

"Could the radio have been damaged?" Mary Rose asked.

"Possibly," Rodgers said. "But again, they're butting right up against their maximum cruising speed. These guys are in a hurry."

Jabbing at the keys with his index fingers, Rodgers asked the computer to check on military facilities in the southwestern section of eastern Anatolia. Unlike the rest of Turkey, which was mountain or desert, Anatolia was mostly flat plateau with areas of low hills.

The screen quickly flashed a red X for negative.

"They're not headed for an emergency landing," Rodgers said. "These guys are after something."

Outside, over the low hum of the air-conditioner, Mary Rose could hear the putter of a motor approaching the van. She continued to read the transcript as it scrolled up one of the monitors.

''. . . are out of our radar range and we are not picking up your signal. Is there a problem? Why do you not answer?''

"Maybe someone's gotten into the country and they're chasing them down," Mary Rose suggested.

"Then why wouldn't they report that to base?" Rodgers shook his head. "No, something isn't right here. I'll tell the TSF what we've got and see what they say."

"Don't you think they'd have been alerted if there were a problem?" Mary Rose asked.

"To the contrary," Rodgers said. "Out here, the rivalries between government factions make Washington politics seem like triple-A ball. They're almost as intense as the rivalries between religious factions."

There was a knock on the door. Mary Rose leaned over, turned the handle, and peeked out. It was Private Pupshaw.

"Yes?" she said.

"Colonel Nejat Seden is here to see General Rodgers," the hulking Pupshaw said.

"Please send him in, Private," Rodgers replied without looking over.

"Yes, sir," Pupshaw replied.

The private stepped aside and Mary Rose opened the door. She smiled pleasantly as a short, light-skinned man entered. He was powerfully built, with a neatly trimmed mustache and deep-set eyes that were also the darkest Mary Rose had ever seen. His curly black hair was damp and pressed down. From a motorcycle helmet, she guessed. He wore a .45 in a belt holster.

Seden returned her smile. He bowed his head. "Good afternoon to you, miss," he said. His English was thickly accented, with the lengthened vowels and clipped consonants of his native tongue.

"Good afternoon," Mary Rose replied. She had been warned that Turkish men, even enlightened ones, would be no more than courteous to her. Though Turkey had long ago granted equal rights to women, equality was a myth in the minds of many Muslim men. As Op-Center's staff psychologist Liz Gordon had told her, "The Koran decrees that women should always cover their heads, arms, and legs. Women who do not are regarded as sinners." Yet this man had a warm smile for her. He seemed to possess a sweet, natural charm.

Colonel Seden turned to General Rodgers and saluted. Rodgers returned the salute. Seden took two steps toward Rodgers and handed the general a crisply folded yellow paper.

"My orders, sir," Seden said.

Rodgers looked at them quickly, then turned back to the screen. "You've come at an opportune moment," the general said. "We have one of your choppers on the screen . . . here." He pointed to a sharp red object moving across an ever-changing green grid.

"That's strange," Seden said. "Military helicopters usually travel in pairs for security. Do you know where this one is from?"

"It came in from Mardin."

"Border patrol," said Seden.

"Yes," said Rodgers. "The radio operator there has been trying unsuccessfully to raise it. What kind of armaments do you put on those ships?"

"Typically, General, there is a machine gun and a side-mounted rotary cannon," Seden replied. "Usually the cannon is 20mm with a rotating barrel with one hundred fifty or so shells."

"Where could it be headed in such a hurry?" Mary Rose asked.

"I don't know that," Seden replied. He didn't take his eyes off the screen. "There's nothing out that way. There are no military targets and the villages are small and not strategic in any way."

"You're sure there are no terrorist groups based in any of them?" Rodgers asked.

"I'm certain," Seden said. "Nor has there been any movement to the region. We watch all of them very closely."

"Couldn't this simply be a hijacking?" Mary Rose asked. "Someone hides the chopper before it can be spotted, then uses it later for any number of things."

"That is unlikely," replied Seden. "It is easier for helicopters to be purchased in Russia or India and smuggled into our country in pieces."

"In pieces?" Mary Rose said.

"On boats, by air, or by land, amidst shipments of machine parts," Seden said. "It isn't as difficult as you might think."

"On top of which," said Rodgers, "the Turkish Air Force is certainly looking for this chopper by now."

"But not there," Seden said. "Somewhere along its original flight plan."

"We've picked it up," Mary Rose said. "Other radar is sure to. It will be found before very long."

"Obviously, whoever has it doesn't care," Rodgers said. "They're planning to use it now. Colonel, do you want to let the Air Force know where it is?"

"In another moment," Seden said. "I'd prefer to tell them where it's headed rather than where it will not be when they arrive."

Mary Rose gave a sideward glance at the officer. She caught Mike Rodgers doing the same. She could tell from his expression that the general was thinking the same thought she was, *Is Seden interested in gathering intelligence or in delaying them?*

The colonel watched as the map scrolled with the chopper. "Can I possibly see a larger view of the area?"

Rodgers nodded. He touched a key, and an expanded view of the region appeared on the screen. The chopper was now a small red dot.

Seden watched the screen for a moment and then said, "General, may I ask—do you know the range of the helicopter?"

"It's around four hundred miles, depending upon the load they're carrying." Rodgers looked back at Seden. "Why? What are you thinking?"

The Turk replied, "The only conceivable targets are several dams along the Firat Nehri—what you call the Euphrates." He pointed at the river, then traced its course southward through Turkey into Syria. "The Keban Dam, the Karakaya Dam, and the Ataturk Dam. All of them are within range."

"Why would anyone want to attack them?" Mary Rose asked.

"It's an old conflict," Seden said. "Islamic law calls water the source of life. Nations may fight over oil, but it's a trifle. Water is what stirs the blood—and causes it to be spilled."

"My friends at NATO tell me that over the last fifteen years or so, the dams of the Greater Anatolia Project have been a sore subject," Rodgers said. "They allowed Turkey to control the flow of water into Syria and Iraq. And if I'm not mistaken, Colonel Seden, Turkey is now embarked on an irrigation project in southeastern Anatolia which will reduce the water supply of those nations even further."

69

"Forty percent less water will reach Syria and sixty percent less to Iraq," Seden replied.

"So some group, perhaps Syrians, steals a Turkish chopper," Rodgers said. "They keep the military guessing as to whether it actually has been stolen. Guessing just long enough for them to strike their target."

"The Ataturk is the largest dam in the Middle East, one of the largest in the world, General," Seden said gravely. "May I use a telephone?"

"Over there," Rodgers said. He pointed to the computer at the side of the van. "And you'd better hurry. That chopper is just about a half hour from the first of the dams."

Seden walked around Mary Rose. He went to the cellular phone, which was cradled on the side of the monitor and hooked directly into the ROC's uplink. He punched in a number. As he spoke softly in Turkish, he slowly turned his back toward them.

Mary Rose and Mike Rodgers exchanged a brief look. When Seden's back was completely turned, Rodgers tapped a few keys on the other computer. Then he turned to watch the simultaneous translation of the colonel's conversation.

NINE

Monday, 4:25 p.m., Halfeti, Turkey

The Ataturk Dam on the Euphrates River is named after Kemal Ataturk, the venerated twentieth-century political and military leader. The Armistice that ended World War I also ended nearly six centuries of Ottoman rule over Turkey. But because the Turks had sided with the Germans, the losing side, the Greeks and British felt free to seize portions of the nation for themselves. The Turks felt differently, and in 1922 Kemal and the Turkish Army drove the foreigners out. The following year, the Treaty of Lausanne created the modern-day Republic of Turkey.

Ataturk established the new republic as a democracy rather than as a sultanate. He instituted a Swiss-style legal system to replace the Sheriat or Islamic code, and adopted the Gregorian calendar to replace the Islamic one. Even the turban and fez were banned in favor of European-style headwear. He founded secular schools, gave women basic rights for the first time, and adapted a Latin-based alphabet to replace the old Arabic one.

As a result of his massive transformation of Turkish

society, Ataturk caused significant resentment to build among the Muslim majority.

Like all Turks, fifty-five-year-old Mustafa Mecid knew the life and legend of Ataturk. But Mustafa wasn't preoccupied with the Father of the Turks. As assistant chief engineer of the dam, he thought mostly about keeping kids from playing on the walls of the dam.

Unlike the more spectacular, high-rising concrete gravity dams, or the sweeping, concave arch dams, embankment dams are long and wide and relatively low. Under the waters of the reservoir side is an upstream shoulder that slopes toward a peak like the side of a pyramid. On the top of the dam is a narrow wave wall with a walkway behind it. The walkway falls away as a sloping downstream shoulder. Typically, the downstream side is stepped. There's a berm halfway down to give the top level of stone a base on which to rest. A drainage layer is located halfway between the berm and the next level, a downstream toe. The effect, viewed from the side, is like a downward-sloping W. The core of the embankment dam is a high column of clay surrounded by sand. A thick layer of stone surrounds the core.

Large embankment dams typically contain fifty million cubic meters of water. The volume of the Ataturk dam is eighty-five million cubic meters. Not that that mattered much to Mustafa. He couldn't see most of the water. The enormous reservoir twisted away behind artificial promontories and breakwaters. The end of it was lost in the hazy distance.

Twice each day, at eleven in the morning and at four in the afternoon, Mustafa left his two coworkers in the small control room at the base of the dam and went looking for kids. That was when they came there to dive from the wave wall into the cool waters.

"We know it is safe to dive here," they would always say. "There are no rocks or roots underwater here, *Saa-Hib*."

They always called him their *Saa-Hib*, their friend, though Mustafa suspected that they were laughing at him. And even if they were sincere, he couldn't allow them to stay here and swim. If he did, the wall would be lined with children. Then the tourists would come. Soon there would be more weight on the dam than it was designed to take.

"And then they would blame the collapse of the dam and the flooding of southern Anatolia on Mustafa Mecid," he said, running his fingers through his full brown beard.

The fifty-five-year-old Turk was happy that he had two grown daughters. Young men were so physical. He watched his sister's children and didn't know how she coped with them. Mustafa's own poor father had sent him to the Army when he was sixteen because he was always getting into trouble with neighbors and teachers and employers. Even when Mustafa was in the Army— stationed on the Greek border near the Gulf of Saros— he made life more difficult for smugglers and undercover operatives than any Turk since His Eminence Ataturk himself. And when he married, his poor wife could hardly keep up with him. More than once she accused him of having a twin brother who crept into their bed in the middle of the night.

Mustafa turned his face toward the skies. "I think, Blessed Lord, that you made Turkish men for the same reason you made hornets. To go here and there and to work. And in doing all of that, to stir up others and to keep them busy." Mustafa smiled brimmingly, proud of his gender and his nation.

He walked briskly, his hiking boots crunching loudly

on the walkway. Its gravel surface had been designed to deter bare feet—designed by some college engineer whose soles weren't calloused from a childhood of walking barefoot. The radio hooked to his belt hung against his right hip. From under the brim of his forest-green cap he looked north, across the reservoir. He breathed deeply as the warm breeze washed over him. Then he looked down ten feet at the waves that slapped gently against the dam. The water was choppy, clear, soothing. He stopped for a moment and enjoyed the solitude.

And then, from the south, Mustafa heard what sounded like a motorbike. He turned and squinted in that direction. There was no dust rising from the dirt roads of the surrounding hillsides. Yet the sound from behind the hillsides grew closer.

Suddenly, the drone became the distinctive beating of a helicopter rotor. He tugged down the brim of his hat and looked toward the rich blue sky. Recreational fliers regularly flew over the reservoir, though of late more and more helicopters had been coming this way. Kurdish terrorists had established a presence around Lake Van and on Mount Ararat to the east, on the border with Iran. According to the radio reports, the military kept track of them by air and sometimes attacked them as well.

Mustafa watched as a small, black helicopter shot up over the treetops. For a moment he was looking at the underbelly. Then he was staring at the front of the craft as it nosed toward him. The helicopter skimmed the green canopy, agitating the leaves as it passed over them.

As the chopper descended, the orb of the sun was reflected in the dark cockpit windshield. Mustafa was blinded for a moment, but he could hear the drone growing louder.

"What are they doing?" he wondered aloud.

When the sunlight finally rolled off the windshield,

Mustafa saw what they were doing. He saw, but there was nothing he could do about it.

The helicopter had cleared the trees and was flying directly toward the center of the dam. He saw a man raise the machine gun so that it was pointed in his direction. On the pilot's side of the helicopter, the rotary cannon was pointed lower.

"They are out of their minds!" Mustafa yelled.

The Turk turned and started running back the way he'd come. The helicopter was less than two hundred yards away and moving in fast. He could feel the gun on him. He felt it the way any battle-seasoned soldier felt danger, by God whispering into his ear and fear tightening his groin.

Without breaking his stride, Mustafa suddenly threw himself to his right, toward the water. He hit it hard and his boots quickly filled with water. But even as he'd jumped he'd heard the machine gun spit death. As he brought his knees toward him and struggled to undo the laces, Mustafa thanked God for having spoken to him.

His lungs ached as he worked on his shoes. His eyes were open, and he saw the bubbly trails of the bullets as they slashed around him. A few came perilously close, and Mustafa gave up on the shoes. He swam to the wall of the dam, dug his fingers into the spaces between the stones, and crept up the sloping side. He stopped just below the surface and lay with his belly against the wall. He heard the muffled roar of the guns as the helicopter bore down. The dam shook beneath him, but at least he felt safe here. He wondered how his coworkers were doing. The fire didn't seem directed at them, and he hoped they were all right. He also hoped that the men in the helicopter didn't make a second pass. He didn't know what they hoped to accomplish with this attack, and he began to fear for the security of the dam.

When he could hold his breath no longer, he turned his face upwards and poked his mouth from the water. He sucked down air—and immediately lost it as something punched him hard in the belly.

TEN

Monday, 4:35 p.m., Sanliurfa, Turkey

Mike Rodgers began to doubt that the attack would ever materialize.

The assault of watermelon and manure that the Turkish Security Forces had warned about was probably a fiction. Rodgers's sixth sense told him that the TSF had invented the warning in order to send Seden out here to observe them. Not that the colonel was a fraud. The colonel had asked his headquarters for aerial reconnaissance of the chopper. The request had been rushed through channels, and the Air Force was getting ready to launch a pair of F-4 Phantoms from a base east of Ankara. What Colonel Seden told Rodgers coincided exactly with the clandestine translation Rodgers had run.

Of course, the whole thing could be a setup, Rodgers thought with an intelligence officer's natural and healthy skepticism. The TSF might just want to see how the helicopter and F-4s registered on state-of-the-art ROC equipment. Perhaps they'd report their findings to the Israeli military, with whom they had a partnership. In exchange for mutual naval support and continued upgrades of aging Turkish jet fighters, the Israelis would have access to Turkish air space. The two nations would also share intelligence. Knowing the capabilities of the ROC, Tel Aviv might deny Op-Center the freedom to use it there. Or conversely, they might press to have access to it. First, however, they had to know what it could do.

Not that any of this would change the way Rodgers conducted his business. To the contrary. There was nothing in the Regional Op-Center that Rodgers worried about Seden seeing. The general had erased the translated conversation the colonel had had with TSF headquarters, and the On-Line Mole program had been shut down before he arrived. The ROC capacities on view were sophisticated but not revolutionary. Indeed, Rodgers would welcome a report from Seden to his superiors that TSF secrets and military data were safe. That would make it easier to bring the ROC back into Turkey and get the facility into other NATO countries. As Rodgers had told Mary Rose while they waited for Seden to arrive, being informed enabled a team leader to craft an appropriate intelligence, military, or diplomatic response. It allowed a leader to feed the party line to an enemy or even to an ally. It was being caught by surprise that was dangerous.

And now they waited for the F-4s to report back. Though Colonel Seden had been offered the relatively comfortable driver's seat up front, he graciously declined. He stood at ease and spent most of the time gazing out the front window. Only occasionally did he wander over to check the helicopter's progress. Rodgers noticed that when he did he no longer looked vaguely put out to be there. His eyes were alert and very interested.

Because he is a loyal Turk, Rodgers wondered, or because he is not?

For her part, Mary Rose clearly wished that Seden would leave. Rodgers knew that she had other programs to test-run. But Rodgers had E-mailed her from his station and told her to wait. Instead of working, she brought up one of the war simulations Mike Rodgers kept on file for relaxation. In alarmingly quick succession, the young woman lost the Battle of San Juan Hill for Teddy Roosevelt and the Rough Riders in 1898, helped El Cid bungle the siege of Valencia during the war with the Moors in 1094, and enabled the formerly victorious George Washington to be defeated by the Hessians at Trenton in 1776.

"That's the value of simulations," Rodgers told her. "It lets you appreciate how large the shoes of those giants really are."

Seden watched Mary Rose fight the last battle during her "break," and seemed vaguely amused. Then he turned. He happened to glance at the helicopter display on Rodgers's monitor when the green screen began turning blue. The color was changing from the center out. The helicopter remained an orange silhouette in the center of the screen.

"General?" Seden said with real urgency.

Rodgers looked over. "Temp flux," he said urgently. "Something just happened out there."

Mary Rose turned around as the blue spread to the corners of the monitor. "Whoa," she said. "Something that's generating a lot of cold in a hurry. This grid is over a mile square."

Seden bent closer. "General, are you sure it's cold and not heat?" he asked. "Could the helicopter have dropped a bomb?"

"No," Rodgers said. He was bent over the keyboard,

quickly punching keys. "If it had dropped a bomb, the screen would have gone red."

"But what could have chilled so much air so quickly?" Mary Rose asked. "That's gone down from seventy-eight to fifty-odd degrees. A cold air mass wouldn't move in that fast."

"No, it wouldn't," Rodgers said. He consulted his meteorological database, then looked at a computerized geophysical chart. He called up a four-mile-square view of the region and asked the satellite to give him specific heat readings.

The helicopter was a step-five AHL—average heat level. That meant it generated a heat signature where the engine was one hundred degrees, plus or minus five. Anything at that heat level showed up orange on the monitor. Above it was a step-six red or a step-seven black. Below it was a step-four green, a step-three blue, a step-two yellow, or a step-one white, which was freezing.

According to the geophysical chart, the mean ground temperature of this region around the Euphrates was sixty-three degrees. That fell within the step-four levels they had been showing. Step three started at fifty-three degrees. Whatever was happening out there was pulling the temperature down at least ten degrees at a speed of forty-seven miles an hour.

"I don't understand," Seden said. "What is it that are we seeing?"

"A massive cooling around the Euphrates," Rodgers said. "According to the anemometer simulation, that's almost strong gale speeds. Are gales possible out there?"

"I've never heard of any," Seden said.

"I didn't think so," said Rodgers. "Besides, a wind like that would've taken out the helicopter."

"But if it isn't air, " Seden said, "what is it?"

Rodgers looked at the screen. There was only one explanation, and it made him sick to contemplate it. "My guess is it's water," he said. "I'm going to notify Op-Center. I think, Colonel, that someone just punched a hole in the Ataturk Dam."

ELEVEN

Monday, 4:46 p.m., Halfeti, Turkey

As they swept along the Euphrates, Ibrahim had peered through the waves of heat rising from Mahmoud's busy 20mm cannon. The ripples had distorted the reservoir and its mighty dam as their attack ravaged it.

The Syrian's hands had been resting on the stock and trigger of the side-mounted machine gun. It hadn't been time for him to act, so he'd watched chunks of stone explode inward along the center of the dam, chewed up by the barrage. Though Walid kept the chopper steady, Ibrahim kept his legs braced firmly on either side of the backpack, which lay between them.

As the helicopter flew over the dam, Ibrahim had seen one large piece of stone strike the dam engineer as he tried to surface. The blow probably hadn't been enough to kill him, though that wouldn't matter. In just a few moments the engineer would be dead.

The helicopter had come in low over the dam, and Walid swung it around sharply for another pass. As they'd flown toward the control house, Ibrahim had peppered the structure with fire from his machine gun. Though one Turk died in the doorway, Ibrahim's task had not been to kill the occupants. It had been to keep them crouched under tables or chairs, away from the windows and from the radio. Walid hadn't wanted anyone to see in which direction they were headed when they left. If they couldn't get back to Syria, they wanted to get as close as possible before they were pursued.

In the back seat, Hasan was tossing out strips of aluminum to jam signals from the control house. At the same time he was monitoring military communications on a radio headset. If someone in the control house did manage to get a message out, perhaps by telephone, and they were pursued, the plan was to land the helicopter and scatter. Then they would make their way individually to one of two safe houses. The huts were located in southern Anatolia on the Syrian border, run by Kurdish sympathizers.

The helicopter had swung around for another pass. Once again Mahmoud's powerful 20mm shells had slammed against the center of the dam. Shards of stone flew in all directions as the cannon fire pounded down. The attack wasn't designed to weaken the dam. It was being used to create a foothold for the package between Ibrahim's legs.

Now that the moment was nearly upon them, Ibrahim unzipped the backpack to make sure that everything was in order. He looked down at the four sticks of dynamite bound neatly in a pack with electrical tape. There was a timer hooked to an ignition cap on top. He ran his finger along each of the wires and fuses to check the connections. They were secure. The nails were also fast, the heads taped to the inside of the bag. The entire package would sit firmly in place when lodged amid the bullet-shattered stones.

Walid lowered the helicopter to just a foot above the dam. Ibrahim hopped out, placed the bag in the largest crevice, and set the timer for one minute. Then he climbed back into the chopper and it soared off.

The young Syrian pulled off his sunglasses and looked back. He saw the sun rippling along the top of the water. Birds pecked at the fish, and the sky behind them was unusually clear. Then, in an instant, the tranquility was rudely destroyed.

Ibrahim winced as a yellow-red burst of flame grew quickly from the top of the dam. The sound reached them a moment later and caused the helicopter to shudder. Hasan and Mahmoud also looked back as the long stone expanse folded outward at the center. As it did, it pulled the sides of the sweeping structure with it. The reservoir came cascading over the crumbling top of the dam, swallowing the fireball and turning it to steam. The giant wave disgorged the stones it had swallowed, spilling them over the shattered top of the wall. The flood pushed down the center of the dam in a giant V shape that reached almost to the base. Water poured through the breach, easily brushing aside the ends of the earthen dam and crashing onto the trees below. The steam quickly dissipated as churning white breakers slapped away the control house and carried its shattered remains into the valley beyond.

The sound of the deluge filled the cabin, dwarfing the roar of the rotor. Ibrahim couldn't even hear his own shout of triumph. He saw but did not hear Mahmoud praise Allah.

As the helicopter raced south over the thundering waters, Hasan suddenly tapped Walid on the shoulder. The pilot half turned. Hasan held his hand out, palm down, and swooped it forward. Then he held up two fingers. Two jets were on their way.

Hasan was clearly annoyed. The helicopter had been flying too low to be spotted by radar, and he'd apparently heard no transmisison from the control house radio. Yet somehow the Air Force knew what had happened here.

"I am sorry, my *akhooya,* my brother!" Hasan shouted.

Walid held up his hand. "We put our trust in the word of God!" he shouted back. "It is written, 'He that flees his homeland for the cause of God shall find numerous places of refuge.' "

Hasan did not appear consoled, though the other members of the team seemed exultant. The mission had been a success and their place in Paradise was secured.

Still, no one was quite ready to give up. As Walid guided the helicopter over the vast, swelling Euphrates, Mahmoud began loading another belt into his cannon. Ibrahim turned to his left to help him. Paradise notwithstanding, they would fight for their lives and for the privilege of continuing to do the work of Allah in this world.

Suddenly, Walid shook his head. *"Saa-Hib!"* he shouted. "Friend! You will not need that."

Mahmoud leaned toward him. "Not need?" he yelled back. "Who will do battle for us?"

Walid replied, "He who is the Sovereign of the Day of Judgment."

Ibrahim looked at Mahmoud. Both men believed in Allah and they had faith in Walid. But neither of them believed that the strong hand of the Lord would reach down and protect them from the Turks.

"But Walid—" Mahmoud said.

"Trust in me!" Walid said. "From safety you will see the sun set."

As Walid flew on with some purpose in mind, Ibrahim

contemplated their chances of surviving. The nearest Turkish Air Force base was two hundred miles to the west. Traveling at maximum cruising speed, the fighter planes—deadly American-made Phantoms, most likely—would be here in about twenty minutes. The helicopter would still be far from the Syrian border. From his Air Force days he knew that each of those jets probably carried eight heat-seeking Sidewinder missiles under each wing. Any one of those rockets would be enough to destroy the chopper long before the jets could be seen or heard. And the Turks *would* shoot them from the sky rather than let them leave the country.

Still, Ibrahim thought, let the Phantoms come. He looked away from his brother. The Ataturk Dam, the pride of Turkish arrogance, was in ruins. The Euphrates would flow as it did in ancient times, and the Syrians would have more water for their needs. Towns for dozens of miles downriver would be flooded. Villages upriver, which depended upon the reservoir, would be without water for their homes and crops. Government resources in the region would be sorely burdened.

As Ibrahim turned and looked back at the maelstrom, he was reminded of a passage from the Koran:

"Pharaoh and his warriors conducted themselves with arrogance and injustice in the land, thinking they would never be recalled to Us. But We took him and his warriors, and We cast them into the sea. Consider the fate of the evildoers."

Like the taskmasters of Egypt and the sinners drowned in Noah's flood, the Turks had been punished with water. Ibrahim was briefly moved to tears by the glory of what had just transpired. Whatever suffering might await him, it could only enhance the sense of holy purpose that filled him now.

TWELVE

Monday, 9:59 a.m., Washington, D.C.

Bob Herbert rolled his wheelchair into Paul Hood's office. "Mike was right as usual," the intelligence chief said. "The NRO confirms that the Ataturk Dam's been heavily damaged."

Hood exhaled tensely. He turned to his computer and typed in a single word: "Affirmative." He appended this to his emergency Code Red E-mail of 9:47 a.m. which contained Mike Rodgers's initial evaluation. Then he sent the confirmation to General Ken Vanzandt, the new Chairman of the Joint Chiefs of Staff. He also copied it to Secretary of State Av Lincoln, Secretary of Defense Ernesto Colon, Central Intelligence Agency Director Larry Rachlin, and super-hawk National Security Advisor Steve Burkow.

"How close is the ROC to the affected region?" Hood asked.

"They're about fifty miles to the southeast," Herbert said. "Well out of the danger zone."

"How well is 'well?' " Hood asked. "Mike's idea of a buffer zone isn't the same as other people's."

"I didn't ask Mike," Herbert said. "I asked Phil Katzen. He had experience with the great Midwest flood of 1993 and he did some quick computations. He says that within the fifty miles there's a good fifteen-to-twenty-mile cushion. Phil figures the Euphrates will rise about twenty feet straight down through Syria to Lake Assad. That won't hurt the Syrians much, since a lot of that area is seasonally dry as toast and deserted. But it's going to flood out a lot of Turks who live in villages around the river."

Darrell McCaskey arrived as Herbert was speaking. The slim, forty-eight-year-old former FBI agent, now interagency liaison, shut the door behind him and leaned quietly against it.

"What do we have on the perpetrators?" Hood asked.

"Satellite reconnaissance showed a Turkish 500D leaving the site," Herbert said. "Apparently, it was the same helicopter stolen from the border patrol earlier in the day."

"Where's it headed?" Hood asked.

"We don't know," Herbert said. "There're a pair of F-4s looking for the chopper now."

"Looking for it?" Hood said. "I thought we had it on satellite."

"We did," Herbert said. "But sometime between one picture and the next it disappeared."

"Shot down?"

"Nope," Herbert said. "The Turks would've told us."

"Maybe," Hood said.

"All right," Herbert agreed. "Even if they didn't, we'd have spotted the wreckage. There's no sign of the helicopter for a radius of fifty miles from the last place it was seen."

"What do you make of that?" Hood asked.

"I honestly don't know," Herbert said. "If there were any caves in the area which were large enough, I'd say they flew right in and parked it. We're still looking, though."

Hood was annoyed. He wasn't like Mike Rodgers, who enjoyed putting clues together and solving mysteries. The banker in him liked information orderly, complete, and now.

"We'll find the chopper," Herbert added. "I'm having the last satellite photograph analyzed to get the exact speed and direction of the 500D. We're also running a complete study of the area's geography. We'll try to find a place like a cave or canyon where a helicopter could hide."

"All right," Hood said. "In the meantime, what do we do about the ROC? Just leave it?"

"Why not?" Herbert asked. "It was designed for on-site reconnaissance. You can't get any more on-site than this."

"That's true," Hood agreed, "but I'm more concerned about security. If this attack is a taste of things to come, the ROC is relatively vulnerable. They've only got two Strikers covering four open sides."

"There's also a Turkish security officer," McCaskey added.

"He seems like a good man," Herbert said. "I checked him out. I'm sure Mike did too."

"That's three people," Hood said. "Just three."

"Plus General Michael Rodgers," Herbert said respectfully, "who is a platoon unto himself. Anyway, I don't think Mike would *let* himself be evacuated now. This is the kind of thing he lives for."

Hood sat back. Rodgers's career as a soldier included two tours of Vietnam, command of a mechanized brigade in the Persian Gulf, and leading a covert Striker operation into North Korea. Rodgers wasn't going to run from a terrorist attack on a dam.

"You're right about that," Hood admitted. "Mike will want to stay. But Mike isn't the one who has to make that decision. We've also got Mary Rose, Phil, and Lowell in the saddle and they're all civilians. I just wish we knew whether the attack was an isolated event or the first salvo of something larger."

"Obviously, we'll know more when we find out who's responsible," McCaskey said.

"Well give me *something* to chew on," Hood said. "Who do you think was behind this?"

"I've spoken with the CIA and with the Turkish Special Forces, and also with the Mossad in Israel," McCaskey said. "They're all saying it's either Syrians or Muslim fundamentalists within Turkey. There's a strong argument for both. The Muslim Fundamentalists desperately want to weaken Turkey's ties with Israel and the West. By attacking the infrastructure, they place a burden on the populace and turn them against the government."

"If that's the case," Hood said, "we can expect more attacks."

"Right," McCaskey replied.

"Yeah, but I'm not going for that one," Herbert said. "The fundamentalists are already pretty damn strong in Turkey. Why would they try to take by force what they can conceivably win on the next ballot?"

"Because they're impatient," McCaskey pointed out. "Iran is paying a lot of their bills and Tehran wants to see results."

"Iran has already put Turkey in the 'win' column," Herbert replied. "It's just a matter of time. Their big playground now is Bosnia. They were outfitting the Bosnians with arms and advisors during the Balkan war. Not only are those advisors still there, they're multiplying like guppies. That's how the fundamentalists plan on getting into the heartland of Europe. As far as Turkey goes, Iran's going to let the political situation move at its own pace."

"Not if Turkey continues to rely more and more on Israeli military assets and on financial aid and intelligence from the United States," McCaskey said. "Iran doesn't want another U.S. stronghold in their backyard."

"What about the Syrians?" Hood interjected. McCaskey and Herbert always went at each other like this, passionately but respectfully. Darrell Consensus and Bob Gut Instinct, psychologist Liz Gordon had once called them. That was why Hood had asked McCaskey to pop in when Herbert phoned that he had news about the attack. Between the two of them, Hood always ended up with a concise but comprehensive overview of a situation—though it was necessary to keep them from turning it into a political science debate.

"With the Syrians we have two possibilities," McCaskey said. "The terrorists could be Syrian extremists who are sold on the idea of the Middle East becoming Greater Syria—"

"Adding it to their collection, like Lebanon," Herbert said bitterly.

Hood nodded. It was the terrorist bombing of the U.S. Embassy in Beirut in 1983 that had cost the intelligence officer his wife and the use of his legs.

"Correct," said McCaskey. "Or what seems more likely is that the dam-busters are Syrian Kurds."

"They're Kurds, all right," Herbert said confidently. "Syrian extremists don't do anything without the approval of the military, and the military takes its marching orders from the Syrian President himself. If the Syrian government wanted to spark hostilities with Turkey, they wouldn't do it this way.''

''What would they do?'' Hood asked.

''They'd do what aggressor nations always do,'' Herbert said. ''They'd hold war games on the border, massing troops there and provoking an incident to draw the Turks over. The Syrians would never set foot in Turkey. As we used to say in the military, they like receiving. It goes back to 1967 when Israeli tanks rolled in on the third day of the Six-Day War. Defending their homeland makes Syrians look and feel like freedom fighters instead of like aggressors. That helps to rally other Arab nations around them.''

''In addition to which,'' McCaskey added, ''except for 1967, the Syrians generally like to fight proxy wars. They gave arms to Iran to fight Iraq in 1982, let the Lebanese kill each other during fifteen years of civil war, then went in and set up a puppet regime—that sort of thing.''

Herbert looked at McCaskey. ''Then you agree with me?''

''No.'' McCaskey grinned. ''You agree with me.''

''So assuming Bob is right,'' Hood said, ''why would Syrian Kurds attack Turkey? How do we know they weren't acting as agents for Damascus? They may have been sent to Turkey to pick a fight.''

''The Syrian Kurds would sooner attack Damascus than Turkey,'' Herbert said. ''They hate the current regime.''

''The Kurds have also become increasingly empowered by the Palestinian example,'' McCaskey said. ''They want their own state.''

''Though even getting that won't bring them peace,'' Herbert said. ''They're Sunni Muslims and they don't want to be mixed with the Shiite Muslims and the rest of the population. That's the big war they've been fighting in Turkey, Iraq, and Syria. But put the Sunnis together in a new Kurdistan and their four branches—the Hanafites, Malikites, the Shafites, and the Hanbalites—will start tearing each other apart.''

"Maybe not," McCaskey said. "The Jews have strong differences of opinion in Israel, but they coexist.''

"That's because the Israelis believe more or less the same thing in terms of religion," Herbert said. "It's politics where they differ. With the Sunnis, there are some very basic, very serious religious differences.''

Hood learned forward. "Would the Syrian Kurds be acting alone or with other Kurdish nationalists?''

"That's a good question," McCaskey said. "If the Kurds are behind the dam attack, it's much more ambitious than anything they've tried in the past. You know, raiding weapons depots or attacking military patrols, that sort of thing. My feeling is that for something this big they'd have needed the help of the Turkish Kurds, who've been fighting their government from strongholds in the east for the last fifteen years or so.''

"And joining with them," Hood said, "what would the Syrian Kurds hope to do?''

"Destabilize the region," Herbert replied. "If Syria and Turkey were to bash away at one another while the Syrian and Turkish Kurds unified, they could become a power in the region by default.''

"Not only by default," McCaskey said. "Assume they use the distraction of war to dig in all along the Turkish and Syrian border. Infiltrate villages, cities, and mountains, set up mobile camps in the desert. They could wage an intractable guerrilla war like Afghanistan lasting for years.''

"And whenever the pressure got too intense in one country," Herbert said, "the Kurds could simply slip into the other. Or else they join with the Kurds in Iraq to bring that country into the fray. Can you imagine an ongoing war involving those three nations? How long before nuclear or chemical weapons are used? How long before Syria or Iraq realizes that Israel is supplying the Kurds—''

''Which they've been doing for years,'' said Mc-Caskey.

''—and starts chucking missiles at them?''

''Eventually,'' McCaskey said, ''when there's a peace settlement, it will have to deal with the Kurdish issue in order to be effective. So the Kurds get a homeland, Turkey embraces the fundamentalists, and democracy and the United States are the big losers.''

''*If* there's a peace settlement,'' Herbert said portentously. ''We're talking about thousands of years of animosity being unleashed on a large scale. If that genie is ever let out of the bottle, it might be impossible to put him back in.''

Hood understood. He also knew that it wasn't the responsibility of Op-Center to plan for a war in the Middle East. His job was to spot ''hot situations'' and manage them if they became ''crises.'' Once they evolved from that into ''policy problems,'' it was up to the White House to handle them. The President would let him know what help was needed and where. The question was, what could be done to manage this developing crisis?

Hood turned to his keyboard and typed in the extension of his executive assistant, Stephen ''Bugs'' Benet. A moment later the young man's face appeared on the screen.

''Good morning, Paul,'' Bugs said, his voice coming from speakers mounted on the side of the monitor.

''Morning, Bugs,'' Hood said. ''Would you please get

Mike Rodgers for me? He's still at the ROC."

"Right away," Bugs said. His image winked off.

Hood glanced at Herbert. "What's Mike doing to find that missing helicopter?"

"Same thing we are," Herbert replied. "Analyzing data. He's in a better position to scan communications in the region, so I'm sure he's doing that too. He'll be following all the procedures we wrote up for ROC operations."

"What's the minimum security requirement you established for the ROC?" Hood asked.

"Two Strikers when the facility is in the field," Herbert said. "That's what they've got now."

Bugs reappeared on the screen. "General Rodgers is not available," he said. "He's gone out to do field work."

Hood's mouth tightened. He knew the general well enough to smell a euphemism when he heard one. "Where did he go?"

"Mary Rose said he took Colonel Seden and left about ten minutes ago," Bugs told him. "They took the Turkish officer's motorcycle."

"Uh-oh," Bob Herbert said.

"What about the computer cell phone?" Hood asked. "Can you reach Mike on that?"

"The general phoned Mary Rose to check reception a few minutes after he went out into the plains," Bugs said. "The satellite uplink worked fine, but he told her not to call unless it was an emergency. Just in case anyone was listening in."

"Lots of cross talk in open spaces like that," Herbert said. "Zero security."

Hood nodded at Herbert. On military missions, Op-Center personnel typically carried secure TAC-SATs. They had their own parabolic dishes which allowed them to uplink securely with satellites, then broadcast directly to Op-Center. But those units were relatively cumbersome. Though the ROC carried one TAC-SAT, Rodgers obviously wanted to travel light.

Hood was angry with Rodgers, and deeply concerned about him being out without Striker backup. But he couldn't pull anyone from the ROC without compromising security procedures, and he didn't want to recall Rodgers. The general was his own man and he hadn't broken any rules. Besides, it wasn't Hood's place to second-guess his Deputy Director from nine thousand miles away.

"Thanks, Bugs," Hood said. "Stay in touch with the ROC and let me know at once if they hear anything."

"Will do, Chief," Bugs said.

Hood clicked Benet off and regarded Herbert. "So. It looks like Mike's gone off to do some first-hand recon."

Herbert absently punched the keys on the speakerphone of his armrest. "Yeah. Well, that's Mike's style, isn't it?"

"Why wouldn't he have taken the ROC?" McCaskey asked. "At least then he'd have been able to do a thorough job."

"Because he knew he was going into a dangerous situation," Hood said. "And you know Mike. He wouldn't want to jeopardize the facility or the crew. That's also his style."

Hood looked at Herbert, who was looking at him. The intelligence chief shut his eyes and nodded.

"I'll find him," Herbert said. He speed-dialed the NRO on his wheelchair phone. "I'll see if Viens can push everything else aside again and get us a nice clear satellite snapshot of Rodgers of Arabia."

"Thanks," Hood said. He looked at McCaskey.

"The usual?" McCaskey asked.

Hood nodded. The former G-man knew the drill. If a group claimed credit, McCaskey would have to run a check through other domestic and foreign agencies to see if they had the resources. If not, who were they covering for and why? If so, he would have to run their modus operandi through the computer to determine what their next likely move was and how long they'd wait. Then McCaskey and his advisors would have to ascertain whether diplomacy would forestall other attacks, whether the perpetrators would have to be hit militarily, and what other targets they were likely to strike.

"Put Liz in on this," Hood said.

McCaskey nodded as he left. Psychological profiles of Middle Eastern terrorists were especially important. If the terrorists were motivated solely by politics, as most Kurds were, they were less likely to be suicidal. That being the case, security against air and ground attacks was possible. If the terrorists were motivated by religion and politics, as the larger majority of Kurds were, then they were not only happy but honored to give their lives. In that case, killers could strike anywhere. They might wear six to eight sticks of TNT in a specially designed belt supported by shoulder straps. Or they might carry a backpack loaded with fifty to sixty pounds of plastique. Wires running from the explosives through two batteries were attached to a switch. This switch was usually kept in the bomber's pants pocket, which allowed him to trigger the blast anytime, anywhere. Those kinds of attacks were virtually impossible to protect against; those kinds of terrorists were damn near impossible to reason with. The most frustrating and ironic part was that a single terrorist was far more lethal than a group. A lone operator had total tactical flexibility and the ability to surprise.

Herbert clicked off his phone. "Viens is on the case

for us. Says he can get the 30-45-3 away from the Defense Department in about ten minutes. It's one of the older jobs, no infrared capacity, but we'll get good daylight pictures.''

The designation 30-45-3 referred to the third satellite looking down on the longitudes thirty to forty-five degrees east of the prime meridian. That was the region which included Turkey.

''Viens's a damn fine man,'' Hood said.

''The best.'' Herbert turned. He snickered as he wheeled toward the door. ''At least Stephen's keeping his sense of humor about the investigation. He told me there're so many nails in his coffin he's thinking of nicknaming the division the Iron Maiden.''

''We won't let Congress close the lid on him,'' Hood promised.

''That's a nice sentiment, Paul. But it'll be real difficult to make happen.''

''I like the difficult, Bob.'' Hood smiled faintly. ''That's why I'm here.''

Herbert glanced back as he opened the door. ''Touché.'' He winked as he rolled into the hallway.

THIRTEEN

Monday, 5:55 p.m., Oguzeli, Turkey

Ibrahim and the radio operator Hasan stood on the windy plain as Mahmoud knelt between them. They had Czechoslovakian Samopal submachine guns lying across their shoulders and Smith & Wesson .38s tucked into holsters on their belts. There were hunting knives sheathed on their hips.

Ibrahim held Mahmoud's weapons as his brother bent low on the hard earth. Tears trickled down the older man's dark cheeks and his voice cracked as he quoted the Holy Koran.

"He sends forth guardians who watch over you and carry away your souls without fail when death overtakes you. . . ."

Just minutes before, Walid had deposited his three passengers and their backpacks and weapons on this dry hillside. He'd given Mahmoud a gold ring he wore, one which was topped with two silver daggers crossed beneath a star. It was the ring which identified him as a leader of the group. Then he'd taken off again and flown the helicopter back toward the flood. Racing headlong into the raging waters, he'd allowed the helicopter to be swallowed up. A geyser of spray and steam had briefly marked its death. Then the three survivors had watched in horror as the helicopter's shattered remains were carried away by the torrent.

Walid had sacrificed himself and the chopper because it was the only way to erase the ship from Turkish radar. The only way to keep the team from being shot from the skies. The only way to protect the others so that they might continue the important work of the Kurdistan Workers' Party.

Mahmoud finished his prayer, but he continued to bow low. His voice soft and sorrowful, he asked, "Why you, Walid? You were our leader, our soul."

"Mahmoud," Ibrahim said softly, "patrols will be covering this region soon. We must go."

"You could have shown me how to fly the helicopter," Mahmoud said. "My life was not as important as yours. Who will lead the people now?"

"Mahmoud," Ibrahim said more insistently. *"Min fadlak*—please! *You* will lead us. He gave you the ring."

"Yes." Mahmoud nodded. "I will lead you. It was Walid's dying wish. There is still a great deal to be done."

Ibrahim had never seen such sadness and then anger in his brother's expression. And it occurred to him then that perhaps this was something else Walid wanted. The fire of hate in the hearts and eyes of his soldiers.

As Mahmoud stood, Ibrahim handed him his Parabellum and a .38.

"Thank you, my brother," Mahmoud said.

"According to Hasan," Ibrahim said with quiet confidence, "we can reach Sanliurfa by nightfall. We can stay in the foothills and hide if necessary. Or there is some traffic in the region. Perhaps we can capture a car or truck.''

Mahmoud turned to Hasan, who was standing a respectful distance away. "We do not hide," he said. "Is that understood?''

"Aywa," said both men. "Yes."

"Lead us, Hasan," Mahmoud said. "And may the Holy Prophet guide us to our home . . . and to the homes of our enemies.''

FOURTEEN

Monday, 6:29 p.m.,
Oguzeli, Turkey

Before coming to the Middle East, Mike Rodgers had done what he always did. He'd read about the region. Whenever possible, he'd read what other soldiers had said about a nation or people. When he was here for Desert Shield and then Desert Storm, he'd read T.E. Lawrence's *Seven Pillars of Wisdom* and reporter Lowell Thomas's *With Lawrence in Arabia*. They were two views of the same man and the same region. This time he'd re-read the memoirs of General Charles "Chinese" Gordon of Khartoum as well as an anthology about the desert. Something by Lawrence—the English author D.H., not the soldier T.E.—which had been published in the latter had stayed with him. That Lawrence had written in part that the desert was "the forever unpossessed country." Rodgers had liked that phrase very much.

Like the polar regions, the desert could be borrowed but not owned. Unlike the polar regions, where ice could be melted for water and there was relatively solid ground for construction, the desert had moods. Now broiling, now cool. Savagely windy one minute, utterly still the next. One had to bring not only water and shelter but commitment. Unlike the Arctic or Antarctic, a traveler didn't get off a boat or a plane, move inland a mile or two, take pictures or readings, then depart. From ancient times, when camel caravans crossed these regions, if a person came to the desert it was with the intention of crossing it. And here in these high, dry lands where the earth was not just sandy but parched, where travel was measured in yards instead of in miles, crossing it required luck as well as stamina.

Thanks to radios and motorized travel, traversing the desert or Turkey's dead meadows was not the purgatory it had been until the turn of the century. But they were still places of staggering desolation. After a half hour of riding on the back of Colonel Seden's motorcycle, Rodgers had noticed that even the ranks of insects had thinned and then dwindled to nothing.

Rodgers leaned forward on the big Harley. The wind knifed through his short-cropped graying hair and pushed hard against his shoulders. He looked at the small compass that was bracketed to the top of the dashboard, just above the tachometer. They were still headed in the direction where the helicopter had last been seen, along the outer perimeter of the flood. He looked at his watch. They should be arriving in another twenty minutes or so.

The sun was low behind the hills, its ruddy light fast fading. Within minutes the sky was as star-filled as any Rodgers had ever seen.

Colonel Seden half turned. "We are nearing the plains," he shouted back. "Above this region there are dirt roads. They are not well traveled, but at least the ride will not be so bumpy."

Those were the first words Seden had spoken since

they left. That was fine. Rodgers himself wasn't a talker.

"A Navy fast-attack craft in rough seas is bumpy," Rodgers yelled back. "This is fine."

"If you can believe it," Seden said, "the temperatures in this region drop to near freezing before dawn. From October to May the roads are often closed here because of snow!"

Rodgers knew that from his reading about the region. Only one thing in this part of the world was unchanging. It wasn't the desert winds or sands or borders, or the local and international players who made the Middle East their battleground. It was religion and what people were willing to do for it. Since the days of the priest-dominated Sumerians who flourished in southern Mesopotamia in the fifth millennium BC, people here had been willing to fight for religion, to slaughter humans and beasts for it, and also to die for it.

Rodgers understood that. Roman Catholic by birth and by choice, he believed in the divinity of Jesus. And he would kill to defend his right to worship God and Christ in his own way. To Rodgers, that was no different from fighting and killing and bleeding to protect the flag and principles of his beloved country. To strike a blow for honor. But he wasn't self-righteous about his faith. He would never raise anything but his voice to try to convert anyone.

The people here were different. For six thousand years they had sent millions of people to dozens of afterlifes populated by hundreds of gods. Nothing was going to change them. The best Rodgers hoped for by coming here was to fight a better holding action.

Seden shifted gears as they climbed a hill. Rodgers watched the bright headlight as it bobbed across the dirt road. Unlike the region they'd just crossed, there were rocks, low scrub, and contours in the terrain.

"This road," said Seden, "will take us directly to—"

The colonel's body jerked to the right an instant before Rodgers heard the gunshot. Seden fell back and knocked Rodgers from his seat just as the motorcycle tipped over. Rodgers hit the road hard and rolled back several feet. Seden managed to hold on as the bike struggled up the road on its side for a few yards. It pulled the colonel part of the way before he slipped off.

Rodgers's right side burned, his arm and leg having been torn open by the pebbles in the road. The motorcycle headlight was pointed back toward them. Rodgers could see that Seden wasn't moving.

"Colonel?" Rodgers said.

Seden didn't answer. Fighting the pain, Rodgers got his elbow under him and crawled toward the colonel. He wanted to get the Turk off the road before a vehicle came over the top and ran them down. But before Rodgers could reach him he felt a gun pressed to the back of his neck. He froze as boots crunched on the road. Rodgers watched as two men went to examine Seden.

The Turk stirred. One man disarmed him and pulled him off the road while another went and moved the motorcycle. The man behind Rodgers grabbed him by the collar and pulled him to the side of the road as well. They were dragged behind a high, narrow hillock.

The man pressed the gun back against Rodgers's neck and said something to him in Arabic. He was not a Turk.

"I don't understand," Rodgers said. He showed no fear in his voice. By their actions, these men appeared to be guerrilla terrorists. The breed did not respect cowardice and refused to negotiate with cowards.

"American?" asked the man behind him.

Rodgers turned to look at him. "Yes."

The man called over someone named Hasan, who had

been checking the motorcycle. Hasan had a narrow face, very high cheekbones, deep-set eyes, and curly, shoulder-length black hair. Hasan was given a command in Arabic. Acknowleding it, Hasan pulled Rodgers to his feet. With the gun still at the general's neck, he began patting him down. Hasan found the general's wallet in his front pants pocket. He took Rodgers's passport from one shirt pocket and his cellular phone from another.

Rodgers's documents identified him as Carlton Knight, a member of the environmental resources department of the American Museum of Natural History in New York. It was a coin toss as to whether these men would buy that. Seden's uniform clearly identified him as a colonel in the Turkish Security Forces. Rodgers was going to have to come up with a good reason why he was out here with a TSF officer.

Personal safety, Rodgers decided. After all, hadn't these men just attacked him?

All other things being equal, Rodgers wasn't sure whether it was good to be identified as an American. Some Middle Eastern groups wanted the sympathy of the American public, and murder didn't get them that. Others wanted the support of Arab extremists, and murdering Americans won them that. If these were the same people who blew up the dam, there was no telling what they might do.

There was only one thing of which Rodgers was certain. The motorcycle was obviously the first vehicle these men had seen—and because of the flooding, it was probably the only one that would be along. They were going to have to make this situation work for them.

Hasan ignited a cigarette lighter and read the passport. "Kuh-ni-git," he said phonetically. He regarded Rodgers. "Why are you out?"

"I came to Turkey to check on the status of the Euphrates," Rodgers said. "When the dam came down, I was rushed to the area. They want my opinion on the short- and long-term ecological damage."

"You came with him?" Hasan asked.

"Yes," Rodgers said. "The Turks were worried about my safety."

Hasan translated for the man behind him, an angry-eyed soul named Mahmoud. The other man was tending to Seden's wound.

Mahmoud said something and Hasan nodded. He looked at Rodgers. "Where is camp for you?" Hasan asked.

"To the west," Rodgers said. "At Gazi Antep." The ROC was to the southeast, and the general did not want to lead them there.

Hasan snickered. "You have not enough gas in this motorcycle for that ride. Where is camp?"

"I told you, it's at Gazi Antep," Rodgers said. "We left our fuel can at a gas station on the way. We were supposed to pick it up on our return." Since Hasan was not a Turk, Rodgers assumed that he wouldn't know whether or not there was a gas station in that direction.

Hasan and Mahmoud spoke. Then Hasan said, "Give me the telephone number of your camp." He snapped the phone open under the lighter. He looked at Rodgers and waited.

Though Rodgers remained outwardly calm, his heart and mind began to race. His main objective was to protect the ROC. If he refused to give them the number, they would surely suspect he wasn't who he said he was. On the other hand, they knew who Colonel Seden was and hadn't killed him. So they would probably hold him as well, at least until they got out of the country.

"I'm sorry," Rodgers said. "I don't know the number. This phone is for them to call me."

Hasan stepped closer. He held the lighter close to Rodgers's chest, the flame burning low under his chin. Slowly, he began to raise the lighter.

"Are you speaking the truth?" Hasan asked.

Rodgers forced himself to relax as the heat spread across the soft flesh of his neck. Everyone who worked behind the lines in Vietnam was taught the rudiments of surviving torture. Beatings, burning with lighted cigarettes, electric current applied to sensitive areas, standing chin-deep in water for days on end, and having your arms pulled behind you as you're hoisted to the top of a pole. All of those were practiced by the North Vietnamese, and sampled by Special Forces operatives who went over there. The key was not to be tense. Tension only tightened the flesh, stretching the skin cells and exacerbating the pain. Tension also focused the mind on the pain. Victims were told to try to count to themselves, divide the suffering into manageable segments of three or five seconds. They had to think of making it to the next plateau rather than to the end.

Rodgers counted as the heat intensified.

"The truth," Hasan urged.

"It is . . . the truth!" Rodgers said.

Mahmoud spoke harshly to Hasan. The young man switched off the flame and sneered at the American. Hasan handed Mahmoud the telephone and then walked over to Colonel Seden.

The third terrorist was standing behind the Turkish officer. He held a pistol pointing down at the top of colonel's head. Seden was sitting up, his back propped against the terrorist's legs. The colonel's head had been crudely bandaged with a sleeve from his jacket. The other sleeve had been used to make a tourniquet for his bloody right arm. He was barely conscious.

Hasan knelt beside Seden. He lit a cigarette, took a few puffs, then held the lighted tip to Seden's chin. The dazed Turk shrieked. Hasan quickly cupped his hand on the colonel's mouth.

Hasan said something in Turkish. Seden shook his head violently. Hasan put the lighted cigarette to Seden's left earlobe. The Turk screamed again. He tried to push Hasan's hand away. The man standing beside him used his free hand to pin the Turk. Hasan withdrew the cigarette.

Suddenly, Mahmoud called Hasan back. The young man jogged over. There was hurried, quiet conversation.

Rodgers tried to turn and see what was going on, but Mahmoud pushed his face back around with the barrel of the gun. Vigorously alert because of the searing pain in his neck, Rodgers listened attentively. He heard a beep on the cellular phone. Hasan had pressed a button. Why?

And then with sickening swiftness the answer came to him. Mahmoud had summoned Hasan, the group's linguist, to read the English words on the phone. Above one of the buttons was the word "Redial." The camp was the last place Rodgers had called. Mahmoud was calling it back.

Hasan was standing just a foot away. Rodgers could hear the phone ringing, and he was numb as he waited to see who picked up and what they said. Of all the stupid, goddamn slipups—

"Hello?"

It was Mary Rose. Hasan seemed surprised to hear a woman's voice, but he said nothing. Rodgers silently prayed for Mary Rose to hang up. He was tempted to shout for her to clear the ROC out, but didn't think they could do it in time. Not if these three killed him and Seden and went after it.

"Hello?" she repeated.

Don't say anything else, Rodgers thought. Please God, Mary Rose, don't say a word—

"General Rodgers, I can't hear you," she said. "I don't know if you can hear me, but if you can I'm going to hang up."

She did. So did Hasan. With a look of triumph, he closed the phone and stuffed it back into Rodgers's shirt pocket. He spoke with the other two men for a minute. Then he glared at Rodgers.

"General Rodgers," he said. "You are not an environmentalist, I think. The American military is working with Turkish Security to find who? Us, perhaps?" Hasan moved his face closer until he was practically nose-to-nose with Rodgers. "So—you have found us. And this person who answered the phone. She is not in Gazi Antep."

"She is," said Rodgers. "At the police department there."

"There are mountainous regions between us and Gazi Antep," Hasan said disdainfully. "Your telephone would not have gotten through them. The only flat lands are to the southeast."

"This has a satellite uplink," Rodgers lied. "It goes over mountains."

The man behind Colonel Seden said something in Arabic. Hasan nodded.

"He says you're a liar," Hasan hissed. "This 'uplink' requires a plate . . . a dish. We do not have time for this. We need to get to the Bekka Valley."

The Arab turned angrily back to Colonel Seden. The officer was more alert than before and breathing heavily from his ordeal. Hasan knelt beside him again and flicked on the lighter. Rodgers could see the Turk's expression in the light of the flame. It was defiant, God bless him.

Hasan asked Seden something in Turkish. The colonel didn't answer. Hasan jammed a handkerchief in his mouth, grabbed a handful of the officer's hair to hold his head steady, then put the flame under Seden's nose. The colonel kicked roughly at the ground, his cries muffled by the handkerchief. This time, Hasan didn't remove the flame. Seden's screams rose higher and he writhed violently to try and get away.

Hasan shut the flame. He removed the handkerchief from Seden's mouth. He spoke closely into Seden's ear. The colonel was panting, his legs and arms trembling. Rodgers could tell from his condition that Hasan was about to "get inside" him. That was the point in torture when the pain and not the mind was in control of the body. The will had been broken and the conscious mind was only concerned with preventing further pain.

Hasan put the handkerchief back in the colonel's mouth. He moved the lighter toward Seden's left eyebrow. Seden shut his eye, but Rodgers knew that wouldn't help.

The flame burned the hair of his eyebrow and crept up along his forehead. Seden was about to break. Rodgers didn't want him to have to live with that guilt—if either of them survived.

"Stop!" Rodgers said. "I'll work with you."

Hasan removed the flame. He let go of Seden's hair. The Turk folded forward at the waist.

"What do you want?" Rodgers asked. It was time to change tactics. He would stop stonewalling and try to compromise and disinform.

"At first, General, we wanted you to come as our

hostages," Hasan said. "But now we want something else."

Rodgers didn't have to ask what. "I will help you hide or leave the country," Rodgers said. "But I won't take you to my camp."

"We know this land. We can find it without you," Hasan said confidently. "But we will not need to. Your people must have vehicles where they are. You are going to tell them to come and get you."

"I don't think so," Rodgers replied.

Hasan walked toward the general. "If Mahmoud and I approach your camp in the dark with the colonel's motorcycle, wearing what is left of your clothes, do you think we will be stopped?"

"My people will challenge you, yes."

"But not before we get very close with our weapons. And they will hesitate before firing," Hasan said. "We will not hesitate. We cannot."

Rodgers extrapolated quickly. Firebrand Private Pupshaw might not hesitate to open fire at the bike, but Private DeVonne might. And if Phil Katzen, Lowell Coffey, or Mary Rose Mohalley were taking the watch tonight, they might not even be armed. Rodgers couldn't justify the almost certain loss of life, especially if these men ended up taking the ROC anyway.

"What guarantee have I that you won't kill the colonel and me after I place the call?" Rodgers asked.

"We could have killed you already," Hasan replied. "We could have telephoned your camp, said we found you bleeding and unconscious. They would have come for you. No, General. The fewer deaths, the better."

"The more hostages the better, you mean."

"God is compassionate and merciful," Hasan said. "If you cooperate, then we will follow His example."

112

"Your flood killed innocent people as well as believers," Rodgers said. "Where was your mercy then?"

"The believers have gone to the High Pavilions of the Lord," Hasan replied. "The others were content to dwell in our stolen homeland. They are victims of their own greed."

"Not their greed," Rodgers said. "The greed of generations long dead."

"Nonetheless," said Hasan, "if they continue to live there, they will continue to die."

Mahmoud spoke impatiently to Hasan, who nodded.

"Mahmoud is correct," Hasan said to Rodgers. "We have talked enough. It is time to telephone." He opened the phone and handed it to Rodgers. "Press only the redial button. And don't try and warn them. It will only lead to bloodshed."

Rodgers looked at the phone. The thought of giving ground offended him utterly. His heart told him to crush the damn thing and be done with these three. He asked himself, What will your people think if you surrender for them? If you don't give them the chance to fight or withdraw on their own? But this wasn't a question of them not having a choice. By resisting he sentenced those people to death. By surrendering for now, he might be able to negotiate the release of some of the team or disable the ROC's key technologies. At least that was something.

Rodgers hesitated as he swallowed the bile of self-reproach.

"Quickly!" said Hasan.

Rodgers looked at the phone. He reached down slowly and touched redial. He raised the telephone to his ear, and Hasan leaned close to listen.

As he did, Rodgers knew that everything he'd just told himself was nonsense. No one was going to hand him a telephone and order him to lead his countrymen into an ambush.

FIFTEEN

Monday, 6:58 p.m.,
Sanliurfa, Turkey

Lowell Coffey II was dozing in the driver's seat of the ROC when the phone rang. He awoke with a jolt, fumbled with the phone for a moment before finding the right button to push, then answered.

"This is the mobile archaeological research center," he said.

"Benedict, it's Carlton Kuhnigit."

Lowell wasn't fully awake. But he was awake enough to recognize Mike Rodgers's voice and to know that his own name wasn't Benedict. In fact, the only Benedict he knew of was Benedict Arnold the traitor, who'd plotted to surrender West Point to the British during the American Revolution. Since Mike Rodgers had zero sense of humor, there had to be a reason he'd referred to him as Benedict. There also had to be a reason that Rodgers had intentionally mispronounced the name of his Carlton Knight pseudonym.

All of this the attorney considered in the instant it took him to reply with a jaunty, "Hi there, Mr. Kuhnigit." At the same time Coffey pressed the record button on the top of the phone cradle. Then he opened the driver's side window and snapped his fingers. Phil Katzen and Mary Rose were eating a chicken they'd bought in the market that morning and had cooked over a campfire. Coffey pointed to them and indicated that they should come in quickly but quietly. They put their paper plates down and hurried over. "How are things going?" Coffey asked.

"Not so well," Rodgers said. "Benny, the colonel and I had this damn accident out here."

"Are you okay?"

"More or less," Rodgers said. "But I want you to tell Captain John Hawkins to pack up and get out here as soon as possible."

Katzen and Mary Rose rushed in.

"I'll tell Captain John Hawkins to do that," Coffey replied. The attorney looked at Mary Rose. He pointed to the computer and wriggled his fingers as though he were typing.

Mary Rose gave him a thumbs-up "got-it" and sat down at the keyboard. She typed in the name.

"Where are you?" Coffey asked. Not that he needed Rodgers to tell him. Coffey would let Mary Rose and the ROC do that. But he wanted to give Rodgers the opportunity to talk, to pass along any other information.

"Have you got map Three P-as-in-perps handy?" Rodgers asked.

"Right here," Coffey said. "Just let me open it up." His mind was speeding. Someone who understood English was obviously listening in, but not someone who spoke colloquial English or knew American history. Otherwise, that person would have known that perps meant perpetrators. The person also would have known who Benedict Arnold was.

So what's he saying? Coffey asked himself. Was Benedict Arnold Colonel Seden? Or did Mike mean that he was being forced to betray the ROC? In any case, there was treason afoot and three people were holding him.

"Ready with the map," Coffey lied.

"Okay," Rodgers said. "We're off the road about a quarter mile after the dirt road begins. There's a hill on the east side of the first rise. See it?"

"Sure do," Coffey replied.

"I'll be waiting for you there."

"You need any medical supplies?" Coffey asked.

"Just a couple of bandages. Also a shot of whiskey for the colonel. I think you better hurry, okay?"

Coffey knew that Rodgers didn't drink. He was guessing that someone had been shot. "I understand, Carlton. We'll be there ASAP." Coffey hesitated. "Are you sure you'll be all right until we get there?"

"I think I'll live, Benny," Rodgers replied.

Coffey hung up and walked toward Katzen. "Okay," he said gravely, "what I got from this is that Mike and the colonel have been caught by three people. They don't speak English very well. Apparently they read his Carlton Knight ID and called him Kuhnigit. Sounds like Seden was shot and Mike was forced to call us. And since Mike isn't a swearing man, I'm guessing he mentioned the 'damn' accident for a very specific reason reason."

"Like he stumbled on the guys who blew up the Ataturk," said Katzen, who was standing behind Mary Rose.

"Or they stumbled upon him," Coffey said.

"Here," Mary Rose said. "Captain John Hawkins. According to the database, Hawkins was an English sailor who was ambushed by the Spanish in Vera Cruz in 1568."

Katzen shook his head slowly. "Only Mike Rodgers would know something like that."

Coffey had slipped into Mike Rodgers's seat. He called Op-Center on the secure line built into the computer. "Mary Rose," he said, "Mike told me he's about a quarter mile up the dirt road. Can we get a closer look at that?"

"Right away," she said. It took just over a second to bring up a map of the region. "They were going across the desert to the plains, which puts them right . . . here." She zeroed in on the region where the road began. "Do you have any other information?"

"Yes," Coffey said. "He said that they were at a hill on the east side of the first rise."

"I see it," she said. She called up the computer-simulated relief map. "That's north-south coordinate E, east-west coordinate H. I'll contact the NRO. See if they can get us visuals."

"I'm going to brief Privates Pupshaw and DeVonne in case we have to move out," Katzen said.

Coffey nodded as the seal of the National Crisis Management Center appeared on the screen—the organization's formal name, though no one at Op-Center ever used it. He typed in his personal access code, and a menu appeared offering all the different departments. Coffey selected Office of the Director. A prompt appeared asking him to input the full name of the person with whom he wished to speak, surname first. This procedure helped to screen crank calls from hackers who managed to get this far into the program.

Hood, Paul David

A computerized voice told him to wait a moment. Almost at once, Bugs Benet's face filled the screen.

"Good afternoon, Mr. Coffey," Benet said.

"Bugs, we've got a major situation here," Coffey said. "I need to talk to Paul."

"I'll tell him," Benet said.

Hood was on the secure digital uplink within seconds. "Lowell, what's up?" he asked.

"Paul, we just heard from Mike out in the field," Coffey said. "From the sound of things, he found the terrorists he was searching for. And it looks like they've got him and the TSF colonel as their prisoners."

"Hold on," Hood said. His expression darkened and his voice had dropped considerably. "Let me bring Bob Herbert in on this."

A few seconds later the screen split down the middle. Hood was on the left side, Herbert on the right. The intelligence chief's thinning hair was disheveled. He looked even grimmer than Hood.

"Talk to me, Lowell," Herbert said. "Do you have any idea what these bastards want?"

"Not a clue," Coffey said. "All we're supposed to do is go out there and get Mike and the TSF officer who went with him."

"Out where?" Herbert asked.

"Into the plains," Coffey said.

"Now?" Herbert asked.

"Immediately," Coffey replied. "Mike was pretty explicit about us leaving at once."

"Meaning the guys who are holding them must need a lift out of the area," Herbert said, "possibly out of the country. Maybe that chopper they had was too hot to keep flying."

"Where are they located?" Hood asked.

"About a ninety-minute drive north of here," Coffey said. "Mary Rose is in touch with the NRO to try and get some precise visuals."

"Did Mike put a time limit on how long it should take you to get there?" Herbert asked.

"No," Coffey said.

"Did the captives make any other demands?" Hood asked. "Do you have to bring the ROC?"

"No," Coffey said.

"Is there any indication that they even know about the ROC?" Herbert asked.

"None," said Coffey.

"At least that's something," Hood said.

"Excuse me," Mary Rose said, turning around. "Stephen Viens says he can give us an infrared photo in about two or three minutes. He's still got the 30-45-3 in the neighborhood."

"Bless him," Coffey said. "Paul, Bob, did you hear that?"

"I heard," said Hood.

"Lowell, did Mike say anything else?" Herbert asked.

"Not much," said Coffey. "He didn't seem to be in pain or under duress. He passed all the information along calmly, using oblique references to Benedict Arnold and some old English sea captain who we found out was ambushed. It was clear he was trying to tell us that he was being forced to say what he was saying and that we'd better watch out."

"These jerks'll want hostages," Herbert said. "If we don't fire, chances are they won't either."

"Are you saying that we should give them a ride?" Hood asked.

"I'm just giving you the facts," Herbert said. "If it were up to me I'd shoot the bastards dead. Fortunately, it isn't up to me."

"Are Privates Pupshaw and DeVonne ready to go out?" Hood asked.

"They were eating when the call came in," Coffey said. "Phil is briefing them now. What do we do about the Turkish government? The TSF will be calling when their man doesn't check in."

"You negotiated our way in there," Hood said. "What are we obliged to tell them?"

"Depends what we decide to do," Coffey said. "If we start shooting we'll be in violation of about twenty different international codes. If we kill anyone, we're in deep doo. If it's a Turk, we're in very deep doo."

"What if we shoot the terrorists who blew up the dam?" Hood asked.

"If we can prove it, and let the TSF share credit, then we'll probably be heroes," Coffey said.

"I'll have Martha get in touch with them," Hood said. "She can brief them and ask them to lay low."

"Lowell," Herbert said, "Mike didn't promise them a certain kind of transportation."

"Not as far as I know."

"Which means if you go out there with the ROC," Herbert continued, "we can follow you even if we don't have satellite imaging. I can listen in through the computer."

"Negative," said Katzen. "I think Mary Rose should lobotomize the hardware."

"I disagree," Herbert said. "That'll leave you defense—"

"Picture about to come in!" Mary Rose said. "NRO should be downloading it to you as well, Paul."

In exactly .8955 seconds, the monitors filled with the same green-tinted photograph showing the site described by Rodgers. Op-Center and the ROC were still voice-linked.

"There they are," Herbert said.

Rodgers was sitting against the motorcycle. It looked

as if his hands were tied to the handlebars. His feet were also bound. The TSF officer was lying on his belly, his hands lashed behind him. A third man was sitting on the side of the hill, smoking. There was a submachine gun in his lap.

"They're still alive," Hood said. "Thank God for that."

Katzen, Private Pupshaw, and Private DeVonne entered then. They stood between the two stations and had a look at the photograph.

Coffey leaned toward the screen. "I only see three people."

"Maybe Mike meant that there were only three people altogether," Hood suggested.

"No," Coffey said. "He told me there were three perps. I can play back the tape if you want, but that's what he said."

"The other two could be out on stakeout," Herbert said. "It would make sense for them to have gone ahead and see who comes in. Make sure Mike didn't send for the cavalry or something."

"Even if they're out watching the road," Hood said, "we've got two Strikers they may not know about. If the captors think that Mike was a run-of-the-mill spook, they may not expect an armed escort to come for him. Especially one that knows exactly what they're riding into."

"Which brings us back to whether you take the ROC," Herbert said. "I still think you should leave everything active. Paul?"

Hood thought for a moment. "Phil, you're against it."

"If anything happens to us, we'd be giving them the key to the candy store," Katzen said.

"Lowell?" Hood asked.

"Legally, Paul, we might have problems," Coffey

said. "Our geographical playing field was pretty carefully delineated to both the Turks and Congress."

"Jesus!" Herbert yelled. "Mike's being held hostage and you're talking about our legal limitations!"

"There's something else," Katzen said. "The Strikers. If someone's watching the van, they may see them. If we dismantle some of the equipment, we can hide them in the battery compartment."

"The battery compartment," Herbert said. "Privates, how do you feel about that?"

"I like it, sir," Pupshaw said. "We go in completely unseen."

Hood asked if everyone was finished with the photograph. They were. He had the face-to-face visuals restored.

"Okay," Hood said. "We go in and we take the lobotomized ROC. Who runs the operation?"

"We can't call it a military rescue," Coffey said. "We need Congressional approval for that and it'll never come in time. So on the books at least it has to be a civilian operation."

"Agreed," said Hood. "The Strikers dress-down, weapons handy but hidden. Who runs the operation?"

No one answered. Coffey looked at the three faces on the green-lit screen. "I guess I'm elected," he said unenthusiastically. "I've got seniority."

"By two days over Phil," Herbert said. "Shit, Lowell, you've never fired a gun. At least Phil has."

"To scare away nesting harp seals," Coffey said. "He never shot *at* anybody. That makes us both virgins."

"Not me," said Mary Rose. "When I was at Columbia I shot once a week at a pistol club on Murray Street in Manhattan. And I once pulled a gun on an intruder who busted into my dorm room. I don't care who goes

123

and who runs this, but I'm going with them."

"Thanks, M.R.," Hood said. "Phil, you did lead some pseudo-military Greenpeace escapades, didn't you?"

"Very pseudo." Katzen grinned. "Shotguns with blanks. I did three in Washington State, two in Florida, two in Canada."

"You feel up to running this?"

"If it has to be done, I'll do it."

"That isn't what I wanted to hear," Hood snapped. "Can you take command of this operation?"

Katzen flushed. "Yes," he said. He looked at the determined faces of Mary Rose and the two Strikers. "Hell, yes, I can do it."

"Good," Hood said. "Lowell, I'd prefer it if you stayed behind. Whatever happens, somebody's going to have to be on-site to smooth things with the Turkish government. You're the best man for that job."

"I won't try to change your mind," Lowell said. He looked at his companions and then looked down. Even though he'd offered to go and been ordered to stay, he felt like a coward. "But in fairness to the mission, let's see how things look when we're ready to roll."

"All right," Hood said. "It'll be your call."

"Thanks ever so much." Coffey frowned.

"You realize, Paul," Herbert said, "that by running even a civilian operation covertly, both Turkey and Congress will be up our butts for a very long time. And that's just if things go right. If they go wrong, we'll all be making license plates for the government."

"I understand," Hood said. "But getting Mike out is my only concern."

"And there's something else," Herbert said. "Our sources in Ankara tell us that the Turkish Presidential Council and Cabinet are meeting now to mobilize the military. They want to prevent any further attacks. The ROC may run into some pretty skittish patrols."

"Once we pull the batteries we'll be limited to eyes and ears," Katzen said. "But we'll keep them open."

"I'll see if Viens can keep a satellite eye on things too," Herbert said.

"Thanks, all of you," Hood said. "Now if you'll excuse me, I'm going to phone Senator Fox so she doesn't find out about it from someone in the Ankara bureau of the *Washington Post*."

Hood clicked off. After saying that he was going to find out what other intelligence agencies had on the dam attack, Herbert also excused himself.

When the ROC team was alone, Katzen rubbed his hands together.

"All right, then," he said. "Mary Rose, would you kindly print out the map? You're going to drive. Sondra, Walter—we three are going to have a strategy session with input from the NRO." He turned and offered Coffey his hand. "As for you, wish us luck and then go finish my chicken for me."

Coffey looked at the four and smiled. "Good luck," he said. "You're really, really going to need it."

"Why is that?" Katzen said.

"Because I can deal with the Turks just as well by phone." He took a long, anxious breath. "I'm coming with you."

SIXTEEN

Monday, 12:01 p.m., Washington, D.C.

Paul Hood was preoccupied with Mike Rodgers's plight when he received a call from Deputy Chief of Staff Stephanie Klaw at the White House. Hood was being ordered to report to the Situation Room by one o'clock to discuss the crisis on the Euphrates. He left at once, telling his assistant Bugs Benet to notify him immediately if there were any developments in Turkey. In the absence of both Hood and Mike Rodgers, Martha Mackall would be in charge of Op-Center. Bob Herbert wouldn't be happy about that. She was the kind of career politician he disliked and distrusted. But he'd have to live with it. Martha knew her way around the corridors of power both domestically and abroad.

At this time of day it would take an hour for him to drive from Op-Center headquarters at Andrews Air Force Base to the White House. Op-Center usually had a helicopter at its disposal for quick, fifteen minute trips into the capital. However, there had been trouble with the rotor heads in other Sikorsky CH53E Super Stallions and the entire government fleet had been grounded. That was fine with Hood. He preferred to drive.

Hood hopped right onto Pennsylvania Avenue, which was located just a short distance northeast of the base. Though most government officials had private cars and drivers to take them around the city, Hood eschewed the privilege. He'd also refused it when he was Mayor of Los Angeles. The idea of being chauffeured was just too ostentatious for him. Security didn't concern Hood. No one wanted to kill him. Or if they did, he'd rather have someone try to do him harm instead of going after his wife or children or mother. Besides, driving himself, he could still conduct business by phone. He also had the opportunity to listen to music and think. And what he was thinking about now was Mike Rodgers.

Hood and his second-in-command were very different types of men. Mike was a benevolent autocrat. Hood was a thinking-man's bureaucrat. Mike was a career soldier. Hood had never even fired a gun. Mike was a fighter by nature. Hood was a diplomat by temperament. Mike quoted Lord Byron and Erich Fromm and William Tecumseh Sherman. Hood occasionally remembered lyrics from Hal David and Alfred E. Neuman's quotes from his son's copies of *Mad* magazine. Mike was an intense introvert. Hood was a guarded extrovert. The two men often disagreed, sometimes passionately. But it was because they disagreed, it was because Mike Rodgers had the courage to say what was on his mind, that Hood trusted and respected him. Hood also liked the man. He truly did.

Hood maneuvered patiently through the thick lunch-time traffic. His suit jacket was folded across the seat and his cellular phone lay on top of it. He wanted it to ring. God, how he wanted to know what was going on. At the same time, he dreaded finding out.

Hood stayed in his lane in the slow-moving traffic.

As he did, he ruminated over the fact that death was an inescapable part of intelligence work. This was something Bob Herbert had pounded into him during the early days of Op-Center. Undercover operatives in domestic as well as foreign situations were frequently discovered, tortured, and killed. And sometimes the reverse was true. Often, operatives had to kill to keep from being discovered.

Then there was Striker, the military wing of Op-Center. Elite teams lost members on secret missions. Op-Center's own Striker had lost two so far. Bass Moore in North Korea and Lieutenant Colonel Charlie Squires in Russia. Sometimes officers were murdered at home and sometimes they were ambushed abroad. Hood's own life had been in jeopardy recently when he and French undercover operatives had helped to break up a ring of neo-Nazis in Europe.

But while death was an understood risk, it was brutal on the survivors. Several Strikers had suffered serious reactive depression due to the death of Commander Squires. For several weeks they had been unable to perform even simple duties. Not only had the survivors shared the lives and dreams of their dead coworkers, they also felt that they'd failed the victims in some way. *Was the intelligence as reliable as it should have been? Were our backup plans and exit strategy sufficiently well thought out? Did we take reasonable precautions?* Merciless, unforgiving guilt was also the price of doing business.

Hood reached the White House at exactly 12:55, though it took him a few minutes to park and get through the security check. Upon finally being admitted, he was met by the slender, gray-haired Stephanie Klaw. Side by side, they walked briskly down the corridor.

"They've just started the meeting," Stephanie said,

her voice as soft as the green carpet underfoot. "I gather, Mr. Hood, that you're still motoring around Washington by yourself?"

"I am."

"You really ought to get a driver," she said. "I assure you, the General Accounting Office will not think that you're taking advantage of your position."

"You know I don't believe in them, Mrs. Klaw."

"I am very much aware of that," she said. "And part of me thinks that's charming. But you know, Mr. Hood, those drivers know the traffic patterns and how to maneuver through them. They also have these really loud sirens to help them get around. Besides, using drivers helps keep the unemployment statistics down. And we like it here when those figures look good."

Hood looked at her. The handsome, wrinkled face was deadpan. He could tell that Mrs. Klaw wasn't making fun of him, but of everyone else who took government limousines.

"How would you like to become my driver?" he asked.

"No, thank you," she replied. "I'm Type A when I get behind a wheel. I'd abuse the siren."

Paul smiled slightly. "Mrs. Klaw, you've been the one bright spot in my morning. Thanks."

"You're welcome," she said. "Your lack of pretension is always a bright spot in mine."

They stopped at an elevator. Mrs. Klaw wore a card on a chain around her neck. It had a magnetic stripe on the back and a photo ID on the front. She inserted it into a slot to the left of the door. The door opened and Hood stepped in. Mrs. Klaw leaned in and pressed a red button. The button read her thumbprint and turned green. She kept her finger on the button.

"Please don't make the President cross," she said.

"I'll try not to."

"And do your best to keep the others from fighting with Mr. Burkow," she added. "He's in a mood over all of this and you know how that affects the President." She leaned closer to Hood. "He's got to defend his man."

"I'm all for loyalty," Hood said noncommittally as she lifted her thumb and the door shut. The ultra-hawkish National Security Advisor was not an easy man with whom to keep the peace.

The only noise in the wood-paneled elevator was the soft whir of the ceiling ventilator. Hood turned his face up to the cool air. After a quick ride he reached the White House sublevel. This was the technological heart of the White House where conferences were held and grounds security was maintained. The door opened on a small office. An armed Marine was waiting for him. Hood presented his ID to the guard. After examining it, the Marine thanked him and stepped aside. Hood walked over to the room's only other occupant, the President's Executive Secretary. She was seated at a small desk outside the Situation Room. She E-mailed the President that Hood had arrived, and he was told to go right in.

The brightly lighted Situation Room consisted of a long mahogany table in the center with comfortable leather-cushioned chairs around it. There was a new STU-5 secure phone, a pitcher of water, and a computer monitor at each station, with slide-out keyboards underneath. On the walls were detailed video maps showing the location of U.S. and foreign troops, as well as flags indicating trouble spots. Red flags marked present armed conflict, while green flags marked latent danger spots. Hood noticed that there was already a red flag on the Turkey-Syria border. Tucked in the far corner of the room was a table with two male secretaries. One took minutes on a Powerbook. The other sat by a computer and was responsible for bringing up any maps or data which might be required.

The heavy, six-paneled door clicked shut by itself. Above the highly polished table, two gold ceiling fans with brown blades turned slowly. Hood gave a general nod to everyone around the table as he arrived, saving a fast smile for his friend Secretary of State Av Lincoln. Lincoln winked back. Then Hood nodded directly at President Michael Lawrence.

"Good afternoon, sir," Hood said.

"Afternoon, Paul," the tall former Minnesota Governor said. "Av was just bringing us up to date."

The President was clearly in a high-energy state. During his three years in office, the President had not enjoyed any headline-making foreign policy successes. Though that would not be enough to lose him the next election, he was a born competitor who was frustrated at not having found the right combination of military strength, economic muscle, and charisma to dominate international affairs.

"Before you continue, Av," the President said, holding up a hand, "Paul—what's the latest on General Rodgers?"

"There's been no change in the situation," Hood said as he made his way to the empty leather chair in the middle of the table. "The Regional Op-Center is headed deeper into Turkey, to the spot from which General Rodgers telephoned." He glanced at his watch. "They should be arriving within the half hour."

"Will the ROC mount a rescue attempt?" asked National Security Advisor Burkow.

Hood sat down. "We're empowered to evacuate our personnel from unstable situations," he said carefully.

"However, we have no idea whether that's feasible at this point."

"Anything's feasible if you want to pay the price," Burkow remarked. "Your people are authorized to use deadly force to rescue hostages. We've got thirty-seven hundred troops at the Incirlik Air-Base, which is right around the corner."

"There are two Strikers onboard," Hood replied. "But as I said, I have no idea what's feasible at this point."

"I want to be notified personally of any developments," the President said, "wherever you are."

"Of course, sir," Hood said. He wondered what the President meant by that last comment.

"Av," the President went on, "would you please continue your briefing?"

"Yes, sir," said Secretary of State Av Lincoln.

The powerfully built former major league baseball star looked at his notepad. He had made a successful transition into politics, and had been one of the earliest supporters of the candidacy of Michael Lawrence. He was one of the few insiders Paul Hood trusted completely.

"Paul," said Lincoln, "I was just telling the others about the Turkish mobilization. My office has been in constant contact with Ambassador Robert Macaluso at our embassy in Ankara, as well as with the U.S. Consulates General in Istanbul and Izmir and the consulate in Adana. We've also been talking with Ambassador Kande at the Turkish Chancery in Washington. All of them have confirmed the following information.

"At 12:30 p.m. our time, Turkey mobilized over a half-million men in their Land Forces and Air Force and put one hundred thousand men on high alert in the Naval Forces, which includes the Naval Air and Naval Infantry. That's nearly all of their total military power.''

"Including reserves?'' the President asked.

"No, sir,'' said Defense Secretary Colon. "They can dig up another twenty thousand troops if they have to, then dip into the nineteen-to-forty-nine-year-old work force for another fifty thousand trainees if necessary.''

"We've been told that the land and air forces are going to take up positions down the Euphrates and along the Syrian border,'' Lincoln went on. "The sea forces are being concentrated on the Aegean and the Mediterranean. We've been assured by Ankara that the naval troops in the Mediterranean will go no further south than the southern tip of the Gulf of Alexandretta.''

Hood looked at the map on his computer screen. The gulf ended about twenty-five miles north of Syria.

"The Turkish forces in the Aegean are to make sure the Greeks stay out of this,'' Lincoln said. "We haven't heard anything definitive yet from Damascus, though the President, his three Vice Presidents, and the Council of Ministers are meeting right now. Ambassador Moualem at the chancery here in Washington says there will be an appropriate response from Syria.''

"Meaning?'' asked the President.

"Some kind of mobilization,'' said General Ken Vanzandt, Chairman of the Joint Chiefs of Staff. "Syria's got its highest concentration of soldiers in bases along the Orontes in the west, along the Euphrates in central Syria, and in the east near the Iraqi and Turkish borders. The Syrian President will probably send half of those troops north, maybe one hundred thousand troops.''

"How far north will they go?'' the President asked.

"All the way,'' said Vanzandt. "To within slingshot distance of Turkey. Since losing the Golan Heights to

Israel in 1967, the Syrians have been pretty aggressive about defending their territory."

"It's interesting that Turkey mobilized nearly six hundred thousand men," said Secretary of Defense Ernie Colon. "That's almost three times the total manpower available to the Syrian Army, the Syrian Navy, the Syrian Air Force, and the Syrian Air Defense Forces combined. Turkey's obviously saying, 'We'll take you on one-to-one. And if any other nations join in, we've got something left over for them too.' "

"That sounds good on the surface," said General Vanzandt. "But the Turks are facing a big problem. They have to fight this kind of terrorism, that's a given. But even if the Syrian military weren't a factor, a Turkish attack against the Kurds is a dangerous proposition. We know that the Kurds have been trying to smooth out their differences. Whether they caused the dam attack or not, it's certain to encourage and solidify the different Kurdish elements. A counterattack by Turkey will inspire even greater unity. There are fourteen to fifteen million Kurds among Turkey's fifty-nine million people, and they're ready to blow."

"Who can blame them?" asked Lincoln. "They've been shot at, gassed in their homes, and executed without trials."

"Hold it right there, Av," said Burkow. "Many of those Kurds are terrorists."

"And many are not," Lincoln replied.

Burkow ignored him. "Larry, what was that business in the Syrian Navy last month?"

CIA director Larry Rachlin folded his hands on the table. "The Syrians did an A-one job keeping this out of the press," he said, "but a Kurdish mole assassinated a general and two aides. When the mole was captured, another Kurdish mole took the general's wife and two daughters hostage and demanded his release. Instead, they sent him his colleague's head. Literally. There was a rescue attempt. By the time it was finished, the general's wife, daughters, and the second Kurd were dead along with two Syrian rescuers.''

"If it's the Turks who are terrorizing the Kurds,'' said the President, "why did this mole turn on the Syrians?''

"Because,'' said Rachlin, "the Syrian President has come to the conclusion, correctly, that his armed forces are full of Kurdish moles. Some of them in very high places. He's vowed to flush them all out.''

Lincoln sat back with disgust. "Steve, Larry, what's the point of all this?''

"The point is that we can't start bleeding all over for the Kurds,'' Burkow said. "We've been good to them in the past. But they're becoming increasingly militant, they're ruthless, and they've got God-knows-how-many moles in the Turkish military as well. If we get mixed up in this those Turkish moles may start turning on NATO assets.''

"Actually, things could be a whole lot worse than that,'' Vanzandt said. "The Kurds have a lot of sympathizers among the Islamic fundamentalist parties in Turkey. Individually or together, those Kurds and their sympathizers could very well take advantage of the confusion of war to try and throw out the secular rulers in both governments.''

"Out of chaos comes more chaos,'' Lincoln said.

"You got it,'' said Vanzandt. "Out with flawed democracy, in with religious oppression.''

"Out with the U.S.,'' Defense Secretary Colon said.

"Out isn't the word for it,'' CIA Director Rachlin added. "Steve's right on the money. They'll start hunting us down not only in Turkey but in Greece. Remember all those Afghan freedom fighters we helped to arm

135

and train to fight the Soviets? A lot of those people have thrown in with the Islamic fundamentalists. Many of them are being directed by Sheik Safar al-Awdah, a Syrian who is one of the most radical clerics in the region."

"God, I'd like to see someone drop-kick that son of a bitch," Steve Burkow said. "His radio speeches have sent a lot of people on one-way bus trips into Israel with bombs tied to their legs."

"His following in Turkey and Saudi Arabia in particular are very strong," Rachlin went on, "and it's gotten stronger in Turkey since Islamic Party Leader Necmettin Erbakan became Prime Minister of Turkey in the summer of 1996. Ironically, not all of the radicalism has to do with religion. Some of it has to do with the economy. In the 1980s, when Turkey went from being a relatively closed market to being a global one, only a handful of people got rich. The rest stayed poor or got poorer. Those kinds of people are easy converts to anything new."

"The fundamentalists and the big urban underclass are natural allies," said Av Lincoln. "Both are minorities and both want things the wealthy, secular leaders have."

"Larry," the President said, "you mentioned Saudi Arabia. What will the rest of the region do if things escalate between Turkey and Syria?"

"Israel is the big question," said Rachlin. "They take their military cooperation agreement with Turkey very, very seriously. Israel's been flying training missions out of Akinci Air Base west of Ankara for two years now. They've also been slowly upgrading Turkey's 164 Phantom F-4s to the more sophisticated Phantom 2000s."

"Mind you," Colon pointed out, "Israel didn't just do that out of the goodness of their hearts. They were paid six hundred million dollars to do that."

"That's right," Rachlin agreed. "But in the event of war, Israel will still continue to provide spare parts, possibly ammunition, and certainly intelligence to Turkey. It's the same kind of arrangement Israel signed with Jordan back in 1994. There will probably be no direct military intervention unless Israel is attacked. However, if Israel permits Turkey to fly from its territory for a two-sided slam at Syria, you can be pretty sure that Damascus will attack Israel."

"For the record," said Vanzandt, "that 'bracketing the enemy' idea works both ways. Syria and Greece have been talking about forging a military relationship so that either of them could hit Turkey from two directions."

"Talk about a marriage made in Hell," said Lincoln. "Greece and Syria have virtually no other common ground."

"Which should tell you how much they both hate Turkey," Burkow pointed out.

"What about the other nations in the region?" asked the President.

"Iran will certainly intensify efforts to promote their puppet parties in Ankara," Colon said, "calling for general strikes and marches, but they'll stay out of this militarily. They don't need to become involved."

"Unless Armenia gets pulled in," Lincoln said.

"Right," said Colon, "which we'll get to in a second. Iraq will almost certainly use the excuse of troop movements to attack Kurds operating on their border with Syria. And once Iraq is mobilized, there's always the possibility that they'll do something to provoke Kuwait or Saudi Arabia or even their old enemy Iran. But as Av said, the big question we have is about Armenia."

The Secretary of State nodded. "Armenia is almost entirely Armenian Orthodox. If the government there fears that Turkey is going to go Islamic, they may have no choice but to jump into any conflict to protect their own border. If that happens, Azerbaijan, which is mostly Muslim, will almost certainly use that as an excuse to try and reclaim the Nagorno-Karabakh region, which they lost to Armenia in skirmishes in 1994."

"And which Turkey has publicly stated belongs to Azerbaijan," Colon said. "That creates tension within Turkey for those who support their religious brethren in Armenia. On top of everything else, we could have civil war in Turkey over events in two neighboring countries."

"This might be a good time to push the expansion of NATO," Lincoln pointed out. "Bring Poland, Hungary, and the Czech Republic into the fold to keep them stabilized. Use them as a breakwater."

"We'll never be able to make that happen in time," Burkow said.

Lincoln smiled. "Then it's best to start right away."

The President shook his head. "Av, I don't want us distracted by that now. Those countries will side with us and we'll support them. My concern is stopping this situation before it gets that far."

"Fine," Lincoln said, raising his hands slightly. "Just a precaution."

Hood looked at the new map which the Situation Room secretary had just put up on the screens. Armenia was situated with Turkey on its western border and Azerbaijan to the east. The Nagorno-Karabakh region in Azerbaijan was claimed by both Armenia and Azerbaijan.

"Obviously," said Lincoln, "the greatest danger isn't that Azerbaijan and Aremenia will go to war. The two of them put together are about half the size of Texas with a combined population of Greater Los Angeles. The danger is that Iran, located directly below them, and Russia, situated directly above them, will start moving troops to protect their own borders. Iran would love to get their hands on that region. It's rich in oil, natural gas, copper, farmland, and other resources. And the hard-liners in Russia would love to get it back.''

"There are also devout Christians in Armenia," said Vanzandt, "and Iran would love to clean them out. Without Armenia to serve as a counterbalance to the mostly Muslim population of Azerbaijan, the entire region becomes a de facto part of Islamic Iran."

"Maybe," said Lincoln. "There are other hair triggers as well. For example, the fifteen million Azeris in the northern provinces of Iran. If they decide to secede, Iran will fight to hold them. And the five million ethnic Caucasians in Turkey will surely fight with their Iranian kin. That puts Iran and Turkey at war with one another. And if the Caucasians fight for independence, chances are good the North Caucasus will be ripped apart by other groups looking to resolve ages-old strife. The Ossetians and Ingush, the Ossetians and the Georgians, the Abkhazians and the Georgians, the Checkens and the Cossacks, the Chechens and the Laks, the Azeris and the Lezgins."

"What's frustrating," said Colon, "is that both Bob Herbert's team at Op-Center and Grady Reynolds's team at the CIA agree with my own people. Damascus probably had nothing to do with blowing up the dam. They'd have to be insane to cut off more than half their own water supply."

"Maybe they want to generate international sympathy," Burkow said. "Videos and photographs of thirsty babies and dying old people would give Syria an instant image-remake. It would help to turn United States sympathy and foreign aid away from Turkey and Israel to them.''

''It would also cause the much larger and better-armed Turkish Army to come marching down their throats,'' Colon replied. ''This dam incident is an act of war. In such a war, the U.S. military and our financial institutions would be obliged by NATO treaty to support Turkey. Israel would also support the Turks, especially if it gave them a chance to hit Syria.''

''Only if Syria rises to the challenge of war,'' Burkow said. ''Turkey might mass an army on the Syrian border. So might Syria. But if Syria chooses not to reply, there'll be no war.''

''And the Arab world would consider them dishonored,'' Colon said. ''No, Steve, that's just too Machiavellian. This makes more sense if it's the work of Syrian Kurds.''

''Why would the Kurds seek to cause an international confrontation?'' asked the President. ''They've been desperate enough to attack host nations. But would they do something on this scale?''

''We've been expecting the different Kurdish nationals to unite for some time,'' said Larry Rachlin. ''Otherwise, they run the risk of getting picked off separately. This could be that unification.''

''Kurdistan in diaspora,'' said Lincoln.

''Exactly,'' said Rachlin.

''The truth is, Steve,'' said Lincoln, ''General Vanzandt is right to worry about what the Kurds might do. As things stand, they're among the most persecuted people on Earth. Distributed throughout Turkey, Syria, and Iraq, they're actively oppressed by all three governments. Until 1991, they weren't even allowed to use their own language in Turkey. Under pressure from the other NATO nations, Ankara reluctantly granted them that but no more. Over twenty thousand Turks have been killed since the rebels started fighting for sovereignty in 1984, and the Kurds are still banned from forming groups of any sort. I'm not just talking about political parties, but even choral clubs or literary societies. If there were a war, the Kurds would inevitably be part of the fighting, and then they'd also be part of the peace process. It's the only way they can ever hope to get autonomy. ''

The President turned to Vanzandt. ''We have to support the Turks. And we also have got to prevent this thing from turning the other way, into Greece and Bulgaria.''

''Agreed,'' said Vanzandt.

''So we've got to try and contain this before the Syrians and Turks go at it,'' said the President. ''Av, what are the chances that the Turks will enter Syria to hunt the bombers?''

''Well, Ankara is pretty upset,'' Lincoln said, ''but I don't think they'll go over the border. At least, not in force.''

''Why not?'' said Vanzandt. ''They've ignored national sovereignty before. In 1996 they mounted some pretty bloody cross-border air attacks on Kurdish separatists in northern Iraq.''

''We've always believed that Turkey was acting with Iraqi approval in that case,'' said CIA Director Rachlin. ''Since the U.S. wouldn't let Saddam attack the Kurds, he let the Turks do it.''

''Anyway,'' said Lincoln, ''there's another reason the Turks are wary of going against Syria. Back in 1987, Turkey discovered that Abdullah Ocalan, the Kurdish guerrilla leader, was living in Damascus. He was sitting in his apartment and ordering attacks on villages in Turkey. Ankara asked Damascus to let a strike team in so they could take him. All Syria had to do was stay out of the way. But Syria didn't want to stir things up with the Syrian Kurds, so they refused. The Turks came very close to ordering a strike team into Damascus."

"Why didn't they?" the President asked.

"They were afraid that Syria had tipped Ocalan off," Lincoln said. "The Turks didn't want to raid the building and not find him there. It would have been politically embarrassing, to say the least."

"I'd say that this dam blast is a helluva lot more provocative than what was happening in 1987," Vanzandt remarked.

"It is," said Lincoln, "but the problem is the same. What if it turns out that Turkish Kurds did the hands-on work, not the Syrian Kurds? Turkey attacks Syria looking for enemies there, and it turns out their own Kurds were responsible. Syria's stock rises in the international forum and Turkey's plummets. Turkey won't risk that kind of an ambush."

"You've got to remember, Mr. President," said Defense Secretary Colon, "this explosion hurts Damascus as much as it does Ankara. My feeling is that it's the unified Kurds who have turned up the heat. They're trying to trigger a war between Turkey and Syria by forcing Turkey to enter Syria looking for terrorists. And the Kurds will keep applying pressure until they get a major incursion."

"Why?" asked the President. "Because they think they'll get a homeland as part of the peace process?"

Colon and Lincoln both nodded.

Hood was looking up at one of the maps. "I don't understand," he said. "What does Syria gain by preventing Turkey from finding Kurdish terrorists? Damascus has got to ensure the security of their other water sources, especially the Orontes River in the west. It looks like it comes right through Turkey into Syria and Lebanon.''

"It does," said Lincoln.

"So if Turkey wants to stop the Kurds," Hood went on, "and Syria needs to stop the Kurds, why won't they join forces? This isn't like the Ocalan affair. Syria doesn't risk stirring up the Kurds. It looks like they're already on the warpath.''

"Syria can't join forces with Turkey," said Vanzandt, "because of the Turkish military cooperation pact with Israel. Syria would sooner support Kurdish political goals to stop them from blowing up other dams rather than join the Turks and eradicate the Kurds.''

"Syria would back one enemy rather than support the friend of another enemy," Colon said. "That's Middle Eastern politics for you.''

"But Syria would have to give up some of its own land to give the Kurds a homeland," the President said.

"Ah, but would they?" asked Av Lincoln. "Suppose the Kurds eventually get what they want, a homeland straddling parts of Turkey, Syria, and Iraq. Do you think for a moment that Syria will stay out of there? They don't play by any rules. They'll use terrorism to exert de facto control over what used to be their territory, and also absorb some of the former Turkish lands into Greater Syria. That's exactly what they've done with Lebanon.''

"General Vanzandt, gentlemen," the President said, "we've got to find some way of guaranteeing the security of those other water sources and also of helping the Turks find the terrorists. What are your suggestions?''

"Larry and Paul, we can talk about internal operations against the terrorists later," said General Vanzandt. "Present the President with some suggestions.''

143

Hood and Rachlin both nodded.

"As for the water," Vanzandt went on, "if we move the *Eisenhower* Carrier Battle Group from Naples to the eastern Mediterranean, we can watch the Orontes while at the same time keeping the seaways secure for Turkish exports. We want to make sure the Greeks don't jump into this."

"That leaves everyone happy," said Steve Burkow, "unless the Syrians suddenly decide in their paranoid way that this is all a United States plot to cut off their water supply. Which, if you ask me, wouldn't be the world's worst idea. That would put Damascus out of the terrorism business right quick."

"And kill how many innocent people?" Lincoln asked.

"Not many more than Syrian-backed terrorists will kill worldwide over the next few years," Burkow replied. He typed his password on the computer and brought up a file. "We were talking about Sheik al-Awdah before," Burkow said as he looked at the screen. "In yesterday's radio speech from Palmyra, Syria, he said, 'We call upon God Almighty to destroy the American economy and society, to transform its states into nations and turn them against one another. To turn its brothers against one another as penance for infidelic evil.' Now, to *my* ears that's a declaration of war. You know how many sickeroos out there are going to hear this and try to make that happen?"

"That doesn't justify blind, preventative strikes," the President pointed out. "We aren't terrorists."

"I know that, sir," Burkow said. "But I'm tired of playing by rules that no one else in the world seems to acknowledge. We pour tens of billions of dollars into the Chinese economy and they use that money to develop and sell military nuclear technology to terrorists.

Why do we allow it? Because we don't want American businesses to suffer by being shut out of China—''

"The issue isn't China," Lincoln said.

"The issue is a chronic goddamn double standard," Burkow shot back. "We look the other way when Iran ships weapons to Muslim terrorists around the world. Why? Because some of those terrorists are bombing other countries. In a perverse way, that gives us allies in the fight against terrorism. We don't have to endure all kinds of criticism for defending ourselves if other nations are defending themselves too. All I'm saying is we've got an opportunity here to hold Syria's feet to the fire. If we cut off their water, we choke their economy. We do that and Hezbollah and the Palestinian terrorist camps in Syria and even our Kurdish terrorists get squeezed."

"Kill the body and you kill the disease," Lincoln replied. "Come on, Steve."

"You also keep the disease from spreading to other bodies," Burkow answered. "If we were to make an object lesson of Syria, I guarantee you Iran and Iraq and Libya would pull in their claws and count their blessings."

"Or redouble their efforts to destroy us," Lincoln said.

"If they did," Burkow replied, "we would turn Tehran and Baghdad and Tripoli into craters wide enough to be photographed from space."

There was a short, uncomfortable silence. Visions of *Dr. Strangelove* flashed through Hood's mind.

"What if we were to turn that around?" Lincoln asked. "What if we were to hold out a helping hand instead of a fist?"

"What kind of hand?" the President asked.

"What would really get Syria's attention isn't just a flow of water but a flow of money," said Lincoln.

"Their economy is in the gutter. They're turning out roughly the same amount of goods as they were fifteen years ago when the population was twenty-five percent smaller. They've gotten mired in an unsuccessful attempt to match Israel's military strength, there's been a big falloff in Arab aid, and they've got insufficient foreign exchange earnings to buy what they need to spur industry and agriculture. They have nearly six billion dollars in external debt."

"My heart grieves," Burkow said. "Seems to me they've got enough money to underwrite terrorism."

"Largely because that's the only kind of pressure they can apply on rich nations," Lincoln said. "Suppose we give Syria the carrot before they sponsor further acts of terrorism. Specifically, we give them U.S. guaranteed credit at the Import Export Bank."

"We can't do that!" Burkow shouted. "For one thing, the World Bank and the International Monetary Fund have to okay any knockdown of debt burdens."

"Donor countries can also write off loans to heavily indebted nations," Hood pointed out.

"Only if the borrowing countries adopt strict market reforms which are monitored by the bank and the fund," Burkow shot back.

"There are ways around that," Hood replied. "We can let them sell off gold deposits."

"And end up buying them ourselves and thereby sponsoring the terrorists who are going to blow our asses up," Burkow said. "No, thanks." He looked back at Av Lincoln. "As long as Syria's on top of the list of terrorist nations, we are forbidden *by law* from giving them financial aid."

"Nuking capital cities strikes you as lawful?" Hood asked.

"In self-defense, yes," Burkow replied with disgust.

"The State Department's annual report on terrorism hasn't had Syria directly involved in a terrorist attack since 1986," said Lincoln, "when Hafez al-Assad's air force intelligence chief organized the bombing of an El Al airliner from London."

"Directly involved." Burkow laughed. "Oh, that's rich, Mr. Secretary. The Syrians are as guilty of terrorism as John Wilkes Booth was of shooting Abraham Lincoln. And not only of terrorism, but of running drug-processing plants for cocaine paste and morphine in the Bekaa Valley, of producing high-quality counterfeit hundred-dollar bills—"

"The issue is terrorism, Steve," Lincoln said. "Not cocaine paste. Not China. Not nuclear war. Stopping terrorism."

"The *issue*," Burkow shouted back, "is giving financial aid to an enemy of this country! You don't want to waste them, that's one thing. But it doesn't mean we have to reward them."

"A token twenty- or thirty-million-dollar loan guarantee as, say, drought relief doesn't constitute aid and it isn't a reward," Lincoln said. "It's merely an incentive to whet their appetites for future cooperation. And coming now, a gesture like that might also help prevent a war."

"Av, Steve," said the President, "all I'm interested in right now is containing and defusing this particular situation." The President looked at Hood. "Paul, I may want you to handle this. Who's your Middle East advisor?"

Hood was caught by surprise. "Locally, I've got Warner Bicking."

"The Kid from Georgetown," Rachlin said. "He was on the U.S. boxing team in the '88 summer Olympics.

Got involved in that tiff over the Iraqi fighter who wanted to defect."

Hood slipped Rachlin an annoyed look. "Warner is a good and trusted colleague."

"He's a loose cannon," Rachlin said to the President. "He critiqued George Bush's policy on asylum on network TV while wearing red trunks and boxing gloves. The press called him 'the flyweight diplomat.' Made a joke of the entire affair."

"I want a heavy hitter, Paul," the President said.

"Warner's a good man," Hood said to the President. "But we've also used Professor Ahmed Nasr to work on many of our white papers."

"I know that name."

"You met him at the dinner for the Sheik of Dubai, Mr. President," Hood said. "Dr. Nasr was the one who left after dessert to help your son with his paper on pan-Turkism."

"I remember him now." The President smiled. "What's his background?"

"He used to be with the National Center for Middle East Studies in Cairo," Hood said. "Now he's with the Institute for Peace."

"How would he play in Syria?"

"He'd be very welcome there," said Hood, still confused. "He's a devout Muslim and a pacifist. He also has a reputation for honesty."

"Hell," said Larry Rachlin, "I'm starting to lean toward Steve on this one. Mr. President, do we really want an Egyptian Boy Scout talking restraint with a terrorist state?"

"We do when everyone else is running off half-cocked," the President said. He glanced at Burkow, but didn't rebuke him. Hood knew that he wouldn't. The men had been friends for too long and been through too many personal and professional crises together. Besides, Hood knew that the President welcomed Burkow saying the things that he, as the Commander-in-Chief, could not. "Paul," the President went on, "I'd like you to go to Damascus with Professor Nasr."

Hood recoiled slightly. Larry Rachlin and Steve Burkow both sat up straight. Lincoln smiled.

"Mr. President, I'm not a diplomat," Hood protested.

"Sure you are," said Lincoln. "Will Rogers said that diplomacy is the art of saying 'nice doggie' until you can find a rock. You can do that."

"You can also talk to the Syrians about intelligence and about banking," the President said. "That's exactly the kind of diplomacy I need right now."

"Until we find a rock," Burkow muttered.

"Frankly, Paul," the President continued. "I also can't afford to send anyone at cabinet level. If I do, the Turks will feel slighted. Personally, I'm as tired of being pushed around as Steve and Larry are. But we've got to try the low-key route. Mrs. Klaw will see that you have the appropriate policy papers to read on the flight. Where is Mr. Nasr?"

"In London, sir," Hood said. "He's speaking at some kind of symposium."

"You can pick him up there," the President said. "Dr. Nasr can fine-tune and help sell whatever you think will work. You can take that kid from GU if you'd like. This will also put you on the scene in case you need to help negotiate for the release of General Rodgers. Ambassador Haveles in Damascus will see to all the security arrangements."

Hood thought about missing his daughter's piccolo solo tonight at school. He thought about how his wife would fear for him going into that part of the world at this particular time. And he thought about both the challenge and pressure of being part of history, of helping to save lives instead of risking them.

"I'll be on a plane this afternoon, sir," Hood said.

"Thanks, Paul." The President looked at his watch. "It's one-thirty-two. General Vanzandt, Steve, we'll have the Joint Chiefs and Security Council meet in the Oval Office at three o'clock. You want to move the battle group, General?"

"I think it would be prudent, sir," Vanzandt said.

"Then do it," said the President. "I also want options in the event of increased hostilities. We've got to keep this from spreading."

"Yes, sir," General Vanzandt said.

The President rose, signaling the end of the meeting. He walked out with Burkow and General Vanzandt on either side, followed by Rachlin and Colon. Secretary of Defense Colon threw Hood a friendly salute as he left.

As Hood sat alone at the conference table, collecting his thoughts, Av Lincoln walked over.

"The first time I ever pitched in the Major Leagues," the Secretary of State told him, "it wasn't because I was ready for the job. It was because three other starters were sick, injured, or suspended. I was eighteen years old and scared spitless, but I won the game. You're smart, you're dedicated, you're loyal, and you've got a conscience, Paul. You're going to bat this assignment out of the ballpark."

Hood rose. He shook Lincoln's hand. "Thanks, Av. I hope I don't dazzle everyone so much that you're out of a job."

Lincoln smiled as they left the Situation Room together. "Considering the stakes, Paul, I hope you do."

SEVENTEEN

Monday, 8:17 p.m., Oguzeli, Turkey

Lowell Coffey was staring through the closed window of the passenger's side of the ROC as the dark countryside slipped by. Mary Rose was driving, and nervously tapping the steering wheel and humming Gilbert and Sullivan to herself, an appropriate piece that Coffey recognized from *Iolanthe*: "Faint Heart Never Won Fair Lady."

Coffey was anxious too, though he calmed himself by half shutting his eyes and picturing himself driving with his father and brother across Death Valley. The three Coffey men always took days-long drives together. The Coffey Beans, his mother used to call them, because they were always packed together in a metal can. He would give just about anything to be able to do that again just one more time. The senior Coffey had died in a small-plane crash in 1983. Lowell's brother had graduated from Harvard two years later and moved to London to work in the U.S. Embassy. Their mother had gone with him. Since then, Coffey didn't feel as if he belonged to anything. He had gone to work for Op-Center not just to have some impact on peoples's lives, as he'd told Katzen, but also to feel as though he were part of a close-knit team. Yet even in the ROC, that sense of belonging wasn't quite there.

What did it take to create that? he wondered. His father spoke of his bomber crew having had that intense camaraderie during World War II. There had been some of that in Coffey's college fraternity. What caused it? Danger? Enclosure? A common purpose? Years of being together? Probably a little of all of that, he decided. But despite their present situation—or perhaps because of it?—there was still a sense of dreamy contentment that came from lowering his lids just a little and pretending that his father was to his left and the mountains he knew were out there were the Panamint Range he had marveled at as a boy.

Phil Katzen was sitting at Mary Rose's terminal in the ROC. He was watching the full-color map scroll by on her monitor. On Mike Rodgers's screen was a radar display of Turkish aircraft operating in central and southern Anatolia. Katzen turned to look at it every few seconds. There were no planes in the region as yet. If there were, he would have been forced to identify himself and do whatever he was told. The Operations and Protocol Manual was explicit about ROC activities in a war zone. The printout was on a clipboard in Katzen's lap.

Section 17:
ROC Operations in a War Zone

Subsection 1:
Undeclared War In Non-Combat Zone
A. If the ROC is conducting surveillance or other passive operations at the invitation of a country which is attacked by an outside force,

or at the invitation of a government which is attacked by insurrectional forces; and participation on behalf of the attacked country is legal pursuant to United States Law (see *Section 9*) and Administration policy, ROC personnel are free to operate away from the field(s) of combat and to work closely with the local military to provide whatever services are required, feasible, or ordered by the Director of Op-Center or the President of the United States. See *Section 9C* for legal operations under the National Crisis Management Center Charter.

B. Any and all activities by ROC or ROC personnel as outlined in *Section 17, Subsection 1A* will be terminated at once if the ROC is ordered to depart the combat zone by a legally empowered officer or representative of the recognized government.

C. If the ROC is present at the invitation of the attacking country in a conflict in which the United States is neutral, ROC personnel are to operate pursuant to United States Law (see *Section 9A*) and provide only those services which do not make the United States a participant in unlawful aggression (see *Section 9B*) or provide intelligence which is designed to protect the lives and property of United States citizens, so long as said action does not bring it into conflict with United States law (see *Section 9A, Subsection 3*) and the laws of the host country.

Subsection 2:
Undeclared War in Combat Zone

A. If the ROC is present in a zone and is caught in a situation of armed conflict, the ROC and its personnel are to retreat with practical speed to a place of safety.

1. If it is not possible to evacuate the ROC, it

153

is to be disabled according to *Section 1, Subsection 2* (self-disablement) or *Section 12, Subsection 3* (external disablement).

2. To remain in the combat zone, permission must be obtained from the legal and recognized government with jurisdiction over said region. Activities in this region are to conform strictly to United States law (see *Section 9A, Subsection 4*) and to the laws of the host country.

a. Where these laws are in conflict, civilians are required to adhere to local law. Military personnel will follow military procedure and United States law.

3. If the ROC is present in the combat zone, or enters a combat zone subsequent to the advent of hostilities; and if the stated purpose of said presence is to study events leading up to and/or including the armed conflict, only military personnel will be permitted to take an active part in the operation of the ROC. They will operate according to the boundaries set out in the NCMC Striker code, *Sections 3 through 5*.

a. If non-military personnel are on the ROC, including but not limited to members of the press, they are not to partake in the activities of the ROC.

B. If the ROC enters a combat zone subsequent to the breaking out of armed conflict, the regulations set forth in *Section 17, Subsection 2A* apply. In addition, ROC must have express permission to enter said region from the legal and recognized government or representatives of said government who have jurisdiction over the combat zone.

1. Absent such permission, ROC can operate only as a civilian facility with its sole objective being the protection of the lives and safety of United States citizens.

a. If said civilians are accompanied by United States military personnel, or if said personnel are the only or sole surviving team onboard the ROC, said personnel will in no way act as a partisan force in the present or evolving conflict, either against or on behalf of the host nation or to further any objectives, goals, or ideals of the government of the United States of America.

1. Said military personnel may employ arms only in self-defense. Self-defense is herein defined as the defense by arms of United States personnel, military or otherwise, who have undertaken to depart the combat zone without attempting to affect the outcome of said combat.

2. Said military personnel may employ arms in the defense of local citizens who are undertaking to exit the region, provided said citizens are not endeavoring to affect the outcome of said hostilities.

According to Lowell Coffey, it was Section 17, Subsection 2, B-1-a-1, which gave them, as civilians, the right to go in and get Mike out. The question they'd wrestled with en route was whether bringing Colonel Seden out constituted a partisan act. Because he was a Turkish soldier who had entered the region with partisan intent, he was not covered by Section 17, Subsection 2, B-1-a-2. However, Coffey said that as long as the colonel was hurt, his evacuation would be acceptable in accordance with the charter of the International Red Cross. According to Section 8, Subsection 3, A-1-b-3, ROC was permitted under to act under the IRC charter to evacuate wounded outsiders at the discretion of the individual in charge.

With just over five minutes to go until they reached the reported location of Mike Rodgers and Colonel Seden, Privates Pupshaw and DeVonne were crouched in the battery cabinets under the raised floorboards. Most of the batteries had been removed and stacked to the side to accommodate the Strikers. As a result, except for the radio, radar, and telephone, the inner workings of the ROC were dead. It was also running on fuel instead of on batteries.

The Strikers hid black nighttime uniforms in a cabinet in the rear of the ROC along with a powerful M21, a sniper version of the M14 combat rifle, an image-intensifier eyepiece. These twin-lens units were designed to be clamped to the front of their helmets. In addition to providing night-vision capabilities, the eyepieces were electronically linked to an infrared sensor on top of each soldier's M21. These sensors were the size of a small video camera, and were capable of identifying targets at 2,200 meters, even behind foliage. The visual data was then relayed to the right-side eyepiece. In a field situation, computers in the Strikers' backpacks would send a monochrome display of maps and other data to the right-side eyepiece. When they emerged from hiding, the plan was for Private DeVonne to immediately retrieve the gear, while PFC Pupshaw reconnoitered through a one-way mirrored window in the back. Though Katzen was in charge of the mission, he had put PFC Pupshaw in charge of the actual rescue attempt, as allowed for by the ROC manual.

"Five minutes to target," Katzen said.

The Strikers snuggled down in their compartments. Coffey went over and helped them replace the compartment tops. After making sure the Strikers were all right, he walked toward Katzen.

"Good thing they're not claustrophobic," Coffey said.

"If they were," said Katzen, "they wouldn't be Strikers."

Coffey watched as the map on the computer monitor scrolled ominously toward the target hill. At least, it seemed ominous to the attorney.

"I have a question," Coffey said.

"Shoot, counselor."

"I've been wondering. Just what *is* the difference between a porpoise and a dolphin?"

Katzen laughed. "Mostly it has to do with the body shape and face," he said. "Porpoises are shaped pretty much like a torpedo with spade-like teeth and a blunt snout. Dolphins have a more fish-shaped body, peg-like teeth, and a snout that looks like a beak. Temperamentally, they're pretty much identical."

"But dolphins seem more lovable because they look less predatory," Coffey said.

"They do, yes," said Katzen.

"Maybe the military should think about that when they design the next generation of submarines and tanks," Coffey said. "They can lull the enemy into complacency with a submarine that looks like Flipper or a tank that looks like Dumbo."

"If I were you, I'd stick to law," Katzen said. He looked toward the front of the van. "Heads up, Mary Rose. According to the map you should be coming up on the rise any moment now."

"I see it," she said.

The small of Coffey's back went ice-cold. This wasn't the same as the jitters he got when he went before a judge or a senator. This was fear. The van went down the sharp dip before the rise. Coffey used both hands to brace himself on the back of Mike Rodgers's empty chair.

"*Shit!*" Mary Rose shouted, and crushed the brake down.

"What is it?" Katzen cried.

Coffey and Katzen both looked out the window. A dead sheep was lying in the center of the road. The carcass was the size of a Great Dane and had coarse, dirty-white wool. In order to stay on the narrow road and avoid the ditches on either side, a driver would have to go over it.

"That's a wild sheep," Katzen said. "They live in the hills to the north."

"Probably hit by a car," Mary Rose said.

"I don't think so," Katzen said. "With an animal that size there'd be tire tracks in the blood beyond."

"So what do you think?" Coffey asked. "That it was shot and put there?"

"I don't know," Katzen said. "Some military units have been known to use animals for target practice."

"The dam-busters, maybe," said Mary Rose.

"No," said Katzen. "They'd probably have eaten it. More likely it was a Turkish unit. Anyway, we've got a pair of Strikers who are going to need fresh air pretty soon. Go over it."

"Wait," Coffey said.

Katzen looked at him. "What's wrong?"

"Is it possible the thing could be land-mined?"

Katzen slumped. "I didn't even think of that. Good catch, Lowell."

"A terrorist might do that to slow down mechanized troops," Coffey said.

Katzen looked out toward the ditches on the right and left. "We're going to have to go off-road."

"Unless that's where the mines are," Coffey said. "Maybe the sheep was put there to send someone off the road."

Katzen thought for a moment. Then he pulled a flashlight from the hook between the two front seats and opened the passenger's-side door.

"This is going to get us nowhere," he said. "I'll pull the damn sheep off the road. If I blow up, you'll know it's safe then."

"Uh-uh," Coffey said. "You're not going out there."

"What choice do we have? The metal detector's tied to the main computer. We broke those batteries down and there isn't time to reassemble them."

"We'll have to make time," Coffey said. "Or at least turn the road check over to the Strikers."

Katzen shouldered past the attorney. "There isn't time for that either." He hopped onto the dirt road. "Besides, you're going to need them to save Mike and the colonel. I've been good to animals," he grinned. "This one wouldn't dare hurt me."

"Please be careful," Mary Rose said.

Katzen said he would, and walked out in front of the van. Coffey leaned out the door. Though the night air was surprisingly cool, his mouth was dry and his forehead was wet. He watched Katzen as the round-shouldered young man followed the flashlight beam into the glare of the headlights. About five yards in front of the van, he stopped and shined the beam around the road.

"I don't see any exposed trip wire," Katzen said. He shined his flashlight on the road and walked around the sheep slowly. "It doesn't look as if the dirt's been dug up." He reached the sheep and shined the flashlight down. The blood glistened a bright, oxygenated red in a wound which was nearly four inches in diameter. Katzen touched the blood. "There's been no coagulation at all. This thing was killed within the hour. And it's definitely a gunshot wound." Katzen bent low and looked under the sheep. He slid his left hand under and felt around. "There's no wire or plastique as far as I can tell. Okay, gang. I'm going to move this sucker."

The pounding of Coffey's heart and temples drowned out the gentle hum of the ROC engine. Coffey knew that it wasn't necessary for the body to be wired. It could simply be lying on top of a mine.

The attorney watched as Katzen set the flashlight on the road and grabbed the sheep's hindquarters. Though Coffey was afraid, it wasn't fear which kept him from joining his coworker. He stayed back because if anything happened to Katzen, he would have to help Mary Rose and the Strikers reach their destination.

Mary Rose squeezed Coffey's hand as Katzen held the sheep tightly and took a step back. The sheep moved an inch, then another. Katzen put it down, went to the other side, bent low, and flashed the light under the carcass.

"I don't see any booby traps," he said.

He returned to the hindquarters and pulled the sheep a little more. After it had moved another few inches, Katzen went back and checked beneath it. Again he saw nothing.

In just over a minute the environmentalist had moved the sheep entirely away from the space it had occupied. There was nothing beneath it, and Katzen quickly pulled it off the road. He was perspiring heavily when he returned to the van.

"So what the hell was that all about?" he complained.

Coffey was looking out into the dark. "The dead sheep could've been the result of army target practice, like we thought," he said. "Or maybe someone *was* out there, watching us. To see who we've got inside."

Katzen shut the door. "Well, now that they think they know," he said, "let's get the hell over this hill."

Mary Rose shifted the van to drive. She breathed deeply before pressing down on the gas. "I don't know about you two, but that did a number on my stomach."

Katzen smiled weakly. "Ditto."

While Mary Rose guided them toward the rise and the hillock beyond, Coffey went back to explain the delay to the Strikers. As the attorney knelt on the floor, he began to feel dizzy. He rested his forehead on his knee.

"Hey, Phil," Coffey said, "are you feeling okay?"

"I'm feeling a little drained," he said. "Why?"

Coffey's ears were beginning to ring. "Because I'm having . . . a little trouble here. Dizzy. Buzzing in my ears. Have you got that?"

When Katzen didn't answer, Coffey turned toward the front of the van. He was just in time to see Katzen fall heavily into the passenger's seat. Mary Rose was leaning forward, her forearms against the steering wheel. She was obviously struggling to keep her head up.

"I'm going to stop," she said. "Something is . . . wrong."

The van slowed and Coffey rose. As he did, he was overcome by a sense of vertigo which brought him back to the floor. He reached along the backs of the two chairs beside the computer stations and struggled to pull himself up. Nausea filled his stomach and rose in his

161

throat and brought him back down again.

A moment later, as black clouds swirled inside his eyes, Lowell Coffey felt himself hoisted up bodily and dragged backward.

EIGHTEEN

Monday, 8:35 p.m., Oguzeli, Turkey

They look without seeing, Ibrahim thought.

The young Kurd had shot the wild sheep and dragged it into the road to stop the van. When the driver braked to avoid hitting it, Ibrahim climbed from the ditch in which he'd been hiding. He crept from the side of the road to the back of the van, plugged the exhaust pipe with his T-shirt, and snuck away again. The windows were closed. Once the door was shut, he knew it would take less than three minutes for the passengers to be overcome by carbon monoxide. He had selected a relatively flat stretch of roadway so that when the driver fainted, the van would simply glide to a stop. Then, removing his T-shirt from the exhaust, Ibrahim entered the van and opened the windows. He was both surprised and delighted to find it filled with computers. The equipment and perhaps the data itself would be useful.

Ibrahim checked the three Americans. They were still breathing. They would survive. Dragging the unconscious man to the front of the van, Ibrahim sat him and the others back-to-back behind the passenger's seat. Using his knife to cut out the seat belts and shoulder harnesses, he tied the three people together by the wrists. Then he bound their legs at the thighs and shins.

He took a last look around the van before slipping into the driver's seat. As he sat down he thought he heard something behind him. It sounded like someone gagging. Noticing the flashlight between the seats, he shined it into the back of the van. For the first time he noticed that there were doors in the floor. Drawing the .38 from his belt holster, he walked over. He stopped at the compartments and looked down.

Each compartment was large enough to hold one person. He heard the retching sound again. There was definitely someone in the left-side compartment.

Ibrahim fought the urge to put bullets into the floor before raising the door. But he knew that whoever was inside would have been incapacitated by carbon monoxide just as the other three had been. Bending, he pointed his gun down and threw open the first door.

There was a woman inside. She was conscious, but just barely so. There was a pool of vomit below her head. Ibrahim opened the other door. There was another soldier inside. He was unconscious. Trapped in the unventilated compartment closest to the exhaust, he had obviously been the most seriously affected of the five. But he too was still alive.

So the American officer did warn these people, Ibrahim thought. They were trying to sneak these two people in to kill them. But Allah was looking out for them, blessed be His mighty name.

Pulling the man out, Ibrahim slipped off his black shirt. Tearing it into strips, he draped the man over the back of the chair and tied his hands to the front legs and his feet to the back legs. Then he went to the woman, threw her over the back of the other chair, and tied her up using the rest of the shirt.

With a self-satisfied smile, he surveyed all his captives one last time before slipping his gun back into his holster and returning to the driver's seat. Flashing the van's headlights three times to signal Hasan to let him through, he put the vehicle into drive and quickly covered the short distance to the hillock.

NINETEEN

Monday, 2:01 p.m., Washington, D.C.

There was a ping from the side-mounted speakers of Paul Hood's computer. Hood looked at the monitor and saw Bob Herbert's code on the bottom of the screen. He pushed Ctrl/Ent.

"Yes, Bob."

"Chief, I know you're in a rush," Herbert said, "but there's something you've got to take a look at."

"Something bad?" Hood asked. "Is Mike okay?"

"It may involve Mike directly," Herbert said, "and I'm sorry. Yeah, it does look pretty bad."

"Send it over," Hood said.

"Right away," Herbert replied.

Hood sat back and waited. He'd been busy downloading classified data onto diskettes to take with him on the airplane. The diskettes were specially designed for use on government flights. The jackets became superheated in a fire, though they could not burn. In the event of a crash, the disks as well as their data would be reduced to slag.

The White House was sending a chopper to Andrews

and putting him and Assistant Deputy Director Warner Bicking on a three p.m. State Department flight to London. Hood was scheduled to meet Dr. Nasr at Heathrow Airport and catch a British Airways flight to Syria an hour later. Hood watched as the computer finished copying files onto diskettes. When the hard drive stopped humming, Hood continued to stare at the blank screen.

"Hold on a second," Herbert said. "I want the computer to animate the stuff for you."

"I'm holding on," Hood said, a trace of impatience in his voice. He tried to imagine what could possibly be worse than Mike Rodgers having been captured by terrorists.

Mike Rodgers a hostage, he thought bitterly. Your wife disappointed in you. A new problem will give you a hat trick. Still, it was a record he didn't feel like shooting for.

Less than two minutes ago Hood had phoned his wife to tell her he wouldn't be able to make daughter Harleigh's piccolo solo at school that night, and almost certainly son Alexander's championship soccer game on Thursday. Sharon had reacted the way she always did when work came before family. She immediately grew cold and distant. And Hood knew she would stay that way until he came back. Part of her reaction was concern for her husband's safety. American government and business leaders abroad, particularly in the Middle East, were neither low-profile nor particularly well liked. And after her husband's experiences with the New Jacobin terrorists in France, Sharon was less complacent than ever about his safety.

Another, possibly larger, part of her reaction was Sharon's oft-voiced concern that time was passing and they weren't spending enough of it together. They weren't building the memories that helped make marriages rich . . . and durable. Ironically, long hours was one of the reasons he'd gotten out of politics and then out of banking. The directorship of Op-Center was supposed to have been about managing a modest staff which managed domestic crises. But after being drawn into a near-disaster in North Korea, Op-Center suddenly found itself an international player, a streamlined counterpart to the bureaucracy-heavy CIA. As a result, Hood's own responsibilities had increased dramatically.

Working hard certainly didn't make him a bad person. It provided a very comfortable life for his family and it exposed their two children to interesting people and events. But on top of everything else, he had to deal with the fact that his freedom to work, and to work hard, made Sharon jealous. She'd been forced to cut back her "healthy cooking" appearances on Andy McDonnell's cable food show to twice a week. There simply wasn't enough time to do a daily segment and shuttle the kids to where they had to go and run the house. Though Hood felt bad for his wife, there was nothing he could do.

Except get home on time, he thought, which sounds great on the surface but isn't practical. Not in a city that operates on international time.

"Here it is," Herbert said. "Watch the left side of the screen."

Hood leaned forward. He saw an extremely jerky motion picture of what looked like the ROC sitting in darkness. From the ID numbers in the lower left corner of the picture, he knew that these were successive NRO photographs being flashed together sequentially, flipbook style. There was approximately a one-second delay between each image.

168

"Am I looking for anything in particular?" Hood asked. "Is that Phil?"

"Yes," said Herbert. "He's pulling a dead something off the road. It looks like a sheep or dog. But that's not what I want you to see. Watch the back of the Regional Op-Center."

Hood did. The darkness seemed to shift slightly behind the ROC, though that could have been caused by atmospheric conditions between the satellite and the target. Suddenly, there was a tiny flash which lasted for just one image. A few seconds later there was another flash in a slightly different spot.

"What was that?" Hood asked.

"I've run it through computer enhancement," Herbert said. "We thought at first that it might have been a moth or an artifact in the image. But it was definitely a reflection, slightly concave and probably coming from a watch crystal. Keep looking, though."

Hood did. He saw Phil Katzen return to the van. He watched it start to move ahead. Then he saw it stop. The van remained parked for several images. Hood leaned closer to the screen. Then the door opened, the light came on inside the ROC, and someone got in.

"Oh, no," Hood said. "God, no."

Herbert froze the image on the monitor. "As you can see," he said, "whoever it is, he's armed. Looks like a .38 in the holster and a Czech Parabellum over his shoulder. According to Darrell, the Syrian Kurds bought crate loads of those from Slovakia in 1994."

Herbert started up the moving image again. For a moment Hood couldn't see anything else because the image had been taken from almost directly overhead. But as he waited, he felt his guilt and every other priority evaporate in the face of what he was watching.

"In about four minutes real time," Herbert said, "the

ROC headlights are going to flash three times. Obviously, whoever is at the controls is signaling someone up ahead.''

"How did this happen?" Hood asked. "Mike wouldn't have told them about the ROC."

"We don't think his captors knew about the Regional Op-Center ahead of time," Herbert said. "They were probably just waiting for Mike's wheels to arrive and lucked out."

"How was it done?" Hood asked.

"My guess is the carjackers set up a watch alongside the road. As a precaution, they must have gassed the ROC as it passed. The way the van slowed seems to indicate that the crew was overcome quickly, although not immediately. The driver had enough time to brake. The good news is that the intruder didn't shoot our people once he got inside."

"How do you know?"

"We would've seen flashes," Herbert said.

"Yes, of course," Hood replied. *That was a stupid question. Pay attention to what the hell's going on.* And then he said, "Unless they were already dead from the gas."

"That's unlikely," Herbert replied. "The crew would be no help if they were dead. Alive they can serve as hostages. Perhaps they can help the Kurds get out of the country. Or," Herbert added gravely, "maybe they can tell the Kurds how to work the ROC."

Hood knew that Mike Rodgers and the two Strikers would die before they helped their kidnappers work the ROC. But Hood did not know whether Katzen, Coffey, or Mary Rose would sacrifice their lives to protect it. Nor did he believe that Rodgers would let them.

"We don't have too many options here, do we?" Hood asked.

"We do not," said Herbert.

According to prescribed Regional Op-Center procedures established by Rodgers, Coffey, Herbert, and their advisors, if the ROC were ever captured, the immediate response would be for someone to hit the "Fry" buttons. Simultaneously pressing *Control, Alt, Del,* and *Cap "F"* on either keyboard would cause a surge from the ROC engine batteries. The current generated by the command would be sufficient to burn out the major circuits in the computers and batteries. For all intents and purposes, the fried ROC would cease to be anything but a gas-powered van. If for some reason the procedure failed, the crew or Op-Center itself was required to destroy the ROC by any means at its disposal. If an enemy were to obtain access to communciations links and codes, national security and the activities and lives of dozens of undercover operatives would be compromised.

Having designed all of that, however, even Rodgers admitted there was no way of knowing what he or anyone would do if the ROC were ever taken. As an experienced hostage negotiator, Herbert had said that it might be worth preserving the operations if some of them could be bartered to keep hostages alive.

But all of that was speculative, Hood thought. We never thought it was ever going to happen.

Hood watched as the ROC's headlights flashed three times. Then the screen went blank.

"Whatever is happening now," Herbert said, "is anybody's guess. It's taking place in darkness. Viens gave this situation Priority A-1, and is trying to get us some infrared reconnaissance. But it'll take at least ninety minutes to reprogram the nearest satellite and turn it around."

Hood continued to stare at the dark image on the monitor. This was one of his worst nightmares. All of their

171

planning, all of their technology had been undermined by what Rodgers called "street fighters." People who fought without rules and without fear. People who weren't afraid to die or to kill. As Hood had learned from the legitimate strikes and bitter riots Los Angeles had endured during his mayoralty, desperation made enemies deadly.

But Hood reminded himself that adversity made strong leaders stronger. He would have to swallow his guilt and disappointment, put aside his sudden desire to kick things, including himself. He was going to have to lead his team.

"Bob," Hood said, "there's a strike force at the Incirlik Air Base, correct?"

"A small one," Herbert said, "but we can only use it inside Turkey."

"Why?"

"Because there are Turks on the team. If U.S. and Turkish troops go into an Arab nation together, that will be considered a NATO action. It'll create a firestorm with our European allies and turn even friendly Arab nations against us."

"Great," Hood said. He cleared the screen and brought up a form document. He began typing. "In that case," he said, "I'm ordering Striker into the region."

"Without prior Congressional approval?"

"Unless Martha can get it for me within the next ninety minutes, yes. Without approval. I can't wait while they diddle."

"Good man," Herbert said. "I'll order the C-141B packed for a desert operation."

"We can put Striker down at the Incirlik if the ROC stays in Turkey or northern or eastern Syria," Hood said. "If the ROC goes into southern or western Syria

172

or Lebanon, we'll have to see about getting them into Israel.''

"The Israelis would welcome anyone wanting to kick terrorist butt," Herbert replied. "And I know just the place to base our team there."

Hood picked up a light-pen and signed the screen. His signature appeared on the Striker Deployment Order No. 9. He saved the document on the hard drive, and then E-mailed it to both Martha Mackall and to Colonel Brett August, the new Striker commander. He put the pen down. Then he rapped the edge of the desk slowly with his knuckles.

"Are you okay?" Herbert asked.

"Sure," Hood said. "I'm probably a hell of a lot better than Mike and those poor devils in the ROC."

"Mike will get them through this," Herbert said. "Listen, Chief. Would it make you feel any better to piggyback to the Middle East with Striker? They'll actually be getting there before you."

"No," Hood said. "I need to talk with Nasr about the Syrian strategies. Besides, you and Mike and all the Strikers have worn uniforms. I haven't. I wouldn't feel right planting myself in a seat of honor I haven't earned."

"Take my word for it," Herbert said. "A ride in a C-141B ain't no day at Disneyland. Besides, it's not like you ran from a uniform. You stayed 1A during the draft. You just weren't called. You think I would've gone if the Selective Service Board hadn't grabbed me by the scruff of the neck and said, 'Mr. Herbert, Uncle Sam wants you?' ''

"Look," Hood said, "I'd be uneasy about it and that's that. Please brief Colonel August and work out the details with him. Fax the finished mission profile to our

173

embassy in London and have them bring it to me at Heathrow. Bugs has my flight schedule.''

"All right, Paul," Herbert said. "But I still think you're overreacting about the C-141B.''

"I can't help that," Hood said. "You're to call me directly with any news. I also want you to get us some on-site help. Does it make any sense to bring in some Kurdish resources?''

"Not to me it doesn't," Herbert said. "If our Kurdish resources were all that goddamn super reliable, we'd have known about the Ataturk blast. We'd know who these terrorists are.''

"Good point. Whoever you get, go into the black budget to pay them. And pay them well.''

"I planned to," Herbert said. "We're talking to some informants now to try and find out exactly where the dam-busters might be headed. I've also got a lead on someone to go in there with Striker.''

"Excellent," Hood said. "I'll call Martha from the car and explain the situation to her. She'll have to go to Senator Fox and the Congressional Intelligence Oversight Committee.''

"You know that Martha's not going to be happy about any of this," Herbert warned. "We're getting ready to mount a covert operation without prior Congressional approval; we're giving money to the Kurdish enemies of her friends in Damascus and Ankara.''

"Friends who aren't going to do a damn thing to help us," Hood pointed out. "She's going to have to live with that.''

"With that," Herbert said, "plus the fact that we planned this without her.''

"Like I said, I'll call her from the car and explain. She's our political officer, for God's sake, not a lobbyist for Turkey or Syria." Hood rose. "Is there anything I'm forgetting?"

"Just one thing," Herbert said.

Hood asked what that was.

"I hope you don't think I'm out of line," Herbert said, "but you've got to try and calm down."

"Thanks, Bob," Hood replied. "Six of my people are in terrorist hands, along with a key to undermining U.S. intelligence efforts. I think I'm pretty calm, all things considered."

"Pretty calm, yes," Herbert said, "but that may not be calm enough. You're not the only one who's on the hot seat. I had supper with Donn Worby of the General Accounting Office last night. He told me that last year, over sixty-five percent of the estimated quarter-million hacker attacks on Department of Defense computer files were successful. You know how much classified data is floating around out there? The ROC is just one front of a large battle."

"Yes," Hood replied, "but it's the one that fell on my watch. Don't tell me there's safety in numbers. Not on this."

"All right," Herbert said, "But I've been through more than a couple of these hostage situations, Paul. You've got the emotional pressure, which is awful, and then you've got additional disorientation. You're forced to work outside our structured environment. There are no checklists, no established procedures. For the next few days or weeks or months or however long this takes, you're going to be a hostage along with Mike—a hostage to the crisis, to every whim of the terrorists."

"I understand," Hood said. "That doesn't mean I have to like it."

"No," Herbert replied. "But you have to accept the process. You also have to accept your part in it. It's the

175

same with Mike. He knows what he has to do. If he can get his people out, he will. If not, he'll have them play word games, make up limericks about God knows what, force them to talk about their families. He'll get them through. That terrible burden's on him. You've got to handle the rest. You've come out of the gate with the right ideas. Now you've got to keep yourself and everyone on this end cool. And that may be pretty rough. We may get intelligence that our people are being mistreated. No food, no water, physical abuse. There are two women in the group. They may be assaulted. If you're not loose, fluid, you're going to crack. If you start to feel vengeful or angry or self-reproachful, you'll become distracted. And then you're going to make mistakes.''

Hood removed the diskettes from his computer. Herbert was right. He was already primed to lash out at Martha, at himself, even at Mike. Who would benefit from that except for the terrorists?

''Go on,'' Hood said. ''What am I supposed to do? How did you deal in these situations?''

''Hell, Paul,'' Herbert said, ''I never had to lead a team. I was a loner. I only had to give advice. That was relatively easy. I was never attached to the people I worked with. Not like we are to Mike. All I know is, people who lead operations like this effectively have got to empty themselves of emotion. Compassion as well as anger. I mean, suppose you find out that one of the terrorists has a sister or a kid somewhere. Suppose you can get to them. Are you prepared to play the same kind of ball they're playing with us?''

''I honestly don't know,'' Hood said. ''I don't want to stoop to their level.''

''Which is something that people like these always count on,'' Herbert replied. ''Remember Eagle Claw in

1980, when the Delta rescue force attempted to get our hostages out of Tehran?"

"Yes."

"Mission parameters forced our guys to set up the Desert I refuel site in a moderately well-traveled area. Minutes after landing, the guys captured a bus with forty-four Iranian civilians. Before the whole operation blew up on them, the plan was to hold the captured Iranians for a day while the commandos went in, then release them from Manzariyeh Air Base, which we intended to capture. Sorry if I sound a little Burkowesque," Herbert said, "but I think we should've held those Iranians and given 'em the same shit treatment our people were getting."

"You would've made martyrs of them," Hood said.

"No," Herbert replied. "Just broken-down prisoners. No press coverage, no burning Iranian flags. Just an eye for an eye. And when word spread among terrorists worldwide that we were prepared to play their game, they would've thought twice before picking on us. You think Israel's still around because they play by the rules? Uh-uh. I've *seen* the view from the high road and it ain't always pretty. If you let compassion affect your judgment, you may end up jeopardizing our own people."

Hood breathed deeply. "If I don't let compassion affect my judgment, then we aren't people."

"I understand," Herbert said. "That's one reason I never wanted a bigger office in this town. You pay for every square inch of it with soul as well as blood."

Hood slipped the diskettes into his jacket pocket. "Anyway," he said, "you weren't out of line, Bob. Thanks."

"You're welcome," Herbert said. "Oh, and one more thing."

"What's that?"

"Whatever you have to face," Herbert said, "you won't face it alone. Don't ever forget that, Chief."

"I won't," Hood said. He smiled. "Thank God I've got a team that won't let me."

TWENTY

Monday, 9:17 p.m., Oguzeli, Turkey

Mike Rodgers was tied uncomfortably to the front of the motorcycle. His arms were above and behind him, tied to the handlebars and dead asleep. His back was pressed against the twisted metal of the fender, and his legs were tied at the ankles and stretched in front of him.

But the discomfort he felt inside was far greater than what he felt outside. Rodgers didn't know for certain what the terrorists had been up to. He knew that one of the men, Ibrahim, had gone up the road and over the rise. His own erstwhile interpreter, Hasan, had walked off to the east, perhaps four or five hundred yards. The pair were probably setting up a two-gun cross fire. One person stayed close to the route of the target, slightly ahead of it. The other went off-road well ahead of the vehicle. There was nowhere the driver could run except to turn around. And if the snipers were good, there usually wasn't enough time for that.

The van was coming and Rodgers hadn't heard any gunfire. Were the terrorists simply hiding, covering their base in case the ROC opened fire?

The van stopped and Ibrahim got out. A few seconds later Hasan came running from the plain and hugged him. The third man, Mahmoud, rose and embraced them both. He had remained behind, and it was clear now that he was their leader. The ROC was facing Rodgers and he couldn't see inside. But it was obvious that the terrorists were in charge. Rodgers only hoped that the Strikers had gotten out and were flanking the terrorists, which is what he would have had them do.

Ibrahim and Hasan entered the van, and Mahmoud hurried over to Rodgers. The Syrian held the submachine gun in his right hand and a hunting knife in his left. Mahmoud sliced away the cord which held him to the handlebars, but left Rodgers's legs tied. Then he motioned for his prisoner to go to the van. Rodgers got into a squatting position, stood, and hopped ahead. It would have been easier to crawl, but that was not something Rodgers did. Though the earth seemed anxious to reject his feet, he managed to keep his balance.

As he approached the van, Rodgers saw Coffey, Mary Rose, and Katzen. The three were splayed groggily on the floor of the ROC. They were tied to the column beneath the passenger's seat, their ankles bound. While Ibrahim left to drag Colonel Seden over, Rodgers hopped up the step. As he looked to the left, toward the back of the van, his flesh went cold.

Pupshaw and DeVonne were draped over the chairs of the computer stations. The Strikers were tied hand and foot to the legs of the chairs and were just beginning to stir. Rodgers felt his bowels tighten. They looked more like hunting trophies than like soldiers.

Whatever had gone wrong didn't matter right now. The fact was that they were all captives. And to determine how they would be treated for however long they were held was going to require a long, complex dance.

The first thing Rodgers had to do was try to help the Strikers. When they woke and found themselves tied like this, not only would their heart and fight be extinguished, but their dignity as well. Though wounded and physically abused, they both could survive this. But without pride, they would have nothing even after they were set free. In training for terrorist situations and in talking to the new Striker commander, Brett August, a former Vietnam POW, Rodgers had learned that more hostages took their own lives a year or two after being released than died in captivity. The feeling that they had been degraded and dishonored left them feeling ashamed. That sense was heightened if the victims were in the military. Rank and medals were the outward recognition of courage and honor, which were the blood and breath of the soldier. When those qualities were compromised in hostage situations, only death could reclaim them. It could be death like a Viking, facing an enemy or presumed enemy with a sword in one's hand, or it could be death like a dishonored samurai, alone with a self-inflicted cut to the viscera. But there was no facing life any longer.

Rodgers also had to run the first of his four remaining military assets up the flagpole for the sake of the Strikers. He had to risk his life. When he was stationed in Cam Ranh Bay in southeast Vietnam, there were always casualties. The physical ones were written in blood. The psychological ones were written in the faces of the soldiers. After soldiers had cradled a friend whose legs or hands or face had been blasted off by a mine, or comforted a buddy dying from a bullet wound in the chest or throat or belly, there were only two ways to motivate them. One was to send them out for revenge. That was what the military psychologists now called a ''spike high.'' Rooted in anger rather than purpose, it was good

181

for quick strikes or fast fixes in tough situations. The second way, which Rodgers had always preferred, was for the leader to put his own life in danger. That created a moral imperative for the platoon to get back on its feet and support him. It didn't heal the scars, but it built a bond, a camaraderie which was greater than the sum of the parts.

All of this Rodgers considered in the time it took him to glance at the Strikers, give the faster-recovering Private Pupshaw a supportive little smile, then look back at the front of the van.

While Hasan checked the crew for concealed weapons, Rodgers felt a gun barrel pressed into the small of his back. Mahmoud pushed him to the left. He wanted him to go into the back of the van.

Rodgers stood where he was and hip-butted the gun aside.

The terrorist spat something in Arabic and used his free hand to push Rodgers through the narrow opening. His legs still bound, the general stumbled and fell into the back. He immediately started to get up again. Mahmoud strode over and aimed the gun barrel at his head. He pointed for Rodgers to stay.

Rodgers started to rise. Even in the dark he could see Mahmoud's eyes go wide.

This was the moment which would define their relationship or end Rodgers's life. As the American struggled to get his feet under him, he continued to stare into his captor's eyes. Many terrorists found it easy to plant bombs, but not so easy to shoot a person they were looking in the eye.

Before Rodgers could get all the way up, Mahmoud raised his foot. He put his heel on Rodgers's chest and angrily pushed him down. Then the terrorist kicked Rodgers in the side and shouted at him again.

The blow forced the air from Rodgers's lungs, but it told him what he needed to know. The man didn't want to kill him. That didn't mean he wouldn't, but it meant that Rodgers could probably push him a little more. Rolling onto his side, Rodgers sat up and got his feet under him again. Once more he tried to stand.

Muttering angrily, Mahmoud swung a roundhouse punch at Rodgers's head. The general hadn't quite gotten up, and simply dropped back onto the floor. The fist flew over him.

"Bahstahd!" Mahmoud screamed in crude English. He stepped back and aimed the gun at Rodgers's midsection.

Rodgers turned his head around. He did not take his eyes off the Arab.

"Mahmoud, la!" Ibrahim yelled. *"Stop!"*

Ibrahim ran over and positioned himself between Rodgers and Mahmoud. They conferred in whispers, the newcomer pointing at Rodgers, at the computers, and then at the ROC crew. After a long silence, Mahmoud threw up his hand and walked away. Ibrahim joined him at the door and helped him carry Colonel Seden inside. He sent Hasan over to talk to Rodgers.

Rodgers had recovered from the kick, and climbed back onto his feet. He stood with his shoulders erect and his chin up. He was not looking at Hasan. In circumstances like these a prisoner tried to avoid the eyes of the interrogator. It created an aloofness, a detachment which the inquisitor had to try to breach. It also helped to prevent the prisoner from seeing the captor as a human being. However benign or compassionate he appeared to be, the man asking the questions was still an enemy.

"You were very close to death," Hasan said to Rodgers.

"It wouldn't be the first time," Rodgers said.

"Ah," Hasan replied, "but it might have be the last. Mahmoud was ready to shoot you."

"To kill a human being is the least injury you can do him," Rodgers replied. He spoke slowly, wanting to make sure that Hasan understood.

Hasan regarded Rodgers curiously as Mahmoud and Ibrahim finished loading Colonel Seden onto the van. They tied him together with the others. Then Mahmoud walked over to Hasan. They spoke briefly, after which Hasan turned to Rodgers.

"It is our intention to drive this bus to Syria," Hasan said. His brow was wrinkled as he concentrated on expressing Mahmoud's wishes in English. "However, there are things which we do not understand about the driving of your bus. There are battery cells in the back and unusual meters in the front. Mahmoud wishes you to explain them."

"Tell Mahmoud that these things are used to find buried foundations, ancient tools, and other artifacts," Rodgers said. "You can also tell Mahmoud that I won't discuss the matter unless he unties my two associates and sits them in those chairs." Rodgers turned when he spoke, and said it loud enough for Pupshaw and DeVonne to hear.

The creases in Hasan's brow deepened. "Do I understand? You wish them to be freed?"

"I insist that they be treated with respect," Rodgers replied.

"Insist?" Hasan said. "Does that mean demand?"

Rodgers turned around and looked at the men standing by the front window. "It means," he said, "that if you don't treat us like people, you can sit in the desert until the Turkish Army finds you. Which will be by daybreak if not sooner."

Hasan regarded Rodgers for a moment, then turned to Mahmoud. He translated hurriedly. When Hasan finished, Mahmoud pinched the bridge of his nose and chuckled. Ibrahim was sitting in the driver's seat. He didn't laugh. He was watching Mahmoud closely. After a moment, Mahmoud withdrew his hunting knife. Then he spoke to Hasan, who turned back to Rodgers.

Rodgers knew what was coming now. The terrorists realized that they couldn't pressure him directly. Mahmoud also saw that he couldn't pressure the Strikers. Threatening to harm them would only ennoble the pair, and they'd welcome that. The terrorists also couldn't afford to kill any of the civilians. The victim might know something useful.

The Syrians needed the team's cooperation, but Rodgers had made a demand they refused to honor. So now they would have to test his military asset: his skin. They had to discover how thick it was. How far he would let his civilian crew be tortured, physically or psychologically or both? While finding that out, they would also attempt to discover who was the weakest link and why, and how that individual might be manipulated.

Hasan faced Rodgers. "In two minutes," he said, "Mahmoud will slice off one of the lady's fingers. He will then amputate one finger every minute until you decide to cooperate."

"Blood won't make the van run," Rodgers said. He was still looking at the front of the ROC. Coffey and Mary Rose were nearly awake now, and Phil Katzen was coming around. Colonel Seden was still unconscious.

Hasan translated for Mahmoud, who turned around in a huff. He walked to the front of the van and cut Mary Rose's left wrist free. Then he straddled her arm and held it against his thigh. He put the knife blade-down in the space between her pinky and ring finger. He pressed down ever so slightly to draw blood and make her jump. Then he looked down at his watch.

Mary Rose was now fully alert. She looked up. "What's going on?" she asked as she tried to pull her hand free.

Mahmoud held on tightly, and he never took his eyes off his watch.

Coffey had also recovered. He was sitting to the left of Mary Rose, and appeared startled when he saw Mahmoud. "What is this?" he demanded, his face puffing with lawyerly indignation. "And who are you?"

"Sit still," Rodgers said, his voice soft but firm.

Mary Rose and Coffey both looked at him for the first time.

"Just stay calm, the two of you," Rodgers said. His brow was thickly knit and his voice was a monotone. Implicit in his stern, even manner was the fact that they were in some difficulty and were going to have to trust him.

Mary Rose seemed confused, but did as she was told. Coffey's chest began to heave, and blossoming horror had replaced the indignation in his expression. Rodgers could just imagine what he was thinking.

"What are you doing, Mike? You know the rules for situations like this. . . ."

Rodgers did indeed know the rules and they were simple. Military personnel were permitted to provide name, rank, and serial number. Nothing more. However, the only mandate for what Op-Center euphemistically called "civilian detainees" was to survive. That meant if the captors wanted information, the hostages were free to provide it. After they were released, the burden was on Op-Center or the military to apprehend the terrorists or else to protect, evacuate, or destroy the newly exposed assets. It was part of the government's characteristic underperform-and-then-overreact syndrome.

Rodgers found the idea repugnant. Civilian or soldier, one's first loyalty was to the country, not to survival. Yet it wasn't his own fierce patriotism that refused to let him capitulate. It was his own little PSYOP, his "psychological operation." He had to be tougher than that. If they didn't win some respect from their captors, this imprisonment—whether it lasted for hours, days, weeks, or months—would be one of abuse and contempt.

"Sifr dahiya," Mahmoud said.

"You have one minute," Hasan informed Rodgers. The young Syrian turned to Mary Rose. "Perhaps the lady is not so stubborn as her leader. Perhaps she would care to show us how some of the driving apparatus operates? That is, while she still can handle it."

"She would not," Rodgers said.

Mary Rose's eyes grew wider with fear. She pressed her lips together and continued to look at Rodgers. He stood straight and strong, her touchstone.

Hasan continued to stare at Mary Rose. "Does this man speak for you?" he asked. "Is it he who will lose his fingers painfully one at a time? Perhaps you want to talk to me. Perhaps you do not wish to be mutilated."

"The knives are in your hands, not ours," Rodgers pointed out.

"Truly," said Hasan, casting a look at Rodgers. "But the farmer who whips his stubborn mule is not cruel. He is doing his work. We are merely doing ours."

"Without imagination," Rodgers charged. "And certainly without courage."

"We do what we must, all of us," Hasan replied.

"Talateen," said Mahmoud.

"Thirty seconds," Hasan said. He gazed at Coffey

and Katzen. "Does someone else wish to help? If any of you cooperate with us now, you will save not just the lady, but also yourself unthinkable suffering."

"*Ishreen!*" Mahmoud barked.

"Twenty seconds," Hasan said. He looked at Coffey. "You, perhaps? Will you be the hero, the one who saves her?"

The attorney regarded Rodgers. Rodgers's gaze was fixed on the windshield.

Coffey took a calming breath. "If the young lady wants my help," he said, "I will give it."

Mary Rose blinked out tears. Then she smiled weakly and shook her head with little jerks.

"*Ashara . . .*" said Mahmoud.

"Ten seconds," said Hasan. He bent close to Mary Rose. "You indicate no, yet I do not believe that is what you mean. Think, young woman. There is not very much time."

"*Tisa . . .*"

"Nine seconds," Hasan said to her. "Soon you will be wet with your own blood."

"*Tamanya . . .*"

"Eight seconds," said Hasan. "Then you will scream piteously to cooperate."

"*Saba . . .*"

"Seven seconds," Hasan said. "And with every finger that is removed, there will be more unendurable pain."

Mary Rose was breathing heavily. There was terror in her eyes.

"She's got more courage than you do," Rodgers said proudly.

"*Sitta . . . khamsa . . .*"

"We will see," Hasan said. "You have five seconds, my young woman. Then you will beg to speak."

Hasan had been smirking slightly during the count-down. But now Rodgers noticed that his mouth had turned down. Had the insult touched him, or was he concerned that they wouldn't get the information after all? Or could it be that Hasan had no stomach for blood-shed, despite his vivid commentary?

"Arba . . ."

"Four," warned Hasan.

Part of Rodgers—a very large part of him—wanted to gamble that Mahmoud wasn't going to go through with this. The Syrians had had nearly two minutes to think about their predicament and also to see what the American team was made of. By capturing the ROC, the Syrians had lost whatever head start they had on the Turks. If they had to leave now, patrols would be every-where. The Syrians needed the ROC and its crew, and might well be wondering if they hadn't underestimated their captives. If maybe they should have done what Rodgers had asked.

"Talehta . . ."

"Three seconds," Hasan said. "Think of the knife cutting through bone and muscle. Over and over, ten times over."

Rodgers could hear Mary Rose panting. But she wasn't talking, God bless her. He'd never been prouder of his own soldiers than he was of her.

"Itneyn . . ."

"Two seconds."

"Monster!" Coffey screamed, and began to struggle against his bonds. The Syrians paid no attention to him. Katzen was awake now and clearly trying to take every-thing in.

"Wehid!"

"The time is up," Hasan said. He looked at Mary Rose.

Mahmoud, however, looked at Rodgers. There was a moment's hesitation, and then something bitter and vengeful came into Mahmoud's eyes. Perhaps he was looking through Rodgers at some other enemy, some distant pain. His upper lip curled, and at that moment Rodgers knew he'd lost.

"Don't!" Rodgers said as the Syrian began to press down with the knife. He was still looking at the windshield, but he nodded so Mahmoud would understand. "Don't do it. I'll get you on the road."

Hasan repeated what Mahmoud already knew. Mahmoud snatched the knife away. There was no triumph in his expression as he tucked it in its sheath and Mary Rose collapsed in tears.

As Hasan squatted beside the woman and began tying her bloody hand back to the chair, Mahmoud motioned Rodgers to come forward. Rodgers walked toward the front of the van, but paused beside Mary Rose. The young woman was sobbing heavily, her head bent back against the chair.

"I'm very, very proud of you," Rodgers said to her.

Coffey leaned his head toward Mary Rose and touched her cheek with his hair. "We're all proud of you," he said. "And we're in this together."

Mary Rose nodded weakly and thanked them.

Mahmoud was glaring at Rodgers. Rodgers ignored him.

"Hasan," Rodgers said, "the lady is bleeding. Do you think you could bind that for her?"

Hasan looked up. "Will you make another showdown if I refuse?"

"If I have to," Rodgers replied. "You'd take care of your mule once it moved, wouldn't you?"

Hasan looked from Rodgers to the wound. He thought for a moment, and after the woman's hand was securely fastened to the column, he pulled a handkerchief from his pocket. He tucked it gently between Mary Rose's fingers. As he did, Mahmoud stepped over and plucked it away.

"La!" Mahmoud screamed. He threw the handkerchief down, stomped once on it, and shouted at Hasan.

Hasan's eyes were downcast. "Mahmoud says to tell you that the next time I take orders from you, he will amputate my hands and yours."

"I'm sorry," Rodgers said, "but what you did was right." He regarded Mahmoud. It was time to use his third military asset: surprise. "Hasan, tell your commander that I'll need help replacing the batteries."

"I will help you," Hasan said.

"You can't," Rodgers lied. "Only one person has that knowledge. Tell Mahmoud I'll need Private DeVonne's help. That's the woman he has tied up in back. Tell him if he wants to get to Syria he's going to have to let her go."

Hasan cleared his throat. Rodgers couldn't remember the last time he saw a man looking so alone. The Syrian informed his superior of Rodgers's needs. Rodgers watched as Mahmoud's eyes grew smaller and his nostrils grew larger. It had been a direct hit. Rodgers enjoyed seeing him broil in the instant it took him to reach the only decision he could make.

Mahmoud waved a finger sideways, and Hasan went into the back of the van. Then in a flash, Mahmoud kicked Rodgers down. Hasan didn't stop to help the fallen general. He stepped over him and hurried into the back to cut Private DeVonne loose. He freed her feet first, then bound them together before releasing her hands.

The Striker tried to turn and help Rodgers, but Hasan pushed her along. While he led her to the battery compartments in the rear of the ROC, Rodgers pulled himself up. He placed both hands on the computer stations and swung his bound feet forward as though he were on parallel bars.

That was part one of the surprise. Part two would come later, when they began replacing the batteries and turning things on. The ES4 satellite would immediately read the increased electromagnetism and send a heads-up signal to Op-Center. Paul Hood would have a number of options then, which ranged from simply watching them to destroying them.

As Rogers moved to where Hasan and Private DeVonne were waiting, he could feel Mahmoud still glaring at him. That pleased him enormously for it told him that his fourth and final military asset had proved effective: He had managed to drive the first small wedge between the commander and one of his soldiers.

192

TWENTY-ONE

Monday, 2:23 p.m.,
Washington, D.C.

Colonel Brett August had been giving his Strikers a
lecture in military science when his pager sounded. He
looked down at the number: It was Bob Herbert. August's cool blue eyes shifted back to the seventeen Strikers in the room. They were all sitting tall at their old
wooden desks. Their khaki uniforms were clean and
crisply pressed, their Powerbooks open in front of them.

The beeper had interrupted a lecture on a bloody attempt by Japanese officers in February 1936 to set up a
military dictatorship.

"You're in command of the rebel force in Tokyo that
day," August said as he headed for the door. "When I
come back, I want each of you to present an alternate
plan for staging the coup. This time, however, I want it
to succeed. You can retain or jettison the assassination
of former Prime Minister Saito and Finance Minister
Takahashi if you like. You can also think about taking
them hostage. Holding them could have been used very
effectively to manipulate public opinion and official reaction. Honda, you're in charge until I return."

PFC Ishi Honda, the Striker communciations expert, rose and saluted as the officer left the classroom.

As the colonel strode down the dark corridor of the F.B.I. Academy in Quantico, Virginia, he didn't bother to wonder what Herbert wanted. August was not a man given to speculation. His habit was self-evaluation. Do your best, look back, then see how you can do better next time.

He thought about the class and wondered if he should have given them the hint about hostage-taking. Probably not. It would have been interesting to see if anyone had come up with that.

Overall, he was pleased with the progress Striker had made since his arrival. His philosophy on running a military outfit was simple. Get them up in the morning and push the body to the limit. Have them work with free weights, climb ropes, and run. Do knuckle-push-ups on a wood floor and one-arm chin-ups. Take a good, long swim, followed by breakfast. A four-mile hike in full gear, jogging the first and third miles. Then a shower, a coffee break, and classes. The topics there ranged from military strategy to infiltration techniques he'd learned from a colleague in the Mista'aravim, the Israeli Defense Force commandos who masqueraded as Arabs. By the time the soldiers got to their classes, they were glad to sit down and their minds were remarkaby alert. August ended the day with a baseball, basketball, or volleyball game, depending upon the weather and disposition of the team.

Striker had come a long way in just a few weeks. Physically, he'd pit them against any crisis, against any strike force in the world. Psychologically, they were healing from the death of Lieutenant Colonel Squires. August had been working closely with Op-Center psychologist Liz Gordon to help them deal with the trauma.

Liz had focused on two avenues of therapy. First, she'd helped them to accept the truth: that the mission in Russia had been a success. The Strikers had saved tens of thousands of lives. Second, based on computer projections for the mission-type, she'd showed them that their losses were well under what the military considered "an acceptable range." That kind of cold, behind-the-lines assessment couldn't cure the hurt. But Liz hoped that it would soothe some of the guilt the team felt and restore their confidence. So far, it appeared to be working. In the last week, he'd noticed that the soldiers were more focused during training, and were also laughing more during downtime.

The tall, lean colonel moved quickly without appearing to hurry. Though his eyes were gentle, his gaze was fixed straight ahead. He didn't acknowledge the FBI officials who passed him. In the short time since he'd taken command of Striker, August had sought to isolate himself and his team from outside influences. More than the late Lieutenant Colonel Squires, August believed that a strike force must not only *be* better than other personnel, it must *think* it's better. He didn't want to be hanging from a cliff with a superior force closing in and his people wondering whether they were good enough to shut the enemy down. Fraternizing with outsiders diluted the focus, the sense of unity and purpose.

August's office was located in the FBI's executive corridor. He entered his code on the keypad on the jamb and entered. He always felt a whole lot better when he closed the door on what he called the White Shirts. It wasn't that he didn't like or respect them. The opposite was true. They were smart, brave, and dedicated. They loved their country no less than he. But their fate scared him. To August, they were like Scrooge's visions of Christmas Yet to Come. The colonel never wanted to become desk-bound and comfortable, which was why he'd resisted Mike Rodgers's suggestion that he leave his post as a NATO officer and come to Washington. Yet because Mike Rodgers was a childhood friend, and because Striker was a singularly sharp and aggressive unit, August had agreed to check them out.

He'd been drawn to the greatest challenge of rebuilding and leading a team that had been demoralized by the death of their commanding officer. And of course there'd been the appeal of being with Rodgers himself. Since they were kids, they'd shared a passion for building model airplanes and reminiscing about old girlfriends. Rodgers had gone so far as to find one of August's childhood sweethearts as an inducement for him to return to the U.S.

It had worked. When August had gotten together with Barb Mathias, the elementary school princess who'd been his first serious crush, he'd known he wasn't returning to NATO. He'd bought a Ford for driving and a Rambler for fixing up on weekends, moved into the Quantico barracks, and become a bonafide man-at-arms for the first time since Vietnam. The Striker team was young but enthusiastic, and the high-tech gear was awe-inspiring.

August shut the door behind him. He walked to the gunmetal desk and hit the autodial on his secure telephone. Bob Herbert picked up.

"Afternoon, Colonel," Herbert said.

"Good afternoon, Bob."

"Turn on your computer," Herbert said. "There's a signed directive. Countersign and E-mail it back."

August's belly burned with anticipation as he booted up the HP Pavilion and input his identification code. He still wasn't speculating, but he was eager and damned curious. In just a few seconds Paul Hood's order appeared on the screen. August read it. Striker Deployment Order No. 9 simply ordered him and his full Striker team to chopper from Quantico to Andrews Air Force Base and board the waiting C-141B. August picked up the electronic pen on the desk and signed the screen. He saved the document and returned it to Herbert.

"Thanks," Herbert said. "Lieutenant Essex of General Rodgers's staff will meet you at the field at fifteen hundred hours. He'll have the mission overview. We'll download the details once you're airborne. However, I can tell you this much, Colonel, and it isn't pretty. Mike and the Regional Op-Center have been captured by what appear to be Kurdish terrorists."

The burning sensation rose in August's throat.

"Either you retrieve the facility," Herbert continued, "or according to the playbook, we close up shop. It may be necessary for us to do that before you get there, but obviously we're going to try and avoid that. Understood?"

Close up shop, August thought. Destroy the ROC regardless of where it is or who's inside. "Yes," the colonel said. "I understand."

"I don't go way back with General Rodgers like you do," Herbert went on, "but I enjoy and respect the hell out of him. He's the only guy I know who can quote Arnold Toynbee in one breath and lines from Burt Lancaster movies in the next. I want him back. I want them all back."

"So do I," August replied. "And we're ready to go get them."

"Good man," Herbert said. "And good luck."

"Thank you," August said.

The colonel hung up the phone. After a moment, he drew breath slowly through his nose. He let himself fill with air from the belly up, like a bottle. The "big belly" was a trick a sympathetic prison guard had taught August when he was a POW in Vietnam. August had been sent into North Vietnam to find a Scorpion team which the CIA had recruited from among persecuted North Vietnamese Catholics in 1964. The thirteen commandos had been presumed dead. Years later, word reached Saigon that they were still alive. August and five others were sent out to find them. They discovered the ten surviving Scorpions in a prison camp near Haiphong . . . and joined them. The Viet Cong guard, Kiet, had to do what he was doing in order to feed his wife and daughter. But he was a humanist and a Taoist who secretly taught his creed of "effortless survival" to the captives. It was as much Kiet's quietistic outlook as August's own determination which had enabled him to survive.

August exhaled, stood quietly for a moment, then left the office. His step was quicker than before, his eyes more intense.

As August tried to assimilate the shock of what had happened, he didn't think of Mike Rodgers or the ROC. He thought only about getting his team airborne. That was another trick he'd learned as a POW. It was easier to deal with a crisis if you bit it off in digestible chunks. Suspended by your wrists nose-deep in a rank, fly-covered cesspool, or baking in a coffin-sized cage under the noon sun, you didn't wonder when you were going to get out. That kind of thinking would drive you mad. You tried to last as long as it took for a cloud to travel from one treetop to another, or until a five-inch-long spider crossed an open patch of earth, or until you counted off one hundred slow Buddah Belly breaths.

He *was* ready, he told himself. And so was his team. At least they'd better be. Because in about half a minute he was going to start kicking Striker ass as it had never been kicked before.

TWENTY-TWO

Monday, 3:13 p.m., over Chesapeake Bay

The State Department 727 took off from Andrews at 3:03, and was quickly swallowed by the low-hanging clouds over Washington. The customized jet would remain in the clouds for as long as possible. That was standard State Department procedure to keep them from being visually sighted and targeted by ocean-based terrorists. It made for a safer ride, albeit a bumpy one.

Paul Hood knew very few of the other forty-odd passengers. There were a number of brawny, silent DSAs—Diplomatic Security Agents—a handful of tired-looking reporters, and a lot of career diplomats with leather briefcases and black suits. There had been a good deal of pre-takeoff networking going on, and ABC State Department correspondent Hully Burroughs had already organized the traditional plane pool. Everyone who had wanted to play kicked in a dollar and picked a number. An official timekeeper had been named and when it was time to land, would count off the seconds from the time the pilot told everyone to buckle in until the instant the wheels touched the ground. Whichever passenger guessed the correct number of seconds between the two events won the pot.

Hood had avoided it all. He'd taken the window seat and put young Warner Bicking on the aisle. Hood had found that chronic talkers tended to talk less if they had to lean over. Especially if they'd already had a few drinks.

Hood's pager beeped at 3:07. It was Martha calling, probably to continue the conversation they'd begun in the car. She hadn't been happy about the fact that the President had sent him to Damascus instead of her. After all, she'd argued, she'd had more diplomatic experience than anyone at Op-Center and she knew some of the players. She'd wanted to get on the plane or meet him in London, requests which Hood had denied. For one thing, he'd explained, this was the President's idea, not his. For another, if she were gone, then Bob Herbert would be left in charge of Op-Center. Hood didn't want him doing anything but working on saving the ROC and its crew. Martha had gotten off the phone angry.

Hood was not permitted to use his cell phone until ten minutes into the flight, so he waited until the flight attendant gave the okay for electronic equipment to be used. Before calling back, Hood booted his laptop. Since the phone lines were not secure, Martha would have to refer him to coded information on the diskettes if there were any new developments.

When Martha picked up the phone, Hood knew that she was no longer quite so angry. He could tell at once from Martha's hollow monotone that something had happened.

"Paul," she said, "there's been a change in the weather where you're headed."

"What kind of change?" he asked.

"It's gone up to seventy-four degrees," she said.

201

"Winds are from the northwest. Nice red sunset."

"Seventy-four degrees, northwest winds, red sunset," he repeated.

"Correct."

"Hold on," Hood said.

He reached into his small carrying case and removed the red-tabbed diskette from its pocket. That already told him that things weren't good. The situation somewhere was code red. After booting the diskette, Hood carefully typed in the code 74NW on the computer. The machine hummed for several seconds, then asked for Hood's authorization code. He punched in PASHA, which stood for Paul, Alexander, Sharon, Harleigh, and Ann—his mother's name—and then he waited again.

The screen went from blue to red. He clicked the mouse on the white letters OP in the upper left corner.

"Warner," Hood said as the file opened, "I think you'd better have a look at this as well."

Bicking leaned over as Hood began scrolling through the file:

Op-Center Projection 74NW/Red

1. Subject: First-Stage Syrian Response to Turkish Mobilization.

2. Provocation Scenario: Syrian and Turkish Kurds jointly strike inside Turkey.

3. Response Scenario: Turkey moves five-six hundred thousand troops to Syrian border to prevent further incursions. *(Access 75NW/Red for larger Turkish response.)*

4. Result: Syria mobilizes.

5. Likely Composition of Syrian Force: Available manpower is 300,000, distributed between Syrian Army, Syrian Navy, Syrian Air Force, and Syrian Air Defense Forces. Police and Security Forces consisting of 2,000 troops would be assigned to defend Damascus and the President. Additional conscripts would be culled from workforce within the first three days of mobilization. Total additional force of 100,000 men between the ages of 15-49 would be fielded within two weeks. Inadequately trained, the conscripts would probably suffer casualties of 40-45% within the next two weeks. Syria would be betting on the fact that wars in the region tend to be brief.

6. *Turkish Diplomatic Efforts:* Intensive. Would not want war.

7. *Syrian Diplomatic Efforts:* Moderate. Given highly secular Turkish government, Syria's ninety% Muslim population (11.3 million of 13 million) would accept a conflagration as a *jihad* or holy war.

8. *Time Frame for Initial Conflict:* Given an emotionally charged environment created by terrorist activities, there is an 88% chance that hostilities would occur within the first forty-eight hours. As reactions cool, there is a 7% chance that hostilities would occur in the next twenty-four hours and a 5% chance that hostilities would occur thereafter.

9. *First Wave Initial Conflict:* Turkey will not want to be the aggressor for fear of triggering Greek response. However, current policy permits the pursuit of terrorists by strike force if "the nature of the crime is of such a nature to warrant pursuit. (Access *Turkish Military White Papers 1995-1997*, file 566-05/ Green.) To discourage internal discord resulting from inactivity or perceived weakness, a measured Turkish response is deemed extremely likely. Syrian response to a Turkish incursion will be swift and absolute. A multi-force retaliation is likely within and without Syrian borders.

(Access *Syrian Military White Papers 1995–1997*, file 566-87/Green.)

10. *Second Wave Initial Conflict:* Turkey will attack any Syrian troops within its borders but almost certainly will not move into Syria. That would surely arouse Muslims living within Turkey. At that point, both sides will have shown sufficient muscle to withdraw and stand only to lose from further hostilities. Diplomatic efforts will intensify and are considered likely to prevail. The small uncertainty factor will be influenced largely by concomitant response from neighboring nations (see 11., below).

11. *Projected Response from Surrounding Countries:* It is expected that all nations in the region will assume some form of defensive military posture. Several are likely to take offensive steps.

A. *Armenia:* The government will support Turkey unless Turkey supports Azerbaijan. In either case, a military response is unlikely against any target but Azerbaijan. Government security forces will watch the Kurdish minority very closely but will not be likely to take military measures against them. (Access *Armenian White Paper*, file 364-2120/S/White, for U.S. response to Armenian situations.)

B. *Bulgaria:* Of the 210,000 active soldiers, only the Frontier Troops are likely to be mobilized. The population is 8.5% Turkish. There is no reason why Turkish forces should cross the border. Unless they do so, the Bulgarian troops will avoid confrontations.

C. *Georgia:* The government will back Turkey but make no military gestures.

D. *Greece:* Mediterranean patrols by the Hellenic Navy will be increased. Confrontations may erupt if Turkish patrols are encountered. If a second wave

of hostilities erupts between Turkey
and Syria, Greece will most likely remain neutral while moving against Aegean territory claimed by both Ankara
and Athens. (*Access Imia Islet file,
645/E/Red.*)

   E. *Iran:* Iran will almost certainly
remain militarily inactive. Fifth column activity will certainly increase.

   F. *Iraq:* During any first-wave hostilities, Baghdad will increase attacks
on Iraqi Kurds to prevent them from
joining with Turkish and Syrian Kurds.
During a second wave, Baghdad may seek
to press old claims against Kuwait.
(*Access Wadi al Batin file 335/NW/Red.*)

   G. *Israel:* Israel's partnership with
Turkey covers only mutual military maneuvers. It is not a mutual defense
pact, though Israeli intelligence resources will be placed at Turkey's disposal. If a second wave of hostilities
erupts, Israel may agree to flying limited sorties.

   H. *Jordan:* Jordan exercises joint air
force maneuvers with Israel. While they
would remain neutral in an Israeli war
with Arabs, they will join a Turkish
war against Syria if the United States
permits them to.

Hood cleared the screen. "Any chances the weather
will change again?" he asked Martha.

"It looks like the front at 11F-Frank is not happening," she replied.

Hood scrolled back. He repeated what Martha had
said for Bicking's benefit. Iraq hadn't moved against the
Kurds, but he knew that wouldn't last. Recent intelligence reports put the Iraqi military at over two million
strong. Many of those men were young newcomers, untested in battle and probably scared. Others were veter-

ans, many of them itching to avenge their humiliation during the Persian Gulf War.

"We're also thinking that 11D-David and 11G-George may move in sooner than expected," Martha said.

Hood was not surprised by either of those. With elections coming up, the Greek President needed to do something blazingly patriotic to win the right wing. Taking long-disputed lands from an embattled Turkey would accomplish that. As for Israel, the hardline government would love the opportunity to strike at an enemy under the auspices of defending an ally.

"What're things like on the home front?" Hood asked.

"The meteorologists are watching and talking," Martha said. "A few picnics have been called off in the area, but only one umbrella has been broken out."

That meant military leave in the region had been canceled and U.S. troops were on a low-level Defcon One alert.

"I'll keep you up to date," Martha said, "but I can tell you there are a lot of long faces at the weather headquarters."

The weather headquarters was the White House. "They're worried about storms, I'm sure," Hood said, "and they'll probably get a few."

"They can live with a few," Martha said. "It's a big one they're worried about."

Hood thanked her and hung up. He turned to Bicking. The spindly twenty-nine-year-old was a former associate professor of social sciences at Georgetown University. His area of expertise was Political Islam, and he was one of four political experts recently added to the Op-Center team to advise Paul Hood on foreign affairs.

"What's your take on this?" Hood asked.

Bicking twirled a longish lock of black hair around his index finger. It was a habit he had whenever he was thinking. "There's a very, very good chance that it'll all blow up. And when it does, it could well drag the rest of the world along with it. From Turkey it can move up through Greece and Bulgaria into Romania and Bosnia. With the Iranian presence there, they can drop-kick this thing up into Hungary, Austria, and straight into Germany. There are two million Turks living in Germany. Of those, half a million are Kurds. They'll pop for sure. At the same time it can move from Turkey in the other direction, up through southern Russia."

"Don't pull any punches," Hood said. "Give it to me straight."

"Sorry," Bicking said, "but you've got all these ancient hatreds being fanned and interacting—Turkey and Greece, Syria and Turkey, Israel and Syria, Iraq and Kuwait, and various combinations and multiples thereof. The smallest thing can trigger any of them. And once those locusts start hopping—"

"You've got a swarm," Hood said.

"*The* swarm," Bicking replied.

Hood nodded unhappily. Suddenly, there was going to be a lot more to do in Damascus than save the ROC.

Bicking twirled his hair a little faster. He peered at Hood from under heavily lidded eyes. "Here's a thought," he said. "Let me work on the ROC situation while you and Dr. Nasr concentrate on preventing a major conflagration."

"There may not *be* a lot of time to work on the ROC situation," Hood said. "If there's even a remote chance that it will be used by the Kurds, the President is going to order the ROC found and destroyed."

"Pronto," Bicking added. "And finding it won't be

a problem. As soon as they uplink, the military will have a signal to lock on to—''

Hood grabbed the phone and dialed. "That's how we buy time."

"How?"

"If the captors manage to turn on the ROC, the signal has to go through the satellite. When it does, there may be a way Matt Stoll can shut it down. If the ROC is dead in the water, we may be able to convince the President to give us time to negotiate a release."

Bicking twirled rhythmically. "It's good," he said.

Hood waited for the connection to go through. The plan to destroy the ROC was a simple one. There was no self-destruct button. It had to be designed as a completely unarmed facility in order to be allowed into many foreign nations. Instead, wherever it went, it could be taken out by a Tomahawk missile, which could be launched from ground, air, or sea and had a range of over three hundred miles. Equipped with terrain-following computers, it could hit the ROC virtually anywhere.

Stoll's assistant answered the phone. He put Matt on at once.

"Are we secure?" Stoll asked breathlessly.

"No," Hood said.

"All right, then listen," the computer expert told him. "You know that missing rock and roll group?"

"Yes," Hood said. They didn't have code phrases to describe the situation with the ROC, so Stoll was improvising.

"There's an ambient level of juice which radiates out when their amps are on," Stoll said. "Bob lost that when the rockers pulled the plug earlier."

"I understand," Hood said.

"Okay. Now our high-flying friend the ES4 is beginning to pick up a signal again."

The ES4 was the Electromagnetic Spectrum Satellite Surveillance System. The sensors were a component in a chain of multi-purpose satellites which read terrestrial radiation in frequencies from 10^{29} to zero hertz and in wavelengths from 10^{-13} centimeters to infinity. These readings included gamma rays, X-rays, ultra-violet radiation, visible light, infrared, microwaves, and radio waves.

"So we now know exactly where the band is?" Hood asked

"Yes," Stoll replied. "But not what they're doing."

"No audio yet," Hood said.

"Zippo," said Stoll. "What's significant, though, is that the band leader's not in any rush to get on-line again."

"How can you tell?"

"According to the tests we ran back here before they left, you can get from zero to sixty, so to speak, in about four minutes and change. You follow?"

"Yes," Hood replied. The batteries which had been removed inside the ROC could be replaced in a little over four minutes.

"At the rate El Supremo's plugging things in," Stoll went on, "the bandwagon won't be up to full power, nor the wheels turning, for another fifteen minutes or so. That's twenty-five minutes in all."

"Which means the other band's still in charge of the equipment," Hood said.

"Very likely," Stoll said.

So Rodgers was stalling and the Kurds were in control. Hood also knew that if Bob Herbert and Matt Stoll were drawing these conclusions from the ROC readings, so was the CIA and the Department of Defense. If they decided that the ROC was fully operational and in enemy hands, it was doomed.

"Matt," Hood said, "is there any way we can shut the band down if it comes online?"

"Sure," Stoll said.

"How would you do it?"

"We'd send a command to the uplink," Stoll said. "Tell it that as soon as a signal from the band hits the receive reflector, it should ignore all other signals from that source. That'd take about five seconds."

"Give the bandleader fifteen seconds," Hood said. "If he's going to try to get a message to us, he'd do it right away. Then shut it down. He'll understand what we're doing and why."

"Okay," Stoll said. "We'll still keep an eye on them, though."

"Right." The ES4 would be able to follow their electromagnetic trail until the NRO satellite was turned on them in just a few minutes. If Hood could keep the President from issuing a destruct order, they'd have a chance of getting the team out. "Matt, I want you to write this up and get it to Martha. Tell her to send it over to the White House with my recommendation that we watch and wait. Meanwhile, you get things ready to close the door if our band opens it."

"It's as good as done," Stoll said.

Hood hung up and briefed Bicking. They both agreed that if the ROC could be shut down, the President would give Striker time to get it back. Despite pressure from National Security Chief Steve Burkow, who believed in security at any price, the President would not be anxious to take out his own team. Not if the hardware in the ROC could be neutralized.

Hood and Bicking began to study the Syrian position papers which had been loaded into their computer. But

Hood had trouble focusing, and announced that he was going off to the galley. Bicking said he'd start highlighting Administration positions while Hood was gone.

The Op-Center Director got a Diet Pepsi from one of the two male flight attendants, and sipped it while he stood looking back at the cabin. The thickly cushioned seats were arranged in two rows of two with a wide aisle. Passengers were huddled over computers.

Typically, an hour or so of work got done before drinks and restlessness and reporters desperate to file stories turned the trip into a social gathering. There were two small tables in the back for conferences and working meals. They were empty right now, but wouldn't be around five when snack sandwiches were served. Beyond them was the door which led to the modest office and sleeping quarters used by the Secretary of State when he was aboard.

Hood wondered how the most powerful nation in the history of civilization, with awesome technological resources and a great army, could be sandbagged by three men with guns. It was inconceivable. But even as he wondered about it, Hood knew that it wasn't the Kurds who were holding the U.S. hostage. It was ourselves, our own self-restraint. It would be a simple matter to target pockets of Kurds and blast them one by one until our people were released. Or to capture and murder the families of their leaders. But civilized, twentieth-century Americans would not do to anyone else what they did to us. We played by the rules. That was one of the qualities which kept any superpower from becoming an abomination like the Third Reich or the Soviet Union.

That was also what gave other people the courage to lash out at us, Hood thought as he finished the soda and crushed the can. He went back to his seat determined to make all of this work through the system. He believed passionately that the American way was the best way in the world, and he took comfort knowing that history-buff Mike Rodgers believed that too.

"The Kurds and the Islamic fundamentalists don't have a corner on political zeal," Hood said as he looked at the computer screen. "Let's figure out how to do the rest of this."

"Yes, sir," Bicking replied as he began twirling his hair again.

TWENTY-THREE

Monday, 10:34 p.m.,
Oguzeli, Turkey

Ibrahim sat in the driver's seat watching the power gauge as each battery was replaced. As the digital numbers increased incrementally, he tried various buttons to see how the lights, air-conditioning, and other devices worked. There were many panels and buttons he didn't understand.

Mahmoud stood beside him, leaning against the dashboard and smoking a cigarette. The Kurd's arms were crossed and his tired eyes never left the Americans in the rear of the van. Hasan was back there with them, holding a flashlight and watching what they were doing.

The other prisoners were all awake. They were sitting silently where the Kurds had left them. Katzen, Coffey, Mary Rose, and Colonel Seden were tied to the base of the passenger's side seat. Private Pupshaw was still draped over the chair at the computer station. Neither food nor water had been offered, nor had it been requested. No one had asked to go to the bathroom.

Ibrahim looked out the window. As soon as power had begun returning to the controls, he'd opened the window to let out Mahmoud's cigarette smoke. The Bedouin-grown tobacco he favored was sickly-sweet, like insect repellent. Ibrahim didn't understand how his brother could enjoy it.

But then, he didn't understand how his brother could enjoy a lot of things. Confrontations, for example. Mahmoud had genuinely liked the showdown with the American. They had both lost a little stature during that, and Ibrahim could tell that his brother was looking forward to the next one.

For his part, Ibrahim knew that this work was necessary, yet he did not enjoy it. He caught his reflection in the sideview mirror. He studied it with a curious blend of satisfaction and hatred. They had done a good job today, but what right did he have to be alive? Walid had fought so long and so diligently. Tonight he should have been thanking Allah in prayer, not in person.

As he stood looking at himself, Ibrahim noticed for the first time the side mirror itself. It was dish-like, curved to provide a wide view of the road. But the setting was also curved, far more than style would seem to dictate. Curious, he took his knife and worked it behind the mirror.

The American leader, the one called Kuhnigit, stopped what he was doing and said something to Ibrahim. Hasan said something back. The American spoke again. Ibrahim glanced back. Kuhnigit did not look as confident as he had before, and Ibrahim wondered if he was on to something. Hasan pointed back to the opening in the floor and said something in English. The American bent down and went back to work. Ibrahim kept working on the mirror.

The glass came free at the sides, but remained attached in the center. Only it wasn't glass, it was something much lighter. Almost like silvery cellophane.

214

Ibrahim leaned out the window and had a look at it. There was something behind it—a horn of some kind. It looked like a transmitter.

No, he thought, not a transmitter. A radio dish like the big ones they used in the Air Force.

Ibrahim replaced the mirror and looked back. The American had stopped replacing the batteries and was glaring at him. Hasan was saying, "Work—*work*!"

The American stood unsteadily on his bound feet for just a moment, then leaned against one of the dark computer stations. Hasan walked over, grabbed him by the shoulder, and pulled him back to the pit.

Ibrahim climbed from the seat. He tapped his knife in his open palm. "There's something wrong here," he said to Mahmoud.

Mahmoud sucked on his cigarette, then ground it out on the floor. "What could be wrong, other than the worm's pace of the American?"

"I don't know," said Ibrahim. "If I were to let my imagination go, I would say that the frame of that mirror appears to be a very small radio transmitter." He swept the knife point across the van. "And there are all of these computers and monitors. Suppose they are not used for finding buried cities. Suppose these people are not scientists and guards. Suppose all of this is a disguise."

Mahmoud stood up suddenly. The exhaustion seemed to leave him. "Go on, my brother."

Ibrahim pointed the knife at Rodgers. "That man didn't act like a scientist. He knew just how far to go when you threatened the girl."

"As if he'd done this before, you mean," Mahmoud said. "*Aywa*—yes. I had that same feeling but I did not know why."

"Everyone has even been very quiet," Ibrahim said. "No one has pleaded or asked for a drink." He pointed from Pupshaw to DeVonne. "Those two took their bondage without complaint."

"As though they had been trained," Mahmoud said. "And would security guards have secreted themselves as these two did?"

"Not security guards," said Ibrahim, "but commandos." Mahmoud looked around the dark van as though he were seeing it for the first time. "But if not for research, then what is this place?"

"A reconnaissance station of some kind," Ibrahim said tentatively. Then, more confidently, he said, "Yes. I believe it could be."

Mahmoud grasped his brother's arms. "Praised by the Prophet, we can use such a thing—"

"No!" said Ibrahim. "No—"

"But it can help to get us out of Turkey," Mahmoud said. "Perhaps we can listen to military communications."

"Or they to us," Ibrahim replied. "And not from the ground but from up there." He pointed at the sideview mirror with the knife. "It is quite possible that they are already watching us, waiting to see where we move."

Mahmoud looked from his brother to Rodgers, who was bent over the pit in the floor and had resumed working on the batteries. *"Abadan!"* the Syrian cried. "Never! One way or another I will blind them." He snatched Ibrahim's knife from him. Turning to Mary Rose, he bent and cut away the rope which held her to the chair. Her hands and feet were still tied together and he threw her forward, onto her face. Then he handed Ibrahim the knife and knelt beside the young woman. He grabbed her hair so tightly that she screamed. He pulled his .38 from its belt holster and pressed the barrel of the gun against the base of her neck.

Rodgers stopped working again. He didn't get up.

"Hasan!" Mahmoud shouted. "Tell the American that I know what this vehicle is. Tell him I wish to know how it works." Mahmoud sneered, "And tell him that this time he has until I count to three."

TWENTY-FOUR

Monday, 3:35 p.m., over Maryland

Lieutenant Robert Essex was waiting for Colonel August when the Striker chopper set down at Andrews Air Force Base. The lieutenant handed him a diskette with a pressure-sensitive piece of silver tape on top. Only August's thumbprint on the diskette, scanned by his computer, would allow him to access the data.

While August accepted the diskette, Sergeant Chick Grey hustled the sixteen-soldier Striker team onto the C-141B. A converted C-141A Lockheed StarLifter, the C-141B had a fuselage which was 168 feet and four inches long—twenty-three feet, four inches longer than its predecessor. The retooling of the aircraft added flight-refueling equipment which increased the troop carrier's normal operating range of 4,080 miles.

The aircraft's crew of five helped the Strikers stow their gear. Less than eight minutes after the soldiers had arrived, the four powerful Pratt & Whitney turbofans carried the jet into the skies.

Colonel August knew that Lieutenant Colonel Squires used to chat with the crew about everything from favorite novels to flavored coffee. August understood how that could relax the team and make them feel closer and more responsive to the commander. However, that was not his style. And that was not the style he taught as a guest officer at the John F. Kennedy Special Warfare Center. As far as he was concerned, one of the tenets of leadership was to make it impossible for the team to know you too well. If they didn't know which buttons to push, how to please you, then they had to keep trying. As his old Cong jailor used to tell him, "We keep together by keeping apart."

The poorly insulated cabin was loud and the bench was hard. That too was how August preferred things. A cold, bumpy plane ride. A landing craft in choppy waters. A long and exhausting march in the rain. These things were the tannin which toughened the soldier's hide.

Led by Private First Class David George, the Strikers began going through the inventory of what had been placed onboard the plane. Op-Center maintained an equipment depot at Andrews which was stocked with gear for any climate and equipment for any mission. Included in the cargo for this trip were the standard "takedown" fatigues with desert coloration, as well as desert-camouflage face scarves and flop hats. Equipment included bullet-proof Kevlar vests, rappelling belts, ventilated assault boots for hot climates, goggles with shatterproof lenses, and gadget bags which were worn around the waist. There were compartments for additional ammo magazines, a flashlight, concussion grenades, flat-sided M560 series fragmentation grenades, a first-aid kit, rappelling rings, and Vaseline to apply to areas rubbed raw by walking, climbing, crawling, and tight straps. Weapons provided for the team were Beretta 9mm pistols with extended magazines and Heckler &

Koch MP5 SD3 9mm submachine guns. The MP5s boasted a collapsing stock and an integral silencer. Since he'd first used them, August had found the weapon's sound suppressor to be both clever and effective. The first stage absorbed the gases while the second sucked up the muzzle blast and flame. The bolt noise was concealed by rubber buffers. Fifteen feet away, the gun was deadly silent.

Bob Herbert was obviously anticipating some close-in encounters.

The team had also been equipped with six motorcycles which had heavily muffled engines, as well as a quartet of FAVs. The Fast Attack Vehicles each carried three passengers and were designed to travel across the desert at speeds in excess of eighty miles an hour. The driver and one passenger sat up front, with an additional gunner in the elevated back seat. The FAVs were armed with .50-caliber machine guns and 40mm grenade launchers.

Colonel August already had a good idea where they were going when he pushed his thumb on the diskette. The tape recorded the thumbprint, the "A" slot of the computer read the print, and the diskette was booted up.

There was an overview of what had happened to the ROC, along with the photographs Herbert had shown to Hood. The evidence collected by Herbert pointed to Syrian Kurds as the perpetrators, possibly in league with Turkish Kurds. Apparent confirmation came less than an hour ago, when Herbert learned from a deep undercover operative working with the Syrian Kurds that there had been highly secret meetings between the two groups several times over the past few months. A dam assault had been discussed at one of those meetings.

As August had suspected, their own destination was

either Ankara or Israel. If they went to Ankara, they'd be landing at the NATO base north of the capital. If Striker went to Israel, they'd be landing at the secret Tel Nef Air Base near Tel Aviv. August had been there just a year before and remembered it well. It was as low-tech and as safe a base as he had ever visited. The perimeter was surrounded by high barbed-wire fences. Outside the fence, every two hundred feet, was a brick outpost with a sentry and a German shepherd. Fifteen feet beyond them, also surrounding the perimeter, was five feet of fine, white sand. Buried within it were land mines. In over a quarter of a century, very few people had attempted to break into the base. None had been successful.

From Ankara, the team would fly east to a staging area within Turkey. From Tel Nef, the Striker team would be flown or would drive to the border of Turkey or Syria. If, as Herbert believed, the ROC was in the hands of Syrian Kurds, chances were very good that they would be headed to the Bekaa Valley in western Syria. That was a stronghold for terrorist operations and a place where the ROC would be of great use. If the Syrian Kurds were in league with Turkish Kurds, they could be planning to stay in Turkey and make for the eastern Kurdish strongholds around Mt. Ararat. However, that could be risky. Ankara was still waging unofficial war on the Kurds holed up in the southeastern provinces of Diyarbakir, Mardin, and Siirt and in the eastern province of Bingol.

Because of the Syrian government's own support of other terrorist groups in the Bekaa, particularly the Hezbollah, that was a more likely destination. Herbert was convinced that the Syrians would never allow Striker into that region.

"Whatever your destination," Herbert wrote, "we do

not yet have Congressional Oversight Intelligence Committee approval for the incursion. Martha Mackall expects to get it, though perhaps not in time to suit our schedule. If the terrorists are still in Turkey, we expect to get you permission to enter the country and set up a control and reporting center until we get COIC approval. If the terrorists enter Syria, Striker will not have the authority to enter the country."

The corner of August's mouth turned up slightly. He reread the passage ". . . Striker will not have the authority. . . ." What Herbert had written didn't mean that Striker shouldn't enter the country. When he first came to Op-Center, Mike Rodgers had encouraged August to spend several nights reviewing the language in other Op-Center/Striker communiques. Often, as August well knew, one's orders were to be found in what wasn't said rather than what was.

What August had discovered was that when Bob Herbert or Mike Rodgers did not want Striker to move ahead they always wrote, "You *do* not have the authority. . . ."

Clearly—or rather, obliquely—this was a case in which Herbert wanted Striker to act.

The rest of the material on the diskette consisted of maps, possible routes to various locations, and exit strategies in the event of non-cooperation from the Turks and Syrians. It was going to take fifteen hours to reach Tel Nef. August began reviewing the maps, after which he'd look at the game plans for surround-and-rescue missions in mountainous or desert terrain.

Because of his years with NATO, August was very familiar with most of the geography of the region and also with the various mission scenarios. Striker's tactics were culled from the same U.S. military branches from which the soldiers themselves were drawn. What was unfamiliar to August was having to evacuate someone so close to him. But as Kiet had helped to teach him in Vietnam, the unfamiliar was nothing to be afraid of. It was simply something new.

As the colonel looked over the maps, Ishi Honda approached. August looked up. Honda was holding the TAC-SAT secure phone, which was patched into the C-141B's dish.

"Yes, Private?" August asked.

"Sir," he said, "I think you'd better listen to this."

"What is it?"

"A broadcast which came into AL four minutes ago," he said.

AL was the active-line receiver, a phone line which automatically paged Bob Herbert and the Striker radio operator when it rang. If Striker was on a mission, the call was relayed to the TAC-SAT. Only a few people had AL's number: the White House, Senator Fox, and ten of the top people at Op-Center.

August looked up at Honda. "Why wasn't I told about it when it came in?" he demanded sharply.

"Sorry, sir," Honda said, "but I was hoping I could figure the message out first. I didn't want to waste your time with incomplete data."

"Next time, waste it," August said. "I might be able to help."

"Yes, sir. Sorry, sir."

"What've you got?" August asked.

"A series of beeps," Honda said. "Someone dialed us and then hit more numbers which keep repeating."

August took the receiver, then held an index finger over his open ear so he could hear. There were nine tones followed by a pause, and then the same nine tones were repeated.

"It's not a phone number," August said.

"No, sir," said Honda.

August listened. It was an eerie, discordant melody. "I assume that each tone corresponds to letters on the telephone."

"Yes, sir," said Honda. "I ran through the possible combinations but none of them make any sense."

Honda handed a note paper to August. The colonel read it and then read it again: 722528573. August looked at the receiver. The possible number of combinations were damn near incalculable. The colonel looked at the message again. It was definitely a code, and there was only one person who would be sending a coded communique via AL.

Mike Rodgers.

"Private," August said, "is there any way this could have come from the ROC?"

"Yes, sir," Honda said. "They could have used one of the phones built into the computer."

"It would have to have been turned on, with someone typing the number into the keys."

"That's right, sir," Honda said. "Or they could have patched a cell phone into the computer and pumped it out through the dish. That might have been easier to key up in private."

August nodded. The ROC was being powered up again. One of the crew would probably have to have done that. Their hands would have to be free, which meant they might have had time to get out a message.

"Op-Center should have gotten this message as well," August said. "See what they make of it."

"Right away," Honda replied.

The radio operator sat down next to August. As Private Honda phoned Bob Herbert's office, August didn't even try to concentrate on the maps while he waited for Honda to see what Op-Center made of it. But the fact that it was in code and very, very short did not give him a good feeling about Rodgers's situation.

TWENTY-FIVE

Monday, 10:38 p.m.,
Oguzeli, Turkey

This time, Mike Rodgers did not have a choice.

Mahmoud had the desire to kill. Rodgers could see it in his eyes. The general didn't even wait the full count of three. As soon as Hasan had translated the order to cooperate, Rodgers had held up his hands.

"All right," he said firmly. "I'll tell you what you want to know."

Hasan translated. Mahmoud hesitated. Rodgers stared into his eyes.

Mahmoud clearly liked having his foot on Rodgers's neck. Rodgers had allowed him to enjoy it even more by capitulating at once. For the Syrian, knowing that he'd won decisively might be all that prevented him from killing Mary Rose out of vengeance or pique. And there might still be a way to stop the Kurds, especially if Op-Center received and understood Rodgers's telephone message. The general had slipped the cellular phone from his shirt pocket where Hasan had placed it earlier that evening. He'd programmed it when he was bent over the pit. A few minutes later, when he'd stood and leaned against the computer station, he'd slipped the phone into its cradle. That automatically jacked it into the uplink. The connection overrode the phone's internal battery; it wouldn't start dialing until the computer came back on.

When Rodgers went back to the pit he connected the battery to several of the ROC's noisiest systems. When the computer snapped back to life, so did the ROC air-conditioner and the security system, which beeped unobtrusively because a window was open. The Syrians did not hear the faint click of the telephone dialing and redialing. Two minutes later all of the batteries were connected. Rodgers swung his bound legs from the battery well.

"Hasan," Rodgers said gently, "would you tell your colleague that everything is ready and that I'm going to cooperate? Tell him I'm sorry for having misled him about the nature of the van. Promise him that it won't happen again."

Rodgers let his gaze slip down to Mary Rose. The poor woman was breathing slowly. She looked as if she were trying not to vomit.

Mahmoud pulled her up by the hair.

"Son-of-a-bitch!" Private Pupshaw grunted, tugging against his bonds.

"Stow that, Private," Rodgers warned. He was trying to ignore the knot of outrage in his own gut.

Hasan nodded approvingly in Rodgers's direction. "I am pleased that you see this our way now."

Rodgers didn't say anything. There was nothing to be gained by explaining how he felt about a gun-wielding man threatening a bound, unarmed civilian. All the general wanted to do right now was keep the terrorists in the front of the van, away from the computer station.

Mahmoud handed Mary Rose to Ibrahim, who held

her tightly with one arm across her chest. The Syrian leader approached Rodgers. As he did, the general hopped forward. He stopped at the computer station opposite the one to which he'd connected the telephone. He lay a reassuring hand on Pupshaw's shoulder.

Mahmoud spoke to Hasan, who translated.

"Mahmoud wishes you to talk," Hasan said.

Rodgers looked at Mahmoud. Some of the anger had left his face, which was good. Rodgers wanted to keep things slow and chatty, give Op-Center time to receive and decode the message. He also wanted to buy time for them to turn a satellite on the ROC if they hadn't already. And he suspected that if he told them some of what the ROC could do, they wouldn't imagine that it could do more—such as access highly secure computers in Washington. If the terrorists learned the full capabilities of the ROC, national security and undercover lives would be compromised. And Rodgers would have no choice but to get to either keyboard and hit *Control, Alt, Del,* and *Cap "F"*—fry the facility, whatever the cost.

"This is a United States surveillance facility," Rodgers said. "We listen to radio communications."

As Hasan explained to Mahmoud, Rodgers felt Pupshaw squirm.

"General, let them kill us instead," the Striker whispered.

"Quiet," Rodgers reprimanded him.

Hasan turned back to Rodgers. "Mahmoud wishes to know if you knew about the work we did today."

"No," Rodgers said. "This is the first time our facility has been used. We're still working on it."

Hasan translated. Mahmoud spoke and pointed to the small satellite dish.

"Can you send a message from here?" Hasan asked.

"A satellite message?" Rodgers asked hopefully. "Yes. Yes, we can."

"Computer messages as well as voice messages?" Hasan inquired.

Rodgers nodded. If Mahmoud saw the ROC as his personal megaphone, so much the better. Op-Center could keep track of them by watching or listening to them.

Mahmoud smiled and said something to Ibrahim. Ibrahim answered confidently. Mahmoud spoke again, and this time Ibrahim put his other arm around Mary Rose's chest and pulled her from the van.

"What are you doing?" Mary Rose asked fearfully. "General! *General*—"

"Leave her alone!" Rodgers demanded. "We're doing what you want!"

He began hopping forward. "If you want someone, take me," he said.

Hasan held him back. Rodgers grabbed the Syrian's hair, but couldn't keep his balance. Hasan threw him down into the nearest battery well. Sondra reached out to help Rodgers, but he waved her away. If anyone was going to get knocked around, he wanted it to be him. She sat on the edge of the well.

"I have treated you well!" Hasan shouted. He spat in the general's face. "Animal! You don't deserve it!"

"Bring her back," Rodgers snarled at Hasan. "I'm doing what you asked."

"Be silent!"

"No!" Rodgers shot back. "I thought we had an agreement."

Mahmoud walked over and pointed the gun down at Rodgers. The Syrian's face was impassive as he spoke to Hasan.

Hasan ran his fingers through his hair. "You angered

me for nothing, Mr. Rambo,'' he said. ''Ibrahim is taking the woman to the Turk's motorcycle. He will follow us at a distance. Mahmoud has ordered that you use these computers to turn off the satellite. If we are stopped, her eyes will be cut out and she will be left in the desert.''

Rodgers swore at himself. He'd blundered into this and made an enemy of Hasan. He had to step back and try to think logically.

Hasan pulled Rodgers up and threw him into the free chair by the computer station. As he did, Mahmoud spoke.

''Mahmoud says you have wasted too much time,'' Hasan told him. ''We want to see this van from a satellite.''

Rodgers shook his head. ''We don't have that capaci—''

Mahmoud turned and kicked Sondra in the face. She had seen the boot coming and rolled with it, lessening the impact. It spilled her onto her side, but she sat up again quickly, defiantly.

Rodgers felt the kick as well. It had punted logic into a remote end zone. He looked at Hasan. ''You tell Mahmoud that if he touches one of my people again, he will get nothing, ever.''

Mahmoud spoke hurriedly to Hasan.

''Mahmoud says he will beat her to death unless you obtain the capacity we requested,'' Hasan replied.

''You are on United States property,'' Rodgers said. ''Tell Mahmoud that we don't obey dictators, whatever the price.'' Rodgers glared at Hasan. ''Tell him, damn you.''

Hasan obliged. When he had finished, Mahmoud went to kick Sondra again. Since her hands were free, she was able to cross her forearms and block the blow. At the same time she turned her hands inward, facing one another, and caught his shin. Holding it, she pushed his leg up and he stumbled back.

"Atta way, Private," Coffey said under his breath.

Screaming with fury, Mahmoud stomped down on the woman's right kneecap then kicked her in the chin. She wasn't fast enough to react to the blows and sprawled back against the wall. Mahmoud walked over and stomped her belly. Her arms slipped to her sides and she gasped for breath.

"For Christ's sake, stop!" Katzen said.

Mahmoud kicked Sondra twice in the chest, and this time she moaned. Then he kicked her in the mouth. With each blow Katzen's eyes burned with greater anger, first at the Syrians and finally at Rodgers.

"He's going to kill her," Katzen said. "Jesus, *do* something!"

Rodgers was proud of his Striker. She was ready to give it all for her country. But he couldn't allow it. Despite what he'd said about dictators, democracy would be better served by the likes of Sondra DeVonne living, not dying.

"All right," Rodgers said. "I'll do what you ask."

Mahmoud stopped, and Sondra tried to pull herself into a sitting position. There was blood on her cheek and mouth. She opened her eyes and looked at Katzen, who exhaled tremulously.

Rodgers held on to the table and swung himself into the empty chair. He put his hands on the keyboard. He hesitated again. If it were just himself and Pupshaw, maybe even Katzen and Coffey, he could tell the Syrians to go to hell. But by giving in to their first demand, he'd shown that his skin could be penetrated. By attacking Hasan, Rodgers had lost the ability to divide the terrorists. That had been stupid. But he'd been tired and afraid for Mary Rose, and it was over and done. Now he had only two assets left: his life and surprise. As long as he could work the ROC for these men, he would stay alive. And as long as he stayed alive, he could always surprise them.

Provided you keep your wits, Rodgers reminded himself. No more temper.

Mahmoud spoke. Hasan nodded.

"We want to see Ibrahim in the picture," Hasan told Rodgers. "Be certain you show him."

As Hasan and Mahmoud both looked over his shoulder, Rodgers opened the NRO software. He followed the on-screen prompts, typed in the coordinates, and asked for a visual of the site. He held his breath when the computer indicated that his request was "already working."

Dammit, Rodgers thought. Godammit. The Syrian could also read English.

"Already working," Hasan said. He translated for Mahmoud, then said, "This means that someone else has already asked for this information. Who?"

"It could be any military or intelligence office in Washington," Rodgers answered truthfully.

Less than twenty seconds later they were looking down at themselves from space. The image was a quarter mile across, standard surveillance distance.

Mahmoud seemed pleased. He said something to Hasan.

"Mahmoud wishes you to find out who else is looking at us."

There was no point in lying anymore. They'd only beat Sondra to death, then turn on someone else. Rodgers hit a flashing satellite icon, and a short list of image-share outlets appeared. The National Reconnaissance Office and Op-Center were the only names on it.

Hasan explained what they said, and then Mahmoud spoke.

"You are to shut the eye of the satellite," Hasan said.

Rodgers didn't hesitate. One of the keys to the hostage game was knowing when to up the ante and knowing when to fold. It was time to fold this hand.

The ROC could not shut down the 30-45-3. That command would have to come from the NRO. However, he could send up a steady stream of digital noise which would cover an area some ten miles across. That would make the ROC invisible to every form of electronic reconnaissance, from normal light to electromagnetic.

Rodgers accessed the software which had been designed to protect the ROC from being seen by enemy satellites. After loading it and removing the safeguards built into the system, all that remained was for him to push "Enter."

"It's ready," Rodgers said.

Hasan translated. Mahmoud nodded. Rodgers pressed the button.

The three men watched as the monitor grew thick with color static until the image broke up. Hasan leaned over Rodgers and clicked the satellite icon. The NRO and Op-Center both disappeared from the image-share list.

Mahmoud stood back and smiled. He spoke to Hasan at length, then turned and pulled his tobacco pouch from his shirt pocket.

Hasan regarded Rodgers. "Mahmoud wishes me to make certain that you have done what you promised."

"I have," said Rodgers. "You can see that."

"I saw an image vanish," Hasan said. He pointed toward Rodgers's shirt pocket. "Use your telephone. Call your headquarters. I will speak with them."

Rodgers felt nervous, but he had to appear calm. Maybe Hasan had just been pointing at him, not at the pocket where he'd placed the phone. Rodgers nodded and casually reached for the telephone on the side of the computer. He lifted it from the cradle and immediately tried to work his thumb onto the *stop* button. The last thing he wanted was for the Syrians to hear the pulsing of the numbers he'd sent out.

Hasan's hand flashed out. He grabbed Rodgers's wrist. He hadn't hit the button yet.

"What are you doing?" Hasan asked. "Where is your telephone?"

"I lost it somewhere," Rodgers said.

"Lost it where?" Hasan asked.

"I don't know," Rodgers replied. "Outside, I suppose. Or on the floor here. It could have happened any one of the times I was tripped or pushed or knocked around."

Hasan's brows came together. "What's that?"

"What?" Rodgers asked.

Hasan looked at the phone. "It is dialing."

"No, it isn't." Rodgers smiled benignly. He had to make Hasan feel foolish if he continued this line of questioning. "It's clicking because of the static we're sending up to the satellite. If it were a number, someone would have picked up. Watch. When we put in a new number, it will be fine."

Hasan didn't appear to be buying that. But he was distracted when Mahmoud spoke sharply. It sounded to Rodgers as if he were pressing Hasan, and Hasan answered testily.

Hasan exhaled loudly, then glared at Rodgers. "Dial the number and then introduce me," he said. "I will do the rest."

Rodgers waited while Hasan released his wrist. Then he clicked the *stop* button, waited for the dial tone, and punched in Bob Herbert's number. Since the main dish

233

on the driver's side of the van was being used to create the digital noise, the "mirror" dish on the passenger's side would create the uplink with the communications satellite Op-Center used.

Within ten seconds, Bob Herbert's startled assistant was summoning the intelligence chief to the phone.

TWENTY-SIX

Monday, 3:52 p.m., Washington, D.C.

Martha Mackall had been conferring with Op-Center Press Officer Ann Farris about how best to present Paul Hood's mission in the media. Martha was seated behind her desk and Ann was working on a leather couch, her laptop resting back near her knees. Together, the women plugged phrases like "exploratory intercession" and "interpositive mediation" into Ann's rough-draft press release. The trick was to position the post-flood mission as a diplomatic one rather than as intelligence-oriented, Hood's directorship of Op-Center notwithstanding.

Suddenly, it seemed as if a second flood had washed over Martha's office. First came Bob Herbert, who wheeled in with word that they had broken the repeating phone code from the ROC.

"We broke the pulse signal," he said proudly. "The beeps represent the numbers 722528573. That has to stand for RC2BKVKRD, which appears to translate as 'ROC to Bekaa Valley Kurds.' Our people are being taken to the Syrian Kurd stronghold in the Bekaa."

Even as Herbert was explaining the code, his wheelchair phone rang. He snatched it up. It was Chingmy Yau, one of his assistants, informing him that they'd lost the ROC on every one of their satellites.

"How can that be?" Herbert demanded. "Are you sure there isn't an equipment failure on this end?"

"Positive," said Chingmy. "It's as if someone nuked an area ten miles across. There's nothing but static."

"What about the Rhyolite?" Herbert asked. The Rhyolite was a small, orbiting radio telescope in a 22,300-mile-high geostationary orbit. Guiding a high-gain beam to earth, it was able to detect even the faintest electronic signals. The most common of these signals was side-lobe energy, radio beam energy which spilled at angles from the main beam. Sigint specialists were usually able to decipher the primary messages from the contents of this leakage.

"The Rhyolite's gone out too," Chingmy replied.

"It's got to be interference from the ROC," Herbert said.

"That's what we decided," Chingmy said. "We're working on reestablishing contact. But it's as if someone threw a blocking program into the ROC computers. They just don't want to let us in."

Herbert told his assistant to update him one way or the other. Less than a minute later, before he could return to discussing the Bekaa Valley message with Martha, his phone rang again.

"Yes, Ching?" he said. Only it wasn't his assistant this time.

"I have someone who wishes to speak with you," said the caller.

Herbert slapped the speaker button and fired a look at Martha. *"Mike,"* he mouthed.

Martha turned to her computer keyboard and typed:

Priority One: Triangulate call on Bob
Herbert's cell phone.
Expedite.

She E-mailed the message to Radio Reconnaissance Director John Quirk, then listened to Herbert's conversation.

"What do you see when you look for your van?" asked the caller.

"First tell me," said Herbert, "with whom have I the pleasure of speaking."

"One who holds your van and its crew of six," the caller replied. "If you wish it to remain a crew of six instead of five, please answer."

Herbert swallowed his quick temper. "We see nothing when we look for the van," he replied.

"Nothing? Describe this nothing."

"We see color static," said Herbert. "Confetti. Glitter."

Herbert was watching Martha. She received a "Mapping in progress" reply from Quirk. From this point it would take the RRD another twenty-five seconds to position the caller.

"Is there anything we can do for you all?" Herbert asked pleasantly as he slipped into his old Philadelphia, Mississippi, drawl. "Maybe we can talk about this, uh—this situation? Find a way to help you."

"The only assistance we require is the following. We wish you to make certain that the Turkish government does not stop us from reaching and then crossing the border," the caller said.

"Surely, sir, you must understand that we don't have the authority to do that."

"Get it," the caller said. "If I ring you again, it will

237

be so you can hear the sound of the bullet which ends the life of one of your spies.''

A moment later the line went dead. Martha gave Herbert a thumbs-up.

"The ROC is exactly where the ES4 placed it," Martha said. "Right outside of Oguzeli, Turkey. It hasn't moved."

"But it will," Herbert said.

Martha swung her high-backed chair around so she was facing away from the others. Then she phoned her assistant and asked him to ring the Turkish Ambassador's office at the Chancery in Washington.

While she waited, Herbert tapped the armrests of his chair.

"What are you thinking, Bob?" Ann asked.

"I'm thinking that I can't get anyone over to Oguzeli in time to follow the ROC," he said. "And if we try to watch it from space, all we'll get is ten miles of video and audio garbage."

"Is there any other way you can do it?" Ann asked.

"I don't know," Herbert said angrily. He was mostly angry at himself that this had happened. Security was one of his areas of responsibility.

"What about the Russians?" Ann asked. "Paul is pretty close to General Orlov. Maybe their operations center in St. Petersburg can see it."

"We had a scrambler built into the ROC so they couldn't," Herbert said. "Paul may be close to Orlov, but Washington and Moscow are still just dating." He punched his open palm. "The world's most sophisticated mobile intelligence unit and it gets coldcocked. Worse, the terrorists have access to our new SINC-GARS-V."

"What's that?" Ann asked.

"Single-Channel Ground and Airborne System

VHF," Herbert said. "It's a radio which hops at random over a wide range of frequencies during a single broadcast. Most SINCGARS-V, like the ones used by the U.S. Army, make a few hundred hops a second. Our unit makes seven thousand hops. Even if it's picked up by an enemy satellite, it's virtually impossible to decode. The people who have the ROC have both the transmitter and receiver."

Martha waved them quiet as she spoke with the ambassador's executive secretary. Herbert sunk into a brooding silence. When Martha was finished, she turned the chair around. She was frowning.

"There's a bit of a setback," she said.

"What happened?" Ann asked.

"In fifteen minutes I'll be talking to Ambassador Kande about the terrorists' request for non-intervention," Martha said. "But her deputy assistant doesn't think we'll be able to swing any kind of a deal for them. The ambassador has been given marching orders to do whatever's necessary to help find the dambusters and bring them in, dead or alive. Fact is, I expect I'll get a lot of pressure to tell the Turks what we know."

"Can't say I blame them," Herbert said, still brooding. "We could use a little more of that spirit in this town."

"Blind justice?" Martha asked. "Lynch mob justice?"

"No," Herbert replied. "Plain old justice. Not worrying about repercussions, like what nation is going to cut off our oil supplies if we do this, or which corporation is going to pull their billions from our banks if we do that, or which special interest group is going to get pissed off and uppity because we came down hard on some of their twisted brethren. *That* kind of justice."

"Unfortunately," Martha said, "that kind of justice and this kind of country weren't made for each other. Due process is one of the things which made this country great."

"And vulnerable," said Herbert. He exhaled. "Let's do this over a table of frozen yogurt when we're all done." He pointed toward Martha's computer. "Would you bring up a map of Turkey for me?"

She obliged. Herbert wheeled toward the desk.

"There are about three hundred miles of border between Turkey and Syria," he said. "If we've interpreted Mike's covert message correctly, and I think we have, the ROC is headed toward the Bekaa Valley. That starts about two hundred miles southwest of Oguzeli."

Martha measured the distance with her thumb and index finger. She compared it to the scale on the bottom. "I make it to be less than a hundred miles of border between Oguzeli and the Mediterranean."

"And the ROC'd be entering in a corridor much narrower than that," Herbert said. "With the Euphrates flooded by the dam blast, they'll probably stay pretty wide to the west of the river and then shoot straight down. That gives them a border window of about seventy miles to drop down through."

"That's still a lot of area to cover, isn't it?" asked Ann.

"And flyovers by Turkish jets or helicopters wouldn't be exactly low-profile," Martha said.

"We might not need aerial recon," Herbert said, "and seventy miles isn't bad if you know where to look." He reached the computer and traced a line down through Turkey into Lebanon. "A lot of that terrain isn't going to be ROC-friendly. There are only one or two good roads in that region. If I can find someone with contacts along those roads, we may be able to spot them.''

"A Racman," Martha said.

Herbert nodded.

"Excuse me," said Ann. "A rack man?"

"R-A-C-man," said Herbert. "The Redcoats Are Coming. Instead of Paul Revere, Samuel Prescott, and William Dawes on horseback warning the militias of Lincoln and Concord, we use a phone relay of people watching from their windows or hilltops or market-places. They report the target's progress to the Racman, who reports to us. It's primitive but efficient. Usually, the only potential problems with the system are leaks along the Racline, someone warning the target that they are a target.''

"I see," said Ann.

"But that usually isn't a problem with the people I'm thinking of using," Herbert said.

"Why not?" asked Ann.

"Because they cut the throat of anyone who turns on them," Herbert replied. He regarded the map. "If the Bekaa's our arena, then Striker will have to land in Tel Nef. Assuming they get Congressional approval to go forward from there, they move north into Lebanon and into the Bekaa. If a Racman can meet them there, we've got a chance of getting everyone out.''

"And possibly saving the Regional Op-Center," Martha added.

Herbert wheeled around. "It's a shot," he said as he rolled quickly toward the door, "and a good one. I'll let you know what I can set up.''

When he was gone, Ann shook her head. "He's amazing," she said. "Goes from James Bond to Huck Finn to Speed Racer in the space of a few minutes.''

"He's the best there is," Martha said. "I only hope that's good enough to do what has to be done.''

TWENTY-SEVEN

Monday, 11:27 p.m., Kiryat Shmona

This is better, thought Falah Shibli.

The swarthy young man stood in front of the dresser-top mirror in his one-room apartment and adjusted his tribal red-and-white checkered *kaffiyeh*. He made sure the headdress sat squarely on his head. Then he brushed lint from the collar of his light green police uniform.

This is much, much better.

After serving seven long and difficult years in the Sayeret Ha'Druzim, Israel's Druze Reconnaissance unit, Falah had been ready for a change. Before joining the local police force, he couldn't even remember the last time he'd worn a clean uniform. His darker Sayeret Ha' Druzim greens had always been crusted with dirt or sweat or blood. Sometimes it was his own blood, more often than not it was someone else's. And he'd usually worn a green beret or helmet, rarely his own headdress. If only his head were sticking up from a foxhole or over a wall, he didn't want an overanxious Israeli mistaking him for an infiltrator and shooting at him.

Falah took one last look at himself. He was as proud

of his heritage as he was of his adopted land. He turned off the dresser light, shut off the fan on his nightstand, and opened the door.

The cool night air was refreshing. When the twenty-seven-year-old first joined the small police force in this dusty northern town, he'd asked for a night job directing traffic. His work with the Sayeret Ha'Druzim had been so intensive, not to mention so damned *hot,* he needed the break. Let the years of sunburn fade a little so the wrinkles around his eyes didn't stand out quite so much. Let the old wounds heal—not just the torn muscle from gunshot wounds, but the still-calloused feet from the long patrols, the flesh ripped by crawling over sharp rocks and thorns to capture terrorists, the spirit rent by having to shoot at fellow Druze.

Very few terrorists came through this kibbutz town. They picked their way through the barren plains to the east and west. Except for the occasional drunk driver or stolen motorbike or car accident, this job was blessedly uneventful. It was so quiet that on most nights, he and the owner of a local bar, a former Sayeret Ha'Druzim gunner team commander, were able to spend a half hour trading gossip. They did so in special forces fashion, standing under streetlights on opposite sides of the road and blinking the information in Morse code.

As Falah stepped onto the wooden stoop that was too small to be called a porch but had a folding chair on it anyway, the phone rang. He hesitated. It was a two-minute walk to the station house. If he left now, he'd be on time. If it was his mother calling, it would take at least that long just to tell her he had to go. On the other hand, it could be his adorable Sara. She'd been talking about taking a day off from her bus route. Perhaps she wanted to see him in the morning. . . .

243

Falah went back into the apartment and snatched up the old, black dial phone.

"Which of my ladies is this?" he asked.

"Neither," said the man's voice on the other end.

The tall, dark-haired young man moved his heels together. His shoulders drew back. Coming to attention was conditioning which never left when your former commander addressed you.

"Master Sergeant Vilnai," Falah said. He said nothing more. After acknowledging a superior, the soldiers of the Sayeret Ha'Druzim responded with silent attention.

"Officer Shibli," said Sergeant Vilnai. "A jeep from the border guard will be arriving at your apartment in approximately five minutes. The driver's name is Salim. Please go with him. Everything you need will be provided."

Falah was still at attention. He wanted to ask his former superior, "Everything I need for where and how long?" But that would have been impertinent. Besides, this was an unsecured line.

"I have a job here—" Fallah said.

"Your shift has been taken care of," the sergeant informed him.

Just like my job, Falah thought. "Take this position, Falah," the sergeant had said. "It will keep your skills in good repair."

"Repeat your orders," said the NCO.

"Border patrol jeep, driver Salim. Pickup in five minutes."

"I'll see you around midnight, Falah. Have a pleasant ride."

"Yes, sir. Thank you."

The caller hung up. After a moment, so did Falah. He stood there staring at nothing in particular. He'd known

244

this day would probably come, but so soon? It had only been a few weeks. Just a few. He'd barely had time to get the burning sun of the West Bank out of his eyes.

Will I ever? he asked himself as he went back outside.

The question bothered Falah as he sat heavily in the chair and looked up at the brilliant stars. It bothered him almost as much as why he'd picked up the goddamned telephone. Not that it would have made a difference. Master Sergeant Vilnai would have climbed into a Jeep and come to the station house to get him. The Sayeret Ha'Druzim NCO always got what he wanted.

The charcoal-gray jeep arrived on schedule. Falah pushed off on his knees and walked around to the driver's side.

"ID?" he said to the baby-faced driver with a buzz cut.

The driver removed a laminated card from his shirt pocket. Falah examined it in the glow of the dashboard light. He handed it back.

"Yours, Officer Shibli?" the driver asked.

Falah scowled and pulled the small leather billfold from his pants pocket. He opened it to his police ID card and badge. The driver's eyes shifted from Falah to the photo, then back again.

"It's me," Falah said, "though I wish it weren't."

The driver nodded. "Please get in," he said, leaning across the seat and opening the door.

Falah obliged. Even before the door was shut the driver had swung the jeep around.

The two men headed north in silence along the ancient dirt road. Falah listened to the pebbles as they spat noisily from under the jeep's tires. It had been a while since he'd heard that sound—the sound of haste, of things happening. He decided that he didn't miss it, nor had he expected to hear it again so soon. But they had a saying in the Sayeret Ha'Druzim: *Sign for a tour, sign for a lifetime.* It had been that way ever since the 1948 war, when the first Druze Muslims along with expatriate Russian Circassians and Bedouins volunteered to defend their newborn nation against the allied Arab enemy. Then, all of the non-Jews were bunched together in the infantry group called Unit 300 of the Israel Defense Force. It wasn't until after the 1967 Six-Day War, when Unit 300 was a key to turning back King Hussein's Royal Jordanian Army on the West Bank, that the IDF and the Unit 300 leader Mohammed Mullah formed an elite Druze reconnaissance splinter group known as Sayeret Ha'Druzim.

Because they were fluent in Arabic, and because they were parachutist-qualified, it was common for Druze recon soldiers to be recalled into active service and dropped into Arab nations to gather intelligence. These assignments could last anywhere from a few days to a few months. Officers preferred to draw on retired soldiers for these assignments since it saved them from having to raid active units. They preferred most of all to draw on soldiers who had fought with the IDF when they invaded southern Lebanon in June of 1982. The Sayeret Ha'Druzim were in the front lines of the battles around the Palestinian refugee camps. Many of the Israeli Druze were forced to fight their own relatives serving in the Lebanese armed forces. Moreover, the Sayeret Ha'Druzim were obliged to support the fierce historic enemies of their people, the Maronite Christian Phalangists, who were warring against the Lebanese Druze. It was the ultimate test of patriotism, and not every member of the Sayeret Ha'Druzim passed. Those who did were revered and trusted. As Sergeant Vilnai had wryly observed, ''Proving our loyalty gave us the honor of being first in line to get shot at in subsequent conflagrations.''

Falah had been too young to serve in the 1982 invasion, but he'd worked undercover in Syria, Lebanon, and Iraq, and dangerously in the open in Jordan. The Jordanian assignment had been the last, not to mention the shortest and most difficult. While patrolling a border sector in the Jordan Valley after a terrorist attack on the town of Mashav Argaman, Falah had gone ahead of his small force of soldiers. He noticed that a hole had been cut through the thick rows of concertina wire which had been stretched along the border—a sign of infiltration. The single set of tracks led back into Jordan. Afraid that he might lose the terrorist, Falah raced ahead alone, pushing a quarter mile into the desert hills. There, following the footprints and his nose, he entered a gully. Moving ahead cautiously, he spotted a man who fit the description of the assassin who had shot a local politician and his son. Falah didn't hesitate. One couldn't in this part of the world. He swung his CAR-15 around as the Jordanian turned and aimed his AK-47. The guns fired simultaneously and both men went down. Falah had been wounded in the shoulder and left arm. The Jordanian had been killed.

Hiding from a Jordanian patrol which had heard the shots, Falah waited until nightfall before crawling back toward the border. He was pale and weak when his unit finally found him inside Jordan.

Falah was told he'd get a medal. All he wanted was coffee laced with cardamom. He received both—the coffee first, happily. He recovered quickly, and in nine weeks was back on active patrol. When his hitch ended, Falah decided it was time to pursue another line of work. He hadn't considered becoming a police officer. Though there was a great demand for military-trained personnel, the pay was low and the hours long. But Master Sergeant Vilnai had arranged this job for him. It was such an open display of personal concern that Falah could hardly decline the position—even though he knew that Vilnai's real motive was to keep his dischargee in good physical condition and close to the Sayeret Ha'Druzim's regional base at Tel Nef.

The ride to Tel Nef took just over a half hour. Once inside the nondescript base, Falah was driven to a small, one-story brick building. It was empty. The real office was in a bunker ten feet below reinforced concrete. There, it was safe from Syrian artillery, Iraqi Scuds, and most any other conventional weapons which might be hurled at it. During its twenty-year history, most of those weapons had been fired at the base.

Falah passed through the staircase checkpoint and walked into the small office shared by Major Maton Yarkoni and Master Sergeant Vilnai. An orderly shut the door behind him and left the two men alone.

Major Yarkoni was not present. He was usually in the field with his troops, which was why Vilnai spent so much time here. Falah was convinced that whereas everyone else in the brigade got too much sunlight, Vilnai got far too little. That would help to account for his chronic bad humor. Studying maps and communiques, keeping track of troop movements, and processing intelligence in this dark, stuffy hole would have made even a Desert Prophet cross.

The barrel-chested Vilnai rose when Falah entered. The former infantryman accepted the sergeant's hand as he offered it across his metal desk.

"You're not in the service anymore," Vilnai reminded him.

Falah smiled. "Am I not?"

"Not officially," he admitted. He held his hand toward a wooden chair. "Sit down, Falah. Would you care for a cigarette?"

The Israeli frowned as he took a seat. He knew what the offering meant. Falah only used tobacco when he was among Arabs, most of whom were chain-smokers. He selected a cigarette from the case on the desk. Vilnai offered him a match. Falah hacked as the first drag went down.

"You're out of practice," the sergeant observed.

"Very. I ought to go home."

"If you'd like," Vilnai said.

Falah looked at him through the smoke. "You're too kind."

"Of course," Vilnai said, "you'll have to crawl under the barbed wire and through the minefield around the base."

"I used to do that for my daily warm-up," Falah smiled.

"I know," Vilnai said. "You were the best."

"You flatter me."

"I find it helps," Vilnai said.

Falah took another drag on the cigarette. It went down more smoothly. "The master puppeteer works his marionettes," he said.

Vilnai smiled for the first time. "Is that what I am? A master puppeteer? There is only one puppeteer, my friend." He shot a look at the white ceiling as he sat down. "And sometimes—no, *most* times—I feel as though Allah cannot decide whether we're performing in a tragedy or in a comedy. All that I *do* know is that the play is as unpredictable as ever."

Thoughts of his own well-being evaporated as Falah regarded his former superior. "What's happened, Sergeant?"

The master sergeant splayed his fingers on his desk

and looked at them. "Shortly before phoning you, I was on a conference call with Major General Bar-Levi in Haifa and an American intelligence officer, Robert Herbert of the National Crisis Management Center in Washington, D.C."

"I've heard of that group," Falah said. "Why?"

"They were part of that New Jacobin takedown in Toulouse."

"Yes," Falah said enthusiastically. "The neo-Nazi hate games on the Internet. That was a beautiful piece of work."

Vilnai nodded. "Very. They're a good outfit with a superb young strike force. Only they managed to stumble down a well in Turkey. You heard about the terrorist attack on the Ataturk Dam."

"That's all they're talking about in Kiryat Shmona," he said. "That and a raw diamond old Nehemiah found in the sand at the kibbutz. It was probably dropped by a smuggler, but everyone's convinced there's a vein under the settlement."

Vilnai looked up sharply.

"Sorry," Falah said. "Please continue."

"The Americans were field-testing a new mobile intelligence facility in the region," Vilnai said. "Very sophisticated, able to access satellites and listen to every form of electronic communication. On their way back to Syria, the Ataturk terrorists—at least, the Americans believe it was the same terrorists—came upon the facility and captured it. Along with this Regional Operations Center, the Syrians were able to take its crew." Vilnai consulted his notes. "There were two strike force soldiers, a General Michael Rodgers, a technician who helped to design the mobile unit and can help the Syrians run it, two NCMC officials, and a Turkish security officer."

"As the Americans would say, a grand slam," Falah observed. "Damascus will be celebrating tonight."

"Damascus does not appear to have been behind this," Vilnai said.

"The Kurds?"

Vilnai nodded.

"I'm not surprised," Falah said. "There have been rumblings about a new offensive for over a year now."

"I've heard those rumblings too," Vilnai admitted. "But I discounted them. Most everyone did. We didn't think they could put aside their differences long enough to make any kind of effective union."

"Well, they have. And this was an impressive show for them."

"An impressive first act," Vilnai corrected. "Our American friend Mr. Herbert believes that the van containing the equipment and his people is still in Turkey but headed toward the Bekaa Valley. A strike team has been dispatched from Washington to try and take it back."

"Ah," Falah said. "And they need a guide." He pointed to himself.

"No," Vilnai said. "What they need, Falah, is someone to find it."

TWENTY-EIGHT

Tuesday, 12:45 a.m., Barak, Turkey

While Ibrahim drove the twenty-five miles to Barak, Hasan had been busy taking inventory of the ROC's cargo. Mahmoud, meanwhile, sat in the passenger's seat, four of his prisoners at his feet. He was teaching himself how to use the radio. Any questions he had were passed from Hasan to Mary Rose. Rodgers had instructed her to answer. He didn't want to push the terrorists again. Not yet. Within minutes, Mahmoud had discovered the frequency used by the Turkish border patrol. Mary Rose showed him how to communicate with them. But he didn't.

The Turkish border town of Barak lies just west of the Euphrates. By the time the ROC arrived, the flood-waters had covered the floors of wood-frame homes, stores, and a mosque in the northeastern sector of the village. The town was deserted, save for a few cows and goats and an old man who sat on his porch, his feet in the water. Apparently, he just hadn't felt like going anywhere.

Ibrahim passed south through the near-lifeless town,

then stopped the ROC less than three yards from rolls of barbed wire strung between six-foot-high posts. The driver said something to Hasan, who nodded and walked over to Rodgers.

The general had been tied between the computer station chairs. He was kneeling and facing the rear of the van. Private Pupshaw was still draped over the chair, and Sondra had been returned to hers. The only concession the Syrians had allowed was to let Phil Katzen to tend to Colonel Seden's bullet wound. Though the Turk had lost a good deal of blood, the wound itself wasn't grave. Rodgers knew that they hadn't done that simply out of mercy. They probably wanted Colonel Seden for something important. Unlike some terrorists who soften toward their hostages as time passes, these three didn't seem to understand concession or compromise. They certainly didn't practice mercy. To the contrary, they had demonstrated their willingness to hurt or kill. On their home ground, with their comrades, there was no telling what they would do. Even if the hostages weren't killed, there was a good chance the men or women would be seriuously abused.

Rodgers realized that he was going to have to try to move quickly against their captors.

Hasan looked down at Pupshaw. "You will come with me," the Syrian said as he cut the bonds around Private Pupshaw's legs.

"Where are you taking him?" Rodgers asked.

"Outside," Hasan said as he led the American from the van.

When Rodgers saw Hasan tie Pupshaw's hands to the door handle on the driver's side, and heard Hasan tell him to stand on the narrow running board, Rodgers knew what the Syrians were planning.

There was just over a quarter mile of "no-man's-land'' between this fence and the one situated at the Syrian border. Rodgers knew that both wire fences were electrified. The Syrians probably knew it too. If they hadn't known it before they arrived, the baked-on insects were a giveaway. Cutting the wire at any point would break the circuit and set off an alarm at the nearest checkpoint. Turkish guards would respond by land or air before anyone could cross in either direction. In this case, Rodgers didn't know whether the sight of hostages would deter the Turks from attacking the van or whether it wouldn't make any difference. They probably wanted to stop the Ataturk bombers so bad that they would shoot first and check IDs later.

Rodgers debated with himself whether or not to tell the Syrians another of the ROC's capabilities. If the terrorists knew, it would be even less reason for them ever to return the van. But the lives of his crew were at risk.

When Hasan returned for Sondra, Rodgers called him over. He had to tell him.

"You don't have to do this," Rodgers said. "Our van is bullet-proof."

"Not the wheels."

"Yes, the wheels," Rodgers said. "They're lined with Kevlar. Nothing is going to happen to the van."

Hasan thought for a moment. "Why should I believe this?"

"Test it. Fire a bullet."

"You would like that," Hasan said. "The Turks would hear."

"And shoot us all," Rodgers said.

Hasan thought again. "If this is so and your tires are bullet-proof, then we can just ride over the wire. Correct?"

"No," Rodgers said. "When the van hits, the metal chassis will still conduct electricity. We'll all be killed."

Hasan nodded.

"Look," Rodgers said, "having my people tied to the side isn't going to stop the Turks. You know that. The border patrol will shoot right through them to try and get to you. Keep them inside and we'll all be safe."

Hasan shook his head. "If the border patrol comes, they may not shoot. They will see one of their own people tied to the outside. And they will want to question us." He bent over Sondra and began to untie her.

"I know these people," Rodgers yelled. "I tell you, they'll try and cripple the van and they won't lose sleep over who dies in the process, even one of their own. And what'll you do if they chase you into Syria?"

"That is the Syrian military's problem."

"Not if we get caught in an artillery cross fire," Rodgers said. "If you'll just give me a little time, we can get across without the Turks even being aware of it."

Hasan stopped untying Sondra. "How?"

"We keep insulated cable in the van for patching into satellite uplinks when we have to," Rodgers said. "Let me rig an arc across the barbed wire so we don't break the circuit. Then I'll cut the wire and you can drive right over the cable. Once we cross the field I'll do the same thing on the other side. It'll be quiet. No alarms and no patrols."

"Why should I trust you to do this?" Hasan asked. "If you were to break the circuit, we wouldn't know until the Turks arrive."

"I don't gain anything by bringing the guards down on us," Rodgers replied. "Even if they don't shoot us, you'd probably kill my people in retaliation. That defeats the purpose."

Hasan considered this, then reported to Mahmoud.

There was a short conversation, after which Hasan returned to the back of the van.

"How long will it take to make these connections?"

"Three quarters of an hour at the most," Rodgers said. "It'll take less time if you help."

"I will help," Hasan said as he retied Sondra and began to untie the general. "But I warn you, if you try to get away, I will kill you and one of your people. Do you understand?"

Rodgers nodded.

Hasan finished removing the restraining rope, and shoved it into his back pocket. Then he retrieved the wire shears from the tool chest in the rear of the van. Rodgers held out his hand, and Hasan hesitated. Mahmoud unholstered his gun and pointed it at Mary Rose. Hasan handed the shears to Rodgers.

While Hasan collected the cable, Rodgers used a staple gun to make a protective, insulated mitt from a pair of rubber mouse pads. When he was finished, he went outside with Hasan.

Rodgers worked quickly under the glow of the headlights. As he bent beside the fence, he couldn't help but think about what he was doing. Not about rewiring the fence. That was rote. He and Hasan cut the cable into two ten-foot lengths, stripped the ends, and used the mitt to wrap them carefully around the two separate but intermeshed coils of barbed wire. Then they laid the cable on the ground and cut the barbed wire. Rodgers used the mitt to pull it aside and staple the end to the post.

No, what Rodgers thought about during those twenty-seven minutes was the fact that it was his job to try to stop these bastards. Now here he was, helping them to escape. He tried to justify his actions by telling himself that they would probably get away regardless. This way, at least, his people wouldn't be hurt. But the idea of being a collaborator, for whatever reason, stuck in his throat and refused to go down.

When they finished, Hasan gave an okay sign to Mahmoud. The leader motioned them back inside. As they entered, Rodgers removed his mitt. He paused to cut Pupshaw free.

Hasan pushed his gun against Rodgers's temple. "What are you doing?" he asked harshly.

"Letting my man back in."

"You presume a great deal," Hasan said.

"I thought we had an agreement," Rodgers replied. "I wire the fence, my people ride inside."

"Truly," said Hasan, "we have this agreement." He pulled the shears away from Rodgers. "But it is not for you to give freedom."

"I'm sorry," Rodgers said. "I was only trying to hurry things along."

"Don't pretend that you are on our side," Hasan said. "Your lie insults us both." Hasan lowered the gun. He used it to motion Rodgers inside.

Rodgers watched the gun from the corner of his eye. As he stepped up on the running board, his sense of duty began to gnaw at him again. That and the humiliating reality of having just had a gun pressed to his head. He was a United States soldier. He was a prisoner. His job should be to try and escape, not to take orders from a terrorist and abet enemies of a NATO ally.

Rodgers quickly considered his options. If he turned and threw himself against Hasan, he might be able to get the gun, shoot the Syrian, then turn the weapon on the other two. Certainly in the dark, on the ground, he'd have a decent chance of success. And if he waited until Pupshaw was free, the private would seize the initiative and probably tackle Mahmoud, who was right behind him inside the van. With luck, the only ones who would be at risk were himself and Pupshaw. Even if they lost their lives, the others were still valuable hostages. The Syrians probably wouldn't kill them.

Action was clearly on Pupshaw's mind as well. Rodgers could tell from the way the private's dark eyes followed him, waiting for his lead. Rodgers knew then that if he didn't act, not only would he hate himself, but he'd lose the respect of his subordinates. He had only an instant to decide. He also knew that if he managed to get the gun, he wouldn't be able to hesitate.

Mahmoud said something. Hasan nodded, then pulled the rope from his pocket. He pushed Rodgers in the small of his back.

"Turn around," Hasan said. "I have to tie you up until we reach the next fence."

Shit, thought Rodgers. He'd been hoping they'd leave him free while they transferred Pupshaw inside. Now, if he acted it would have to be alone—with Pupshaw tied up in the line of fire. Rodgers glanced at the private, whose gaze was unwavering.

Rodgers extended his hands toward Hasan. The Syrian tucked his gun in his waistband and slipped the rope around Rodgers's wrists. Rodgers's hands were held palms-together. Slowly, imperceptibly, he curled the third and fourth fingers of his left hand slightly so that the tips of all four fingers were even. Then, pressing the fingers one against the other, he drove the solid line of fingertips into Hasan's throat. The Syrian gagged and reached for Rodgers's hand. As he did, Rodgers's right hand shot down and grabbed the gun. He fired twice into Hasan's chest. As the Syrian tumbled soundlessly to the ground, Rodgers stepped into the van and aimed at Mahmoud.

"Use me as a shield!" Pupshaw shouted.

Rodgers had no intention of doing so. But before he

could shoot around the private, Ibrahim gunned the engine. Rodgers was thrown to the floor as the ROC raced forward. The passenger's door was still open with Pupshaw tied to the handle. The private was bucked off the running board and his lower body was dragged alongside, under the door, as the van sped ahead.

Mahmoud vaulted from the passenger's seat and threw himself on top of Rodgers. As the American tried to bring the gun around, the Syrian drew his knife. Rodgers was able to move Mahmoud's arm to the side. But with incredible speed the Syrian literally fed the knife to his finger tips, pinched the hilt between his thumb and index finger, turned the knife around, and grasped it facing the other way. Once again the knife was pointing down at Rodgers. He was forced to let go of the gun to concentrate on Mahmoud's knife hand. The general grabbed the wrist with one hand and tried to pry his fingers from the hilt with the other.

Suddenly, Ibrahim braked. Mahmoud and Rodgers were thrown against the prisoners who were tied to the base of the passenger's seat. The van's noisy advance became the deathly quiet of late night as Ibrahim drew his own weapon. Shouting at Mahmoud, he aimed at Rodgers's head.

Mary Rose screamed.

Before Mahmoud could fire, the wail of a siren reached them from across the plain. A patrol must have heard the shot. Without hesitation, Ibrahim threw the van into reverse. When they reached Hasan's body, Mahmoud jumped out and pulled it in. He was dead. His eyes were wide and unseeing. Blood stained his shirtfront and was seeping into the fibers around the side.

There was more conversation, probably about whether to kill Rodgers. Though Ibrahim was shaking with rage, the Syrians obviously decided that a gunshot would only tell the Turks exactly where they were.

Mahmoud pulled the dazed and bloodied Pupshaw inside and tied him back to his chair, while Ibrahim kicked Rodgers in the head before tying him to the chair leg, his back on the floor. They drove off, Ibrahim leaning heavily on the gas pedal.

Mahmoud punched Rodgers several times as they drove. Each time he struck the American's jaw, Mahmoud spit in his face. He stopped only when they reached the fence. Grabbing the mitt and the shears, Mahmoud went out to cut them through. There was no longer any need to be secretive. He sliced the wire quickly, pulling each strand to the side and wrapping it around the post.

Rodgers looked up through bloodstained eyes. He saw Sondra struggling hard to get free.

"Don't," he said through his swollen jaw. He shook his head slowly. "You're going to have to survive . . . to lead them."

When the last strand was cut, Ibrahim pressed on the gas and the van tore across the border. He stopped to let Mahmoud in. Evidently having had enough of punishing Rodgers, Mahmoud settled into his seat. As he sat in silence, picking pieces of bloody flesh from his ring, Ibrahim continued into the night.

TWENTY-NINE

Monday, 6:41 p.m., Washington, D.C.

"You don't have to tell me," Martha Mackall said as Bob Herbert wheeled into her office. "The ROC has gone into Syria."

Herbert's wheelchair was reflected over and over in the framed, hanging gold records Martha's father Mack Mackall had earned during his long singing career. He parked, frowning, in front of her desk. "We picked up the description from a radio broadcast by the Turkish border patrol. My expression tell you that?"

"No." She tapped a pencil eraser against her computer monitor. "This did. I've been watching the computer lines we hacked in Turkey and elsewhere. It reminds me of when the stock market started to fall in '87, all that computerized trading kicking in and making it worse."

"It *is* like computerized trading," Herbert said. "Only it's computerized warfare. CARfare, they're calling it."

"That's a new one on me," Martha said. She rubbed her tired eyes. "Care to translate?"

"It's Computerized Armed Response," Herbert said. "Every government is choosing the appropriate response based on its own simulation programs."

Martha made a face. "If that's CARfare, then I've got bumper-to-bumper traffic up here. The Turkish Security Forces say their border patrol crossed into Syria, lost the target, and retreated. As a result of the crossing, Syria's calling up its reserves and Turkey is mobilizing more troops and sending them toward the border. Israel has gone on maximum alert, Jordan is about to begin moving tanks toward its borders, and Iraq is shifting troops possessively toward Kuwait."

"Possessively?"

"They're geared for a long camp-out," Martha said, "just like before Desert Shield. And to top it off, Colon just notified us that the Department of Defense has ordered the U.S. carrier battle group into the Red Sea."

"Defcon?"

"Two," she said.

Herbert seemed relieved.

"Supply lines have already begun forming from the Indian Ocean, just in case they're needed. Publicly, we're showing support for our NATO ally. Privately, we're prepared to kick whatever ass is necessary to try and contain the whole damn thing in case it blows up. The President is determined not to let this spread into Turkey and Russia."

"Probably as determined as Syria and Iran will be to see it spread there," Herbert replied.

"They *are* an opportunistic bunch," Martha said, "but they don't want to see the region turned into a war zone. Don't forget, Syria sided with us during Desert Storm."

"They gave us a couple of jets and permission to get ourselves killed defending their water supplies," Herbert said. "Never mind them. What's so damn frustrating is that no one else wants to see this happen. And most of the players realize they've been snookered by a small band of Kurds."

"It's *The House That Jack Built*," Martha replied.

"What do you mean?"

"That's a little epigram from my side of the fence," she said. "These are the rats who tweaked the cat, who crossed the border and woke the dog, who engaged the cat and woke the menagerie that sent the fur flying in the House That Jack Built."

Herbert sighed. "It's more like *The House on Haunted Hill*," he said. "One nightmare after another."

"We move in very different cultural circles," Martha replied with an arched brow.

"Life would be boring otherwise," Herbert said. "Anyway, the good news is that my friend Captain Gunni Eliaz of the First Golani Infantry Brigade in Israel put me in touch with an operative who knows the Bekaa just about as well as anyone. He's already on his way there, posing as a Kurdish freedom fighter, to see what he can find out. I've got Matt working on geographical surveys of the region, looking for possible destinations for the ROC."

"What is he checking for?"

"Caves, mostly," Herbert said. "Ironically, in blacking out our satellite view, the Syrians left us with a clue to where the ROC is. We always know that it's within the ten-mile-wide window we can't see through. We'll collate all of that information with known PKK bases of operation and see if we can select the most likely spot. And we may still pick up some stray remark in a telephone or radio communication."

"Then it will be up to this Israeli of yours and Striker

to get them out," Martha said. "Or it will be up to a Tomahawk to take them out."

As she was speaking, Herbert's phone beeped. He scooped it up. After a moment, he poked a finger in his other ear. "There's *what*?" he demanded. His eyes shifted absently from the floor to Martha to the ceiling. "What else? Did they find anything else there?" His eyes moved around again. "Nothing at all? Okay, Ahmet. *Tessekur*. Thanks very much." He hung up. "Shit."

"What?" Martha asked.

"There's a narrow zone between two barbed wire fences at the Turkish-Syrian border," Herbert said. "The Turkish border patrol heard a shot there and raced over. That was where the ROC crossed into Syria. The patrol found fresh blood beside six deep tire fans."

"Tire *fans*?"

"A tire rut with dirt blown out behind it like a paper fan," Herbert said. "It's caused by a fast, sudden start."

"I see," Martha said. "Six tires. So it was the ROC." Herbert nodded.

"And it was running from something."

"They weren't being chased yet," Herbert said. "The Turks say the ROC got past an electrified fence by setting up a diversionary arc. They were already through before the Turks heard a gunshot and realized that they were there. The ROC took off long before the border patrol arrived. Something else caused the ROC to bolt."

"Bob, I'm totally confused," Martha said impatiently. "First, who do they think was shot and why?"

"They don't *know*," Herbert said. He shut his eyes. "I don't know. I've got to think. Why would the ROC take off? Because they were afraid someone heard the gunshot? That's possible. That isn't what's important. The question is, who was shot? If one of the hostages had been killed, the Syrians probably would have dumped the body behind.''

"And if they were wounded?" Martha asked.

"Unlikely," Herbert said.

"How can you be sure?"

"The Turks say the shot echoed," Herbert said. "The ROC is soundproofed. It would have swallowed most of the blast. In order to be wounded, a hostage probably would have been trying to run away in the dark. The gun would have fired, the hostage would have fallen, and the ROC would have driven to where he or she was. It didn't. It was right by the fence. No," Herbert said. "I know Mike Rodgers. My guess is that they were about to cross into Syria, so he decided to try and stop them."

"And failed," she stated flatly.

Herbert fired her a look. "Don't say it like he screwed up. The fact that he or someone else may have made the effort at all is a helluva thing. A helluva big thing."

"I didn't mean any disrespect," she said indignantly.

"Yeah, well, it sounded like that."

"Calm down, Bob," Martha said. "I'm sorry."

"Sure," he said. "The sideline generals are always sorry. I lost my wife and my legs to a military miscalculation. It's bad, but it's like everything else. Real easy to quarterback when you're watching the game tapes, not so easy when you're on the field."

"I never said any of this was easy," Martha said. She drummed her long, rounded nails on the desk. "Want to see if we can get back to fighting the enemy?"

"Yeah, okay." Herbert sucked down a breath. "I've gotta think this whole thing through."

"Let's start with some hypotheses," Martha said. "Suppose Mike hurt or killed one of his captors. There will be repercussions."

"Correct," Herbert said. "The question is, against who?"

"Would it be against one of the hostages?"

"Not necessarily," Herbert said. "There are three options. First of all, they won't kill Mike. Even if they don't know his military rank, they've got to know he's the leader. He's a valuable hostage and they'll want to hold onto him. Though they may torture him as an example to the others not to try to escape. That rarely works, though. You watch someone beat a fellow prisoner, it scares you into wanting to get away." Herbert laid his neck back on the barbershop-style headrest. "That leaves two other possibilities. If a terrorist was killed in the exchange, they may execute one of the hostages. They'd select the person by lot, the short straw drawing the bullet in the back of the head. Mike would be forbidden from participating, though he'd be forced to watch the murder."

"Jesus," Martha said.

"Yeah, that's a rough one," Herbert said. "But it also breeds a sense of resistance among hostages. Terrorists tend to use it only when they want to send a body back to someone, to show that they mean business. So far, no one but us has been notified that anyone's taken our team hostage."

"Then scenario number two is unlikely," Martha said hopefully.

Herbert nodded. "But the terrorists can't let an escape attempt go unpunished. So what do they do? They go to option three, which is an old favorite of Middle Eastern terrorists. They hit a target of equal importance to the hit they took. In other words, if a lieutenant was killed, they take out a lieutenant somewhere else. If a nonmilitary leader was killed, they go after a political figure."

Martha stopped drumming. "If the Kurds are behind this whole operation, they don't have many quick-strike options."

"Correct again," said Herbert. "We don't think they've infiltrated any of our bases overseas, and even if they had, they wouldn't show their hand for something like this. They'd probably hit an embassy."

"They've got the greatest numbers of followers in Turkey, Syria, Germany, and Switzerland," Martha said. She looked sharply at Herbert. "Would they know about Paul's trip?"

"Damascus has been informed," Herbert said, "but it won't be announced publicly until he lands in London." Herbert began wheeling toward the door. "If Damascus knows, the Kurds may also know. I'm going to inform Paul and also warn our embassies in Europe and the Middle East."

"I'll handle the Middle Eastern embassies," Martha said. "And Bob? I'm sorry about before. I really didn't mean any disrespect to Mike."

"I know," Herbert said. "But that isn't the same as showing him respect."

He left, leaving Martha wondering why she'd bothered.

Because they put you in charge here, that's why, she told herself. Diplomacy wasn't supposed to be pleasant, just effective.

Calling her assistant Aurora, Martha put everything but the safety of American diplomats from her mind as she had the young woman begin placing overseas calls, beginning with Ankara and Istanbul.

THIRTY

Tuesday, 2:32 a.m.,
Membij, Syria

Ibrahim did not stop the van until he was ten miles within Syria. He wasn't sure whether the Turkish border patrol had followed him. He didn't hear them, but that didn't mean they weren't back there following the van's tracks. Even if the enemy were in pursuit, however, the Turks wouldn't dare come as far as Membij. It was the first sizable town on this side of the border, and even at this hour the unauthorized intrusion of foreigners would raise the citizens to resistance.

As it was, the arrival of the long, white van woke more than a few of the townspeople. They came to their windows and doors and gawked as the magnificent vehicle passed. Ibrahim didn't stop, but drove on to the south, past the town, wanting to attract as little attention as possible. His captives and the van weren't a Syrian trophy but a Kurdish prize. He intended to keep it that way.

Only when Ibrahim stopped, only when he looked down at Mahmoud, who was squatting protectively over the body of Hasan, did Ibrahim permit himself to cry for his fallen comrade. Mahmoud had already spoken a prayer, and now Ibrahim said his part from the Koran.

Kneeling and bowing his head low, Ibrahim offered softly, " 'He sends forth guardians who watch over you and carry away your souls without fail when death overtakes you. Then are all men restored to God, their true Lord.' "

And then Ibrahim's tear-filled eyes turned back to the man who had done this monstrous deed. The American was lying on his back on the floor of the van where Mahmoud had left him. His face was swollen where he had been beaten, but there was no sadness in his eyes. The accursed eyes were looking up, indignant and unmoved.

"Those eyes will not be defiant for very long," Ibrahim vowed. He reached for his knife. "I will cut them out, followed by his heart."

Mahmoud clasped a hand on his wrist. "Don't! Allah is watching us, judging us. Vengeance is not the best way now."

Ibrahim wrested his arm free. " 'Let evil be rewarded with like evil,' Mahmoud. The Koran knows best. The man must be punished."

"This man will submit to God's judgment soon enough," Mahmoud said. "We have other uses for him."

"What uses? We have hostages enough."

"There is much more to this van than we know. We need him to tell us of it."

Ibrahim spit on the floor. "He would sooner die. And I would sooner kill him, my brother."

"Someone will die for what happened to Hasan. But we are home now, my brother. We can radio the others. Tell them to seek out and strike down one of our enemies. This man must suffer by living. By watching his companions suffer. You saw how he broke before, when I threatened to cut the woman's fingers. Think of how much worse the days ahead can be for him.''

Ibrahim continued to look back at Rodgers. The sight of him filled the Kurd with hate. ''I would cut his eyes out just the same.''

''In time,'' said Mahmoud. ''But we're tired now, and in mourning. We're not thinking as clearly as we should. Let's contact the commander and have him decide how best to avenge the deaths of Hasan and Walid. Then we'll blindfold our prisoners, finish our journey, and rest. We've earned that much.''

Ibrahim looked back at his brother, then at Rodgers. Reluctantly, he sheathed his knife.

For now.

THIRTY-ONE

Tuesday, 7:01 a.m.,
Istanbul, Turkey

Situated on the shimmering blue Bosphorus where
Europe and Asia meet, Istanbul is the only city in the
world which straddles two continents. Known as Byzan-
tium in the early days of Christianity, when the city was
built along seven great hills, and as Constantinople until
1930, Istanbul is the largest city and most prosperous
port in Turkey. Its population of eight million people
swells daily, as families migrate from rural regions looking for work. The new arrivals invariably come at night
and erect shanties on the fringes of the city. These
homes, known as *gecekondu* or "built at night," are
protected by an ancient Ottoman law which declares that
a roof raised during the darkness cannot be torn down.
Eventually the shantytowns are razed, new housing
blocks rise in their place, and new shanties are erected
beyond them. These shacks stand in dramatic contrast to
the wealthy apartments, chic restaurants, and fancy bou-
tiques of the Taksim, Harbiye, and Nisantasi districts.
The Istanbullus who live there drive BMWs, wear gold
and diamond jewelry, and weekend in their *yali*, wooden

271

mansions nestled on the shores of the Bosphorus.

American Deputy Chief of Mission Eugenie Morris had been the overnight house guest of charismatic Turkish automobile magnate Izak Bora. Because the U.S. consulate in Istanbul was secondary to the embassy in Ankara, commercial as well as political interests were dealt with here in a less formal, less bureaucratic manner. The forty-seven-year-old diplomat had gone to a dinner party at Mr. Bora's *yali* with American business representatives, and had stayed until all the other guests had left. Then she had dismissed her driver and a second car carrying two members of the Diplomatic Security Agency. These men literally rode shotgun for any official who went out on government or private business. DSA agents were authorized to use appropriate force to protect their charges. And because they were attached to an embassy or consulate, they were immune from prosecution for their actions.

When the two cars returned at seven a.m. the following morning, Eugenie was waiting inside the foyer of the *yali* with Mr. Bora. A liveried butler opened the door for them and then followed, carrying the guest's overnight bag. One DSA agent waited outside the low iron gates of the mansion as the portly businessman walked her along the short, stone path. The other agents sat behind the wheel with the motor running. Behind the mansion, the Bosphorus sparkled whitely in the early morning sunlight. The leaves of the trees and the petals of the flowers in the garden also shone brightly.

Eugenie stopped when her host did. He waved his hands at a hornet which seemed intent on nesting in his hooked nose. The DSA agent stood with his wrists crossed in front of him. His hands were inside his dark sports jacket, ready to draw his .38 if necessary. In the car, behind the nearly opaque bullet-proof windows, his companion had a sawed-off shotgun and an Uzi at his disposal.

Mr. Bora ducked in an ungainly fashion, then watched with triumph as the hornet flew off toward the water. Eugenie applauded his maneuver, and they continued toward the gate.

A motorcycle hummed in the distance. The DSA agent standing by the fence half turned to keep an eye on it as it approached. There was a boy sitting tall in the seat, wearing a black leather jacket and a white helmet. There was a canvas messenger's bag slung around his neck with the tops of envelopes sticking out. The DSA agent looked for telltale bulges under his jacket and in his pocket. The fact that the jacket was tightly zippered made it unlikely that he'd be reaching inside for a weapon. The agent kept an eye on the bag. The cyclist continued on past the cars without slowing.

As the agent looked back toward the compound, something fell from the thick canopy of leaves. Both Eugenie and Mr. Bora stopped to look at it as it clunked on the stones at their feet.

The DSA agent tried and failed to open the gate as he looked at the top of the tree. "Get back!" he shouted as the hand grenade exploded.

Before the couple could move, a gray-white cloud erupted on the walk. At once, the boom of the grenade was followed by the dull *thucks* and metal *clangs* of shrapnel as it struck tree, iron, and flesh. The DSA agent fell away from the gate, his chest shattered. Eugenie and Mr. Bora went down as though they'd been cut down by a scythe. Both writhed on the walk where they fell.

A moment after the explosion, the driver of the state car shifted it forward. He rammed through the open gate with his steel-reinforced fender, then pulled up beside the fallen Deputy Chief of Mission. Behind him came the DSA car. The driver swung it around sideways and emerged with a shotgun. Protected by the car, he stood and fired into the treetops. His shell cut a fat path through the branches, stripping them clean and causing a rain of damp green glitter.

Submachine-gun fire from the tree sent the agent ducking back down behind the car. The ski-masked gunman then turned his fire upon the Deputy Chief of Mission, stitching a bloody path across Eugenie's white blouse and jacket. She shuddered as the bullets struck, and then she stopped moving. The gunman ignored Mr. Bora, who was lying on his side and slowly clawing his way back toward the house. His butler had already run back and was crouched in the foyer, a phone pressed to his ear.

The DSA driver rose from behind the car. As he prepared to fire a second shot into the trees, he heard a *clunk* and looked down. A second hand grenade was rolling toward him. Only this one had come from behind. As he dove back into the car, he saw the motorcyclist standing down the road, behind a tree.

The grenade exploded, causing the car to leap slightly. But even before it had settled, the agent had grabbed the Uzi from the glove compartment. He needed rapid fire now, not just power. He rolled outside, lay low on the ground, and aimed at the motorcyclist. The man was already speeding toward him, coming around the cars and using them for protection.

The agent aimed to his side, shooting under the chassis. He nailed the tires and the motorcycle skidded toward the car, smacking into the other side. As he was about to crawl under the car to reach the biker, he heard a *thunk* on the roof. He looked up and saw the man who had been in the trees. He'd jumped down and was standing in a wide-legged horse stance, pointing a revolver down at him. Before he could fire, the driver of Eugenie's car pulled his own .45 and fired two shots from behind the gunman. One slug passed through each of the man's thighs and he dropped heavily to his side, slid onto the hood of the car, and tumbled onto the ground. Several hand grenades rolled from the deep pockets of his black sweater.

The DSA agent crawled under the open door of the car, stood next to the hood, and disarmed the moaning gunman. He scooped up the extra grenades and placed them all inside his car. Then he cautiously made his way to the man who had been on the motorcycle. The swarthy young man was lying on his back, a broken right arm and left leg bone jutting raggedly through his pants and jacket. Seven other hand grenades had spilled from his delivery bag.

One of them was in his left hand on his chest. He'd pulled the ring and let the safety lever pop off.

"Down!" the DSA agent yelled.

The driver hit the dirt behind his car, and the DSA agent jumped over the hood of his own vehicle. A instant later the first grenade exploded, taking the seven others with it in a series of loud, echoing bangs.

The car lurched and shook as sharpnel hit it, the tires screaming as they burst. The DSA agent was squatting behind one of them and he felt his feet go numb as a piece of metal tore through the heel. But he continued to squat, leaning against the car to present as shielded a profile as possible.

When the explosions were over, he rose painfully behind his Uzi.

The two assassins were dead, torn apart by their own hand grenades. The driver of Eugenie's car was holding the arm which was holding the gun, but at least he was standing. Mr. Bora had made it back to the house and was lying inside the foyer, his butler crouching behind him. The rest of the household staff was standing behind them, concealed in the shadows.

A moment later, sirens ripped through the sudden quiet. Four carloads of Turkish National Police arrived, their Smith & Wesson .38s drawn. Police swarmed around the grounds and through the house. The DSA agent set his Uzi on the car roof, just so the Turks would know he was one of the good guys. Then he limped over to his fallen colleague. He was dead, as was the Deputy Chief of Mission.

The driver walked over, still holding his gun and his bloody arm. He caught an officer's eye and pointed to the wound. The officer said an ambulance was coming.

Both men ducked into their cars to radio their superiors at the embassy. The reaction to the deaths was cool and economical. Emotions were always kept inside in situations like this. The press, and through them the enemy, couldn't be allowed to see how scared or upset you were.

When the men were finished, they met by the DSA agent's car.

"Thanks for tagging that guy on the roof," the agent said.

The driver nodded as he leaned carefully against the back door. "You know, Brian, there's nothing you could've done about any of this."

"Bull," he said. "We should've gone in to get her. I told Lee that, but he said the lady didn't like being crowded. Well, shit. Better crowded than what she got."

"And if we'd gone in we'd all be dead," the driver said. "They were expecting us to meet her in there. What'd they have, fifteen grenades between them? It was household security that screwed up. I'm betting that guy was in the tree since last night waiting for Ms. Morris.

The other asshole on the bike must've been following us."

Three ambulances arrived, and while several paramedics took care of the men's wounds before carrying them off, others ran inside to check on Mr. Bora. He was carried out on a gurney, moaning in Turkish how this never would have happened if he hadn't been such an internationalist.

"That's how they win," the DSA agent said as he was loaded into an ambulance beside the other American. "They scare guys like him into playing ball with just the home team."

"It doesn't take much to scare a guy like Mr. Bora," the driver replied as he looked from the agent to the IV in his arm. "Let's see what happens when they have to duke it out with the United States of America."

THIRTY-TWO

Tuesday, 5:55 a.m.,
London, England

Paul Hood and Warner Bicking were met at Heathrow Airport by an official car and a DSA vehicle with three agents. The Americans had expected to spend the two hours between flights at the airport. However, an airport official met Hood at the gate with an urgent fax from Washington. Hood walked off to a corner to read it. Bob Herbert had arranged for them to ride with an embassy official to the U.S. Embassy at 24/31 Grosvenor Square in London. It was important, the fax said, for Hood to use the secure phone there. He and Bicking were shown to a secure area of the terminal where international dignitaries were hurried safely through customs.

The ride through the very light early morning traffic was swift. Hood was surprisingly alert. He'd managed to catch three hours' sleep on the plane, and he could still taste the weak coffee he'd swigged two cups of before deplaning. Together, it would be enough to keep him going for now. If he could grab three or four more hours of sleep on the next leg of the trip, he'd be fine when they hit Damascus. Hood was also alert in part because of his curiosity and concern about the mystery fax. If it had been good news, Herbert would have indicated that.

Bicking sat beside Hood, his legs crossed and his foot rocking eagerly. Though he had worked straight through the seven-hour flight, studying the various CARfare scenarios, he was more alert than Hood.

Bicking is young enough to do that, damn him, Hood thought as he watched an early morning mist begin to dissipate. There was a time when Hood could do that too, during his banking years. Breakfast in New York or Montreal, a late dinner in Stockholm or Helsinki, then breakfast the following morning in Athens or Rome. In those days he could go for forty-eight hours without sleep. He even *disdained* sleep as a waste of time. Now, there were times when he got into bed and he didn't even want his wife to touch him. He just wanted to lay down and savor the sleep he had earned.

Shortly after the car had gotten underway, the driver handed Hood a sealed envelope from the ambassador. It contained their local itinerary and indicated that Dr. Nasr would be meeting them at the embassy at 7:00 a.m.

Ordinarily, Hood savored London. His great grandparents were born in the Kensington section, and he responded in an almost spiritual way to the city's history and character. But as the car drove by the centuries-old buildings, still charmed or haunted by the ghosts of the courageous and the nefarious, all Hood could think about was Herbert, the ROC, and why the DSA car was so tight on their tail. Usually, the diplomatic security teams traveled with the length of a car or two between them. He also wondered why there were three agents in the car instead of two. That was all their companion, an embassy assistant, should have merited.

Hood's questions were answered when he was shown

to an office in the stately old embassy building and he was able to place his call to Herbert. The intelligence chief told him about the assassination in Turkey and what appeared to be a failed attempt by hostages to escape when the ROC crossed into Syria. He also speculated that the assassination may have been a response to that. When Hood asked why, Herbert briefed him on a few facts which wouldn't be making their way into the press just yet.

"One of Mr. Bora's household domestics is a Turkish Kurd," Herbert said. "He let the assassin in."

Hood looked at his watch. "It happened less than an hour ago. How do they know for certain who did what?"

"The Turks asked a lot of questions with rubber hoses and choke holds," Herbert replied. "The servant admitted his orders came from Syria. But except for the code name Yarmuk, he didn't know from who or where. We're running checks on Yarmuk. So far the only thing that's come up besides a river is a battle from 636 A.D., when the Arabs defeated the Byzantines and recaptured Damascus."

"Sounds like someone's tipping their hand," Hood said.

"My thoughts exactly," Herbert said. "Only we can't let Damascus know because for one thing, they might not believe us. And for another, if they did believe us, they might throw in with the Kurds just to keep the peace there."

"What about the motorcyclist?" Hood asked. "Was he a Kurd or was he a freelancer?"

"Oh, he was one of them," Herbert replied "Up to his chin. He'd been living in a shack on the outskirts of Istanbul for four weeks. Our guess is that he'd been sent from the eastern Turkish combat zones as part of a team designed to hit targets in Istanbul after the initial dam strike. His fingerprints were on file in Ankara, Jerusalem, and Paris. He's got a helluva record for a twenty-three-year-old. All of it as a Kurdish freedom fighter. And the grenades he was carrying were the kind the Kurds have been using in eastern Turkey. Old style, without safety caps. East German.''

"The Kurds probably have fifth columnists ready to act in other cities as well," Hood said.

"Undoubtedly," Herbert replied. "Though the ones in Ankara have probably scattered like cockroaches by now. I've notified the President. My feeling is that the Kurds probably intend to turn Ankara, Istanbul, and Damascus into killing grounds as part of their overall plan."

"To stir up a war that'll give them a homeland as part of the peace settlement," Hood said. "That was something we talked about at the White House."

"I think that assessment is dead-on," Herbert said. "The only good news I've got is that we've managed to put an Israeli Druze soldier inside the Bekaa Valley to look for the ROC. Though we've got a ten-mile-wide stick in our eye, our Sayeret Ha'Druzim veteran should be able to pinpoint the location for us. Striker should be arriving in Israel in another five hours or so. They can link up in the Bekaa then."

"What are you hearing from Ankara and Damascus?" Hood asked.

"Ankara is scrambling for information like we are, but Damascus is starting to get tense. Major General Bar-Levi in Haifa has been in touch with his deep undercover Mista'aravim personnel in the Jewish Quarter."

"Those are the Arab impersonators?"

"Right," Herbert said. "Actually, they're trained special forces operatives who see and hear damn near every-

281

thing. They say there's been an unprecedented crackdown on Kurds. Arrests, reports of beatings, real hardball. I've got a feeling that's going to get worse very quickly." Herbert paused. "You know, Paul, about Mike. If he *did* spill blood trying to retake the ROC, I'm hoping the attack on Deputy Chief of Mission Morris was in response to that."

"Why?"

"Because it means that the Kurds wanted to pay him back without hurting him directly," Herbert said. "You know who used to do that all the time?"

"Yeah, I do," Hood said. "Cecil B. DeMille. If he wanted to put the fear of God in an actress, he yelled at her makeup person or costumer. Scared her without leaving any bruises."

"Very good, Paul." Herbert said. "I'm impressed."

"You hear things like that running L.A.," Hood said. He looked at his watch and got annoyed with himself. He'd looked at it less than a minute before. "I'm going to have to get going, Bob. I'm meeting Dr. Nasr back at the airport. And you know how I attract traffic."

"Like Job attracts afflictions."

"Right. On top of which, I feel goddamned useless."

"No more useless than I feel," Herbert said. "I put out a warning to all our embassies as soon as I figured out about the ROC border incident. Got to the DSAs in all of 'em, but Ms. Morris slipped through the net. The bastards knew our M.O. and went after the stray lamb."

"Not your fault," Hood said. "You responded quickly and correctly."

"And predictably," Herbert said, "which is something we've gotta change. When the enemy knows where your people are and how to get to them, and you don't, you've got problems."

"Twenty-twenty hindsight—"

"Yeah," said Herbert. "I know. Most businesses you learn your lessons by losing money. In our business we learn by losing lives. It stinks, but that's the way it goes."

Hood wished there were something else he could say. But Herbert was right. They discussed some of the Striker parameters, including the fact that the team would be on the ground in Israel before Congress was back for the day. And that it might well be necessary for Striker to move before the Congressional Intelligence Oversight Committee had a chance to okay their actions. Hood told Herbert he'd sign a Director's Order taking full legal responsibility for any Striker activities. He had no intention of letting Striker sit in the desert if they had a chance to rescue Rodgers and the team.

Herbert wished Hood well on his mission to Damascus and hung up. Sitting alone in the dark, quiet room, Hood took a moment to consider what he was prepared to do. To save six people they only hoped were still alive, he was committed to risking the lives of eighteen young commandos. The math didn't make sense, so why did it seem right? Because that was the job Striker was trained for, the job they wanted to do? Because national honor demanded it, as well as loyalty to one's colleagues? There were many excellent reasons, though none of them neutralized the terrible burdens of command and the execution of those commands.

Where is Mike Rodgers, the walking Bartlett's, when you need him? Hood mused as he rose from the heavy lacquered chair.

Hood's footsteps were swallowed by the Persian rug as he crossed the room and rejoined Warner Bicking, who was waiting for him in the outer office. An embassy secretary offered Hood coffee, which he accepted gratefully. Then Hood, Bicking, and a young official chatted about the developments in Turkey as they waited for Dr. Nasr.

Nasr arrived at five minutes to seven. He entered the main hallway and approached briskly. The native Egyptian stood a few inches over five feet tall, but he walked like a giant. His head and shoulders were pulled back, and his sharp salt-and-pepper goatee was pointed ahead like a lance. Nasr's eyes were also sharp behind his thick-lensed glasses, and his crisp, light gray suit was nearly the same shade as his wavy hair. He smiled generously when he saw Hood and extended his small, thick hand from half a room away. The gesture made him seem paternal now rather than self-impressed.

"My friend Paul," he said as Hood rose. Their hands locked tightly, and Nasr reached up to pat Hood on the back. "It's so good to see you again."

"You're looking very well, Doctor," Hood said. "How's your family?"

"My dear wife is fine and getting ready for a new series of recitals," he replied. "All Liszt and Chopin. To hear the *Funeral Procession of Gondolas No. 2* is to weep. Her *recitando* is glorious. And her *Revolutionary Etude*—superb. She'll be playing in Washington later in the year. You will be our special guests, of course."

"Thank you," Hood said.

"Tell me," Nasr said. "How are Mrs. Hood and your little ones?"

"Last time I checked, everyone was happy and not so little," Hood said guiltily. He turned to where Warner Bicking was standing behind him. "Dr. Nasr, I don't believe you've ever met Mr. Bicking."

"I have not," Nasr said. "However, I did read your paper on the increasing defensive democratization of Jordan. We'll talk on the plane."

"It will be my very great pleasure," Bicking replied as the men shook hands.

As they walked to the car, Nasr between the other two, Hood quickly briefed them on the latest developments. They climbed into the sedan, Bicking taking a seat up front. As the car started out, Nasr lightly stroked the tip of his beard between the thumb and index finger of his right hand.

"I believe you are correct," said Nasr. "The Kurds want and require their own nation. The question is not how far they're prepared to go to get it."

"Then what's the question?" Hood asked.

Nasr stopped playing with his beard. "The question, my friend, is whether the blowing up of the dam was their big gun, or whether they have something even bigger in store."

THIRTY-THREE

Tuesday, 11:08 a.m., the Bekaa Valley, Lebanon

The Bekaa Valley is an upland valley which runs through Lebanon and Syria. Also known as El Bika and Al Biqa, the Bekaa is situated between the Lebanon and Anti-Lebanon mountain ranges. Seventy-five miles long and ranging between five and nine miles wide, it's a continuation of Africa's Great Rift Valley, and is one of the most fertile farming regions in the Middle East. "Coele Syria," the Romans called it: "Hollow Syria." Since the beginning of recorded history, wars have been fought for the control of the wheatfields and vineyards, the apricot, mulberry, and walnut trees.

In spite of the valley's lushness, fewer and fewer farmers work its most remote and fertile areas. These regions are bordered by the tallest peaks and thickest woods. Despite the presence of the Beirut-Damascus highway, the mountains and trees create a very real sense of isolation. From the ground, many of these places can only be reached by a single road. From the air or from the peaks, these same places are hidden by ledges and year-round foliage.

For centuries, these hidden places have given sanctuary to religious sects and cabals. In the modern era, the first group known to have hidden here were the men who helped to plot the the assassination of General Bake Sidqi, the oppressive leader of Iraq, who was slain in August of 1937. In their wake, Palestinian and Lebanese guerrillas came to the valley to train and plot against the formation of Israel and then against the state itself. They came to conspire against the Iran of the Shah, against Jordan and Saudi Arabia and other governments which embraced the infidels of the West. Though archaeologists rarely come to the valley to dig for Greek and Roman ruins anymore, the soldiers have uncovered more caves than the archaeologists ever found. They sell antiquities they discover to raise money, and use the caves as headquarters from which to mount their military and propaganda campaigns. Arms and printing presses, bottled water and gas-powered generators sit side by side in the cool caverns.

With the blessings of the Syrians, the PKK has operated in the Bekaa Valley for nearly twenty years. Though the Syrians are opposed to the idea of a Kurdish homeland, the Syrian Kurds have spent much of their time and efforts helping their Turkish and Iraqi brothers survive the forces sent against them. In fighting Ankara and Baghdad, the Syrian Kurds strengthened Damascus by default. By the time Damascus realized that it might finally be a target as well, the Kurds were too well hidden, too well entrenched in the Bekaa to be easily evicted. And so the Syrian leaders took a wait-and-see position, hoping that the brunt of any assaults would be turned north or east.

Ironically, it was United Nations pressure on Ankara and Baghdad to relax attacks on the Kurds that only recently allowed them to focus on mounting a unified offensive. A series of meetings at Base Deir in the deepest caves of the northern Bekaa followed. After eight months, representatives of the Iraqi, Syrian, and Turkish Kurds devised Operation Yarmuk, a plan to use water and surgical military activity to throw the Middle East into disorder. In command of the base and its operation was a fifty-seven-year-old Southern California-educated Turkish Kurd named Kayahan Siriner. Siriner's longtime Syrian friend Walid al-Nasri was one of his most trusted lieutenants.

Mahmoud had used Hasan's radio to let Base Deir know that they were coming in. They used the same frequency used by the more prosperous farmers in the region to keep in touch with their shepherds, and referred to themselves by code names. Anyone who was eavesdropping electronically would not suspect their real identities. Mahmoud had informed Siriner that they were coming in with several oxen—enemies who were unmanned. Had he told them that he was bringing in bulls, it would have meant that the enemies were armed and the Kurds were the hostages. Still, Siriner knew that Mahmoud could have been coerced into making the broadcast. The Kurd leader would not take any chances.

The appearance of the ROC was preceded by over a minute by the sound of it crawling up the gentle slope. Stones and dead branches cracked thickly beneath its tires, the engine hummed and echoed, and finally it was visible through the trees. The ROC made its circuitous way toward the cave, avoiding the land mines and stopping when the trees became too thick. When the passenger's door opened, four armed Kurds ran out of the cave, each wearing a black *kaffiyeh* and camouflage fatigues and carrying an old NATO Model 1968 submachine gun. Before they could deploy, one man on each side, Ibrahim shut the van down and Mahmoud stepped from inside. He raised his pistol and fired three shots into the air. Had he been a hostage, he would not have been carrying a loaded gun. Shouting his thanks to God and His Prophet, Mahmoud holstered his pistol and walked toward the nearest man. As Mahmoud embraced him, and whispered to him of the loss of Hasan, the other three guards went to the open passenger's door. Ibrahim did not hug the men. His attention was on the blindfolded prisoners, and he didn't relax until they'd been led one by one into the cave. Only when they had been tied up inside did Ibrahim walk over to Mahmoud, who was standing alone beside the van. The guards had returned with earth-colored tarps. They quickly began throwing them over the van.

Ibrahim hugged his brother. "We paid dearly for this one," Ibrahim sobbed.

"I know," Mahmoud said into his ear. "But it was God's will, and Walid and Hasan are with Him now."

"I'd rather they were still with us."

"So do I," Mahmoud said. "Now come. Siriner will want to hear about the mission."

Mahmoud kept his arm around his brother's shoulder as the two of them walked toward the cave. It was the first time Ibrahim had been to the sanctuary of the unified Kurdish freedom fighters. He had always hoped that his coming would have been under different circumstances. Humbly, almost invisibly, as an observer. A witness to history. Not as a hero who felt like a blunderer.

Base Deir was named after the Syrian word for monastery. It was Kayahan Siriner's way of acknowledging the lonely, sacrificial life he and his people led here. The command headquarters was located in an underground section of the cave. A tunnel had been dug in the floor, and cinderblocks had been used to make steps. The tunnel was covered by a trapdoor which, when shut, could not be seen in the floor of the dark cave. The door had been weighted with heavy strips of rubber. If anyone walked on it, their footsteps wouldn't sound hollow. Beyond the trapdoor the cave continued to the north. There, the dozens of PKK soldiers slept on cots and ate around a picnic table. Just past their sleeping quarters the cavern forked. The eastern fork was nearly a straight continuation of the north-running tunnel. Daylight was visible from one end to the other. A dead-end dry gallery, this fork contained the militia's arms and gas-powered generators. The group's field commander, Kenan Arkin, had a station here and in the command headquarters. The tall, gaunt Turk remained in constant contact with the PKK's many factions. The natural cave had ended there, but the soldiers had broken through to a small gorge beyond. Cliffs overhung the gorge on either side, hiding it from the air and making it ideal for training. In the western fork of the cavern were ten small, dark pits. They were lined with wire mesh and covered with circular iron grates. The grates were held in place by iron bars which lay across the center. Each end of the bar was fitted into an iron upright. The eight-foot-deep holes were used as jail cells and held two people each. Sanitation consisted of larger mesh openings on the bottom.

Electric lights had been strung along the roof of the narrow passageway, and Siriner's bunker was protected by an iron door. The door had been made from the hatch and armored plate of a Syrian tank destroyed by the Israelis. It was cool ten feet below the surface of the cave, and within the bunker itself a pair of large fans stirred the musty air. The room was nearly square and roughly the size of a large freight elevator. The walls were naked, and the low ceiling had been covered with a clear plastic tarp. The plastic was pulled tight and bolted in the corner to protect the room in the event of artillery shelling. There were rugs on the dirt floor, a small metal desk, and folding chairs with embroidered cushions. Beside the desk was a shredder. Behind it there was a radio with a headset and stool.

Commander Kayahan Siriner was standing behind his desk when Mahmoud and Ibrahim entered. He was dressed in a drab-green uniform and a white *kaffiyeh* with a red band. He wore a .38 in a holster on his belt. Siriner was of medium height and build, with dark skin and pale eyes. He had a very thin pencil moustache on his upper lip and a ring on his left index finger. The gold band sported two large silver daggers crossed beneath a star. Like Walid, Commander Siriner bore a scar. This one was a deep, jagged scar which ran from the bridge of his nose to the middle of his right cheek. He had obtained the wound as the leader of the Kurdish food parties in Turkey. It was his job to lead small bands against non-Kurdish villages to obtain food. If the villagers didn't give it willingly, the Kurds took it by force. Turkish soldiers were killed out of hand whether they resisted or not.

Commander Siriner did not leave the cave unless it was necessary. Even at night, there was the fear that he might be assassinated by Turkish or Iraqi snipers positioned in the peaks around the base.

It was both a relief and an honor that Siriner was standing. An honor because the commander was showing the men respect for what they'd accomplished. A relief because he attached no blame to them for the loss of Walid and Hasan.

"I thank Allah for your safe return and for the success of your mission," said Siriner, his deep, resonant voice filling the room. "You have come with a trophy, I understand."

291

"Yes, Commander," said Mahmoud. "A vehicle of some kind which the Americans use to spy."

Siriner nodded. "And you are certain that in bringing it here, you yourselves were not spied upon?"

"We used it to blind the satellite, Commander," said Ibrahim. "There is no doubt that they cannot see us."

Siriner smiled. "As their flyovers of the region suggest." He looked at Mahmoud. "Tell me what happened to Walid's ring and to Hasan."

Mahmoud took a step forward. Hasan had radioed the base about Walid's death, and the guard had just informed Siriner of Hasan's death. Now Mahmoud gave their commander the details. The commander remained standing as he spoke. When Mahmoud was finished, Siriner sat down.

"The American is here, in captivity?"

"He is," said Mahmoud.

"He knows how to work the equipment you've captured?"

"He does," said Mahmoud. "Several of the captives appear to know something of its operation."

Siriner thought for a long moment, and then called for a soldier who served as his master-at-arms. The brawny young man hurried into the office and saluted. Military formalities were strictly observed among the twenty-five soldiers who were permanently stationed at the base.

The commander returned the salute. "Sadik," he said, "I want the American leader tortured where the others can hear."

Ibrahim wasn't convinced that the American would break. However, he didn't offer his unsolicited opinion. The only answers Siriner accepted from his people were "Yes, sir," and "I'm sorry, sir."

"Yes, sir," the master-at-arms said.

292

"Mahmoud," said Siriner, "I've heard that there are women prisoners as well?"

"Yes, sir."

Siriner looked back at Sadik. "Select a woman to watch the torture. She will go second. I want this vehicle working for the next part of our operation. It may help us guide the infiltrators."

"Yes, sir."

Siriner dismissed his master-at-arms. He turned back to Mahmoud and Ibrahim. "Mahmoud. I see you wear Walid's ring."

"Yes, sir. He gave it to me before he—left us."

"He was my oldest friend," said Siriner. "He will not die unavenged."

Siriner walked from behind the desk. His expression was a strange mix of grief and pride. Ibrahim had seen the expression before in the faces of people who had lost friends or brothers, husbands or sons to a cause that was equally close to them.

"As we expected, Syrian Army troops have begun moving to the north. Mahmoud. You're acquainted with the role that Walid was to have played in the second phase of our operation?"

"I am, sir," Mahmoud replied. "Upon his return he was going to relieve Field Commander Kenan. Kenan is going to lead the raid upon the Syrian Army outpost in Quteife."

Siriner stood in front of Mahmoud and peered into his eyes. "The raid is vital to our plan. However, Allah is merciful. He has returned you to us. I see in that a sign, Mahmoud al-Rashid. A sign that you and not Kenan are to take Walid's part."

Mahmoud's tired eyelids raised slightly. "Commander?"

"I would like you to lead the Base Deir group to

293

Quteife and then Damascus. Our man there awaits the signal. Set out with the others and I will give it.''

Mahmoud was still surprised. He bowed his head. ''Of course, Commander. I am honored.''

Siriner embraced Mahmoud. He patted his back. ''I know you must be tired. But it is important that I be represented in Damascus by a hero of our cause. Go and see Kenan. He will give you your instructions. You can sleep while you wait for the Syrians.''

''Again, sir, I am honored.''

Siriner moved over to Ibrahim. ''I am equally proud of you, Ibrahim.''

''Thank you, sir.''

''Because of your role in the day's victory, I have special need of you,'' Siriner said. ''I wish for you to remain with me.''

Ibrahim's mouth fell at the edges. ''Sir! I would like to be allowed to go with my brother!''

''That is understandable,'' Siriner said as he hugged Ibrahim. ''But I need a man who has dealt with the Americans and their van. This is not a question of courage but of efficiency.''

''But commander. It was Hasan who spoke—''

''You will remain here,'' Siriner said firmly. He stepped back. ''You drove the van from Turkey. You may have seen something that will prove helpful. And you have experience with machines. That in itself is more than many of my soldiers have.''

''I understand, sir,'' Ibrahim said. He looked narrowly at his brother without moving his head. He fought hard to conceal his disappointment.

''I will have a talk with the Americans,'' Siriner told him. ''For now I want you to rest. You've earned it.''

''Thank you, sir,'' Ibrahim replied.

Siriner looked at Mahmoud. ''Good luck,'' he said,

and then went back to his desk. The men had been dismissed.

Ibrahim and Mahmoud turned smartly, then returned to the tunnel. They stood there facing one another.

"I'm sorry," Ibrahim said. "I belong at your side."

"You will be even closer," Mahmoud said. He touched his chest. "You'll be in here. Make me proud of you, little brother."

"I will," Ibrahim said. "And you be careful."

The men hugged for a long minute, after which Mahmoud walked deeper into the cave to meet with the field commander.

Ibrahim walked toward the makeshift barracks, where he sat on an empty cot and removed his boots. He lay back slowly, stretching toes and leg muscles which were happy to be free of their burden. He shut his eyes. Ibrahim was aware of the soldiers trooping past him, toward the cells.

Siriner would have a "talk" with the Americans. He would torture them. They would break. And then their leader would have nothing to do but help the other Kurds run the computers and drive the van.

It wasn't glorious. He wasn't even convinced that it was useful. But he was tired and perhaps he wasn't thinking clearly.

In any case, he hoped the American *did* break. He wanted him to capitulate, to cry out. What right did any foreigner have to interfere with the fight for Kurdish freedom? And to take the life of a fighter who had displayed compassion as well as heroism was unforgivable.

He listened as the grates creaked open, as two prisoners were pulled out, as the others shouted from their cells. Their cries were like a campfire on a cold night, warming him. Then his mind drifted to the events of the past day and visions of the storm they would unleash before this day was through. He thought of his brother and the pride he felt for what he was about to do. And the warmth settled over him like a blanket.

THIRTY-FOUR

Tuesday, 11:43 a.m., the Bekaa Valley, Lebanon

When she was a young girl, Sondra DeVonne used to help her father Carl as he worked in the kitchen of their South Norwalk, Connecticut, apartment. By day, he managed a fast-food hamburger restaurant on the heavily traveled Post Road. By night, he mixed ingredients by the bowlful looking for a custard recipe which would taste better than anything else on the market. After two years, he came up with a soft ice cream which his wife sold on weekends at Little League games and carnivals. A year after that, he quit his job and opened an ice cream stand on Route 7 in Wilton, Connecticut. Two years later, he opened his second stand. A few months before Sondra joined the United States Air Force, he opened his twelfth Carl's Custard and was hailed as Connecticut African-American Businessperson of the Year.

Watching her father at night, the ten-year-old girl learned patience. She also learned dedication and silence. He worked like an artist, intense and unhappy with distractions. Sondra always remembered the time he'd gotten so much powdered sugar on his face that he looked like a mime. She'd sat on the small, butcher-block kitchen table for nearly sixty full minutes, turning the crank of the ice cream maker and swallowing back a laugh. Had she succumbed, her father would have been deeply offended. For that long, long hour she kept her eyes shut and sang silently to herself—any top-forty tune that would keep her mind off her dad.

This wasn't her small kitchen in South Norwalk. The man in front of her wasn't her father. But Sondra had flashes of being small and helpless again as her hands were pulled behind her and cuffed to a waist-high iron ring. In front of her, on the other side of the cavern, Mike Rodgers's shirt was cut off with a hunting knife. His arms were pulled up and handcuffed to a ring which hung from the stone ceiling of the cavern. His toes barely touched the floor. As an afterthought, the man with the knife cut a bloody pencil-mustache over Rodgers's upper lip.

In the glow of the single overhead bulb, Sondra could see Rodgers's face. He was looking in her direction though not at her. As the blood ran in streams into his mouth and down his chin he was focusing on something—a memory? A poem? A dream? At the same time he was obviously marshaling his energy for whatever lay ahead.

After a few minutes, two men arrived. The first one held a small butane blowtorch. The blue-white flame was already lit and hissing. The other man walked with an imperious strut. His hands were clasped behind him and his pale eyes shifted from Rodgers to Sondra and back again. There was no remorse in those eyes, nor lust. There was just a sense of cold purpose.

The man stopped with his back to Sondra. "I am the commander," he said in a rich, thinly accented voice. "Your name does not matter to me. If you die, it does not matter to me. All that matters is that you tell us everything you know about the operation of your vehicle. If you do not do so quickly, you will die where you are and we will move on to the young lady. She will suffer a different punishment"—he looked at her again—"a far more humiliating one." He looked back at Rodgers. "When we are finished with her we will move to another member of your group. If you elect to cooperate, you will be returned to your cell. Though you murdered one of our people, you did what any good soldier would have done. I have no interest in punishing you and you will be released as soon at it can be arranged. Do you wish to tell us what you know?"

Rodgers said nothing. The man waited only a few seconds.

"I understand you withstood a cigarette lighter in the desert," the man said. "Very good. So that you will know what to expect this time, we will burn the flesh from your arms and chest. Then we will remove your trousers and continue down to the bottom of your legs. You will scream until your throat bleeds. Are you sure you don't wish to speak?"

Rodgers said nothing. The commander sighed, then nodded to the man with the blowtorch. He stepped forward, turned it toward Rodgers's left armpit, and brought it forward slowly.

The general's jaw went rigid, his eyes widened, and his feet jumped from the floor. Within seconds, the smell of burned hair and flesh made the thick air fouler. Sondra had to breathe through her mouth to keep from retching.

The commander turned toward Sondra. He covered her mouth to force her to breathe through her nose. He was simultaneously pushing up on her jaw so that she couldn't bite him.

"It has been my experience," said the man, "that one member of a party always tells us what we wish to know. If you talk now you can save them all. Including this man. Your people were oppressed. They are oppressed still." He removed his hand. "Can you not sympathize with our plight?"

Sondra knew she wasn't supposed to speak to her captors. But he'd given her an opening and she had to try reason with him. "Your plight, yes. Not this."

"Then put a stop to it," the commander said. "You're not an archaeologist. You're a soldier." He nodded toward Rodgers. "This man has been trained. I can see that. I feel it." He stepped closer to Sondra. "I don't enjoy doing this. Talk to me. Help me and you help him. You help my people. You will *save* lives."

Sondra said nothing.

"I understand," the commander said. "But I won't let dozens of women and children die every day because others do not approve of our culture, our language, our form of Islam. Hundreds of my people are in Syrian prisons where they're tortured by the Mukhabarat, the secret police. Surely you can understand my desire to help them."

"I understand," she replied, "and I sympathize. But the cruelty of others doesn't justify your own."

"This is not cruelty," he said. "I would like to stop. I have been tortured. I have suffered for hours with electric wires threaded inside my body so there would be no bruises. A dead animal hung around your neck in a steaming-hot cell leaves no marks. Nor do the flies it attracts or the vomiting it induces. My wife was raped to death by an entire Turkish unit. I found her body in the hills. She was violated in ways which I hope are worse than you can imagine." He looked back at Rodgers. "Other nations have made halfhearted efforts to help us. The United States special envoy tried to bring together the feuding Talabani and Barzani factions in Iraq. He had no budget, no arms for them. He failed. The United States Air Force tried to prevent the Iraqis from bombing Kurds in the north. They succeeded, so the Iraqis simply poisoned their water supply. The Air Force could not prevent that. It is time for us to help ourselves. For one of us to lead all of us.''

This is why we aren't supposed to talk to them, Sondra thought. The man was making perfect sense. And the Kurd was right about one thing. Someone would probably talk. But it couldn't be her. She had taken an oath of allegiance, and part of that oath was to obey orders. Rodgers did not want her to speak. She couldn't. She wouldn't. Living with that shame would be worse than dying.

She continued to look at the commander as Rodgers's handcuffs rattled against the iron ring. After a minute, the torch was moved to Rodgers other side. He jumped this time, and so did she, as the flame was applied. The jaw was no longer so strong. His mouth fell open, his eyes rolled, and his entire body trembled. The tips of his feet kicked up and down vigorously. But he didn't scream.

The commander watched with a relaxed, confident expression as the flame was moved to Rodgers's back. Rodgers arched and shook and shut his eyes. His mouth went wide and there was a gurgling deep in his throat. As soon as Rodgers became aware of the sound he forced his mouth shut.

Though tears formed in her eyes and fear dried her mouth, Sondra refused to say a word.

Suddenly, the commander said something in Arabic. The torturer stepped away from Rodgers and shut off the burner. The commander turned to Sondra.

"I will give you a few minutes to think without having to see your friend suffer." He smiled at her. "Your friend . . . or your superior officer? No matter. Think about the people you can help. Yours as well as mine. I ask you to think about the German people during the Second World War. Were the patriots those who did the bidding of Hitler, or those who did what was right?"

The commander waited a moment. When Sondra said nothing, he walked away. The torturer left with him.

As their footsteps died, Sondra looked at Rodgers. He raised his head slowly.

"Say . . . nothing," he ordered.

"I know," she said.

"We are not Nazi Germany," Rodgers gasped. "These people . . . are terrorists. They'll use the ROC to kill. Do you . . . understand?"

"I do," she said.

Rodgers's head dropped again. Through tears, Sondra looked at the dark, raw burns under his upraised arms. Rodgers was right. These men had killed thousands of people by blowing up the dam. They'd kill even more if they were able to use the ROC to watch troop movements or listen to communications. The Kurds were oppressed, but would they be any better under a warlord like this? He was a man who had suffered, yet he was willing to burn hostages alive and keep them in pits to get his way. If he were Syrian, would he tolerate the Turkish Kurds? If he were Turkish, would he tolerate the Iraqi Kurds?

She didn't know. But if Mike Rodgers was prepared to die to say no to him, she was too.

And then she heard the footsteps returning. Sondra saw Mike Rodgers breathe deeply to bring up his courage and resolve and felt her own legs weaken. She pulled on the handcuffs and wished she could at least die fighting their captors.

The torturer reappeared without the commander. After lighting the burner, he moved toward Mike Rodgers again. And impassively, as though he were igniting a barbecue pit, he turned the flame on Rodgers's breastbone.

And after his head rolled back and he fought for a long moment to keep his teeth clenched, the general finally screamed.

THIRTY-FIVE

Tuesday, 3:55 a.m.,
Washington, D.C.

Bob Herbert started working on his fourth pot of coffee while Matt Stoll finished off his seventh can of Tab. Except for bathroom breaks, neither man had left Stoll's office, even when the night shift came on duty.

The two were examining photographs of the Bekaa Valley which had been taken from 1975 through the present by satellites, infiltrators, and Israeli Sayeret Tzanhanim paratroopers. They knew the ROC was somewhere in the valley, but they didn't know where. An F-16 flyover from Incirlik hadn't provided any clues. The thick tree cover and camouflage undermined visual reconnaissance. And except for the low-watt satellite-killer program, the ROC had apparently been shut down or else hidden in a cave or beneath a ledge. Otherwise, an infrared search might have turned up something. The Air Force plane had also been sending out millimeter-wave microwave signals in an effort to raise the ROC's active-passive radar reflector. Had Rodgers been able to get to the dashboard and switch the ROC transponder on, it would have replied with a coded message. So far, there had been only silence.

With nothing else to go on, the two men looked at photographs. Herbert wasn't certain what he was looking for. But as the pictures filled Stoll's twenty-inch monitor, the intelligence chief tried to think like the enemy.

According to Turkish intelligence, which was confirmed by Israeli intelligence, there were nearly fifteen thousand PKK soldiers. Some ten thousand of those were living in the hills of eastern Turkey and northern Iraq. The rest were divided into pockets of ten to twenty fighters. Some of these people were assigned to specific areas of Damascus or Ankara or other major cities. Others were in charge of training, communications, or maintaining supply lines through the Bekaa Valley. Now, the Bekaa was also apparently the home of a new, aggressive Syrian Kurdish unit. One which was working closely with, or perhaps even joined with, Kurds from Turkey and Iraq.

"So the terrorists capture the ROC," Herbert said.

Stoll let his forehead plunk down on his arms, which were crossed on his desk. "Not again, Bob."

"Yes, again," Herbert said.

"There's got to be something else we can try," Stoll moaned. "The farmers out in the fields contact their hands using cellular phones. Let's listen to them. Maybe they saw something."

"My team is doing that. They've picked up zip." Herbert took a mouthful of warm coffee from a chipped, stained mug which had once sat on the desk of OSS chief Wild Bill Donovan. "So the terrorists capture the ROC. They report back to their headquarters. Since we can't find the terrorists, we have to find the command base. The question is, what do we look for?"

"A command center has to have access to water, and

it'll have generators for electricity and a radar dish for communications and probably heavy tree cover for security," Stoll droned. "We've been through this a zillion times. Water can be trucked in or flown in, generator exhaust can be vented by hose to someplace and dispersed so an airplane heat-sensor won't see it, and a radar dish is easy to hide."

"If you decide to chopper in drinking water, you'd have to make a helluva lot of flights," Herbert said. "Enough so that you stand a good chance of being spotted."

"Even at night?"

"No," Herbert said. "At night you stand a good chance of crashing into some of those peaks, especially if you're using a twenty- or thirty-year-old bird. As for trucks, water can only be trucked in if there's a road nearby. So if the base isn't near a stream—and there aren't very many in this region—it has to be near the highway or at least a dirt road."

"Granted," Stoll said. "But that still leaves us about thirty or forty possible locations for a terrorist base. We keep examining these same pictures and magnifying different sections of them and computer-analyzing the geology of the region, and we still come up with squat."

"That's because we're obviously not looking for the right thing," Herbert said. "Every human activity leaves traces." He was annoyed with himself. Even without some of the high-tech satellite and surveillance tools he'd normally have at his disposal, he should be able to find those traces. Wild Bill Donovan did. Lives and national security depended upon it. "Okay," he said. "We know the command center is somewhere in there. What other trappings would it have?"

Stoll raised his head. "Barbed wire hidden in vines, which we haven't seen. Mines, which we can't see anyway. Cigarette butts, which we could see if we had a satellite that we could turn on the area. We've been through all that.''

"Then let's look at it a different way," Herbert said.

"Fine. I'm game. Fire away.''

"You're a terrorist leader," Herbert said. "What's the most important asset you need in a base?''

"Air. Food. Sanitation. Those are the biggies, I'd guess.''

"There's one more," Herbert said. "A bigger one. The top quality you'd look for is safety. A combination of defensibility and impregnability.''

"From what?'' Stoll asked. "From spies or attack? From the ground or the air? For assault or retreat?''

"Safety from aerial bombardment," Herbert said. "Flyovers and artillery fire are the easiest, safest ways to take an enemy base out.''

"Okay," said Stoll. "So where does that lead us?''

"We know that most of these caves are made of— what did Phil call them in his analysis?''

"I don't remember," Stoll said. "Porous rock, sponge rock, something that sounded like you could quarry it with a good karate chop.''

"Right," said Herbert. "The thing is, that kind of rock only protects the terrorists from surveillance by air, not from attack. What does?''

"Protect from attack? You said that terrorists in the Bekaa move around a lot," Stoll said, "like mobile Scuds. Their best defense is keeping anyone from knowing where they are.''

"True," Herbert said. "But this situation may be different.''

"Why?''

"Logistics," Herbert replied. "If these terrorists are coordinating movements in at least two nations, they have to remain centralized to distribute arms, bomb parts, maps, information.''

"With computers and cellular phones, most of those capacities are pretty transportable," Stoll pointed out.

"Maybe you can move the trappings around," Herbert agreed. "But these guys would also have been training for a series of very specific missions." He took another swallow of coffee. Grounds washed along his gums as he reached the bottom of the cup. He absently spat them back in. "Let's think this through. When any strike force trains for a specific mission, they build replicas of the sites."

"These guys wouldn't have built a mockup of the Ataturk Dam, Bob."

"No," Herbert agreed. "They wouldn't have had to, though."

"Why not?"

"That part was pure muscle. The terrorists didn't have to work out technique and finesse because they just flew in, dropped their bombs, and got out. But if that was simply a precipitating incident, which it almost certainly was, they'll probably have follow-up assaults planned. Assaults which will have to be rehearsed."

"Why?" Stoll asked. "What makes you think those assaults won't be pure muscle as well?"

Herbert drained his mug. There were more grounds in his mouth. He spat them back into the cup before pushing it to the side of the desk. "Because historically, Matt, the first strike in a war or war-phase is big, surprising, and strategic—like Pearl Harbor or the Normandy invasion. It destabilizes and shocks. After that, the enemy is ready, so you have to shift into a more methodical mode. Careful, surgical assaults."

"Like capturing important towns or killing opposition leaders."

"Exactly," Herbert said. "That requires site-specific training. When combined with the other factors about communications, supplies, and commands, that means a more or less permanent base."

"Maybe," Stoll said. He pointed at the monitor. "But not in caves like the soft-rock jobbers we have here. You can't reinforce those. Lookit. They're not very big to begin with, only about seven feet tall and five wide. If you throw in a lot of iron and wood supports, you'd barely have room to move around."

Herbert chewed on a lingering coffee ground for a moment, then absently pulled it out. He looked at it. "Wait a minute," he said. "Dirt."

"What?" Stoll asked.

Herbert held out the dark ground and then flicked it away. "Dirt. You can't build much inside one of those caves but you *can* excavate. The North Vietnamese did it all the time."

"You mean an underground bunker," Stoll said.

Herbert nodded. "It's the perfect solution. It also narrows down our search. You can't blast a tunnel in caves like these or the roof'll come down on you—"

"But you can dig one," Stoll interrupted excitedly. "You've *got* to dig one."

"Right!" Herbert said. "And to dig, you need dirt."

"From the descriptions on those pictures," Stoll said, "most of these caves were cut into the rock shelf by subterranean streams."

"Most," Herbert said as the data came up, "but maybe not all."

Stoll stored the Bekaa photographs and brought up the geological records which Katzen had organized before leaving for the region. Stoll and Herbert both leaned toward the monitor as Stoll ran a word-search for "soil." He came up with thirty-seven references to soil composition. The men began reading through each reference, looking for anything which suggested a recent excavation. They crawled through a mass of figures, percentages, and geological terms until something caught Herbert's eye.

"Hold it," Herbert said. He slapped his hand on the mouse and scrolled back a page. "Look at this, Matt. A Syrian agronomical study from January of this year." Herbert began scanning down. "The team reported an anomaly in the Thicket of Oaks region of the Chouf Mountains."

Stoll glanced at notes he'd been taking. "Ohmigod. That's the area where the ROC is."

Herbert continued reading. "It says here the A horizon or topsoil there is characterized by unusually high biotic activity as well as an abundance of organic matter which is typically found in the B horizon substratum. Movement typically occurs from A horizon to B, carrying fine-grained clay downward. This concentration of substratum material suggests one of two things. First, that an effort was made to enrich the soil with more active earth, and then abandoned. Or second, it could be the result of a nearby archaeological dig. The level of biological activity suggests the deposits were placed here within the last four to six weeks."

Stoll looked at Herbert. "An archaeological dig," he said, "or else a bit of bunker-building."

"Absolutely possible," Herbert replied. "And the time frame fits. They found the soil four months ago. That means the digging was done five to six months ago. That would have been enough time to put together a base and train a team."

Stoll began typing commands.

"What are you doing?" Herbert asked.

"The NRO routinely photographs the Bekaa," Stoll

said. "I'm bringing up the recon files of the region for the last six months. If there was any digging, they may not have done it all by hand."

"Yeah, those caves might just be wide and tall enough," Herbert said. "And if they brought in a backhoe or bulldozer, even at night—"

"There would be deep tire tracks," Stoll said. "If not from the equipment itself, then from the truck or flatbed which carted it in."

When the files were loaded, Stoll accessed a graphics program. He pulled up a file and typed *Tire Treads*. When the menu appeared, he typed, *No Automobiles*. The computer went to work. Just over a minute later, it offered a selection of three photographs. Stoll asked to see them. All three showed distinct tread-bar marks in front of the same cave. It was the cave from which the soil had been excavated.

"Where's the cave?" Herbert asked.

Stoll asked the computer to find the cave in its geography file. It took just a few seconds for the coordinates to come up.

Stoll held up his can of Tab. "Here's dirt in your eye," he said as he triumphantly slugged the rest of it down.

Herbert nodded quickly as he snapped up his cellular phone, put in a call to Major General Bar-Levi in Haifa, and told him about the map which was about to be modemed over.

THIRTY-SIX

Tuesday, 1:00 p.m., Damascus, Syria

Over the past twenty years, Paul Hood had been to dozens of crowded airports in many cities. Tokyo had been big but orderly, packed with businesspeople and tourists on a scale he'd never imagined. Vera Cruz, Mexico, had been small, jammed, outdated, and humid beyond imagining. The locals were too hot to fan themselves as they waited for departures and arrivals to be written on the blackboard.

But Hood had never seen anything like the sight which greeted him as he entered he terminal of the Damascus International Airport. Every foot of the terminal had people in it. Most of them were well dressed and well behaved. They held baggage on their heads because there wasn't room to keep it at their sides. Armed police stood at the gates of arriving aircraft to keep people out if necessary and help passengers get off planes and into the terminals. After the passengers deplaned, the doors of the gate were shut and they were on their own.

"Are all of these people coming or going?" Hood asked Nasr. He had to shout to be heard over persons who were crying for family members or yelling instructions to friends or assistants.

"They all appear to be going!" Nasr shouted back. "But I've never seen it like this! Something must have happened—"

Hood elbowed sideways through the mob at the gate entrance. He thought he felt a hand reach for his inside jacket pocket. He stepped back against Nasr. His passport or wallet would both be valuable if people were trying to leave Syria. His arms tight at his sides, he got on his tiptoes. A white piece of cardboard with his name written in black was bobbing above heads about five yards away.

"Come on!" Hood shouted at Nasr and Bicking.

The men literally pushed their way to the black-suited young man who was holding the sign.

"I'm Paul Hood," he said to the man. He wormed his arm behind him. "This is Dr. Nasr and Mr. Bicking."

"Good afternoon, sir. I'm DSA Agent Davies and this is Agent Fernette," the young man yelled, cocking his head toward a woman standing to his right. "Stay close behind us. We'll take you through customs."

The two agents turned and walked side by side. Hood and the others fell in, following closely as their escorts alternately shouldered, elbowed, and pushed their way through the crowd. Hood wasn't surprised they didn't have a Syrian security contingent. He wasn't high-ranking enough to merit one. Still, he was surprised that there were so few police here. He was dying to know what had happened, but he didn't want to distract their escorts.

It took nearly ten minutes to push through the main terminal. The baggage area was relatively empty. While they waited for their luggage, Hood asked the agents what had happened.

"There's been a confrontation at the border, Mr. Hood," Agent Fernette replied. She had short brown hair and a clipped voice, and looked about twenty-two.

"How bad?" Hood asked.

"Very bad. Syrian troops surrounded Turkish troops which had crossed the border looking for the terrorists. The Syrians were fired upon and fired back. Three Turkish soldiers were killed before the rest of the border patrol managed to work their way back into Turkey."

"There's been worse," Nasr said. "This panic is for that?"

Fernette turned her dark eyes on him. "No, sir," she said. "For what followed. The Syrian commander pursued the Turks into Turkey and wiped them out. Executed the soldiers who surrendered."

"My God!" Bicking cried.

"What is his background?" Nasr asked.

"He's a Kurd," Fernette replied.

"What happened after that?" asked Hood.

"The commander was dismissed and the Syrians withdrew," the woman said. "But not before the Turks moved some of their regular army troops and tanks to the border. That's where it sits the last we heard."

"So everyone's trying to get out," Hood said.

"Actually, not everyone," said Fernette. "Most of the people here are Jordanians, Saudis, and Egyptians. Their governments are sending in planes to evacuate them. They're afraid that their countries may come in on the side of the Turks and they don't want to be here if they do."

After gathering their bags, Hood and the others were led to a small room on the far northern side of the terminal. There, they were hurried through customs and taken to a waiting car. As he climbed into the stretch limousine with its American driver, Hood smiled to himself. The President had to fly him to the other side of the world to get him into one of these.

The ride north into the city was quick and easy. Traffic on the highway was light, and the driver came in around the city to Shafik al-Mouaed Street. He turned west and drove toward Mansour Street. The U.S. Embassy was located at Number Two. Both roads were deserted.

Nasr shook his head as they headed down the narrow road. "I've been coming here all my life." There was a catch in his voice. "I've never seen the city so deserted. Damascus and Aleppo are the oldest continuously inhabited cities in the world. To see it like this is terrible."

"I understand it's even worse in the north, Dr. Nasr," said Agent Fernette.

"Has everyone left the city or are they indoors?" Hood asked.

"A little of both," said Fernette. "The President has ordered the streets to be kept clear in case the army or his own palace guards have to move around."

"I don't understand," Hood said. "All the activity is taking place one hundred and fifty miles north of here. The Turks wouldn't be reckless enough to attack the capital."

"They're not," said Bicking. "I'll bet the Syrians are afraid of their own people. Kurds, like the officer who led the attack at the border."

"Exactly," said Fernette. "There's a five p.m. curfew. If you're out after that, you're going to prison."

"Which is someplace you don't want to be in Damascus," Agent Davies said. "People are treated rather harshly there."

315

Upon reaching the embassy, Hood was greeted by Ambassador L. Peter Haveles. Hood had met the career foreign service man once, at a reception at the White House. Haveles was balding and wore thick glasses. He stood a few inches under six feet, though his rounded shoulders made him seem even shorter. He'd gotten this post, it was said, because he was a friend of the Vice President. At the time, Haveles's predecessor had remarked that a man would only give this post to his worst enemy.

"Welcome, Paul," Haveles said from halfway down the corridor.

"Good afternoon, Mr. Ambassador," Hood replied.

"Was the flight pleasant?" Haveles asked.

"I listened to oldies on audio channel four and slept," Hood said. "That, Mr. Ambassador, is pretty much my definition of pleasant."

"Sounds good to me," Haveles said unconvincingly. Even as the ambassador shook hands with Hood, his eyes had already moved to Nasr. "It's an honor to have you here, Dr. Nasr," Haveles said.

"It's an honor to be here," Nasr replied, "though I wish the circumstances were not so grim."

Haveles shook Bicking's hand, but his eyes returned quickly to Nasr. "They are grimmer than you know," Haveles said. "Come. We'll talk in my office. Would any of you care for something to drink?"

The men shook their heads, after which Haveles turned and extended a hand down the corridor. The men began walking slowly, Haveles between Hood and Nasr and Bicking beside Hood. Their footsteps echoed down the corridor as the ambassador talked about the ancient vases on display. They were top-lit, and looked quite dramatic in front of nineteenth-century murals showing events from the reign of the Umayyad Caliphs during the first century A.D.

Haveles's round office was at the far end of the embassy. It was small but ornate, with marble columns on all sides and a central drum ceiling reminiscent of the cathedral at Bosra. Light came through a large skylight in the top of the dome. There were no other windows. The guests sat in thickly padded brown armchairs. Haveles shut the door, then sat behind his massive desk. He seemed dwarfed by it.

"We have our sources in the Presidential Palace," he said with a smile, "and we suspect they have sources here. It's best to speak in private."

"Of course," said Hood.

Haveles folded his hands in front of him. "The palace believes that there is a death squad in Damascus. The best information they have is that the team will strike late this afternoon."

"Do we have corroboration?" Hood asked.

"I was hoping you could help us there," Haveles said. "At least, that your people could. You see, I've been invited to visit the palace this afternoon." He looked at the antique ivory clock on his desk. "In ninety minutes, in fact. I've been invited to remain there for the rest of the day, talking things over with the President. Our chat is to be followed by dinner—"

"This is the same President who once kept our Secretary of State waiting for two days before granting him an audience," Dr. Nasr interrupted.

"And kept the French President sitting in an antechamber for four hours," Bicking added. "The President still doesn't get it."

"Get what?" Hood asked.

"The lessons of his ancestors," said Bicking. "Through most of the nineteenth century, they used to invite enemies to their tents and seduce them with kind-ness. Pillows and perfume won more wars out here than swords and bloodshed.''

"Yet those victories still left the Arabs in disunity," Dr. Nasr said. "The President does not seek to seduce *us* with kindness. He abuses foreigners in an effort to seduce his Arab brothers."

"Actually," said Haveles, "I think you're both miss-ing the point. If I may finish, the President has also in-vited the Russian and Japanese ambassadors to this meeting. I suspect that we will be with him until the crisis has passed."

"Of course," Hood nodded. "If anything happens to him, it'll happen to you and the others."

"Assuming the President even shows up," Bicking pointed out. "He may not even be in Damascus."

"That's possible," Haveles admitted.

"If an attack occurs," said Dr. Nasr, "even with the President away from the palace, Washington, Moscow, and Tokyo will find it impossible to support whoever staged the attack, whether it's the Kurds or Turks."

"Exactly," said Haveles.

"They could even be Syrian soldiers masquerading as Kurds," said Bicking. "They conveniently kill everyone except the President. He survives and becomes a hero to millions of Arabs who dislike the Kurds."

"That's also possible," Haveles said. He looked at Hood. "Which is why, Paul, any intelligence you can come up with will be helpful."

"I'll get in touch with Op-Center right away," Hood said. "In the meantime, what about *my* meeting with the President?"

Haveles looked at Hood. "It's all been arranged, Paul."

Hood didn't like the smooth way the ambassador had said that. "When?" he asked.

Haveles grinned for the first time. "You've been invited to join me at the palace."

THIRTY-SEVEN

Tuesday, 1:33 p.m., the Bekaa Valley, Lebanon

Phil Katzen crouched on the mesh floor of the dark pit. He had quickly grown accustomed to the stale smell in his little prison. To the stench of the sweat and waste of those who had been incarcerated before him. Any lingering discomfort he felt passed when Rodgers's torture began. Then it was the smell of burning flesh which filled his nostrils and lungs.

Katzen had wept when Rodgers finally screamed, and he was weeping still. Beside him, Lowell Coffey sat with his chin against his knees and his arms around his legs. Coffey was staring through Katzen.

"Where are you, Lowell?" Katzen asked.

Coffey looked up. "Back in law school," he said. "Arguing in moot court on behalf of a laid-off factory worker who had taken his boss hostage. I do believe I'd try that one differently now."

Katzen nodded. School didn't prepare a person for much. In graduate school, he had taken specialized courses as part of his training for extended visits to other countries. One of these was a semester-long series of lectures by visiting professor Dr. Bryan Lindsay Murray of the Rehabilitation and Research Center for Victims of War in Copenhagen. At that time, just over a decade before, nearly half a million victims of torture alone were living in the United States. They were refugees from Laos and South Africa, from the Philippines and Chile. Many of those victims spoke to the students. These people had had the soles of their feet beaten mercilessly and had lost their sense of balance. They had had eardrums punctured and teeth pulled, tacks thrust under fingernails and toenails and cattle prods pushed down their throats. One woman had been enclosed in the bell, a glass dome which remained over her until her sweat had reached her knees. The course was supposed to help students understand torture and help them to deal with it if they were ever captured. What a big, fat intellectual sham that'd been.

Yet Katzen knew that one thing he'd learned in the lectures was true. If they survived this, the deepest scars would not be physical. They would be emotional. And the longer the captivity went on, the less treatable their post-traumatic stress disorder would be. Fits of panic or chronic despondency could be brought on by re-experiencing anything they had suffered today. The smell of dirt or the sound of a scream. Darkness or a shove. Perspiration trickling down their armpits. Anything.

Katzen looked at Coffey. In his fetal position and distant expression he saw himself and the others. The time they'd spent tied up in the ROC had enabled them to pass through the first phase of the long emotional road hostages faced—denial. Now they were moving through the numbing weight of acceptance. That phase would last for days. It would be followed by flashbacks to happier times—which was where Coffey was already headed—and finally by self-motivation.

If they lived that long.

Katzen shut his eyes, but the tears kept coming. Rodgers was snarling now, like a caged dog. His chains rattled as he tugged against them. Private DeVonne was talking to him calmly, trying to help him focus.

"I'm with you," she was saying to him in a soft but very tremulous voice. "We're all with you. . . ."

"All of us!" Private Pupshaw shouted from the pit to the left of Katzen's. "We're all with you."

Rodgers's snarls soon became screams. They were short, angry, and agonized. Katzen could no longer hear Sondra's voice over his cries. Pupshaw was swearing now, and Katzen heard Mary Rose vomiting in the pit to the right. It had to be her. Seden was still unconscious.

There wasn't a civil, dignified human sound to be heard. In a few short minutes, the terrorists had transformed a band of educated, intelligent people into desperate or frightened animals. If he weren't one of them, he might have admired the simple skill with which it was done.

He couldn't just sit there. Turning, Katzen dug his fingers into the mesh and pulled himself to his feet.

Coffey looked up at him. "Phil?"

"Yeah, Lowell?"

"Help me up. I want to stretch too but my goddamn legs are like rubber."

"Sure," Katzen said. He put his hands under Coffey's armpits and helped him to his feet. As soon as Coffey was standing, Katzen released him tentatively. "You okay?"

"I think so," said Coffey. "Thanks. How about you?"

Katzen turned to the mesh side of the pit. "Shitty. Lowell, I have to tell you something. I didn't get up to stretch."

"What do you mean?"

Katzen looked up at the grate. Rodgers was shrieking now in clipped bursts. He was fighting the pain and losing. "Oh, for God's sake *stop*!" Katzen moaned. He looked down and shook his head from side to side. "Jesus God, make them stop."

Coffey wiped his forehead with his handkerchief. "It's kind of ironic," he said. "We're in God's backyard and He isn't even listening. Or if He is," Coffey added apologetically, "He's got a plan that's not making much sense to me."

"To me either," Katzen said. "Unless we're wrong and these other people are right. Maybe God *is* on their side."

"On the side of monsters like this?" Coffey said. "I don't think so." He took two halting steps across the pit and stopped beside his coworker. "Phil? Why did you get up? What were you going to do?"

"I was thinking of stopping this."

"How?" Coffey asked.

Katzen put his head against the mesh wall of the pit. "I've dedicated my life to saving endangered animals and ecosystems." He lowered his voice to a loud whisper. "I've done that through action, by risking my life."

"You've got a streak of steel in you," Coffey said. "I've told you that many times. Me? I don't know how well I'm going to stand up under—under that." He looked up quickly and then back. He leaned closer conspiratorially. "If you're thinking of trying to get the hell out of here, I'm with you. I'd rather die fighting than cringing. I think I'm strong enough for that."

Katzen looked at Coffey in the faint light falling from above. "I'm not thinking about starting a war, Lowell. I'm thinking about ending one."

"How?"

323

Katzen shut his eyes as Rodgers howled louder than before. It was only a short cry because the general bit it off. But it tore through Katzen's bowels. After a moment, he leaned closer to Coffey.

"When the ROC is turned on, when it's completely on, the locator will go on too," Katzen said. "Op-Center is sure to locate it. When they do, the military will blow the hell out of it and the terrorists with it. It won't be used against anyone."

"Wait a minute. Are you suggesting we *help* these people?"

"They're burning Mike alive," Katzen said, "and God knows what they'll do to Sondra. By taking some kind of initiative we have a chance of living. Or at least dying with dignity."

"Helping these bastards isn't dying with dignity," Coffey said. "It's treason."

"To what?" Katzen asked. "A rule book?"

"To your country," Coffey said. "Phil, don't do this."

Katzen turned his back on Coffey. He reached up and wrapped his fingers around the grate. Coffey came around to face him.

"I've fallen way short of my potential in a lot of ways," Coffey said. "I can't now. I couldn't live with myself."

"This isn't your doing," Katzen said. He pulled himself up so that his mouth was pressed against the cool iron. "Stop it out there!" he yelled. "Come get me! I'll tell you what you want to know!"

Silence fell in pieces. First Pupshaw, then the hiss of the burner, then Rodgers and DeVonne. It was broken as footsteps crunched on the dirt. Someone shined a flashlight down at Katzen. The environmentalist dropped back down to the bottom of the pit.

"You've decided to speak?" asked a deep voice.

"Yes," Katzen said. "I have."

Coffey turned away from him and sat back down.

"What is your group?" the deep voice demanded.

"Most of these people are environmental researchers," Katzen said. He shielded his eyes against the bright light. "They were here studying the effects of dambuilding on the ecosystem of the Euphrates. The man you're torturing is a mechanic, not anyone's 'superior officer.' I'm the one you want."

"Why? Who are you?"

"I'm a United States intelligence officer. The Turkish colonel and I came along to use some of the equipment in the van to spy on Ankara and Damascus."

The man above was silent for a moment. "The man beside you. What is his specialty?"

"He's an attorney," Katzen said. "He came along to make sure we didn't break any international laws."

"The woman we have out here," said the man. "You say that she's a scientist?"

"Yes," said Katzen. He prayed to God that the man believed him.

"What is her specialty?"

"Culture media," Sondra said. "Gelatinous substances containing nutrients in which microorganisms or tissues are cultivated for scientific research. My father holds patents in those areas. I worked with him."

The man switched off the flashlight. He said something in Arabic. A moment later the grate was lifted. Katzen was pulled out at gunpoint. He stood before a dark-skinned man with a scar across his face. To the left, from the corner of his eye, he could see Rodgers hanging from his wrists. Sondra was tied to the wall on the right.

"I don't believe that you are environmentalists," said

325

the commander. "But it's no matter if you're willing to show us how to work the equipment."

"I am," said Katzen.

"Tell him nothing!" Rodgers gasped.

Katzen looked directly at Rodgers. His legs weakened as he saw the general's mouth, which was still contorted with pain. As he looked at the dark, glistening areas of burned flesh.

Rodgers spat blood. *"Stand where you are! We don't take orders from foreign leaders!"*

The dark-skinned man spun. He swung a fist hard at Rodgers's jaw. The blow connected audibly and snapped the general's head back. "You take orders from a foreign leader when you're the guest of that leader," the man said. He turned back to Katzen. His mood was less amiable now. "Whether you live depends only on whether I like what you show me."

Katzen looked at Rodgers. "I'm sorry," he said. "Your lives are more precious to me than that principle."

"Coward!" Rodgers roared.

Sondra pulled at her chains. "Traitor!" she hissed.

"Don't listen to them," the commander said to Katzen. "You've rescued them all, including yourself. That is loyalty, not treason."

"I don't need your stamp of approval," Katzen said.

"What you need is a firing squad," DeVonne said. "I played your game because I thought you had a plan." She looked at the commander. "He doesn't know anything about the van. And I'm not a scientist."

The commander walked up to her. "You're so young and so talkative," he said. "After we see what the gentleman does know, my soldiers and I will come back and speak with you."

"No!" Katzen said. "If any of my friends are hurt, the deal is off!"

The commander turned suddenly. In the same motion, he slapped Katzen with a vicious backhand. "You do not say *no* to me." He regained his composure at once. "You will show me how to operate the vehicle. You will do so without any further delay!" He slid his left hand behind Sondra's head and held it tightly. Then he seized her jaw with his right hand and squeezed her mouth into an O. "Or will you work better hearing her cry as we use a knife to pry out her teeth one by one?"

Katzen held up his hands. "Don't do that," he said as the tears began to flow again. "Please don't. I'll cooperate."

The commander released Sondra as a man pushed Katzen from behind. He stumbled ahead. As he walked past the Striker, her eyes felt more lethal than the gun at his back. Dark slits, they cursed him to his soul.

Katzen winced as he walked through the cave into the sunlight. Tears continued to flow. He wasn't a coward. He'd protected harp seals by shielding them with his own body. He simply couldn't let his friends suffer and die. Even though, after this day, he knew that these people who had been so important to him for over a year would be his friends no more.

THIRTY-EIGHT

Tuesday, 12:43 p.m.,
Tel Nef, Israel

Shortly after noon, the C-141B landed in the fields outside the military base. Colonel August and his seventeen soldiers were already dressed in their desert takedown fatigues and camouflage face scarves and flop hats. They were met by Israeli troops who helped set up tents which would conceal their cargo.

Captain Shlomo Har-Zion met Colonel August with a typed message. It was written in matte gray-ivory ink on a white background which reflected the sun. August had experience with these kinds of field documents. The medium guaranteed that the information would not be read by reconnaissance personnel who might be positioned in the surrounding hills. The details were not spoken of. Electronic surveillance and lip-readers were used extensively by Arab infiltrators.

August tempered the reflectivity by moving the paper around as he read the message. It indicated that Op-Center had found a likely location for the ROC and the hostages. An Israeli operative had been dispatched to the area and would reconnoiter ahead of Striker. He would contact Captain Har-Zion directly. If the intelligence proved correct, then Striker was to move in at once. August thanked the superior officer and told him he'd join him shortly.

August helped as the Strikers and the Israelis off-loaded and prepped the vehicles. The six motorcycles were rolled out under a camouflage canopy and stored in the tents. The four Fast Attack Vehicles came next. Engine connections were checked to make sure that nothing had shaken loose during the flight. The .50-caliber machine guns and 40mm grenade launchers were also carefully examined to make sure that the mechanisms and sights were clean and aligned. The C-141B left quickly after refueling, lest it be spotted from the hills or by Russian satellites. The information would be relayed quickly to hostile capitals in the region and used against Washington at a later date.

While the team examined their equipment, August and Sergeant Grey went to a secure, windowless building at the base. With Israeli advisors the two Strikers reviewed maps of the Bekaa region, and talked with the Israelis about possible dangers in the area. These included land mines as well as farmers who might be part of an early warning network. The Israelis promised to listen for shortwave transmissions and jam any they might pick up.

Then there was nothing to do beyond what August did worst.

He had to wait.

THIRTY-NINE

Tuesday, 1:45 p.m.,
the Bekaa Valley, Lebanon

Falah had walked most of the night and slept briefly before the sun came up. The sun was his alarm clock and it had never failed him. And the darkness was his cloak. That had never failed him either.

Fortunately, Falah had never required a great deal of sleep. As a young boy growing up in Tel Aviv, he'd always felt that he was missing something if he slept. As a teenager, he'd known he was missing something when the sun went down. And as an adult, he had too much to do in the dark.

One day it will catch up to you, he thought as he made his way

Equally fortunate, after being driven to the Lebanese border, Falah had been able to make most of the first leg of his journey before resting. It was a seventeen-mile trek to the mouth of the Bekaa, and he found an olive grove well away from the dirt road. Covered with fallen leaves for warmth and concealment, Falah had the Lebanese Mountains to the west and the foothills of the Anti-Lebanon range to the east. He made certain there was a break in the peaks where he rested. That would allow the rising sun to kiss him before it cleared the mountains and woke others in the valley.

Virtually every village in Syria and Lebanon has its own preferred style of dress and cloth. Wraps, robes, trousers, and skirts with distinctive patterns, colors, tassels, and accoutrements are more varied here than anywhere in the world. Some of the styles are based on tradition, others are based on function. Among the Kurds who had moved into the southern Bekaa, the only traditional article of clothing is the headdress. Before leaving Tel Nef, Falah had gone into the "closet," a well-stocked wardrobe room, to dress for his role as an itinerant farm worker. He'd selected a ratty black robe, black sandals, and a characteristic black, stiff, tasseled headdress. He'd also chosen heavy, black-framed sunglasses. Under the torn, loose-fitting robe, Falah wore a tight rubber belt strapped to his waist. Two waterproof pouches were attached to it. One, on his right hip, contained a fake Turkish passport with a Kurdish name and an address in a Kurdish village. He was Aram Tunas from Semdinli. The pouch also contained a small two-way radio.

The other pouch contained a .44 Magnum revolver which had been taken from a Kurdish prisoner. A coded map printed with food dye on dried lambskin was tucked into the pouch with the radio. If he were captured, Falah would eat the map. Falah was also given a password which would identify him to any of the American rescuers. It was a line Moses had uttered in *The Ten Commandments*: "I will dwell in this land." Bob Herbert had felt the password for the ROC's Middle East mission should be something holy, but not something from the Koran or the Bible that someone might say inadvertently. When challenged after giving the line, Falah was to say that his name was the Sheik of Midian. If he were captured and the password tortured or drugged from him, chances were good an imposter would not think to ask for the second part. The impersonator would then give himself away by answering with the name on Falah's passport.

The Israeli also carried a large cowskin water pouch over his left shoulder. Over his right shoulder was a duffel bag with a change of clothes, food, and an EAR—an Echelon Audio Receiver. The unit consisted of a small, collapsible parabolic dish, an audio receiver/transmitter, and a compact computer. The computer contained a digital recorder as well as a filter program which was based on principles of the Doppler effect. It allowed the user to choose sounds by echelon or layer. At the press of a button on the keypad, the audio which reached the listener first was eliminated to make way for that which came next. If the acoustics were good enough, the EAR could hear around corners. The audio data could also be stored for later transmission.

Less than five minutes after he woke, Falah was bent over a stream, sucking water through a minty reedstalk. As he savored the cool water his radio vibrated. With the throw of a switch, the radio could be made to beep. However, when he was working undercover or stalking an enemy who could be concealed anywhere, that was not something Falah desired.

Crouching, Falah chewed on the reed as he answered. He never sat down in the open. In an emergency, it took that much longer to get to his feet.

"Ana rahgil achmel muzehri," he answered in Arabic. "I am a farmer."

"Inta mineyn?" asked the caller. "Where are you from?"

Falah recognized the voice of Master Sergeant Vilnai,

332

just as Vilnai had surely recognized his. For the sake of security, the two men went through the exchange of codes just the same.

"Ana min Beirut," Falah replied. " I am from Beirut." If he'd been injured he would have answered, *"Ana min Hermil."* If he'd been captured he would have said, *"Ana min Tyre."*

As soon as Falah had said that he was from Beirut, Master Sergeant Vilnai said, "Eight, six, six, ten, zero, seventeen."

Falah repeated the numbers. Then he pulled the map from the pouch. There was a drawing of the valley with a grid sketched on top of it. The first two numbers of the sequence directed Falah to a grid box. The second pair of numbers indicated an exact spot within the grid. The final two numbers referred to a vertical location. They meant that the cave he sought was situated point-seventeen miles up the side of a cliff, probably along a road.

"I see it," Falah said. Not only did he see it, but it was the perfect place for a military base. There was a gorge behind it which could easily accommodate helicopters and training facilities.

"Go there," Vilnai replied. "Reconnoiter and signal if affirmative. Then wait."

"Understood," the young man said. *"Sahl."*

"Sahl," Vilnai answered.

Sahl meant "easy" and it was Falah's individual sign-off. He had selected the word because it was ironic. Due to Falah's high success rate, his superiors had always chided him that he'd picked the word because it was true. As a result, they kept threatening to give him more dangerous assignments. Falah dared them to find more dangerous assignments.

After replacing the radio, Falah took a moment to

study the map. He groaned. The cave he sought was nearly fourteen miles away. Given the incline of the hills and the rough terrain here, and allowing for a short rest, it would take him approximately five and a half hours to reach his destination. He also knew that as soon as he entered the valley his radio would be ineffective. In order to communicate with Tel Nef he'd have to use the EAR's uplink.

Spitting out the reed he'd been chewing, Falah pulled up a few more for later. He tucked them in the deep cuff of his robe and started out. As he walked, he ate the map for breakfast.

Falah was out of condition. When he reached the cave shortly after noon, his legs felt like sacks of sand and his once-tough feet were bleeding at the heels. There were large calluses on the balls of both feet and his skin was greasy with sweat. But the discomfort was forgotten as he arrived at his destination. Through the dense copse he saw rows of trees and a cave. Between the woods and the cave, on a sloping dirt road, was the white van. It was covered with a camouflage tarpaulin and was guarded by two men with semiautomatics. A quarter mile away was a road-cut which led behind the mountain.

Falah crouched behind a boulder some four hundred yards away. After unshouldering his duffel bag he dug a small hole. He carefully collected the dirt in a neat pile beside it. Then he looked around for a large clump of grass. Finding one, he removed it and set it on top of the mound of dirt.

Now that he was ready, Falah turned his attention to the cave. It was located roughly sixty feet up the side of a cliff, just above the tree line. It was accessible only by a sloping dirt road. He took a quick look at the ground-level terrain. He knew there would be land mines within and around the copse, though he would have no problem finding out just where those mines were. When Striker arrived, he would simply surrender to the Kurds. They would come and get him. Wherever they walked would be mine-free.

As he watched, Falah saw a man emerge from the cave. The man was dressed in a khaki shirt and shorts. He was followed by a man who held a gun to his back. Someone else was there, although he didn't come out of the cave. He stood in the shadows of the entrance, watching. The prisoner was led into the van.

Falah opened the duffel bag and withdrew the three parts of the EAR. The computer was slightly larger than an audio cassette. He set it on the rock. Then he withdrew the satellite dish. Folded, it was approximately the size and shape of a small umbrella. At the press of a button, the black dish fanned open like a small umbrella as well. He pressed a second button, and a tripod shot out from the other side. He stood it on the rock as well and plugged it into the computer. Then Falah fished out the earphones. He plugged them in, turned on the unit, and guessed the distance to the cave. After fine-tuning it to within a foot of the entranceway, he listened.

He heard Turkish being spoken in the front of the cave. He told the computer to go to the next layer. Someone was speaking Syrian.

". . . is the timetable?" a man asked.

"I don't know," said another man. "Soon. He has promised the leader to Ibrahim and the women to his lieutenants."

"Not to us?" another man grumbled.

There's evidence of the Turkish and Syrian Kurdish collaboration, Falah thought. He wasn't surprised, merely gratified. When he was finished, he'd transmit the recording to Tel Nef. From there it would be relayed to Washington. The American President would probably inform Damascus and Ankara. The conversation was also evidence of other captives being held at this location. Before contacting Tel Nef, Falah decided to probe deeper into the cave.

He went ten feet at a time. He heard more Syrian, more Turkish, and finally English. It was muffled and difficult to understand. Knowing how the Kurds worked in the hills, the speakers were probably being kept in prison pits. He picked up only a few words.

"Treason . . . sooner die."

". . . will."

He listened for a few moments longer, then programmed new coordinates into the computer. Sitting sturdily on its tripod, the dish began to turn. The Israeli communications satellite Falah needed to contact was in a geostationary orbit directly over Lebanon and eastern Syria.

As Falah waited for the dish to establish the uplink, one of the Arabs ran from the van. He hurried over to the dark figure standing in the cave entrance.

Falah pushed the "cancel" button on the uplink. Then he physically picked up the dish, turned it back toward the cave entrance, and entered the distance into the computer. He listened.

". . . turned on a computer inside," the man from the van was saying. "It told us there was a satellite dish out there."

The man in the shadows calmly asked where it was.

"To the southwest," the other man replied, "within five hundred yards—"

That was all Falah needed to hear. He knew there was no way he'd be able to outrun the Kurds and no way he could take them on. He had only one option. With an oath, he pressed a button to send a silent signal back to the base. Then he folded the satellite dish and tripod and swept the entire unit into the hole he'd dug. He reached into the pouch around his waist and dropped the radio in as well. Finally, he pulled off his sandals and dropped them in. He filled the hole with the dirt, then placed the sod on top of it. Unless someone was looking, they wouldn't see that the soil beneath the grass had been disturbed. Grabbing his duffel bag, Falah crept toward the northeast. As he headed toward the cave he saw over a dozen Kurdish soldiers run from the cave. They fanned out in columns of three, carefully avoiding the mines.

Falah crawled mostly on grass and stone so he would leave as few tracks as possible. When he was roughly one hundred yards from where he'd buried the dish and radio, the young Israeli lay the duffel bag on the ground beside him. He put on the other sandals so his footprints wouldn't match those around the rock. Then he scooped up his bag and ran off, reviewing again the details of the life of Aram Tunas from Semdinli.

FORTY

Tuesday, 2:03 p.m.,
Quteife, Syria

The Syrian Army base at Quteife was little more than a few wooden buildings and rows of several dozen tents. There were two twenty-foot-tall watchtowers, one facing northeast and the other southwest. The perimeter was surrounded by a barbed-wire fence strung from ten-foot-high posts. The base had been erected eleven months before, after Kurdish troops from the Bekaa Valley had constantly attacked Quteife for supplies. Since then, the Kurds had stayed away from the large village.

The twenty-nine-year-old communications officer, Captain Hamid Moutamin, knew that the raids and then the peace were intentional. When Commander Siriner had decided where he was going to set up his own base in the Bekaa, he'd wanted the Syrians to establish a small military presence close by. Access to the Syrian military was an important part of Siriner's plans. Once the base at Quteife had been built, Captain Moutamin had used his ten years of exemplary military service to get himself transferred there. That too was important to Commander Siriner's plan. When both goals had been accomplished, Commander Siriner had gone ahead and established his own base in the Bekaa.

Moutamin was not a Kurd. That was his strength. His father had been a traveling dentist who serviced many Kurdish villages. Hamid was his only son, and after school or on vacations he often accompanied his father on short journeys. Late one night, when Hamid was fourteen, their car was stopped by Syrian Army troops outside of Raqqa, in the north. The four soldiers took the gold his father used for fillings, as well as his tobacco pouch and wedding band, and sent them on their way. Hamid wanted to resist, but his father wouldn't let him. A short while later the elder Moutamin pulled the car over. There, on the deserted road, under a bright moon, he suffered a heart attack and died. Hamid returned to the home of one of his father's Kurdish patients, an elderly printer named Jalal. He telephoned his mother and an uncle came to get him. The funeral was one of sadness and rage.

Hamid was forced to leave school and go to work to support his mother and sister. He worked at a radio factory on an assembly line where he had time to think. He nursed his hatred of the Syrian military. He continued to visit Jalal, who, after two years, cautiously introduced him to other young people who had had run-ins with the Syrian military. All of them were Kurds. As they exchanged stories of robbery, murder, and torture, Hamid came to believe that it was not just the army but the entire government that was foul. They had to be stopped. One of Jalal's friends introduced him to a young visiting Turk, Kayahan Siriner. He was determined to create a new nation in the region where Kurds and other oppressed people would live in freedom and peace. Hamid asked how he could help. Siriner told him that the best way to weaken any entity was from within. He asked

Hamid to become what he detested. He was to join the Syrian military. Because of his experience on the assembly line, Hamid was assigned to the communications corps.

For just over ten years Hamid served his Syrian commanders with seeming loyalty and enthusiasm. Yet during that time he secretly communicated troop movements to Syrian Kurds. His information would help them to avoid confrontations, steal supplies, or ambush patrols.

Now he had been given his most important assignment. He was to inform the base commander that by chance he'd intercepted a message from a Turkish Kurd. The man was alone, on the eastern side of the Anti-Lebanon range. He was a quarter mile west of the village of Zebdani, just within the Syrian border. Apparently, said Hamid, the man had been based there for quite some time and was reporting on Syrian troop movements. Hamid provided the base commander with the infiltrator's exact location.

The commander smiled. No doubt he saw a promotion for himself to a more prestigious base if he could find and break a Kurd spying for the Turks. He dispatched a unit, twelve men in three jeeps, with orders to surround and take the prisoner.

Hamid smiled inside. Then he took a break and made sure the motorcycle he intended to take was fueled up.

FORTY-ONE

Tuesday, 2:18 p.m., Zebdani, Syria

Mahmoud was gently nudged awake after having slept for over two hours. He opened his eyes and squinted into a dark face framed by a cerulean sky.

"The soldiers are near," said Majeed Ghaderi. "They are coming, just as Hamid said they would."

"Allah be praised," Mahmoud replied. He took a moment to stretch on his grassy bed, then climbed to his feet. He wasn't rested, but the nap had been enough to take the edge off his exhaustion. Retrieving his canteen, he turned his face up and spilled water on his eyes. He rubbed it in vigorously and looked at Majeed.

Majeed was Walid's cousin and had been his devoted aide. He had been instructed not to wake Mahmoud until it was almost time to attack. The teenager had been quiet during the ride through the mountain pass, and his eyes were still red from crying for his dead cousin. But now that the moment was at hand, there was strength in those eyes and eagerness in his voice. Mahmoud was proud of the boy.

"Let's go," said Mahmoud.

Mahmoud followed Majeed. They crossed ruts cut by melting snows and backed carefully around large boulders to the PKK position.

There were fourteen Kurdish sharpshooters deployed in the low peaks. A radio had been placed beside a rock below. A campfire had been built and snuffed. The Syrians would spot those. Then, following regulations, they would leave their Jeeps and crouch behind them. They would set up a covering fire, and one soldier would walk ahead to examine the site. And they would find themselves in a lethal cross fire from fifty feet above. The Syrians covering the peaks would be taken out first. By the time the others shifted their fire to above, they would be dead. As many of the Syrians as possible would be shot in the head. Hopefully, their uniforms would not be stained with blood. The Kurds needed ten of them.

Mahmoud joined the others. They watched as the Jeeps moved in. They raised their weapons. They waited until the soldiers had climbed out and taken their positions. When Mahmoud nodded, they raised their rifles. When he nodded a second time, they fired.

Many of the Kurds on the cliff hunted wild turkey, boar, and rabbit to feed their families. And because bullets were scarce, all of them were accustomed to hitting their targets on the first shot. The first volley involved ten Kurds firing at the soldiers closest to the foothills, including the soldier who had gone to examine the campsite. Nine of the Syrians died instantly. A tenth was wearing a helmet. He took two shots to the throat before he went down. The remaining Syrians looked up. They froze for the moment it took them to spot the gunmen. In that moment the remaining Kurds opened fire. The rest of the Syrians went down.

Pistol drawn, Mahmoud led a contingent of Kurds down the hill. All of the Syrians were dead. Mahmoud waved to the others in the foothills, and they hurried down. Ten bodies were stripped, and then all of the dead were piled into one Jeep. Dressed as Syrian Army regulars, ten of the Kurds climbed into the remaining two Jeeps. As the rest of the team covered up all signs of the encounter, Mahmoud brushed dirt from his colonel's stripes and led his team through the arid plain.

Because Turkey and Syria had both closed their borders to tourists and travelers, the M1 highway was relatively deserted. Upon reaching the modern road, Mahmoud and his party of nine turned south for the twenty-five-minute ride to Damascus . . . and the end of over eighty years of suffering.

FORTY-TWO

Tuesday, 1:23 p.m.,
Tel Nef, Israel

Master Sergeant Vilnai and Colonel Brett August had been in the underground cinderblock radio room for over an hour. For most of that time, they'd looked at detailed aerial maps of the Bekaa on a computer screen. Beside them, raven-haired radio operator Gila Harareet listened for word from Falah.

A few minutes earlier the men had been joined by the base commander Major Maton Yarkoni. The veteran of the 1973 Yom Kippur War had a bull-like face and a short but powerful build. August had heard he possessed a disposition to match. When the major arrived, he began discussing the Israeli high alert that had gone into effect when Syria sent its forces northward. If fighting erupted, Israel stood ready to aid the Turks.

"Neither Israel nor NATO can afford to see Turkey torn apart by warring factions," said Major Yarkoni. "NATO needs a palisade against Islamic fundamentalists. And like Syria, Israel needs the water. It's worth fighting a war now to keep the nation intact."

"What will NATO do?" asked Vilnai.

"I've just spoken with General Kevin Burke in Brussels," said Yarkoni. "In addition to the increased U.S. military presence in the Mediterranean, NATO troops in Italy have been upgraded to Defcon Two."

"Smart move," August said. "Before joining Striker I served with NATO in Italy. Five'll get you ten that the move to Defcon Two is to force Greece to choose sides now. Either they're in this with their NATO allies to help defend Turkey, or they're going to side with Syria. And if Greece joins Syria, they're going to catch the Italian boot up their butts."

Master Sergeant Vilnai shook his head slowly. "The Middle East goes to war and NATO fractures. The world has become much too micro-aligned."

"Tell me about it," August said bitterly.

"One nation sides with another nation, but factions within those nations sympathize with factions in other nations. Soon there'll be no nations."

"Only special interests," Colonel August said. "A world of quarreling warlords and grabby kings."

As they were speaking, a red light flashed on the console. The radio operator listened intently as a digital tape recorder captured the message. The message consisted of two short beeps and a long one followed by another long one. The message repeated once and then shut down.

The radio operator removed her headphones. She turned to the computer which sat beside the radio.

"Well?" Yarkoni asked impatiently.

"It was a coded emergency signal," the youthful radio operator replied. She replayed the taped message directly into the computer. A decoded message appeared on the computer monitor. She read, "Captives here. Enemy party approaching. Attempting to evade."

"Then they spotted him," Yarkoni said.

The only change in August's demeanor was a tightening along the jaw. He was not a man who showed much emotion. "Is there any way we'll be able to contact him again?"

"Very unlikely," Vilnai said. "If Falah's in danger he'll have abandoned the radio. He can't afford to be captured with it. If he believes he can outrun the pursuers, he'll try to do so. If he's successful, perhaps he'll return to the radio. If he feels that he's cornered, he'll adopt his Kurdish identity and present himself to the PKK as a potential new recruit."

August looked down at the radio operator. He didn't see her. He saw the faces of the ROC crew. Every minute he'd waited had been haunted by one thought: that when they finally reached the ROC they'd arrive too late. It had made sense to wait for intelligence. But now that intelligence would not be forthcoming, there was no longer any reason to delay.

"Major," August said, "I'd like to move my team in."

Yarkoni looked into the taller man's eyes.

"We know where the cave is," August pressed, "and Master Sergeant Vilnai and I have studied the approaches from the west and east." The Colonel moved closer to the Major. His voice was tense, just above a whisper. "Major Yarkoni, it isn't only the ROC crew that's at stake. If this cave is the PKK headquarters, we can take them out. We can shut down this war before it gets started."

Yarkoni lowered his chin. The darkness of those bull's eyes deepened. "All right. Go. And may God look after you."

"Thank you," August said. The men exchanged salutes, after which the American officer hurried up the stairs.

Master Sergeant Vilnai downloaded the maps onto diskettes. Then he followed August to the staging area just inside the barbed-wire barricade.

Ten minutes later the four Fast Attack Vehicles were tearing through the hilly, heavily treed countryside at eighty miles an hour. They were moving in wedge formation, with two FAVs in the front and two behind them at a forty-five degree angle. They bracketed the six desert bikes which were arranged in two rows of three. The FAVs' .50-caliber machine guns and 40mm grenade launchers were armed, the gunners ready to repulse any attack with warning fire first, deadly force second.

Colonel August was in the lead FAV. From Tel Nef, the ride to the border was twenty minutes. Israeli gunships would take off in five minutes from Tel Nef and cross the border to create a distraction. Once the Lebanese and Syrian troops were drawn away, Colonel August and his Strikers would be able to drive in. From there, it would be less than a half-hour drive to their destination.

The satellite-generated maps had been loaded from the diskettes onto the code-operated computers onboard the FAVs. As Striker sped through the lush terrain of northern Israel, the greenest section of the country, August and Sergeant Grey reviewed attack options and exit strategies. If there was any indication that the hostages were still alive, the Strikers would use any means necessary to get them out. If it were possible to save the ROC, they would. If not, they would destroy it. If they had to kill to achieve any of these goals, August was prepared to do so.

When he and Grey were finished, the colonel slipped on his sunglasses. He hadn't been on a combat mission since Vietnam, but he was ready. He gazed through the thick trees at the smoky mountains in the distance. Somewhere among them Mike Rodgers was a prisoner. Striker would rescue Mike or, if his oldest friend were dead, August was prepared to do one thing more.

He would personally take out the sonofabitch who had killed him.

FORTY-THREE

Tuesday, 2:24 p.m., Damascus, Syria

Paul Hood's impression of Damascus was that it was a gold mine.

Perhaps he'd been Mayor of tourist-friendly Los Angeles for too long, or perhaps he'd become jaded. The mosques and minarets, the courtyards and fountains were all spectacular, with their ornate facades and meticulous mosaics. The gray and white walls surrounding the Old City in the southeast section of Damascus were at once battered and majestic. They had helped protect the city from attacks by the Crusaders in the thirteenth century, and they still bore signs of those ancient sieges. Long stretches of wall had been destroyed or breached, and had been left in historic disrepair.

But as he looked at the sights from the darkened window of the embassy limousine, Hood wasn't thinking about the past. His one thought was that if this region of the world were at peace, if this nation were not a sponsor of terrorism, if all people could come and go freely here, Damascus would be a more popular tourist destination. With that money Syria could find ways to desalinize water from the Mediterranean and irrigate the desert. They could build more schools or create jobs or even invest in poorer Arab nations.

But that isn't the way of things, Hood told himself. Though this was an international city, it was still a city whose leaders had an agenda. And that agenda was to carry Syrian rule into neighboring nations.

The meeting with the President was going to take place in the heart of the Old City, at the palace built by Governor Assad Pasha al-Azem in 1749. This was partly for security reasons. It was easier to guard the President behind the still-formidable walls of the Old City. It was also to remind the citizens that whether they agreed or disagreed with their President, a Syrian ruled in a palace which had been built by an Ottoman governor. Foreigners were their enemies.

For the most part, that was propaganda and paranoia. Ironically, today it was true. As Bob Herbert had put it when Hood called Op-Center from the embassy, "It's like the broken watch that's right twice a day. Today, the Turkish and Syrian Kurds are the enemy."

Herbert told Hood that operatives in Damascus had reported movement among the Kurdish underground. That morning, beginning at 8:30, most of them had begun leaving their five safe houses scattered around the city. These were houses Syria allowed them to keep to plot against the Turks. Shortly before noon, when Syrian security forces realized there might be a plot involving the unified Kurds, they went to the safe houses. All of them were deserted. Herbert's people had managed to keep up with a handful of the forty-eight Kurds. They were all in the vicinity of the Old City. Some of them were sitting along the banks of the Barada River, which flowed along the northeastern wall. Others were visiting the Muslim cemetery along the southwest wall. None of the Kurds had gone inside the walls.

Herbert said that he had not passed this information on to the Syrians for two reasons. First, it could very well expose his own intelligence sources in Damascus. Second, it might cause the Kurds to panic. If there were a plot against the President, then only the President and those close to him would be targets. If the Kurds were forced to act prematurely, a firefight might erupt in the streets. There was no telling how many Damascenes might be killed.

Hood did not bother telling Herbert that he might be one of those targets close to the Syrian President.

The embassy car entered the southwest sector of the Old City. The walls had fallen along a five-hundred-yard stretch here, and security was extremely thick. Jeeps had been parked fender-to-fender along the edges of the wall, leaving only a fifty-yard gap in the middle. This area was lined with over a dozen soldiers, all of them armed with Makarov pistols and AKM assault rifles. Tourist passports were being checked, and locals had to show identification.

The ambassador's car was stopped by a tough-looking corporal. He collected passports, then used his field phone to call the palace. After each passenger in the car had been okayed, they were sent through. Before proceeding to the palace, the driver waited for the DSA car behind them to be cleared. They took al-Amin Street northeast to Straight Street, and went left. They turned right on Souk al-Bazuriye and drove three hundred yards. They passed the oldest public baths in Damascus, the Hamam Nur al-Din, as well as the nine-domed Khan of Assad Pasha, a former residence of the builder of the palace.

The palace was located just southwest of the Great

Mosque or the Umayyad Mosque. Named for the Muslims who renovated it early in the eighth century, the mosque is built on the ruins of an ancient Roman temple. Before that, three thousand years ago, a temple dedicated to Hadad, the Aramean god of the sun, stood on this spot. Though burned and attacked repeatedly over the years, the mosque still stands and is one of the holiest sites in Islam.

The palace is no less imposing than the Great Mosque. Three separate wings surrounded the great court, a quiet retreat with a large pond and abundant citrus trees. One wing was for the kitchen and domestics, another for receiving guests, and the third was the living quarters. On the south side of the palace was a spacious public receiving area with marble walls and floor and a large fountain.

The palace was typically open to the public, though the private apartments were shut when the President came here. Today, the entire palace was closed and the President's personal security force patrolled the grounds.

After parking along the northwest side of the palace, the DSA agents were shown to a palace security room while the ambassador and his party were conducted to a large receiving room down the corridor. The heavy drapes were pulled and the crystal chandelier was brightly lit. The walls were covered with dark wood paneling, ornately carved with religious images. The room was appointed with richly inlaid furniture. In the center of the wall opposite the door was a large *mahmal* or pavilion which contained a centuries-old copy of the Koran. Designed to be carried on the back of a camel, the *mahmal* was covered with green velvet embroidered with silver. On top was a large gold ball with silver fringes. The gold was real.

Japanese Ambassador Akira Serizawa was already

present, along with his aides Kiyoji Nakajima and Masaru Onaka. Gray-haired presidential aide Aziz Azizi was also present. The Japanese bowed politely when the American delegation entered. Azizi smiled broadly. Ambassador Haveles led his group over and shook each man's hand. Then he introduced Hood, Dr. Nasr, and Warner Bicking in turn. After presenting his team to Azizi, Haveles took the Japanese ambassador aside. Still smiling, Azizi faced the rest of the American contingent. He had on black-rimmed glasses and a neatly clipped goatee. He also wore a white earphone with a wire which ran discreetly along his collar to the inside of his white jacket.

"I am delighted to meet you all," Azizi said in very precise English. "However, I am familiar by reputation only with the distinguished Dr. Nasr. I have recently read your book *Treasure and Sorrow* about the old Mecca caravan."

"You honor me," Nasr replied with a slight incline of his head.

Azizi's smile remained fixed. "Do you really believe that the Bedouin would have attacked the caravan and left twenty thousand people to die in the desert had they not been driven by despair and starvation?"

Nasr's head rose slowly. "The Bedouin of that time and that place were barbarous and greedy. Their needs had little to do with their misdeeds."

"If my eighteenth-century ancestors were barbarous and greedy, as you say," Azizi replied, "it is because they were oppressed by the Ottomans. Oppression is a powerful motivator."

Bicking had been chewing the inside of his cheek. He stopped and eyed Azizi. "How powerful?" he asked.

Azizi was still smiling. "The desire for freedom can

cause frail grass to split a walk or a root to break stone. It is very powerful, Mr. Bicking.''

Hood wasn't sure whether he was listening to an historical discussion, a foreshadowing of things to come, or both. Regardless, Azizi was like a cat on a fence, and Nasr looked like he wanted to find a shoe. Excusing himself as the Russian contingent arrived, the presidential aide withdrew.

''Anyone care to tell me what just happened?'' Hood asked.

''Centuries of ethnic rivalry just clashed,'' Bicking said. ''Egyptian versus Bedouin. Mr. Azizi's a Hamazrib, I'll bet. Successful at adapting to host cultures but very, very proud.''

''Too proud,'' Nasr grumbled. ''Blind to the truth. His people *do* have a history of cruelty.''

''Certainly their enemies think so,'' Bicking said with a snicker.

Hood stole a look at Azizi. He was walking the Russians over. He hadn't done that when Haveles's group entered.

''Could his little freedom speech have been a warning about the Kurds?'' Hood asked quickly.

''The Bedouin and the Kurds are fierce rivals,'' Bicking said. ''They wouldn't be helping each other, if that's what you mean.''

''It isn't what I mean,'' Hood said. ''You saw how he set up Dr. Nasr. Maybe Ambassador Haveles hit it on the head when he said we could be used as bait.''

''Maybe he was also being just a touch paranoid,'' Bicking said.

''Ambassadors always are,'' Nasr remarked.

After the Russian group of four was introduced, Azizi said that the President would be joining them shortly. Then he turned and motioned to a domestic who was standing in the doorway. The domestic motioned to someone who was standing to the side, out of sight. Hood had a photo-flash vision of camouflage-clad terrorists rushing in with semi-automatics and cutting them all down. He was relieved when liveried men in white walked in carrying trays.

That's only because the President isn't here yet, he thought. That was when the terrorists would arrive.

The Russian Ambassador had lit a cigarette and, with his translator, had joined the other two ambassadors in a corner of the room. Azizi walked over to the door and stood there while the rest of the men mingled and ate *shawarma*—finely cut pieces of lamb—or *khubz*—spicy, deep-fried chickpea paste on unleavened bread. As the men speculated on the nature of the bombing in Turkey and the ramifications of the troop movements, Hood noticed Azizi put an index finger to the earphone. The presidential aide listened for a moment, then looked into the room.

"Gentlemen," he said. "The President of the Syrian Arab Republic."

"So he really *is* going to show," Bicking said, leaning close to Hood. "I'm surprised."

"He had to," said Nasr. "He has to show he is fearless."

The men stopped talking. They turned to face the door as footsteps clattered smartly down the marble hallway. A moment later the aged President entered the room. He was tall and dressed in a gray suit, white shirt, and black tie. His head was uncovered and his nearly white hair was slicked back. He was flanked by a quartet of bodyguards. Azizi fell in beside the presidential party as they walked toward the group of ambassadors.

Standing between Bicking and Nasr, Hood frowned.

"Hold on. That bodyguard on the left—his trousers are sticking to his legs."

"So?" Bicking said.

The bodyguard looked at Hood as Hood looked at him.

"That's static electricity," Hood said. He began moving toward the bodyguard for a better look. "On the plane I read an Israeli E-mail bulletin. It said that electromagnetic fuses in pants pockets are being used to trigger bombs around the waist or—"

Suddenly, the bodyguard shouted something which Hood didn't understand. Before the other bodyguards could close ranks, the man was engulfed in a fireball. The blast knocked everyone down and blew the crystal from the chandelier. Hood's ears rang as black smoke rolled over him and shards of shattered glass rained down. He couldn't hear his own coughs as he lay on the floor choking.

He felt a hand pull at his jacket sleeve. He looked to his right. Bicking was waving smoke away. He shouted something. Hood couldn't hear him. Bicking nodded. He pointed at Hood and held his thumb up, then down.

Hood understood. He moved his legs and arms. Then he held up a thumb. "I'm okay!" he shouted.

Bicking nodded just as Dr. Nasr came crawling toward them from the settling smoke. There was blood on his neck and forehead. Hood crept over and examined his face and head. Nasr had been closer to the blast, but the blood wasn't his. Hood indicated that his colleague should lie where he was. Then he turned and tapped Bicking on the top of his head.

"Come with me!" Hood said. He pointed to himself, to Bicking, and then to where the presidential party had been standing. Bicking nodded. Hood motioned with his hand that the younger man should stay low in case there was shooting for any reason. Bicking nodded again. Together they wormed their way toward the door.

As they neared the blast site, they were hit with the distinctive, acrid smell of nitrite—like the lingering smell of freshly ignited matches. A moment later, the carnage was visible through the rising smoke. There were sprays of blood on the marble walls and puddles on the floors. The first body they encountered was that of the terrorist. He had been blown over the others. His legs and hands were gone. Bicking had to stop and look away. Hood continued on. As he moved along on his elbows, sweeping aside particles of glass, Hood wondered why no one had come to investigate the explosion. He considered sending Bicking out for help, but decided against it. He didn't want him running into overly anxious security forces who might gun him down.

Upon reaching the bodyguards, Hood found them all dead. The blast had dismembered and torn off the bulletproof vests of the two men nearest the explosion. Two other men were still tucked inside their vests, but their heads and limbs were riddled with two-inch nails and small ball bearings—the preferred projectiles of suicide bombers. Hood crawled around them to where the President and Azizi lay. The President was dead. Hood moved on to Azizi. He was alive but unconscious, bleeding from his chest and right side. Kneeling, Hood gently began pulling away the bloody fragments of clothing. He wanted to see if the bleeding could be stopped.

Azizi shuddered and moaned. "I knew—knew this would happen."

"Lie still," Hood said into his ear. "You've been injured."

"The President—" he said.

"He's dead," Hood informed him.

Azizi opened his eyes. *"No!"*

"I'm sorry," Hood said. Through the frustrating thickness in his ears he heard shots. It sounded as if they were coming from outside the palace. Were there more terrorists trying to get in or guards firing at fleeing accomplices? The gunfire grew louder with each new volley. Hood began to fear that the shots weren't being directed away from the palace but toward it.

Azizi squirmed with pain. "He is not—" Azizi choked. "He is not the President."

Hood continued to pull away blood-drenched pieces of the man's jacket. "What do you mean?"

"He was . . . a double," Azizi said. "To draw . . . his enemies out."

Hood scowled as the words sunk in. Score one for paranoia, he thought. He patted Azizi's shoulder. "Don't exert yourself," he said. "I'll see if I can stop the bleeding and then call for an ambulance."

"No!" said Azizi. "They must . . . come here."

Hood looked at him.

"We have been waiting," Azizi said weakly. "Watching . . . for them."

"For who?"

"Many . . . more," Azizi replied.

Hood winced as he cleared the last remnants of shirt from Azizi's chest. Blood was pumping out in half-inch-high squirts. He didn't know what to do for the man. Sitting back on his heels, he held Azizi's hand.

"Why won't you let me call for a doctor?" Hood asked.

"They have to . . . come in."

"They," Hood said. "You think there may be more terrorists?"

"Many," Azizi wheezed. "The bomber . . . was Kurd. Many Kurds . . . missing. Still in Damascus—"

Suddenly but peacefully, almost as if he were moving

358

in slow motion, the Syrian's head rolled to the side. His breathing slowed as the spurts of blood continued. A moment later Azizi's eyes closed. There was a long exhalation and then silence.

Hood released Azizi's hand. He looked to his right as Nasr crept through the smoke. He was followed by the three ambassadors. The Russian looked stunned. Haveles was holding him by an elbow and leading him ahead. The Japanese Ambassador was walking behind him, a little unsteady. Their aides, most of them shell-shocked, walked a few paces behind.

"My God," Haveles said. "The President—"

"No," said Hood as his ears began to clear. "A look-alike. That's why the President's security forces haven't come in yet. They used this man to smoke out a mole."

"I sold the President short," Haveles said. "He was expecting to win allies by having us dead and him alive."

"He'd have gotten that too if the bomber hadn't panicked," Hood said.

"Panicked?" Haveles said. "What do you mean?"

Hood watched as the blood stopped pumping from Azizi's chest. "The infiltrator counted on the other bodyguards looking ahead and not seeing him. But he didn't count on someone inside noticing the static charge when he armed the electromagnetic fuse." Hood indicated the shattered remains of the bomber. "He must have been put in place years ago to have gotten this kind of access."

"Who was he?" Haveles asked.

"Azizi thinks—thought he was a Kurd," Hood said. "I agree. There's something going on here that's larger than sending Syria and Turkey to war."

"What?" asked Haveles.

"I honestly don't know," said Hood.

The shots from outside grew louder and closer.

"Where are our security agents?" the Russian ambassador yelled in English.

"I don't know that either," Hood said, more to himself than to the Russian. However, he feared the worst. He peered through the smoke. "Ambassador Andreyev, are all of your people all right?"

"Da," he replied.

"Ambassador Serizawa!" Hood yelled. "Are you okay?"

"We are unhurt!" a member of the Japanese contingent yelled through the smoke.

Hood checked the other blast victims. They were all dead. A half-dozen people and one terrorist had given their lives to smoke out more terrorists. It was insane.

"Warner!" Hood yelled. "Can you hear me?"

"Yes!" came a muffled response from the right. Bicking was probably breathing through a handkerchief.

"Do you have your cellular?" Hood asked.

"Yes!"

"Call Op-Center," Hood said. He listened as explosions popped in the distance. He thought about the Kurds that Herbert's people had tracked to the palace. "Tell Bob Herbert what happened. Tell him we may be under siege here." Then he ducked under the rising tester of smoke and, still stooping, walked toward the door.

"Where are you going?" Haveles asked.

"To try and find out whether we stand a chance of getting out of here."

FORTY-FOUR

Tuesday, 2:53 p.m., the Bekaa Valley, Lebanon

Falah didn't understand it. He was running quickly. Yet as fast as he ran, following a jagged course through the foothills, the Kurds stayed with him. It was almost as if they had a spotter in the mountains, telling them where he was going. But that was unlikely. The tree cover was thick here and he was under it more than he was out of it. Still, somehow they were managing to stay within thirty to fifty yards of him.

Finally, exhausted and curious, Falah stopped. He took off his sweat-soaked headdress, grabbed a stick, and found a patch of grass. Pitching a small tent with the fabric, he slid his head under it and pretended to settle in for a nap. Less than a minute later the Kurds arrived. They surrounded him in a wide circle, then tightened it slowly. He opened his eyes, sat up, and raised his hands.

"Ala malak!" he shouted. "Slow down!"

They kept coming, stomping through the low brush and moving around the trees. Only when the eight men were standing around him shoulder to shoulder, guns pointed down, did they stop.

"What are you doing?" Falah asked. "What do you want?"

One of the men told Falah to keep his hands behind him and rise slowly. He obeyed. He started to ask what they were doing. He was told to be quiet. He obeyed again. The man tied his hands together and slipped the other end of the rope around his throat. Then he patted Falah down. He removed his gun and passport and handed them to a soldier, who ran ahead. Then, with his faced pointed toward the sky, Falah was marched through the rocky foothills to the cave. As he was led up the dirt road he stepped as hard as he could. If Striker decided to move in, they might see his footprints and know where it was safe to walk.

He was led past the van. As he walked by he noticed what he hadn't been able to tell from hiding. That the van was humming and lights were on inside. Either the commandos had been schooled enough in electronics to figure the computers out, which he doubted, or someone had talked under torture. In either case, he had a good idea how they'd been able to track him. He was glad he hadn't been able to send a voice message to Tel Nef. The van would have picked that up for sure. The short, coded burst he'd managed to get out might have slipped through the cracks. Even if it hadn't, it wouldn't mean anything to them.

Falah was led into the cave.

The young Israeli knew something about the groups that worked in this part of the world. The Palestinian groups Hamas and Hezbollah tended to set up shop in villages and on farms, where attacks against them would kill civilians. The Lebanese Freedom Front, devoted to the overthrow of Syrian rule in Lebanon, worked in small, mobile pockets. The PKK worked in somewhat larger groups, but they also tended to stay mobile. Straining to look straight ahead as he reached the cave, what Falah saw was not a mobile unit. There were sleeping quarters, electric lights, racks of weapons, and supplies. He also caught a quick glimpse of what they used to call "Satan's footsteps" in the Sayeret Ha'Druzim. The shallow pits that led from captivity directly to Hell, since no one ever came out of them alive. One thing Falah did not wonder was whether he'd be coming out of this cave alive. His Sayeret Ha'Druzim training didn't merely emphasize the positive. It demanded it.

Still tied, Falah was led down a flight of stairs to what was clearly the group's command center. The finished quality of the room surprised him. These people were not expecting to be driven out. He wondered if this were where the Kurds hoped to make the heart of a new nation. Not in the eastern part of Turkey, where their nation had been located centuries before, but in the west. Down through Syria and Lebanon with access to the Mediterranean.

There was a man seated at the desk reading documents. Another man was sitting behind him. He was squatting on a low stool, listening to a radio, and taking notes by hand. The man who had led Falah here saluted. The man at the desk returned his salute, then ignored Falah as he continued studying what looked like radio transcripts. After what seemed like two or three minutes, the man at the desk picked up Falah's passport. He opened it, studied it for a moment, then put it aside. He looked at the prisoner. A jagged red scar ran from the bridge of his nose to the center of his right cheek. His eyes were deathly pale.

"Isayid Aram Tunas," said Commander Siriner. "Mr. Aram Tunas."

"Aywa, akooya," Falah replied. "Yes, my brother."

"Am I your brother?" Siriner asked.

"Aywa," Falah answered. "We are both Kurds. "We are both freedom fighters."

"Then that is why you came here," Siriner said. "To fight alongside us?"

"Aywa," Falah replied. "I heard about the Ataturk Dam. There were rumors that the men behind it had come to a camp in the Bekaa. I thought I might seek them out and join their group."

"I'm honored." Siriner picked up Falah's gun. "Where did you get this?"

"It is mine, sir," Falah said proudly.

"For how long has it been yours?"

"I bought it on the black market in Semdinli two years ago," Falah replied. That was partly true. The weapon had been purchased on the black market two years before, though Falah hadn't been the one who bought it.

Siriner put the gun back down. The radio operator put fresh transcriptions on Siriner's desk. The commander continued to look at Falah. "We detected someone in the foothills with a radio set," the commander said. "Did you happen to hear or see anyone?"

"I saw no one, sir."

"Why were you running?"

"I, sir?" said Falah. "I wasn't running. I was at rest when your men surrounded me."

"You were perspiring."

"Because it was very hot," Falah said. "I prefer to travel when it's cool. Stupidly, I did not realize I was so near to my goal."

Siriner regarded the captive. "So you wish to fight with us, Aram."

"I do, sir. Very much."

364

The commander glanced at the soldier standing beside Falah. "Cut him loose, Abdolah," he said.

The soldier did as he was told. As soon as his head was free, Falah rolled it around. When his hands were loose, he flexed his fingers. Siriner pointed to Falah's gun. "Take it," he said.

"Thank you," Falah said.

"I have a great deal to do here," Siriner said. "If you serve under me, you will be required to follow orders without hesitation or question."

"I understand," said Falah.

"*Tayib*," Siriner said. "Fine. Abdolah, take him to the prisoners."

"Yes, sir!" the soldier said.

"Two of them are American soldiers, Aram," the commander said. "One man, one woman. I would like you to shoot them in the back of the head with your pistol. When you are finished, I'll have instructions as to the disposal of the bodies. Are there any questions?"

"None, sir," Falah said. He looked at the pistol. Suddenly, he raised it. He aimed at the commander's head, and fired. The hammer clicked on an empty chamber.

Siriner smiled. Falah felt a gun barrel pressed to the back of his neck.

"We watched you from the American van," Siriner said. "It has a variety of electronic devices for watching one's enemies. We saw you run. We knew you were spying on us."

Falah swore to himself. He'd seen the van there, the one the Americans were anxious to get back. He should have remembered it was operational. Those were the kinds of mistakes which cost lives. Including, it would seem, his own.

"It's interesting, isn't it?" Siriner said. "Most spies would have gone so far as to commit the murders. You must be Druze or Bedouin. You have a more sensitive nature.''

Siriner was correct. Israeli operatives who went deep undercover for long periods of time had to do whatever it took to gain access. It was a sad but necessary sacrifice for the greater good. Druze and Bedouin reconnaissance agents and trackers did not work that way.

Siriner smiled as he snatched the .44 from Falah. ''Also, I sell these on the black market in Semdinli. Aram Tunas was a good customer of mine. You look nothing like him. You also think nothing like him. I only emptied one chamber so the gun would not seem to weigh less. You should have fired again.''

Falah felt like a fool. The man was correct. He should have fired again.

Siriner looked at him a moment longer. ''Would you mind telling me who Veeb is?''

''I'm sorry?''

Siriner reached down. He picked up Falah's radio, which had been sitting on the floor behind his desk. ''Veeb. Whoever you were trying to contact with this.''

Falah had no idea what the man was talking about. But that didn't matter. If he said that, no one would believe him. So he didn't bother saying anything.

''No matter,'' Siriner said as he called another man into the room. He handed the newcomer the .44. ''Take this spy outside and execute him. See that his body is returned to the Israelis. Also, use the van to inform the Americans that the corpses of their people will follow if another rescue is attempted.''

With two guns pointed at the back of his head, Falah was led up the stairs. In the Sayeret Ha'Druzim he'd been trained to take out a gun pointed to his back. You turned clockwise if it were in the right hand, counterclockwise if it were in the left hand. You cocked the same-side elbow behind you, waist high. As you turned, you used your elbow to push the gun hand in the opposite direction. The turn left you facing your attacker with the gun pointing away from you.

The maneuver worked even if your hands were tied. But it only worked with one gun. Siriner obviously knew it, which was why he had two guns trained on the prisoner. As he was led from the cave into the sunlight, Falah knew he had just one option. As soon as they were outside he'd try to "reap" the men. He'd drop to the ground, extend his leg back, and sweep it to the side. There was room for that out here, though Falah knew he probably wouldn't get both men before one was able to fire.

While he had grown accustomed to living with death, he had never grown accustomed to failure. If he regretted anything, it was that. That and the fact that Sara, his lovely Kiryat Shmonan bus driver, would never know what had happened to him. Even when the Israelis found his body—and they would; the Israelis will go to almost any length to recover the bodies of soldiers and spies—they wouldn't say anything about it. They couldn't admit he'd ever been in the Bekaa. Falah hated the idea that she might think he'd just left the village and her.

The slanting, late-afternoon sun felt warm as Falah was marched into it. They stopped on the dirt road just outside the cave. A guard was stationed a few yards away, outside the van. He was holding a .38 at his side and watched the men dispassionately.

Blessing his God and his parents, Falah was prepared to die as he had lived.

Fighting.

FORTY-FIVE

Tuesday, 2:59 p.m.,
Damascus, Syria

The two Jeeps had sped up Straight Street toward Souk al-Bazuriye. As they approached, Mahmoud saw smoke rolling from windows on the southeast side of the palace. He smiled. To the northeast and southwest, Kurds were already taking up positions along the wall and firing at the police. Tourists and shoppers and Old City merchants were fleeing in every direction, adding to the chaos. The dozens of Kurds knew who their targets were. As far as the police were concerned, any one of the hundreds of people running, walking, or crawling by could be an enemy.

Mahmoud stood in the passenger's seat. He wanted his people to see him, to see how proud he was. After decades of waiting, years of hoping, and months of planning, freedom was finally at hand. Listening to the Jeep radio he'd learned that even today, the dreaded Mukhabarat secret police had stopped suspected Kurdish rebels and searched them for arms. But the Kurds had hidden their weapons days before. Some of the firearms had been buried in the cemetery, while others had been placed in waterproof boxes in the river. Since late morning, the PKK fighters had stayed close to the weapons by posing as mourners or simply by lolling around the Barada. They didn't retrieve them until after the explosion that signaled the death of the tyrannical Syrian President and the start of a new era.

Gunfire popped on all sides. Though Mahmoud and his infiltrators were supposed to have been right outside the palace when the attack began, he wasn't concerned. His people were fighting bravely and aggressively. Inside, loyal Akbar wouldn't have detonated the bomb unless he was sure he could at least get the President. Akbar was a Turkish officer who was Kurdish on his mother's side and secretly devoted to their cause. A suicide note left in his locker indicated that this was his way of avenging decades of genocide against the Kurds.

Once Akbar made his move, the PKK man in the security office would have taken out any agents who had come with the foreign visitors. All that would remain for Mahmoud and his team to do was finish off any presidential security guards who were still alive and secure the palace. When that was done, Mahmoud would doff his Syrian disguise and notify Commander Siriner to come to Damascus. With Syria's forces gathered in the north along the Turkish border, and Iraq using the distraction to look longingly back at Kuwait, Kurds from three nations would make their way to the city. Many would be killed, but many would make it past the overtaxed military. Speaking in a voice tens of thousands strong, the Kurds would tell of the crimes of the Syrians, the Turks, and the Iraqis. With the eyes and ears of the world upon them, the Kurdish people would demand more than justice. They would demand a nation. Some countries would condemn the methods they'd used to get it. Yet from the time of the American Revolution through the birth of Israel, no nation had ever been born without violence. Ultimately, it was the justness of the cause and not the methods used to which other nations responded.

Police jumped to the side of the road to let the Jeeps through. Officers saluted Mahmoud as he passed. The Syrian police probably thought he was standing up to give them hope and courage.

Let them think that, Mahmoud thought. He was here to help in exactly the same way authorities had always helped his people, with murder and suppression.

The Jeeps rolled up to the west side of the palace. Mahmoud jumped out, followed by his soldiers. The ten men seemed imperious, braving the gunfire as they walked toward the ornate iron fence. They were ushered through the gate by a guard who had been crouching behind a decorative, half-sized marble camel. The guard was a city employee and not part of the presidential security force.

"What's going on?" Mahmoud asked as bullets chewed at the dark green grass around his feet. The Kurdish attackers knew who he was and wouldn't shoot him or his men.

The guard hovered behind the camel as a bullet flew by. "There was an explosion," he said. "It came from the receiving room in the eastern wing."

"Where was the President?"

"We believe the President was in the room."

"You *believe*?" barked Mahmoud.

"We've not had word from inside since before the explosion," said the guard. "That was when one of the security guards radioed another to say that the President was leaving his quarters to attend a meeting."

"One of the security guards radioed?" Mahmoud asked. "Not the President's personal guard?"

"It was one of the palace police," the sentry said.

Mahmoud was surprised. When the President moved anywhere, whether in the palace or the nation, all communications and security were handled by his own elite team. "Has an ambulance been sent for?"

"I've heard nothing," said the guard.

Mahmoud looked toward the palace. It had been over five minutes since the explosion. If the President had been hurt, his personal physician would have been sent for. He would have been here by now. Something was wrong.

Waving his pistol for his men to follow, Mahmoud jogged quickly toward the palace entrance.

FORTY-SIX

Tuesday, 7:07 a.m., Washington, D.C.

Martha Mackall awoke with a start as her pager beeped. She looked at the number. It was Curt Hardaway.

Martha had spent the night at Op-Center, napping in the spartan employee lounge. It had taken her until three a.m. to fall asleep. Martha admitted it herself: When something annoyed her, she was like a dog with a bone. And having to turn Op-Center over to Paul Hood's evening counterpart, Curt Hardaway, annoyed her. Events overseas were just too delicate to leave to his ham-fisted ways. When he'd come on duty, Martha had gone so far as to consult Lowell Coffey's deputy assistant, Aideen Marley, about who had decision-making authority if something happened during the night. Whenever Paul Hood remained at his desk after his shift was over, he still outranked the night crew. But according to the charter, an acting director did not. Until 7:30 a.m., Op-Center belonged to Hardaway.

Martha hoped that nothing had happened. Hardaway was a cousin and protégé of CIA Director Larry Rachlin, and his appointment had been a necessary expedience. In order to keep Op-Center free of CIA influence, the President had wanted an outsider to run it. However, to appease the intelligence community, he was pressured to put in a veteran as Hood's backup. Though the Oklahoma-born Hardaway was an affable man with the intelligence skills necessary for the job, Martha found him to be uninspired and uninspiring. He also had a talent for speaking before thinking things through. Fortunately for Op-Center, the powerful Hood-Rodgers-Herbert triumvirate set very rigid policies during the day, and Hardaway had never been able to muck things up too badly.

Martha picked up the phone on the end table beside the couch. She called Hardaway. He picked up immediately.

"You'd better get on over," he said. "This mess is going to bleed into your shift."

"I'm coming," she said, and hung up. Hardaway was as tactful as ever.

The employee lounge was located near the Tank, a windowless conference room which sat within an electronic web. There wasn't a spy device on Earth that could hear what was discussed inside it. Turning left from the lounge and walking down the curving wall would have brought her past the Tank to the offices of Bob Herbert, Mike Rodgers, and Paul Hood in turn. Martha turned right. Walking briskly, she passed her own office, followed by the office of FBI and Interpol liaison Darrell McCaskey, Matt Stoll's computer area—"the orchestration pit," he called it—and the legal and environmental sections where Lowell Coffey and Phil Katzen worked. The psychological and medical divisions came next, followed by the radio room, the small Striker office for Brett August, and Ann Farris's two-person press department.

As she hurried along, Bob Herbert came wheeling up behind her. "Did Curt tell you what's been going on?"

"No," she said. "Only that there's a mess and it's going to hemorrhage all over my desk."

"A little raw but true," Herbert said. "All hell's broken out in Damascus. I got a call from Warner. They had a suicide bomber at the Azem Palace. He killed the President's double."

"That cobbler?"

Herbert nodded.

"Then the President probably isn't even in Damascus," Martha said. "What about Ambassador Haveles?"

"He was at the palace," Herbert said. "He's shaken but unhurt. Now the palace is under siege. Unfortunately, Warner is still in the room where the bomb went off and can't tell us much. I switched him over to Curt. We're keeping that line open."

"And Paul?" Martha asked.

"He left the room to look for the DSA guys who came with them."

"He should've stayed put," Martha said. "They may show up while he's gone and leave without him."

"I'm not so sure anyone's going anywhere," Herbert said. "Not unless they know some shortcuts by heart. Israeli satellite recon shows fighting on all sides. Looks like about forty or fifty plainclothes attackers in the process of breaching the wall. Syrian Army regulars just showed up to defend the palace. Ten whole men."

"That's what they get for sending their troops north," Martha said. "What's it all mean?"

"Some of my people think it's a Turkish assault with Israeli support," Herbert said. "The Iranians are saying we're behind it. Larry Rachlin's wanted to take the President down for a long time because of Syria's involve-

374

ment with terrorists. But he swears that CIA undercovers aren't a part of this.''

"What do you think?'' Martha asked as she knocked on Hardaway's door. It clicked open. She hesitated before opening it.

"I'm putting my money on the Kurds,'' Herbert said.

"Why?''

"Because they're the only ones who have anything to gain from all of this,'' he said. "Also, process of elimination. My Israeli and Turkish contacts seem as genuinely surprised by what's happening as we are.''

Martha nodded as the two of them went inside.

Skinny, bearded Curtis Sean Hardaway was behind his desk looking at his computer. His eyes were circled with dark rings, and the trash can was filled with chewing-gum wrappers. Mike Rodgers's backup, natty young Lieutenant General William Abram, was seated in a wing chair. His laptop was open on his knees. His thick black eyebrows came together above his nose, and his eyes were alert beneath them. His thin-lipped mouth was relaxed between two ruddy cheeks.

Soft crackling and occasional pops came from the speaker phone on Hardaway's desk.

Hardaway snapped his gum and looked over. "Good morning, Martha. Bob, I haven't heard a word from Warner since you turned him over to me.''

"Just gunfire,'' Abram said in a low monotone, "and static from military communications.''

"So we don't know if Paul found the DSA operatives,'' Martha asked.

"We do not,'' said Hardaway. "The President wants extraction options by seven-fifteen, and frankly there aren't many. We've got the Marine guards at the embassy, but they've got no jurisdiction outside the embassy—''

"Though they can always extricate first and answer questions later," said Abram.

"True," said Hardaway. "We've also got a Delta Team at Incirlik. They can be scrambled and on the palace roof in forty minutes."

"Which creates problems if the Turks are behind this," Abram said, "because we'll be shooting at allies."

"To save our ambassador," Martha said.

"Not if he isn't a target," Abram pointed out. "So far, we have no indication that he or any of the other ambassadors are in any danger."

Hardaway glanced at his watch. "There's one other option, which is to recall Striker and get them into Damascus. We've spoken with Tel Nef. They can get the team back and choppered to the palace within thirty minutes."

"No!" Herbert said emphatically.

"Hold on, Bob," Martha said. "Aideen already cleared it with the Congressional Intelligence Oversight Committee to have them go to the Middle East. Of the three groups, they're the only ones with any kind of authority."

"Absolutely not," Herbert replied. "We need them to get our people out of the Bekaa."

Martha looked at him. "Don't give me 'absolutely nots,' Bob," she said. "Not with Paul and our ambassador in the line of fire—"

"We don't know if they're in immediate danger," Herbert replied.

"Immediate danger?" Martha yelled. "Robert, the palace is under *attack*!"

"And the ROC and its crew are in the hands of terrorists!" Herbert yelled back. "That danger is real and Striker's within shouting range of it. Let them finish the mission they were sent to accomplish. Christ, they may not even have floor plans of the palace. You can't send them in blind."

"Armed and equipped they're hardly blind," Martha said.

"But they've studied the Bekaa," Herbert said. "They prepared for this mission. Look, you've got Warner on the line. Wait till Paul gets back. Let him make the call."

"You know what he'll say," Martha replied.

"Damn right I do," Herbert snapped. "He'll tell you to keep Striker on target and your ambition on a short leash."

"My ambition?"

"Yeah," Herbert said. "You save the ambassador and you score big-time brownie points with the State Department. What do you think, I don't know what your career map looks like?"

Martha stiffened with rage as she looked down at Herbert. "You talk to me like that and you'll find some roadblocks on *your* map—"

"Martha, calm down," Hardaway said. "Bob, you too. You've been up all night. And I'm running out of time here. The Striker issue may be academic in any case. The President plans to decide by seven-thirty this morning whether to destroy the ROC with a Tomahawk missile fired from the USS *Pittsburgh* in the Mediterranean."

"Aw, Christ!" Herbert said. "He was supposed to give us time!"

"He did. Now he's afraid the Kurds will use the ROC against the Syrians and Turks."

"Of course they will," Abram said, "if they aren't using it already."

"You're assuming they've figured out *how,*" Herbert

377

said. "Getting the ROC up and running isn't like starting a goddamn rental car."

"If someone shows them how, it is," Abram said.

Herbert glared at him. "Watch it, Bill—"

"Bob," Abram said, "I know you and Mike are close. But we have zero intelligence on what the terrorists might have done to persuade our people to talk."

"I'm sure your brother officer would appreciate that vote of confidence."

"This isn't about Mike," Martha said. "There are three civilian hostages as well. They aren't made of the same stuff Mike is."

"Not many people are," Herbert said. "Which is all the more reason to get him the hell out! We need him. And we owe it to the others we sent over there."

"If feasible," Martha said. "It may not be."

"Especially if we give *up*!" Herbert barked. "Jesus, I wish we were all on the same page here."

"So do I," Martha replied coldly. "The question is whether the hostages are lost to us and whether we should redirect our assets to Damascus."

"Martha's right," Hardaway said. "If that missile is launched we'll have no choice but to abort the Striker mission. Otherwise, the entire unit may get tagged along with the ROC and its crew."

Herbert folded his hands tightly in his lap. "We've got to give Striker time. Even if the Tomahawk flies, it'll take at least a half hour to reach its target. That may be time enough to get the ROC crew out. But if you withdraw Striker, Mike and the others are dead. Period. Is there anyone in this room who disagrees with *that*?"

No one spoke. Hardaway looked at his watch again. "Two minutes from now I've got to give our recommendation to the President regarding the situation at the palace. Martha?"

"I say we divert Striker," she said. "They're equipped, they're in the field, and they are the only legally defensible option we have."

"Bill?"

"I agree," said Abram. "I also think they're better trained than Delta, certainly better than the Marine guards at the embassy."

Hardaway looked at Herbert. "Bob?"

Herbert rubbed his hands on his face. "Leave Striker alone. They can still get clear of the Tomahawk with a window of five minutes to impact. That gives them at least a half hour to get the ROC crew out."

"We need them in Damascus," Martha said slowly.

Herbert pressed his fingertips to his forehead. Suddenly, he dropped his hands to his lap. "What if I can get someone else to help Paul and the ambassador?"

"Who?" she asked.

"It's a long shot," he said. "I don't know if the Iron Bar will let me have them."

"*Who?*" Martha repeated.

"People who can be there in about five minutes." Herbert picked up a secure phone on a small table near the wing chair. He pressed an unlit line and told his assistant to put him through to Major General Bar-Levi in Haifa.

Hardaway looked at his watch. "Bob, I've got to call the President."

"Tell him to give me five more minutes," Herbert told the hollow-eyed Assistant Deputy Director of Op-Center. "Tell him I will get Paul and the ambassador out without using Striker, or my resignation will be on Martha's desk before noon."

FORTY-SEVEN

Tuesday, 12:17 p.m., the Mediterranean Sea

The Tomahawk is a cruise missile which can be fired from torpedo tubes or from specially constructed vertical launch tubes. There are four kinds of Tomahawk: the TASM or antiship missile; the TLAM-N or land-attack missile equipped with a nuclear warhead; the TLAM-C, a land-attack missile with a conventional warhead; and the TLAM-D, a land-attack missle equipped with low-yield bomblets.

After the twenty-five-foot-long Tomahawk has been launched via rocket booster, small wings snap from the sides and lock into place. The rocket shuts down within a few seconds of firing and the missile's turbofan engine kicks in. By then, the Tomahawk has attained its flying speed of over five hundred miles an hour. As it scoots low over the land or ocean, its guidance unit keeps it on target with input from a radar altimeter. Following a computerized flight path, the Tomahawk quickly reaches its pre-landfall waypoint. This is the site which enables the missile to spot and lock on its first navigation point—typically a hill, a building, or some other fixed structure. After that, the onboard Terrain Contour Matching system or TERCOM carries the Tomahawk from point to point, often through sharp turns, sharp ascents, or dizzying dives. Corroboration of the course is provided by the Digital Scene Matching electro-optical system, a small television camera which compares the actual visuals to those stored in the TERCOM's memory. If there is any discrepancy, such as a parked truck or new structure, the DSMAC and TERCOM will quickly determine whether the rest of the image is correct and that the missile is on-target. If not, it sends a signal home which can be answered with one of two commands: continue or abort.

The TERCOM data is prepared by the Defense Mapping Agency and then forwarded to a Theater Mission Planning Center. From there, it is transmitted via satellite uplink to the launch site. When previously unmapped regions are targeted, up-to-the-minute satellite imagery is employed by the DMA. Depending upon the accuracy of the mapping, the Tomahawk is precise enough to destroy a car-sized target thirteen hundred miles away.

Presidential Directive M-98-13 was received by the communications shack of the USS *Pittsburgh* at 12:17 p.m. local time. The encrypted order was sent digitally, via secure satellite uplink, and was quickly decoded and hand-carried to the submarine's Captain George Breen.

The task directive gave Captain Breen his mission, his target, and his abort code. One of the twenty-four Tomahawks his submarine was carrying was to be launched at 12:30 p.m. local time toward a target in Lebanon's Bekaa Valley. The precise coordinates were provided, backed up by the DMA TERCOM data for the missile itself. If the target were moved, the Tomahawk would switch to a fallback guidance program. The missile would search to the horizon for visual, microwave, electromagnetic, and other characteristics which in combination could only describe the target. It would then lock onto the object and destroy it. The only way to order the missile to self-destruct before reaching its target was if the captain received the abort code HARDPLACE.

Captain Breen signed the directive and passed it to Weapons Officer E.B. Ruthay. Stationed in the control room, he worked with Console Operator Danny Max to load the flight data into the Tomahawk's computer. After it was downloaded and checked, the USS *Pittsburgh* slowed to a speed of four knots. It rose to periscope depth. Captain Breen gave the order to launch the missile. The hydraulically operated doors of one of the submarine's twelve forward-located vertical launch system tubes was opened. The pressure cap used to protect the missile was ordered withdrawn. The Tomahawk was ready for firing.

Captain Breen was informed of the missile's status. After making sure that there were no hostile aircraft or surface ships within detection range, he ordered Ruthay to fire at will. Acknowledging the order, the weapons officer inserted his launch key into the console, turned it, and pressed the firing button. The submarine shook perceptibly as the missile took off on its 455-mile journey.

Within five seconds of ascertaining that the Tomahawk was airborne, Captain Breen gave the order for the submarine to depart the region at once. As the crew took her deeper out to sea, Console Operator Max continued to monitor the missile's progress. During the next thirty-two minutes, he would not leave his station. If the command came from the captain or weapons officer for the mission to be aborted, it would be Max's responsibility to input the code for the satellite uplink and then push the red "destruct" button.

The USS *Pittsburgh* had a long history of firing Tomahawks. This included, most proudly, a flurry of missiles launched during Desert Storm. During that time, all of the Tomahawks had struck their targets. In addition, the submarine had never received an abort command.

This was Max's first firing of a non-test missile. His palms were damp and his mouth was dry. It was a matter of pride that Tomahawk's ninety-five-percent accuracy rate not catch up to the submarine's one-hundred-percent success rate on his watch.

He glanced at the digital countdown clock. *Thirty-one minutes.*

Max also hoped that he wouldn't have to pull the plug on his bird. If he did, it would take weeks for the rest of the crew to let up on the "firing blanks" and "unleaded pencil" jokes.

He watched the data stream in from the blazing missile as it prepared to cross two narrow time zones.

Thirty minutes.

"Fly, baby," Max said quietly, with a paternal smile. "Fly."

FORTY-EIGHT

Tuesday, 3:33 p.m., the Bekaa Valley

Phil Katzen sat at Mary Rose's station inside the ROC. An armed, English-speaking Kurd stood on either side. Each time Katzen was about to turn something on, he had to explain what it was. One man took notes while the other listened. All the while, sweat trickled down Katzen's ribs. Exhaustion burned his eyes. And guilt churned inside of him. Guilt, but not doubt.

Like most boys who'd ever played soldier or watched a war movie, Phil Katzen had asked himself the question often: *How do you think you'd hold up under torture?* The answer was always: *Probably okay, as long as I was just being beaten or held underwater or maybe electrified.* As a kid you think about yourself. You never think: *How would you hold up if someone else were being tortured?* The answer was *very badly.* And that had surprised him. But a lot had happened between the days when he'd played soldier in the backyard and now. He had gone to college at Berkeley. He'd seen the campus paralyzed by student marches for human rights in China and Afghanistan and Burma. He'd helped care for students who were weakened by hunger strikes against the death penalty. He himself had partaken in fish-free weeks to protest Japanese fishing tactics which netted dolphins along with tuna. He'd even gone shirtless for a day to call attention to the plight of sweatshop workers in Indonesia.

Upon obtaining his doctorate, Katzen had worked for Greenpeace. Then he'd worked for a succession of environmental organizations whose funding came and went. In his free time he built houses alongside former President Jimmy Carter, and worked at a homeless shelter in Washington, D.C. He learned that the suffering of parents who couldn't feed their children or the oppression of good souls opposed to tyranny or the pain inflicted on dumb animals was worse than one's own physical pain. It was magnified by empathy and worsened by helplessness.

Katzen had felt sick when Mike Rodgers was being tortured. But he'd felt dehumanized because Sondra DeVonne had been forced to watch, told that her own punishment would be worse. In retrospect, Katzen knew that that was what had broken him. The need to get some of that dignity back for himself and for her. He also knew that the pain he'd caused Mike Rodgers was greater than the torture inflicted by the Kurds. But as he'd discovered with Greenpeace, nothing good came without a price. If you saved the harp seals, you robbed fur traders of their livelihood. If you protected the spotted owl, you put loggers out of work.

Now here he was, showing the people who had tortured Mike how to work the ROC. If he stopped telling them what he knew, his colleagues in the pits would suffer. If he continued, scores of people might be injured or killed—starting with that poor soul the ROC's thermal-imaging system had shown lurking in the foothills.

Yet an equal number of Kurds might also be saved.

Nothing good came without a price.

Most importantly, Katzen had bought time for his fellow hostages. With time came hope, and the hope-sustaining knowledge that Op-Center had not abandoned them. If something could be done to help them, Bob Herbert would find it.

Yet Katzen had also had the basic "S&S" courses—eighty hours of safety and security. All Op-Center personnel were required to take them. Traveling abroad, American government officials were tempting targets. They had to know the fundamentals of psychology, of weapons and self-defense, of survival. Katzen knew that to survive, it was vital to be alert. However tired he was, however unsettled he felt about what was happening, he had to be aware of his surroundings. Hostages could not always count on rescuers to pull them out. Sometimes they had to seize on the distraction of a counterattack to escape. Sometimes they had to counterattack on their own.

Because Katzen had faith in Bob Herbert, he had decided to buy time by working as slowly as possible. He'd also decided to turn on equipment that would be useful to him. Radios, infrared monitors, radar, and the other basics. Since his two captors understood English, he was careful to avoid the Striker frequency. He would record it and listen later, if possible.

It was Katzen who had inadvertently alerted the Kurds to the presence of the lone spy in the foothills. The man had been listening to them with a sophisticated radio, possibly a TACSAT-3. With the help of the ROC's laser imaging system, the Kurds had been able to follow him easily as he tried to get away. Every move he'd made had been radioed to the pursuers in the field. What the Kurds didn't know was that the man had been prepared to beam a signal to Israel. Katzen had watched the man's parabolic dish search for the uplink. As soon as he saw where the dish was headed—there was only the Israeli satellite in that sector of the sky—Katzen had switched to a simulation program which showed a field operative attempting to contact a recon group, code-named Veeb. Veeb, for Victory Brigade, was a group of unknown size and an indeterminate nationality in an unspecified region of the Syrian-Israeli border. The point of the simulation was to use ROC software to find out who and where they were.

After the man was taken, Katzen had used the ROC to listen to everything which transpired in the cave. The man had been speaking in Arabic to the commander, so Katzen had no idea what had passed between them. His two guards understood, of course. Their smug expressions told him that, though they said nothing. When Katzen stole a low-tech look out the front window of the van and saw the prisoner being led out, he had no doubt that the man was going to be executed. He might have been a spy. Or perhaps he'd been a scout for Striker.

Katzen took a nervous breath. The air-conditioner had been cut down to conserve fuel. He mopped his forehead with his handkerchief. He'd risked his life for seals and bears, for dolphins and spotted owls. He wasn't about to stay in the van and let this happen.

"I need some air," Katzen said suddenly.

"Work," the man on his right commanded.

"I need to *breathe,* dammit!" he said. "What do you think I'm going to do? Run away? You know how to follow me on this"—he pointed to the monitor—"and where the hell would I go anyway?"

The man on his left pursed his lips. "Only for a moment," he said. "There isn't much time."

"Fine," Katzen said. "Whatever you say."

The Kurd grabbed the back of Katzen's collar in his fist. He tightened it to a knot and yanked him up. He put his .38 to Katzen's head. "Come," he said, and walked his captive to the closed door of the van.

They started down the two steps, the Kurd pushing Katzen ahead. Katzen opened the door. As he did, he drew on the survival training which had taught him how to use stairs to his advantage. He crouched. For a moment, the gun was pointing at the empty air above him. Making sure he was low and centered, Katzen reached across his chest with his left arm. He grabbed the arm fabric of the jacket his captor was wearing. Then he tugged the fabric toward his shoulder, dipped his shoulder down, and pulled the Kurd over.

The man tumbled head-first over Katzen. He landed on the ground, on his back, and Katzen leapt toward him. The Kurd was already getting up when Katzen landed on him. Katzen's head was facing the Kurd's feet, the gun hand to his right. He turned, raised his fist, and pounded the side hard on the man's wrist. The fingers opened reflexively. Katzen grabbed the .38.

The American took a moment to turn and look for the two men and their prisoner. They had stopped down the road, about twenty yards behind the van. One of the men had turned to look at him.

"*Yu af!*" he cried. "Stop!"

Katzen heard the other Kurd in the van running toward the doorway. Katzen regarded the Kurd on the ground. He'd come out here to save a life, not to take one. But if he didn't do something his own life would be lost. Still facing the Kurd's feet, Katzen raised the .38 and put a slug through the man's right foot.

As the Kurd shrieked, Katzen glanced toward the two executioners. The one who'd looked back at the van turned his pistol toward Katzen. The moment he did so the prisoner twisted like a top to his right, literally rolling his neck off the barrel of the other man's gun. Simultaneously, he cocked his right arm like a chicken wing and raised the elbow head-high. As he turned he rolled the elbow behind him, using it to push the gun aside. For a moment, neither weapon was trained on the captive. The prisoner kept turning until he was at the side of his would-be executioners, facing him. As the gunman turned to retarget the prisoner, the captive lifted his hands so they were on either side of the gunman's wrist—palms turned to one another as though he were about to clap. Then the palms flashed toward the gunman's forearm, one slightly closer to his elbow than the other. When they came together they kept moving, snapping the man's wrist between them. Katzen could hear it break. The gun fell. The captive bent to retrieve it.

All of that happened in an instant, and it was all Katzen saw. Behind him he could hear the Kurd in his heavy desert boots clomping down the steps of the ROC. There were shouts coming from the cave to his left. In a moment they'd have him pinned in a three-way cross fire. There was only one avenue open to him: straight ahead, toward the edge of the dirt road. There was a drop on the other side, he didn't know how far, but a fall could be more forgiving than a rain of bullets. He opted to take it. Hopping off the writhing Kurd, Katzen dropped to his side, rolled several yards, and went over the ledge.

He never seemed to hit the steep slope so much as roll alongside it. Branches cracked as he went down and rocks punched him as he rolled over them. He held tight to the gun and covered his face with that arm as he tried to stop his fall with the other. He heard several gunshots, muted by distance and by the sound of sliding dirt and splitting twigs. But he didn't think that anyone was firing at him. The shots were too far away to be coming from the ledge.

Katzen stopped with a jolt. He'd landed on his back in the crook of a tree growing sideways from the slope. It not only punched the air from him, it felt like it broke a rib. He lay there for just a moment as he drew a slow, painful breath. There were more shots, and Katzen squinted up at the solid blue sky. As he did, someone looked down at him. It was the man who had stayed behind in the van. After a moment, the face was joined by a gun.

Katzen still had the gun he'd taken. His arm was dangling beside him, and when he tried to raise it pain ripped across his chest. His arm shuddered as he tried to lift it again. He let it drop back down.

Panting, Katzen waited for the bullet to strike. But before the man could fire, his head seemed to bounce to the right. It bounced again, and this time it also turned around. The head drooped, the gun fell, and then another head appeared. This time it was the man who had been marched from the cave. He motioned for Katzen to stay where he was.

"As if I can go anywhere," Katzen said to himself.

The man swung over the ledge, sat with his legs stretched before him, and followed them down as if he were on a slide. He held his arms in front of him and jerked them up and down for balance. There was a gun in each. As he neared the tree, he put his feet sole-down and slowed to a stop. Crawling under it for protection, he set the guns down, placed Katzen's .38 beside them, and helped the injured American off the tree. Katzen put his hands under his body and tried to brace himself. He sucked air through his teeth as each move caused fresh pain.

"I'm sorry," said the newcomer. "I wanted to get you under the tree for cover."

"It's okay," Katzen said as he eased to the ground. "Thanks."

"No," said Falah. "My thanks to you. Because of the distraction you caused, I was able to deal with the men who were going to kill me. I also managed to finish the men who had you."

Katzen felt a flash of sadness. Because he'd left the van, four men were dead instead of one. It was a quantitative judgment, nothing more. But it was still a weight on his soul.

"There are more men inside," Katzen said. "Maybe twenty Kurds and six of my own people."

"I know," said the man. "My name is Falah and I'm with—"

"No!" Katzen interrupted. "The machine's still recording audio up there. They don't know how to replay it, but there's no guarantee we'll get it back."

Falah nodded.

Katzen struggled onto one elbow. "My name's Phil," he said "Were you scouting this location for anyone?"

He nodded again. He pointed to Katzen and saluted.

My troops, Katzen thought. Striker. That must have been who he was trying to radio.

"I see," Katzen said. "What where they supposed to do if they didn't hear anything from . . ."

Katzen fell silent as his companion suddenly pushed him back. Then Falah lay flat beside him. Katzen heard it now too: boots crunching on the dirt. He turned his face around so he could look up the slope. A semiautomatic weapon was poked over the side. As Falah huddled close beside Katzen under the tree, the gun was fired. Bullets tore into the tree as well as the earth around

391

them. It continued for only a second, though it seemed much longer.

Katzen looked at Falah to make sure he was all right. He looked up. Broken bark was sticking off the tree at odd, ugly angles. Katzen couldn't help but think that that was the first time a tree had ever saved an environmentalist.

But for how long? he wondered.

Falah brought both guns around. Still lying flat, he held them in front of him, pointing them up the slope. There were more footsteps, followed by silence. And then a horrifying thought hit Katzen. He'd left the goddamn infrared imaging system on in the ROC. It was still running at Mike Rodgers's station. Even though the men who had been taught how to run some of the ROC equipment were dead, anyone could go inside and have a look at the monitor. And anyone who was within two hundred yards of the cave would show up as a red figure on the screen. Bodies hit by gunfire would leak warm, detectable blood.

He and Falah weren't bleeding and the Kurds would know it.

Katzen leaned over so his mouth was right beside Falah's ear. "We're in trouble," he said. "The van can *see* us the way they saw you. The infrared—they know we're not dead."

After a short silence there were more footsteps. There was a high-pitched whimper. Katzen twisted his face so he could look up. A moment later he saw Mary Rose standing at the edge of the slope. Someone was standing behind her. All Katzen could see were his legs through hers.

"You men down there!" shouted a voice from above. "You have a count of five to surrender. If you don't come up your people will be shot in turn, beginning with this woman. *One!"*

"He'll do it," Falah whispered to Katzen.

"Two!"

"I know," Katzen replied. "I've seen how they work this drill. I've got to give myself up."

"Three!"

Falah put a hand on his arm. "They'll kill you!"

"Four!"

"Maybe not," Katzen said. He got up slowly, painfully. "They still need me." He looked up. They were doing a fast count, the bastards. "I'm hurt!" he shouted. "I'm coming as fast as I can!"

"Five!"

"No, *wait!"* Katzen screamed. "I said—"

Suddenly, blood exploded from the top of the slope and sprayed darkly across the blue sky.

"No!" Katzen screamed, his face distorted as Mary Rose fell to her knees and the blood rained toward them. *"God, no!"*

FORTY-NINE

Tuesday, 3:35 p.m.,
Damascus, Syria

The floor of the palace security office was slippery with blood.

The Diplomatic Security Agents were dead. So were the two- and three-agent security forces for the Japanese and Russian ambassadors respectively. They had been gunned down in the small office, a dark and windowless room with two stools and a large, slanting console consisting of twenty small black-and-white television monitors. The images showed bedlam at nearly every entrance, every room.

The man who presumably had shot them, a blue-uniformed palace guard whose station this must have been, was also dead. There was an automatic rifle on the floor beside him and a pair of bullet holes in his forehead. One of the Russians had been able to draw his own pistol. Apparently, the head shots were his.

Paul Hood did not want to linger in the security office. He checked the men for signs of life. Finding none, he remained on his hands and knees and poked his head into the hallway. The sounds of gunfire were all around him. They were no longer distant. The reception room, though only about two dozen yards away, seemed incredibly far. In the other direction, the outside door was much closer. But he wouldn't leave without the others. Tactically, it would make more sense if he could get them here.

Then he remembered Warner Bicking's cellular phone.

Hood turned back into the room. The DSA agents both had cellular phones. One had been shattered by gunfire. The other had been busted when the man fell. None of the other agents had phones. Hood sat back on his heels. He looked around.

This is a security office, goddammit! he told himself. They have to have a telephone.

He ran his hands along the console. They did have one. It was in a lidded recess to the right of the lowest right-hand monitor. Hood lifted the receiver. The lighted numbers were on the handset. He held it in his trembling palm and punched in Bicking's number. Bicking was probably still on the line with Op-Center. Hood wondered if anyone else in history had ever used call waiting in the middle of a firefight.

Hood went back to watching the monitors as the phone range. It beeped twice before Bicking picked up.

"Yes?"

"Warner, it's Paul."

"Jesus God," Bicking laughed nervously, "I'd hoped it wasn't a wrong number. What'd you find?"

"They're all dead in here," Hood said. "Anything from Op-Center?"

"They've got me on hold while they try to get someone to us," he said. "Last I heard was from Bob. He told me something's up but couldn't tell me what."

"He was probably afraid the lines are being monitored." Hood shook his head. "I'm looking at the monitors, though, and I don't see how anyone's going to—hold it."

Hood watched as what looked like a contingent of Syrian Army troops made their way through one of the corridors.

"What's going on?" Bicking asked.

"I'm not sure," Hood said, "but the cavalry may have arrived."

"Where?"

"Looks like it's the other end of the corridor from where I am," Hood said.

"Closer to us?"

"Yes."

"Should I go out and try to meet them?" Bicking asked.

"I don't think so," said Hood. "Seems like they're headed right toward you."

"They probably have orders to get the ambassadors out," Bicking said. "Maybe you'd better come back."

"Maybe," Hood agreed.

The gunfire was growing louder at the other end of the hall, away from the reception room. It wouldn't be long before the rebels reached the security office.

Hood continued to watch the monitors. The troops weren't checking other rooms, nor had they set up any kind of flank watch. They were moving ahead with surprising confidence. Either they had courage or they didn't have a clue as to how bad things were.

Or, Hood thought, they aren't afraid of being attacked.

It was part of Hood's job to do what he called the "PC thing," to presume conspiracies. Part of Op-Center's mission was constantly to ask "What if?" when faced with a murder by a lone assassin or a rebellion by a hitherto underarmed faction. Hood was not obsessed with conspiracies, but he wasn't naive.

The soldiers continued to move ahead purposefully. Hood watched as coverage shifted to another monitor.

"Paul?" Warner said. "Are you coming?"

"Hold the line," Hood said.

"I've got Op-Center still holding—"

"Stay on the line!" Hood ordered.

He bent lower to the monitors. A few seconds later he saw two men with black *kaffiyehs,* brandishing what looked like Makarov pistols, cross the hall behind them. One of the soldiers looked back briefly. He didn't even break his stride.

"Warner," Hood said urgently, "get out of there."

"What? Why?"

"Get everyone together and *move!*" he said. "Bring them here. I don't think the cavalry is on our side."

"Okay," Bicking said, "I'm moving."

"And if they won't leave, don't argue with them. Just get out."

"Understood," Bicking said.

Hood squeezed the phone. More attackers passed with impunity behind the troops. Either the Syrian military was in on this, or these men were only masquerading as Syrian Army regulars. In either case, the situation had just gone from dangerous to deadly.

"Shit!" Hood said as the soldiers turned down the last corridor. "Warner, stay put!"

"What?"

"Stay where you are!" Hood shouted. He'd no longer have to watch the attackers on the monitor. To see them, all he'd have to do was stick his head out the door. His head or—

Hood looked down at the blood-soaked marble. The Russian guard's pistol was there along with the Syrian killer's automatic rifle. All that Hood knew about firing guns was what he'd been taught in the required courses at Op-Center. And he hadn't done terribly well at those. Not with Mike Rodgers and Bob Herbert casually ticking off bull's-eyes at the firing stations on either side of him. But what Hood knew might be enough. If he could drive the Syrians back, that might buy Warner and the others enough time to get out of the reception room.

"Warner," Hood whispered loudly into the phone, "there are soldiers coming toward you. Probably hostile. Hunker down until you hear from me. Acknowledge."

"Hunkering down," Bicking said.

Hood let the phone drop. He lifted the automatic rifle from the thin layer of blood carpeting the marble floor. He got up quickly and felt dizzy. He wasn't sure if it was because he'd gotten up too fast or because his hands and the soles of his shoes were sticky with someone's blood. It was probably a little of both. Moving quickly, Hood stepped over the outstretched arm of one of the DSA men. He stood just behind the doorjamb.

His heart was a mallet, thick and heavy. His arms trembled slightly. He had taken mandatory weapons training, but he had never shot at anyone before. He wouldn't fire to kill. Not at first. But there was no guarantee he wouldn't have to. He'd been the Mayor of Los Angeles and a banker. He'd signed on at Op-Center for a think-tank-type desk job. Crisis management, not wallowing in blood.

Well, things freakin' change, Hood, he pep-talked to himself as he took a slow breath. Either you fire if necessary, or your family attends a funeral. He leaned into the hallway and looked at the soldiers walking toward the reception room. He had the framework of a plan. First, to find out if he could communicate with these people. Second, to see how they'd react to a challenge.

"Do any of you speak English?" Hood asked.

The soldiers stopped. They were nearly twenty feet from the reception room, about three-dozen yards from him. Without turning around, the leader said something to a man behind him. The man stepped forward.

"I speak English," said the man. "Who are you?"

"An American guest of the President," Hood replied. "I just spoke with the commander of the presidential guard by phone. He's asked that all loyal forces meet him in the north gallery at once."

The man translated for the leader. The leader gave an order to a man behind him. Two soldiers left the group and went back the way they'd come.

He's got to check, Hood thought, but he's not using his field radio. If there are presidential guards out there, this man doesn't want them to know he's here.

As the two men trotted around a corner, the leader issued a new order. The group split up again. The leader and four men continued toward the reception area while three men moved toward Hood. Their weapons were in their hands. They weren't coming to rescue him. The question was, did they intend to take the men hostage or kill them? They had already taken several lives in a failed effort to assassinate the President. And they'd killed all the men in this booth. Even if they were taking prisoners, which Hood doubted, he didn't want to subject his country, his family, himself, or the men in the other room to an extended hostage ordeal. As Mike Rodgers had once put it, "In the long run, that's just a different way to die."

Hood hugged the automatic rifle to his waist, the magazine resting along his thigh. Aiming the barrel low, he swung into the corridor and fired at the floor just in front of the group's leader. Hood was startled as casings flew at him from the ejection port, but he continued to hold the trigger. The men down the hall retreated. The three men who were coming toward the security room threw themselves against the wall, behind a large bronze horse, and returned fire.

Hood stopped firing and ducked back behind the jamb. His knuckles were bone-white around the pistol grip. His breathing was fast and his heart was hammering harder than before. The men down the hall also stopped firing. The automatic rifle felt light, nearly empty. Hood picked the bloody pistol up off the floor and checked the magazine. It was about one-third empty. He had seven or eight shots.

Hood knew that there wasn't much time. He'd have to go back into the hallway and fire again, this time aiming higher. He checked the monitor. The leader and his group were hanging back. They'd been joined by a ragtag group of Syrians with guns. The leaders of both groups were conferring. Hood knew that if he waited any longer he'd fall to sheer force of numbers.

He sidled up to the jamb and held both guns facing up. He didn't feel like John Wayne or Burt Lancaster or Gary Cooper. He was just a frightened diplomat with guns.

One who's responsible for the lives of men trapped down the hallway. He listened. He heard no movement outside. Holding his breath this time, he dropped both guns hip-high and swung into the hallway.

And stopped as a soldier stepped right into his face and shoved a pistol barrel up under his chin.

FIFTY

Tuesday, 3:37 p.m., the Bekaa Valley, Lebanon

Before joining Striker, Sergeant Chick Grey had been Corporal Grey of the elite counterterrorist Delta Force. He'd been a private when he'd first reported for training at Fort Bragg. But Grey's two specialties had enabled him to climb the ratings ladder to private first class and then corporal in a matter of months.

His first skill was in HALO operations—high-altitude, low-opening parachute jumps. As his commander at Bragg had put it when recommending Grey's boost from private to PFC, "The man can fly." Grey had the ability to pull his ripcord lower and land more accurately than any soldier in Delta history. He attributed that to having a rare sensitivity to air currents. He believed that also helped with his second skill.

Grey's second skill was marksmanship. As the late Lieutenant Colonel Charles Squires had written when insisting that Mike Rodgers recruit him for Striker, "Corporal Grey is not only a sharpshooter, General. He could put a bullet clean through one of *your* bull's-eyes." The report didn't note that Grey could also go without blinking for as long as necessary. He'd developed that ability when he realized that all it took was the blink of an eye to miss the "keyhole," as he called it. The instant when your target was in perfect position for a takedown.

A few seconds before, perched in a treetop, Grey had been staring through the twelve-power Redfield telescope mounted on top of his Remington 7.62 mm M401 sniping rifle. It had been twenty-odd seconds since he'd blinked. Twenty-odd seconds since the terrorist had walked from the cave holding a gun to the head of Mary Rose Mohalley. Twenty-odd seconds since Colonel Brett August had told him to take the subject out at will. During that time, Grey had not only watched everything that transpired, he'd also listened carefully through earphones plugged into a six-inch-diameter parabolic dish. The clip-on dish had been attached to a branch beside him and provided clear audio from the area surrounding the idle ROC.

There is an instant in every hostage situation when a marksman makes an emotional rather than just a professional commitment to doing what must be done. A life must be taken in order to rescue a hostage. It isn't a point of no return; hostage situations are fluid and one must always be ready to stand down. But it is a form of peacemaking with oneself. If the guilty party doesn't die—swiftly, painlessly—an innocent one may. That realization is black and white. It comes without passing judgment on the larger matter, the merits of the terrorist's cause. At that point, an almost supernatural calm comes over the marksman. Those last seconds before firing are moments of cold and frightening efficiency. The first seconds afterward are moments of equally dispassionate acceptance with just a hint of professional pride.

Sergeant Grey waited until the gunman had uttered the last number of his count before firing. His single shot struck the terrorist in the left temple. The man jerked hard to the right on impact, twisted slightly, and then dropped to his back. His blood sprayed out over the ledge and then poured with him as he fell. When the man's arms went limp, Mary Rose fell to her knees. No one rushed out to claim her. A moment later, someone began clambering up the slope. Grey didn't wait to see the outcome.

Privates David George and Terrence Newmeyer were standing under the tree. The instant the terrorist went down, Sergeant Grey lowered the dish and headphones to Private George, handed his rifle to Private Newmeyer, and climbed down. As he stowed his gear, Sergeant Grey felt only one thing. That there was still a lot to be done.

The three men joined Colonel August and the others. The Strikers had left their vehicles a quarter mile back so the engines would not be heard. Two Strikers had remained behind to protect the FAVs and motorcycles, while the others had moved forward through the tops of the close-growing trees. They'd executed an infrared scan and hadn't detected sentries, so the off-ground route served a double purpose. First, it would keep them from tripping any mines that guarded the cave. Second, if the ROC were working, the reading would indicate that something was moving in the trees—though at this distance the Kurds might think they were some of the flocking vultures that were indigenous to the region.

For the three minutes that Sergeant Grey had been in the tree, Colonel August and Corporal Pat Prementine had been using field glasses to watch what was happening on the ledge approximately three hundred yards away. The other eleven Strikers had been gathered in a tight group behind them. When Sergeant Grey arrived with the two privates, the group absorbed them without seeming to expand.

August looked back at the newcomers. Corporal Prementine, the boy genius of infantry tactics, continued to look out at the ledge.

"Good work, Sergeant," August said.

"Thank you, sir."

"Sir," said Prementine, "no one's gone after the woman."

August nodded. "We're going to have to move that," he whispered. "To bring you up to date, we think that's Phil Katzen and our contact at the foot of the slope. We'll be going out in one or two groups. One group if we need to storm the cave to get our people out. Two if the hostages are—"

"Colonel," Prementine interrupted, "the men are coming out. The bastard's've gone half-and-half."

August swung his binoculars around. Sergeant Grey also squinted back toward the cave. Three of the hostages had been thrown face-down in the dirt outside the cave. Grey could see men inside the cave, but they were hidden by the deep shadows.

"Corporal, mask up and get A-Team over there *now*." August snapped. "Take them inside. We'll handle the perimeter."

"Yes, sir," Prementine said. He moved out with seven Strikers crouching low behind him, single file, as they ran toward the ledge.

"George, Scott!" August barked.

"Sir?" both men replied.

"RAC 'em."

"Yes, sir," said George.

The two privates moved to the equipment locker they'd hauled from the FAV. As David George assembled a charcoal-gray mortar, Jason Scott pulled four shells of RAC—rapid-acting incapacitant—from their insulated storage bag. Within two seconds of exploding, the amber-colored gas would knock out everyone within a twenty-foot radius. Private Scott assisted with the heavy baseplate, and in just over thirty seconds the grenade launcher was loaded and assembled. While Private George peered through the sight, Scott adjusted the traversing and elevating handles to fix the line of fire.

"Sergeant Grey," August said, "back in harness. Night vision. Tell me what you can see inside the cave."

"Right away, sir."

While Grey grabbed his rifle and headed back to the tree, Newmeyer pulled the night-vision goggles from his backpack. The strap was preset to slip over Grey's helmet and hang over both eyes. The Redfield telescope had been fitted with an adaptor to slip over either eyepiece.

"Sergeant," August said, "it looks like the hostages' feet are tied to ropes inside. See if you've got a shot at whoever's holding those ropes."

"Yes, sir," Grey replied. He began climbing back toward the large branch which gave him a clear view over the other trees.

As he ascended, Grey heard Private Ishi Honda's radio beep. The communications operator answered, listened for several seconds, then put the caller on hold.

"Sir," Honda said calmly, "it's Mr. Herbert's office with an AE update."

AE meant "all ears." Though that usually meant that an immediate evacuation was being ordered, Grey continued to climb.

"Shoot," August said.

"Mr. Herbert reports that seven minutes ago, a Tomahawk missile was fired from the USS *Pittsburgh*. It will be reaching the ROC in twenty-five minutes. We are advised to abort.''

"Advised, not ordered," August said.

"No, sir."

August nodded. "Private George."

"Sir?"

"Let the sons of bitches have it."

FIFTY-ONE

Tuesday, 3:38 p.m., Damascus, Syria

When the revolver was pressed under his chin, Paul Hood did not see his life race by. As the other two men disarmed him, Hood was overcome with an almost dreamlike light-headedness. The mind's way of dealing with incomprehensible shock? But he was lucid enough to ask himself what the hell he'd been thinking when he'd decided to take on the terrorists. He was a desk jockey, not a fighter. And he'd been so preoccupied with the leader—where he was going and what he was doing—that he'd forgotten all about the men creeping along the wall. As usual, Mike Rodgers had been right about these things. War, he'd often said, was unforgiving.

The men with Hood's guns stepped back. One of them turned. Hood watched the leader move his band forward. There was nothing smug or triumphant about his opponent's manner. He seemed purposeful—no more, no less—as he stopped by the door and looked down the corridor. He nodded once. The man who was watching him turned back. He said something to the soldier in front of Hood. The soldier grunted and looked at Hood. Unlike the leader, this man smiled.

Hood shut his eyes. He said a mental good-bye to his family. Saliva had collected in his throat. He wished he could swallow, but the pressure from the gun barrel was preventing it. Not that it mattered. In a moment he would never again swallow or smile or close tired eyes or dream—

A shot cracked along the corridor and Hood started. He heard groaning and opened his eyes. The man who'd been standing in front of him was on the floor, holding his left thigh. As Hood watched in shock, the other two men went down. Bullets had punched ugly holes in their legs and lower back. Both men were dead.

Hood looked down the hallway and saw the band of ragtag Syrians striding forward. They were a wall of guns and multicolored robes and intense expressions. As Hood stood there, surprised to be alive and uncertain what to do, the Kurdish leader froze. His men stopped behind him. They were just a few steps away from the door of the reception room. The leader looked at his three fallen soldiers, then turned and began screaming at the Syrians.

Ignored for a moment, Hood ducked back into the security office. Even as he stepped inside, he kicked himself for not thinking to grab one of the fallen men's guns. But it was too late for that, and at least he was alive. Like they used to say in the stock market, bears and bulls can prosper. Pigs don't.

Hood grabbed the phone. "Warner, are you there?"

"Of course!" Bicking said. "What's happening?"

"I'm not sure," Hood said. "Some of those soldiers were just shot by Syrians."

"Great—"

"It may be," Hood said. "I still don't think they were

here to help us. Can you hear what the leader's saying?''

"Hold on," said Bicking. "Let me get closer." A moment later Bicking came back. "Paul? His name is Mahmoud al-Rashid and he wants to know what the Syrians are doing. Apparently he'd already told them he was a Kurdish leader, not a Syrian Army regular."

"What did the Syrians say?"

"Nothing," Bicking replied.

Hood looked at the monitor. "Warner, I've got a feeling those Syrians didn't mistake the Kurds for soldiers. I think they knew exactly who they were."

Mahmoud shouted again.

"What's he saying now?" Hood asked.

"He's ordering the men to identify themselves," Bicking said. "He also wants them to take care of the men they shot."

Hood's heart began to beat faster as he watched the screen. "Mahmoud's raising his gun," he said. "Warner, I'll bet my life they're not with him."

"Maybe they're presidential security forces," Bicking said. "Those guys are long overdue."

"I don't know," Hood said. "Listen, Warner. Get back to Op-Center and tell them what's happening. See if they know anything about an undercover counterstrike."

"Wouldn't they have told me?"

"Not on an open line," Hood said. "Security won't matter now."

Mahmoud stopped talking. There was a very short silence, and then the Syrians suddenly fell back a few paces. They opened fire, shooting as one at the main body of Mahmoud's group.

"Shit!" Bicking screamed into the phone. "Paul, I can't hear anything! Too much noise!"

Several of Mahmoud's men fell before they could return fire. Mahmoud himself was unable to shoot because his men were in the way. Instead, he motioned the surviving members of his group back. As they ran around him he covered their retreat, driving the Syrians back with a waist-high burst of fire. A few were knocked back, but must have been wearing bullet-proof vests. They got back up again. Mahmoud, however, was not wearing a vest. He appeared to take several bullets before turning and hobbling toward the reception room. As soon as he'd turned, the shooting stopped. The Syrians rushed forward again.

When it was quiet, Hood got back on the phone. "Warner, forget about Op-Center. Get to cover. The Kurds'll be there in a second!"

There was no answer.

"Warner, do it *now*!" Hood said. "Warner, do you hear me?"

"I hear you," he said. "But maybe there's something I can do—"

"There *isn't*," Hood said, "except to get your ass into hiding!"

Hood was still watching the monitor as five Kurds entered the reception room. They were followed by their wounded leader. Hood didn't say anything else. If Bicking had managed to hide somewhere, Hood's voice coming over the phone might give him away. He set the phone on its side and continued to stare at the monitor.

As Hood waited, he heard more shots just outside his door. He saw someone coming down the hall. He looked over just as the man who had been about to execute him slid past his door, lying on his back and arching like a worm. He turned onto his side, grimacing horribly for a moment, and then he curled into a tight ball. There were three bloody holes in his chest. His breathing was labored for a moment, and then stopped. His expression did not relax as he died.

Hood felt sick.

A moment later one of the Syrians stepped over the body. He was a big man, about six-foot-five, with a white *kaffiyeh* and a full, black beard. The 9mm parabellum at his side was smoking slightly, and there were two bullet holes in the chest of his khaki jacket. He stood there, his frame filling the doorway on all sides.

"You are Hood?" he asked in stilted English. His gravelly voice seemed to come from a cave.

"Yes," Hood said.

The man kicked over the gun that had belonged to the dead man. It spun over on a sheet of blood. "Keep this," he said as he pulled the bottom of his *kaffiyeh* across his face. "Use it if you must."

Hood picked it up. "Who are you?"

"Mista'aravim," he replied. "You stay here."

"I want to go with you," Hood said.

The man shook his great head. "I was told that Mr. Herbert will personally kick my ass if anything happens to you." He pulled a fresh ammunition clip from the deep pockets of his pants and replaced the spent clip in his parabellum.

"What about the others?" Hood asked.

"Look for videotapes in here," the big man said. "If you find them, take them."

"All right," Hood said. "But the ambassador, my associates—"

"I'll see to them," the man said, "and I'll be back for you." With that, he turned and walked back along the corridor.

There was a sudden surge of gunfire in other parts of the palace. Save for the man's heavy footsteps, it was unnervingly quiet in this wing.

Hood returned to the monitor. He watched as the big man rejoined the others. The Mista'aravim were deep-cover Israeli Defense Force commandos who masquerade as Arabs. Herbert had very close contacts with the Israeli military, and had probably asked for help here. Their undercover nature was why the operative wanted Hood to look for tapes: There mustn't be a record of his face.

The five men stood along the wall on either side of the reception room door. They had divided into two groups and were putting something on the marble walls. Hood suspected that it was C-4. They'd use the plastic explosive to distract the Kurds while at the same time creating an opening through which they could fire.

Hood began searching for the tapes. He found two half-inch videotape machines in a cabinet under the console. He popped the tapes from each. Then he stopped and swore.

The tapes weren't the only records of the Mista'aravim. The Kurds had seen them too. For that, they would have to die. And to make absolutely certain that they did, the Israelis would probably pepper the room with gunfire before they went in. That was how the Israelis worked. Sometimes the good had to be sacrificed with the bad for the benefit of the rest.

But that wasn't how Hood worked. He picked up the phone.

"Warner," he whispered, "if you can hear me, stay put. I think all hell's about to—"

An instant later all hell did break loose. The alabaster walls exploded chest-high on both sides of the door and the masked Israelis stood at the openings. As the Kurds opened fire on them, the faster, more powerful Israeli rifles replied with one, deadly voice.

FIFTY-TWO

Tuesday, 3:43 p.m., the Bekaa Valley, Lebanon

When he saw the spray of blood, Phil Katzen screamed curses at Kurds. Oblivious to the sharp pains in his side, he tried to crawl up the slope to the roadway.

Falah laid his guns down. He put his arms around the American's waist and held him back. "Wait!" he cried. "Wait! Something is not right—"

Katzen pressed his forehead to the dry earth. "They killed her. Shot her without a thought!" He pounded his fists slowly on either side.

"I don't think so," Falah said. "Shhh . . . I think I hear her."

Katzen quieted. He heard the grinding of gears as the ROC drove off. Then he heard whimpering from the ledge. "Mary Rose?" Katzen wondered aloud. Other than the sobbing, there was absolute silence. Katzen glanced over at Falah. "If she's alive, something must have happened to the man who was going to shoot her."

"That is true," Falah said. He retrieved his guns. "It was probably his blood we saw."

"But how?" Katzen asked. "I don't see how any of

413

the other prisoners could have escaped. There were iron grates on those pits.''

"No one escaped,'' said Falah. "If they had there would be shouts, running around. Just the opposite has happened. No one is moving.'' He looked off to the south. He squinted. "If it was the Kurd who was shot, he had to have been picked off. I shut down the radio an hour ago. That would have enough time for a quick 'go' decision and rapid-deployment ingress.''

Striker, Katzen thought. He followed Falah's gaze.

Before Katzen could scan the trees for movement, someone shouted from above. He was yelling in English, threatening to kill three hostages.

"He's not talking to us,'' Falah said. "Someone sniped the killer. He's talking to them.''

"If that's true,'' Katzen said, "the ROC may spot whoever's out there.''

"We can't even take the ROC out,'' Falah said. "It seems the Kurds have moved it.'' He climbed over Katzen and handed him one of the guns. "You stay here. I'm going to try and find them, warn—''

Before he could move farther, there was a faint pop and then a whistle from the southeast. Katzen looked up as a small, black projectile rocketed toward the cave. Another came seconds later, followed by a third. They exploded in rapid succession, sending out thick copper-colored clouds.

"Neo-phosgene!'' Katzen said.

"What?'' Falah asked.

"A new lung agent,'' Katzen said. "It induces asthma-like effects for about five minutes. Striker's the only team that has it.''

At full dispersion the gas seemed to freeze, like cotton. Within moments the liquid content evaporated and the remaining vapor sunk to the ground in a thick pancake. The edges of the pancake crept toward the edge of the slope and spilled over. The men watched as Mary Rose fell forward. Her torso dopped over the ledge and she lay there gasping for breath.

"Come on," Katzen said. "The cloud itself will turn white and non-toxic in about two minutes. We may be able to get our people out before the Kurds recover."

"No," Falah said. "You stay here. Your broken ribs will slow us both down."

"Horseshit," Katzen said. "I'll look after Mary Rose, but I'm coming up."

Falah agreed, and began clawing up the slope. His speed and dexterity momentarily took Katzen aback. Being out of the field so much these days, he sometimes forgot the breathtaking skill with which indigenous people maneuvered in their native terrain.

Stretching out his leg on the side with the broken rib, Katzen tried to immobilize that side as much as possible. Tucking the gun in his belt, he began crawling up. All the while he cast looks above, to the south, and below. Despite being out of the field, he didn't forget the swiftness and surprise with which Striker struck. If neophosgene gave them a five-minute window to get in and wrap things up, they'd be here with everything wrapped up in five minutes or less.

As he was looking south, Katzen heard footsteps on the road above. He looked up. Falah was still climbing and the gas was still brownish, still potent. He couldn't see the road itself, but he saw the edges of the cloud swirl as though people were moving through it. Then someone appeared beside Mary Rose. He was wearing a camouflage uniform and a gas mask. He knelt beside her, put his arms around her shoulders, and carefully pulled her from the slope. Then he put her over his shoulder and was gone.

Falah practically vaulted up the last few yards to the ledge. Standing just outside the clearly defined edge of the gas, Falah looked back at Katzen. The Israeli smiled enthusiastically, gave Katzen a thumbs-up, then ran in the direction of the cave.

There was no longer any need for Katzen to continue his climb. With pain stabbing him from jaw to waist, he gladly settled belly-down on a soft patch of grass. He breathed using the "Buddha" technique he'd learned in first aid. He expanded his belly rather than his chest to minimize the pain of the broken rib.

As he lay there, contentedly listening to a concerto of faint but regular wheezing and the stop-and-start crunch of boots on dirt and pebbles, he was shocked alert by the sound of gunfire. From the echo, it sounded as if it were coming from deep within the cave.

Pulling one knee and his palms underneath him, Katzen struggled to drag himself the rest of the way up the slope.

FIFTY-THREE

Tuesday, 3:45 p.m.,
Damascus, Syria

Mahmoud had been leaning with both hands against a table beside the *mahmal* when the wall of the reception room blew in. He'd wanted to be a part of the defense of their small bastion, but he hadn't the strength. He hadn't even been able to check the room for stragglers who might have survived the blast engineered by their suicide bomber, Saber Mohseni.

Already weakened by a bullet in the leg and another in his left side, Mahmoud was shaken to the ground by the blast. Though shamed by his infirmity, he avoided the scythe of gunfire which slashed once across the room chest-high, and then once back again knee-high. The other Kurds were not so lucky. They'd taken up positions behind chairs and columns in the center of the room, braced for an attack. But the powerful Turkish-made G3 rifles cut them apart.

Lying with his cheek on the cold tile, Mahmoud listened as the gunfire died along with his troops. Unhurt in the latest fusillade, he left his eyes open just a crack. He stared across the floor covered with shattered crystal and broken bodies. He watched as a face appeared in each of the wall-openings. The bottom of their *kaffiyehs* had been pulled across the nose and mouth of each man. Mahmoud had suspected that these were not the President's elite bodyguard. Now he was certain. These men did not wish to be identified. Also, the President's bodyguards didn't shoot to kill. They used gas to debilitate foes so they could capture and torture them. The Syrian President liked to know about possible conspiracies and his inquisitors couldn't question a dead man. Finally, these men had shot blindly into a room containing the holy *mahmal*. No Muslim would have dared commit such sacrilege.

No, these men were not Syrians. Mahmoud suspected that they were Mista'aravim, Israelis who masqueraded as Syrians.

Mahmoud's gun was lying beside him in the dark. He picked it up. He could still help to make the goal a reality. His fingers tensed around the butt. His index finger slid through the trigger guard. There were still Syrian Kurds in the building and they were fighting on. So would he.

The men strode into the reception room. One man remained behind to watch the corridor while the others fanned out. Two men moved along the northern wall, two along the southern wall. They were all walking toward him as they peered through the dark, quickly checking the bodies as they made their way to the rear wall. They seemed to be looking for someone.

Mahmoud was dizzy from the loss of blood, but he fought to stay alert. The men were about twenty feet away. The two walking along the southern wall were making toward an alcove in the rear. The men moving along the northern wall passed a pair of ottomans. The backs of the divans had been splintered by their rifle fire. There were two small cedars in ceramic planters, one on either side of the ottomans. The trees had been chewed nearly in half.

Suddenly, something stirred behind the farthest tree.

"Watch out!" a voice cried in Syrian.

The voice was drowned out as Mahmoud opened fire on the two men near the planters. He put two rounds into the leg of the man nearest him. Then he shot at the second man, who fell, a bullet in his thigh. But as Mahmoud turned to fire at the men on the other side of the room, a dark form descended on him. A strong hand pinned Mahmoud's gun hand to the floor while a fist struck his jaw.

"Get back!" a different voice yelled.

The dark form jumped away. Mahmoud saw two rifles swing toward him. A moment later a shower of 9mm shells ripped into his body. His eyes closed reflexively as bullets punched his right shoulder, his back, his neck, his jaw, and his side. But there was no pain. When the shooting ended there was no sensation of any kind. Mahmoud was unable to move or breathe or even open his eyes.

Allah, I've failed, he thought as he was overcome by sadness. But then consciousness gave way to oblivion and failure, like success, no longer mattered.

FIFTY-FOUR

Tuesday, 3:51 p.m.,
Damascus, Syria

Warner Bicking rose. He held up his hands, one of which was bloodied from the punch he'd delivered to the Kurd's prominent jaw.

"I'm on your side," Bicking said in Syrian. "Do you understand?"

A short man with a high, scarred forehead hoisted his rifle into his armpit. As he walked toward Bicking, he motioned for his companion, a giant of a man, to go to the others. Bicking stole a glance to the right as the big man effortlessly picked up one of the men who'd been shot in the leg. He tossed the man over his shoulder, then lifted up the second.

"I'm an American," Bicking went on, "and these men are my colleagues." He cocked his head toward the planter, where Haveles and Nasr had also sought refuge. They rose.

The man standing watch at the door turned suddenly. "People are coming!"

The short man looked at his big companion. "Can you manage?"

The giant nodded as he shifted the weight of the man on his right shoulder. Then he held his rifle so it was pointing straight ahead, between the man's legs.

The short man turned to Bicking. "Come with us."

"Who are you people?" Haveles asked. The ambassador stepped forward unsteadily. He reminded Bicking of a car-crash victim who was in glassy-eyed shock but still insisted that he was okay.

"We were sent to collect you," the short man said. "You must come now or remain here."

"The representatives of Japan and Russia are in the room as well," Haveles said. "They're in the alcove over—"

"Only you," the short man said. He turned toward the door and motioned to the man standing who was there. The man nodded and headed left down the corridor. The short man turned back. "Now!"

Bicking took the ambassador by the arm. "Let's go. The palace guard will have to handle the rest of this."

"No," said Haveles. "I'll stay with the others."

"Mr. Ambassador, there's still fighting—"

"I'll stay," he insisted.

Bicking saw that there was no point arguing. "All right," he said. "We'll see you later at the embassy."

Haveles turned and took stiff, mechanical steps toward the dark alcove which doubled as a bar area. He joined the other men who had sought safety in the shadows.

The big man headed to the door, followed by the smaller man.

"Our train is pulling out," Nasr said as he walked past Bicking.

Bicking nodded and joined him.

The man who'd gone down the hall returned with Paul Hood. Hood handed the videotapes to the short man, and the group started down the hall. Two of the masked men were in front and the giant was in the rear.

"Where are the ambassadors?" Hood asked. "Is everyone all right?"

Bicking nodded. He glanced at his red knuckles. He hadn't punched anyone in six years. "Almost everyone," he said, thinking about the Kurd.

"What do you mean?"

"The Kurds are all dead and Ambassador Haveles is slightly shaken up," Bicking said. "But he decided to stay. Our escorts here were pretty specific about who they were willing to take."

"Only our group," Hood said.

"Right."

"And it probably cost Bob Herbert a lot of chits to get that."

"I'm sure," Bicking said. "Well, diplomatically, it's probably the smart thing for the ambassador to have done. There'd be a major international shitstorm if a rescue attempt favored Washington. Not that Japan or Russia would spit on an American diplomat if he were burning."

"You're wrong," Hood said. "I think they would."

The men continued down the corridor to a gold door. It was locked. The man in front shot off the knob and kicked the door in. They entered, the man in the rear closed the door, and the man in front turned on a flashlight. The group proceeded quickly through a grand ballroom. Even in the near-dark Bicking could feel the weight of the gold drapes, smell their long history.

There was a sudden clattering of boots outside the door. The three men of the Mista'aravim froze, their weapons turned toward the hallway. The flashlight was doused and the short man hurried back to the gold door.

"Continue straight ahead and wait by the kitchen," the giant man whispered to Hood, Nasr, and Bicking.

They did as they were told. As they walked, Hood looked back. The small man peeked through the hole where the knob used to be. When no one entered, the masked men rejoined them.

The small man said something to the others in Syrian.

"Presidential guards," Bicking translated for Hood as they ran through the enormous kitchen.

"Then this whole thing was a kabuki, as the ambassador suggested," said Nasr. He pushed back his wavy gray hair, which had become disheveled in the excitement. It immediately fell back over his forehead.

"What do you mean?" asked Hood.

"The Syrian President expected this to happen," Nasr said, "just as Ambassador Haveles predicted. He allowed his stand-in and the foreign ambassadors to take the heart of the attack, protected only by palace guards—"

"Who are like museum or bank security personnel in the U.S.," Bicking interjected. "They're trained for one-on-one response. If there's big trouble they have to call for help."

"Correct," said Nasr. "When the President was certain the Kurds had sent in the bulk of their force, he had his elite guards close the door on them."

"The President uses other nations as a buffer against his enemies," Bicking said. "He uses Lebanon to throw terrorists against Israel, Greece to fight Turkey, and helps Iran to create trouble around the world. We should have been prepared for him to do the same with people."

The sounds of gunfire increased. Hood imagined phalanxes of well-armed soldiers moving through the corridors, gunning down any and all opposition. Though wounded Kurds would be captured, he couldn't imagine any of them surrendering. Most would find death preferable to incarceration.

The men stopped at another door. The short leader told the others to wait. After withdrawing a small slab of C-4 from his pocket along with a timed detonator, he opened the door and exited. These people might not be the most personable men Bicking had ever met, but he was impressed by how prepared they were.

"Is Ambassador Haveles going to be safe?" Hood asked.

"That's difficult to say," Nasr admitted. "Whatever happens is a win-win situation for the Syrian President. If Haveles dies, it's the Kurds' fault and the U.S. declines to support them in the future. If he lives, then the elite guards are heroes and the President gets concessions from the U.S."

The short man returned and motioned the others ahead. The group passed through a large pantry to a door which led to a small outdoor garden. It was surrounded by a ten-foot-high stone fence with a ten-foot-high iron gate at the south end. They walked along a slate path through an immaculately manicured waist-high hedge. When they reached the end of the path, the short man stopped them. They waited some twenty feet from the gate. A moment later the lock exploded, blowing a hole in the gate and in the fence. Almost at once, a large truck with a canvas back pulled up to the curb. The short man ran ahead of the others.

The street was free of pedestrians. Either the fighting or the local police had chased them away. The street was also clear of news crews, which could not go anywhere without the government's consent. Though as Bicking thought about it, he realized that the government might have sent undercover operatives to the scene. That was probably why the group had taken the long way around. The men didn't want to be photographed.

The short man pulled the rear flap to one side. Then he motioned to the men at the gate.

As the men approached the truck, they were struck by the strong smell of fish. But that didn't stop them from boarding. Hood, Bicking, and Nasr climbed in first. They helped the giant man carry on his two wounded companions. Then the rest of the team got in. The wounded men lay on empty canvas sacks, while the other men sat on greasy wooden barrels which lined the back. In less than a minute the truck was on its way, headed southeast toward Straight Street. Turning left, the driver sped past the sixteen hundred year-old Roman Arch and the Church of the Virgin Mary. Straight Street became Bab Sharqi Street, and the truck continued northeast.

Nasr peeked out the back flap of the truck. "As I expected," said Nasr.

"What?" asked Hood.

Nasr shut the flap and leaned close to Hood. "We're avoiding the Jewish Quarter."

"I don't understand," Hood said. "What does that mean?"

Nasr bent even closer. "That we are almost certainly in the hands of the Mista'aravim. They would never operate out of that section of the city. If they were ever found out, the repercussions against the Jewish population would be severe."

Bicking had also leaned toward Hood. "And I'll bet everything I own that there's more than fish in these barrels. There's probably enough firepower in this truck to wage a small war."

The truck slowed as it made its way through the very narrow and twisted paths. Tall, white houses hung over the road at irregular distances and angles, their once-white walls burned an unhealthy yellow by the sun. Low dormers and even lower clotheslines rubbed the canvas top of the truck, while bicyclists and compact cars moved at their own unhurried pace and made it even more difficult to maneuver.

Eventually, the truck pulled into a dark, dead-end alley. The men got out and walked over to a wooden door on the driver's side of the alley. They were greeted by two women who helped carry the wounded men in to a dark, spare kitchen. The injured men were placed on blankets on the floor. The women removed their *kaffiyehs* and trousers, then washed the wounds.

"Is there anything we can do?" Hood asked.

No one answered.

"Don't take it personally," Nasr said quietly.

"I didn't," said Hood. "They've got other things on their minds."

"They'd be this way even if their men hadn't been shot," Nasr whispered. "They're paranoid about being seen."

"Understandably," said Bicking. "The Mista'aravim have infiltrated terrorists groups like Hamas and Hezbollah. They have safe houses like these when they need to work in absolute security. But if they were to be seen here it could cost them their lives and—much worse in their minds—compromise Israeli security. They certainly can't be very happy about having had to come out to save a bunch of Americans."

Even as the men spoke, the truck driver and the three masked men rose. While the short man made a telephone call, the others hugged the women. Then they left the dark room. Moments later the gears rattled and moaned as the truck backed from the alley.

One of the women continued to tend to the injured.

The other woman stood and faced the three newcomers. She was in her middle-to-late twenties and stood about five feet-two. Her auburn hair was worn in a tight bun, and her thick eyebrows made her brown eyes seem even darker. She had a round face, full lips, and olive skin. She wore a blood-stained apron over her black dress.

"Who is Hood?" she asked.

Hood raised a finger. "I am. Will your men be all right?"

"We believe so," she said. "A doctor has been sent for. But your associate is correct. The men were not happy about going out. They are even less happy that two of their men have been hurt. Their absence and their wounds will not be easy to explain."

"I understand," Hood said.

"You are in my cafe," the woman said. "You were a delivery of fish. In other words, you cannot be seen outside this room. We will get you to the embassy when we close for the day. I can't spare the people until then."

"I understand that as well."

"In the meantime," she said, "you've been asked to telephone a Mr. Herbert when you arrive. If you don't have your own telephone I'll have to get you one. The call cannot appear on our bill here."

Bicking reached into his pocket and pulled out his cellular phone. "Let's see if this one's still working," he said as he flipped it open. He turned it on, listened for a moment, then handed the phone to Hood. "Made in America and good as new."

"Also not secure," Hood said. "But it will have to do."

Hood walked over to a corner and called Op-Center. He was put through to Martha's office, where she, Herbert, and members of their staff had been waiting for word about the operation. Because it was an open line, he would only use first names.

"Martha—Bob," Hood said, "it's Paul. I'm on a cellular but I wanted you to know that Ahmed, Warner and I are fine. Thanks for everything you did."

Even standing a few yards away Bicking could hear the cheers rising from the telephone. His eyes moistened as he thought of the incredible relief they all must be feeling.

"What about Mike?" Hood asked, being as discreet as possible.

"He's been found," Herbert said, "and Brett is there. We're still waiting to hear."

"I'm on the cellular," Hood said. "Call me the instant you hear anything."

Hood hung up. As he briefed the others, the doctor arrived. The three men stepped to a corner, well out of the way. Then they watched in silence as the doctor gave the wounded men injections of local anesthetics. The woman who had spoken to them knelt beside one man. She lay a wooden spoon between his teeth, then held his arms pressed to his chest to keep him from flailing. When she nodded, the doctor began cutting the bullet from his leg. The other woman used a washcloth and a basin of water to wipe away the blood.

The man began to wriggle from the pain.

"I've always found that the toughest part about being a diplomat is when you have to say and do nothing," Bicking said softly to Hood.

Hood shook his head. "That isn't the toughest part," he whispered. "What's tough is knowing that compared to the people in the front lines, what you do *is* nothing."

At the doctor's request, the woman stopped cleaning the wound to hold the man's leg still. Without asking, Hood handed Bicking the phone, then hurried over. He picked up the cloth, maneuvered his arm between the three bodies, and dabbed at the blood as deftly as possible.

"Thank you," said the woman who had spoken to them.

Hood said nothing, and Bicking could see that it was very, very easy.

FIFTY-FIVE

Tuesday, 3:52 p.m., the Bekaa Valley, Lebanon

The Strikers had taken only what they needed from the FAVs. They were wearing their Kevlar vests beneath their uniforms and their gas masks. Their equipment sacks were packed with neo-phosgene grenades, flares, and several bricks of C-4. They were armed with Beretta 9mm pistols with extended magazines and Heckler & Koch MP5 SD3 9mm submachine guns with additional ammunition. They were also carrying plastic thumb-cuffs. These small, lightweight cuffs incapacitated individuals by locking them thumb-to-thumb, knuckle facing knuckle. The cuffs could also be used to create a daisy chain of prisoners.

The team had its orders, which had been given to them during the flight from Andrews Air Force Base. Since they knew that the target was going to be a cave or a base rather than a moving target, they would separate into two teams. The first team would muscle its way inside and incapacitate the enemy. The second team would back them up. The second team would also be responsible for preventing enemy troops from escaping or reinforcements from getting in.

If there were a difference between Colonel August and his predecessor, Lieutenant Colonel Squires, it was that August advocated team play. Squires invariably broke his unit into heavily armed pairs or individuals, each of which had specific goals in a master plan. If any of the tactical goals were not met, one of three things happened. An alternate plan was shifted into place, a backup team went in, or the mission was aborted. In his years of strike force command, Squires had never had to abort a mission. His infiltration techniques were unobtrusive, effective, and always left the target naked and surprised. But August was different. He preferred to hit hard and keep up the pressure. Instead of causing dominoes to fall in succession, he believed in shaking the table.

Corporal Prementine's A-Team, eight soldiers strong, quickly made their way up the dirt road toward the mouth of the cave. They moved single file behind their submachine guns with orders to shoot first and never mind the questions. By the time they reached the slab of coppery neo-phosgene, it had sunk from waist-high to just below the knees. It swirled thickly as the Strikers walked through—like stirred house paint, Prementine thought. The wiry corporal sent Private William Musicant, the company medic, to find and assist the woman the Kurds had been planning to execute.

Before Musicant could fall out, a voice came from their left, from the side of the slope.

"I will dwell in this land!"

Prementine stopped the Strikers with five fingers held face-high, palm-back. If he closed his fist, it would mean to open fire. The Strikers stood with their submachine guns ready. Though the correct password had been

431

given, Prementine knew that it could have been forced from one of the prisoners. He'd wait for the challenge to be answered before continuing.

They watched as a man climbed up past the cloud of neo-phosgene. His hands were raised. His gun hung by the trigger guard, which was around his left-hand index finger.

"Identify yourself!" Prementine said from under his mask.

"The Sheik of Midian," the man replied.

"Hold where you are," Prementine said. The corporal turned his hand sideways, thumb-back. Everyone was to continue what they'd been doing. Private Musicant went to the slope, while the Strikers pressed along the cliff leading to the mouth of the cave. They were less than twenty yards away.

The corporal made his way through the gas, which was now ankle-high. He stopped a few feet from the newcomer. The man kept his hands raised, but pointed down with his free index finger.

"Another of the hostages is down there alive," he said. "The other five are still inside. I have no idea where your van is. They moved it a few minutes ago. Possibly inside. I believe there's also an area in back to which they could have taken it."

Prementine kept his gun on the man as he looked over. He saw Phil Katzen less than ten feet down. He was painfully making his way up the slope. The environmentalist looked up and gave the Striker an okay sign. Below him, August and his team were just arriving. They fanned out along the bottom of the slope, and four of the eight soldiers began to climb. They would take up positions along the slope. To the right, the Strikers had divided. Three of them somersaulted together

432

through the gas to other side of the cave. No one from inside fired at them.

The corporal regarded the man standing in front of him. "Do you know where the prisoners are?"

"Yes," the man replied.

As they were speaking, Musicant returned. He had set Mary Rose down on the road, clear of the gas.

"Report," Prementine said.

"She's groggy but alive," Musicant replied.

"Take her down to Colonel August's group, then help Mr. Katzen," said Prementine. "And give the Sheik your mask."

"Yes, sir," Musicant replied. He was clearly disappointed not to be going in, but his manner was one of aggressive efficiency.

Musicant handed his gas mask to the man. Falah slipped his gun in his belt and pulled the mask on. As he did, Prementine turned to the Strikers at the mouth of the cave. As two Strikers set up a covering fire into the cave, shooting shoulder-high bursts, the other four pulled the wheezing Kurds and former hostages to one side. Clear of the gas, the Kurds were cuffed. Prementine leaned over the slope and held up two fingers. Two Strikers near the top of the slope scurried up to help recover the ROC personnel. There wasn't time to get them clear of the area. They would be killed with the rest of them if the Tomahawk struck. For now, however, they were moved to the foot of the slope, out of the line of fire.

The six A-Team Strikers regrouped on either side of the cave. They all watched the colonel as he held his hand face-high, palm-forward. An instant later he dropped it. The first two Strikers on either side of the cave tossed flares, then moved in behind them. They

433

hugged the inside wall as the next two Strikers moved in behind them.

The flares revealed five choking Kurds sprawled beneath a thin blanket of neo-phosgene. As the first two Strikers fired short, high bursts into the dying light, the two Strikers behind them moved in to cuff the enemy personnel. Once they'd been taken, the last group of two moved in to drag the prisoners out. When that was done, the two lead Strikers tossed neo-phosgene grenades ahead of them. As they exploded with a dull hiss, the Strikers threw in additional flares and repeated the maneuver.

Outside the cave, Prementine looked at his watch. The Tomahawk was due in seven minutes. He sought out August at the bottom of the slope and held up seven fingers.

August nodded.

Then he held up four fingers.

August nodded again.

Prementine looked at his companion. "We've got four minutes to get in and get the prisoners out." He pointed to the gun. "Use that if you have to. I want my people out of there."

"So do I," said Falah as he started toward the cave.

FIFTY-SIX

Tuesday, 3:55 p.m.,
the Bekaa Valley, Lebanon

Mike Rodgers was standing in the eight-foot-deep prison pit. He stood with his arms stretched above him, his fingers wrapped through the checkerboard grate. That was the only way he could prevent the burns up and down his arms from touching the burns along his sides. As it was, the salty trickle of sweat caused pain which made Rodgers's entire body shake.

Colonel Seden was in the pit beside him. The Turkish officer was awake but in pain. Private DeVonne had been feeding him rice and water until she, Coffey, and Private Pupshaw had been taken away. Except for an occasional moan from Seden and the nervous gum-chewing of the guard, the prison area was quiet.

Rodgers wished he knew why the others had been taken away. He suspected that they had been brought to the ROC. That bastard Phil Katzen must have turned it on and told the Kurds all that he knew about its operation. Then they'd brought out Mary Rose to force her to talk. Rodgers thought he'd heard a gunshot when they had her out there. He hoped they hadn't murdered the poor woman as an object lesson before bringing out the others. He hoped that almost as much as he hoped that the Kurdish commander remained alive until he could kill him.

Rodgers distracted himself by pushing his palms up against the grate to test it. It was unyielding. He poked a finger through the mesh fence that lined the pit, and dug at the dirt beneath the grate. The chicken wire didn't allow him to push his finger very far, and he gave up.

Then the shells exploded outside the cave. Rodgers stood there, listening. He thought he recognized the distinctive pop of Striker's NQ-doubleB—the Not Quite Big Bertha, their nickname for the compact cannon— but he couldn't be sure. The blast was followed by shouts from the front of the cave and from the sleeping quarters.

As he listened to the commotion, Rodgers took his hands from the grate. He stood unsteadily.

"Colonel Seden," Rodgers said, abandoning any pretense about their real identities. "Colonel, can you hear me?"

The colonel didn't answer. But neither did the guard. The fact that he hadn't told Rodgers to be quiet indicated that something unexpected had happened. Rodgers listened closely for a moment. He couldn't hear the popping of the man's gum. The guard wasn't even there.

"Colonel Seden!" Rodgers yelled.

"I hear you," he responded weakly.

"Colonel, can you tell me what's going on out there?"

"They were . . . shouting about a gas attack," said the Turk. "The Kurds . . . were trying to get to their masks."

Then it *is* gas, Rodgers thought. Colonel August's first-stage attack against a stationary position was to use neo-phosgene gas to incapacitate the enemy. Things were going to be happening quickly.

Encouraged and revitalized and wanting to join the fray, Rodgers pushed up on the grate again. Though it sat there like a perforated manhole cover, he couldn't push it up because of the bolt lying across the center. He tried pushing up one side and then the other, but it was too high. He couldn't muster the necessary force. He attempted to pull it down, but hanging there didn't put enough stress on the grate.

Standing under it, looking up, Rodgers suddenly realized that he needed torque to dislodge it. Painfully pulling off his shoes and socks, he fed the socks through the grate. One on the left side, one on the right. He pulled the ends back in and tied the top of each sock to its own bottom. Then he slipped his fingers through one end of the grate. Pulling himself up, he slid his feet into the stirrups he'd made from the socks.

Rodgers was in agony. His burned skin stretched and bled. But he wouldn't stop. He wouldn't let Striker find him caged like an animal waiting to die. He took a deep breath to increase his body weight. Then he jerked down with his arms while simultaneously kicking up with his feet. He felt the grate shudder. He pulled down with his hands and kicked up again. The center of the grate scraped roughly against the bar. The grate sunk a little on one end, rose a little on the other. Rodgers dropped down, his arms aching.

There were sounds of gunfire now. They were short bursts, cover fire. Striker had definitely arrived.

The top of the pit was rimmed by a metal hoop to which the chicken wire had been nailed. The hoop was slightly smaller than the grate and prevented it from turning further. But the rim was made of brass, which was thinner and softer than iron. The grate was already askew. Weight applied to one spot now might cause the hoop to bend and allow the grate to swing in.

Rodgers stood under the grate where it dipped into the pit. He forced his fingers through the tight spot between the hoop and the grate's edge. Holding tight, he hung straight down. Sweat burned his wounds, and he used the pain to fan his rage. He pulled his knees to his chest and dropped them suddenly. That added force to the downward pull. He waited a moment, then did it again. This time there was a loud screech as the edge of the grate pressed against the inside of the hoop. Rodgers felt the hoop give slightly. He continued to hang on the grate as it forced its way through the metal. After a few seconds Rodgers was able to squeeze through the opening. Fire from his wounds continued to fuel his determination. Though the grate was suspended nearly straight down now, Rodgers hung on. He extended one hand and grabbed the bar in the middle—the bar which had locked him in but now offered a way out. As soon as he had a grip on it, he reached out with the other hand. He hung there for a moment, as though preparing to do a chin-up. His arms were weary and shook violently. His fingers were cramped. But if he let go, he knew he wouldn't be able to jump high enough to reach the bar.

With a cry of hurt and anger, Rodgers lifted himself up so that his waist was bent against the bar. He rested there for a moment, then hoisted a leg over it. He lay flat, arms and legs wrapped around the bar, and shimmied the short distance to the side. When he reached the side of the pit, he stood.

And he screamed. He screamed from the suffering he'd endured, and he kept screaming with the inarticulate voice of triumph. Before the scream had died he'd snatched the bar from between the uprights of his former prison.

"I'll come back for you, Colonel," Rodgers said as he strode down the deserted corridor. There was an engine puttering somewhere in the north. When Rodgers reached the turnoff to the main tunnel, a flare erupted well to his right. He turned. Not to the south, to the flare and the opening of the cave. He knew what was down there. Instead, Rodgers turned to the left.

He moved along the corridor with his back close to the wall. He stuck to the shadows and walked with his knees bent. That allowed him to shift his weight from whichever leg was moving and enabled him to put his bare foot down as quietly as possible.

About fifteen yards in, Rodgers saw empty gun racks and two Kurdish soldiers. One soldier was talking on an old shortwave radio. From his agitated manner Rodgers surmised that he was either briefing a field force on the situation here or else calling for reinforcements. He was armed with a holstered pistol. The other soldier was standing guard with an AKM assault rifle. He was drawing hard on his hand-rolled cigarette. Well behind them were a pair of portable generators venting through hoses which ran along the floor deeper into the cavern.

Rodgers was no more than ten yards from the men. He continued along the wall, moving sideways. He tightened his hold on the iron bar. The pain in his arms and sides made him intensely alert. He stopped. The single overhead bulb lit a wide area around them. If he came any closer he'd be seen.

Rodgers took a moment to decide on the best approach. Then he extended his right arm diagonally so that the tip of the bar nearly touched the ground. He would have one shot.

He flicked his wrist back and then snapped it forward

hard, releasing the iron bar. It flew ahead, striking the armed guard in his right shin and bending him hard to that side. A moment after he threw the bar, Rodgers ran at the men. He was there when the guard bent, and he had his hands on the AKMC before the man could straighten and bring it to his shoulder. Rodgers pushed the butt into the man's groin, doubling him over. Then he pounded the side of his fist on the back of his head.

The guard released the weapon and went down. Rodgers drove the stock into the back of his neck and pointed the barrel at the radio operator.

The Kurd raised his hands. Rodgers disarmed the man and motioned for him to get up. He obeyed. Rodgers paused to take the cigarette from the fallen Kurd and poked it between his own lips. Then he retrieved the iron bar and walked the radio operator toward the back of the tunnel where there was a hint of daylight and the generators still puttered noisily.

FIFTY-SEVEN

Tuesday, 3:56 p.m.,
the Bekaa Valley, Lebanon

The A-Team Strikers stopped when they noticed the neo-phosgene gas rising above a portion of the floor of the main cavern. The two point men held up their hands for the others to wait, then went to explore the area.

Corporal Prementine stood with Falah in the mouth of the cave and watched in the dying light of the flare. The section of yellow gas was floating slightly above the rest in an almost rectangular shape. Only heat would cause it to rise like that. Heat from a room underground. An occupied room.

Prementine looked at his watch. The Tomahawk would arrive and detonate in six minutes. If the ROC were within a quarter mile of the cave, in any direction, the explosion would still take them out with it. They didn't have time to get clear. There were still two hostages to locate.

The point men knew that too. One of them reached into his kit and cut off a small block of C-4. He placed it on the door, jabbed in a small timer, and motioned the men back. They all lay flat in the fast-dissipating gas.

He joined them a moment later. Five seconds after that the charge detonated.

Iron fragments blew in all directions, zipping over the heads of several Strikers and barely missing Prementine. Gunfire erupted from underground. It drove Prementine from the mouth of the cave and prevented the Strikers inside from advancing.

Prementine realized that PKK fighters must have been able to get to gas masks and hunker down below. It was going to be difficult to get them out. There were no lights and the Strikers didn't have a clear shot down the stairs. Grenades weren't guaranteed to take down the enemy, and for all they knew Mike Rodgers and the Turkish officer were being held down there.

The Strikers were going to have to take the room, and quickly. That would entail four men moving forward. Two Strikers would jump down one after the other, quickly identify targets, and open fire. With any luck, their bullet-proof vests would take the brunt of the initial barrage. With a bit more luck they would be able to take out the enemy before anyone realized the Strikers were wearing vests. Once they'd established a beachhead, the other two men would have go down and help finish the job.

It was the most dangerous kind of operation. But given the amount of time left, it was the only option they had.

Prementine moved cautiously into the mouth of the cave. The flares had died and he knew that he was brightly backlit against the blue sky. But no one shot at him. He was far enough back so that the men in the underground room couldn't see him. He raised his hands to give the order which would put the four Strikers on alert: two fingers on each hand pointed up. The point men acknowledged the order with a low thumbs-up. But before Prementine could point his fingers ahead and send the men crawling over, he saw movement in the back of the cave.

He made two fists to put the men on hold, then watched as one figure and then another emerged slowly from the darkness. The man in front was a Kurd. He held two large, red plastic containers. The man in behind him held a rifle and a bar with a white handkerchief tied to the end. A lit cigarette hung from his lips. Prementine waited anxiously as they came closer to the light.

"General Rodgers!" he said softly as the bare-chested man came closer to the light. The man with him couldn't be the Turkish officer. Rodgers had the gun barrel pointed to the back of his head.

"He's been tortured," Falah said.

"I see," said Prementine.

"As soon as you can, you should get him out of there," Falah said. "I'll go in to get the other hostage."

Rodgers put the white flag down and raised a fist. He wanted the Strikers to wait. Prementine looked at his watch. The Tomahawk would be arriving in five minutes. They had to notify Op-Center in three minutes in order to have time to abort the detonation. The corporal knew that Colonel August would not make the call unless the area had been taken: If the ROC had been moved to some other site, August would be hard-pressed to explain why he ordered the abort. It was not a valid excuse to say, "To save the team and the hostages." In enemy hands, the ROC could be far more lethal in the long term.

His forehead and collar soaked with sweat, Prementine watched as the Kurd walked through the now-harmless white neo-phosgene. He set the containers down a foot behind the opening and unscrewed the caps. Rodgers stepped up next to him. He motioned for the

443

Kurd to raise his arms. The frightened radio operator did so. Rodgers put the rifle barrel under his chin. Using his bare foot, he gently knocked one container over, then the other. The clear contents spread over the floor and poured into the opening.

Rodgers pulled the Kurd back several paces, then casually dropped the cigarette into the gasoline. He continued to walk back as the room below lit up with a loud *whoosh*.

A rippling wave of heat poured up the stairs, forcing the Strikers to scurry backwards. Shrieks and flame shot up next, followed by burning bodies rushing wildly, sometimes blindly for the stairs.

"Help them!" Corporal Prementine shouted as he ran into the cave. The A-Team rose and Falah rushed in. Together, they pulled bodies from the steps as they emerged. Prementine dodged flames as he raced around the pit to Rodgers's side.

"Glad to see you, sir," he said, saluting.

"Corporal, Colonel Seden is in the back in one of the prison pits," Rodgers said. "The ROC is back there too, down the eastern fork of the tunnel. There are six or seven Kurds guarding it."

Prementine looked at his watch. "There's a Tomahawk due to impact in less than four minutes," he said. "That gives us two minutes to take the ROC." He turned. "A-Team, this way!" he shouted.

The Strikers stopped what they were doing and ran forward. As Prementine waved them down the eastern fork, he pulled his radio from its belt-strap.

"Colonel August," he said, "we need B-Team here as backup. General Rodgers requires medical assistance and there are a lot of wounded Kurds. We're moving ahead to the ROC. Please open the recall line."

"Acknowledged, Corporal," said August.

Prementine saluted Rodgers again as he started down the tunnel. When he arrived, one of his men was already cuffing the Kurd Rodgers had knocked down. The others had continued to the back of the tunnel. The corridor jogged left and right, then opened into a gorge. While the men hugged the wall behind him, Prementine looked out. The ROC was there, roughly fifty yards away. It was sitting under a ledge and facing them. There were two Kurds crouched on the dry brush close to the ROC on either side. At least two men were inside. It didn't appear as if anyone was using the ROC's electronics. Perhaps they didn't know how.

The Strikers had a little over a minute left to "disinfect" the ROC. It was still possible that the Strikers could step on a mine and the Kurds would be able to simply drive the ROC away. The team had to own the vehicle before they called Op-Center.

It struck Prementine as damned ironic that the ROC was bullet-proof and fire-resistant. The only contingency plan which had been designed to deal with a situation like the ROC falling under enemy influence was to destroy it with a missile. Once again he was faced with a situation in which his men would have to charge armed and fortified opponents. And win in sixty seconds.

"Corporal!"

Prementine turned as Colonel August arrived with Privates David George and Jason Scott.

"Yes, sir!" Prementine responded.

"Step aside," August said as the men set down and quickly assembled what they were carrying, their partially dismantled NQ-double B mortar.

"Yes, sir," Prementine said. "But Colonel, that may not—"

"Stow it, Corporal," August said. "I've debriefed

445

Mr. Katzen. He didn't tell the hijackers anything about the ROC's exterior capabilites.''

"Understood," said Prementine.

"Grey, Newmeyer," August said, "set up a cross fire on the ROC. If they fire, fire back. But make sure you don't hit the van or you'll blow our bluff."

"Yes, sir," both men replied as they went to opposite sides of the cave. They stayed just within the shadows. One of the Kurds fired a short burst at Private Newmeyer, who returned fire. No one was hit.

When Privates George and Scott were finished, August took a deep breath. He looked at the two men. "We have to allow the enemy to see us," he said. "I'll draw first fire, you follow."

The men acknowledged the order. August drew his Beretta from its holster and stepped from the dark at the side of the cavern. He moved quickly toward the cave mouth followed by the men.

Prementine looked at his watch. They had thirty seconds to place the call to Herbert. Radio operator Ishi Honda crouched beside him.

"Are you ready, Private?" the Corporal asked nervously.

"I've got Mr. Herbert on the line," he said, "and Mr. Herbert's got the White House on another line. I've briefed him. He knows our situation."

Prementine raised his submachine gun, ready to support the team. But his mind was on the missile and what its warhead would do to all of them if it detonated.

Bullets chewed into the cave floor as August came into view. He aimed at the ROC, fired, and kept walking. Prementine and Musicant also shot at the gunmen, and the Kurds were forced back. Privates George and Scott quickly set up the mortar. George aimed it at the van.

Colonel August holstered his Beretta. He faced the

van and held up his ten fingers so the men in the window could see.

"Ten!" he shouted, and folded a thumb in. "Nine!" he shouted, and dropped his pinky. "Eight . . . seven . . . six . . . five . . . four. . . ."

When he brought down the thumb of the other hand, that was obviously enough for the Kurds. The men on the side of the van scattered into the gorge. The two men who were inside the ROC ran for the passenger's side door. They jumped out and joined their comrades.

"Grey, Newmeyer, cover us!" August shouted. "Striker, advance!" he cried as he led the charge to the van.

Prementine remained behind with Honda. There were ten seconds left on the corporal's watch. Someone fired at August from a hillside. Grey shot back at the gunman and August kept running. He reached the door of the ROC and swung inside, followed by Privates Musicant, Scott, and George.

Prementine's heart drummed as he looked at his watch. There were five seconds left.

August leaned out the door. "It's ours!" he cried.

"Do it!" Prementine said to Honda.

"This is Striker B-Team!" Honda said into the phone. "The ROC is ours! Repeat! The ROC is ours!"

FIFTY-EIGHT

Tuesday, 8:00 a.m., Washington, D.C.

Bob Herbert actually had two lines open to the White House, just in case one of them went down. Martha Mackall's desk phone and also the cellular phone on his wheelchair were both connected to the office of the Chairman of the Joint Chiefs of Staff. Herbert was using the cell phone while Martha listened in on the other line. They were alone now, the night crew having left and the rest of the day team focusing on tensions which were still at a peak in the Middle East.

"Striker has retaken the ROC," Herbert told General Ken Vanzandt. "Request immediate Tomahawk abort."

"Acknowledged and hold," said Vanzandt.

Herbert listened as what he called the "ball and chain of command" made its way from the people at the site, through the military bureaucracy, back to the site again. He would never understand why the soldiers on the scene, the people whose lives were at risk, couldn't simply radio the HARDPLACE abort order to the missile. Or at least to Commander Breen on the USS *Pittsburgh*.

By this time, Vanzandt should have passed the word

to his Naval liaison. With any luck, he would call the submarine directly. And promptly. The missile was due to strike in just over two minutes, and there was no window for error or delay. The time it would take a member of this relay team to sneeze could bring the Tomahawk an eighth of a mile closer to its target.

"This is madness," Herbert grumbled.

"This is a necessary checks-and-balances," Martha said.

"Please, Martha," Herbert said. "I'm tired and I'm scared for our people there. Don't talk to me like I'm a goddamned intern."

"Don't act like one," Martha replied.

Herbert listened to the silence on the other end of the phone. It was only slightly more frustrating than Martha.

General Vanzandt came back on. "Bob, Commander Breen has the order and is passing it to his weapons officer."

"That's another fifteen-second delay—"

"Look, we're moving this as fast as we can."

"I know," Herbert said. "I know." He looked at his watch. "It'll take them at least another fifteen seconds to transmit. Longer if they're—*shit*!"

"What?" said Vanzandt.

"They can't use a satellite to relay the abort code," Herbert said. "The ROC has a window of interference that's going to screw up the download from the satellite."

Vanzandt echoed Herbert's oath. He got back on the phone to the submarine.

Herbert listened as the general spoke to Captain Breen. He wanted to wheel himself into a closet and hang himself. How could he have forgotten to mention that? *How?*

Vanzandt came back on. "They realized the satellite

wasn't responding and switched to direct radio transmission."

"That cost us some time," Herbert said through his teeth. "The missile's due to impact in one minute."

"There's still a bit of a window in there," said Vanzandt.

"Not much of one," Herbert said. "What'd they pack in that Tomahawk?"

"The standard thousand-pound high-explosive warhead," said Vanzandt.

"That'll take out ground zero plus a fifth of a mile in every direction," Herbert said.

"Hopefully, we can pull the plug well before then," said Vanzandt. "And if we do, then just the missile blows. Not the warhead. The team should be okay."

Herbert felt a jolt. "That's not true. What if the missile blows in the cave?"

"Why would it?" Martha asked. "Why would the missile even go into the cave?"

"Because the new generation of missile operates via LOS," Herbert said. He was thinking aloud, trying to figure out if he was right. "In the absence of geographical data, the Tomahawk identifies its target through a singular combination of visual, audio, satellite, and electronic data. The missile probably won't have visual contact because the ROC is behind a mountain, and the satellite's been shut down. But it will pick up electronic activity—probably through the cave, which is the most direct path. And the missile will go after it along that route. Sensors in the nose will warn it to stay away from everything which isn't the ROC, such as the sides of the cave."

"But not people," Martha said.

"The people are too small to notice," Herbert said. "Anyway, it isn't the impact I'm worried about. It's the abort itself. Even if the order is transmitted in time, it'll come when the missile is already inside the cave. Everything in the cave will be caught in the explosion.''

There was a short silence. Herbert looked at his watch. He grabbed the phone to Ishi Honda.

"Private, listen to me!" Herbert said.

"Sir?"

"Take cover!" he yelled. "Any cover! There's a chance the missile's going to abort in your laps!"

FIFTY-NINE

Tuesday, 4:01 p.m., the Bekaa Valley, Lebanon

Mike Rodgers had no desire to watch the B-Team Strikers help the Kurds. They were pulling burning bodies from the hell of the burning headquarters. The Strikers used dirt from the floor of the cave and even their own bodies to extinguish flaming clothes and hair and limbs. Then they began carrying them outside, to the light, where they could be given at least basic first aid.

Rodgers turned his own burned body from the rescue effort. He didn't like what he was thinking and feeling— that he hoped they suffered. Each one of them. He wanted them to hurt the way he did.

The general let his head roll back. Pain continued to flare along his arms and sides. Pain caused by a willful disregard for every legal and moral code. Pain ordered by a man who demeaned his cause and his people by inflicting it.

Rodgers walked back into the cave. He would rescue Seden later. Right now, he wanted to see if there was anything he could do to help take back the ROC. The

ROC which had been his to command, which he had lost.

He listened as he approached. There were gunshots, followed by Colonel August counting down. He arrived just as Ishi Honda radioed Op-Center that the ROC had been retaken.

Rodgers faded back against a wall. This was August's triumph and he had no right to share in it. He looked down and listened. He could hear the relief in the voices of the Strikers as A-Team moved in to secure the van. He felt nearly alone, though not quite. As the Italian poet Pavese had once written, "A man is never completely alone in this world. At the worst, he has the company of a boy, a youth, and by and by a grown man—the one he used to be." Rodgers had the company of the soldier and the man he'd been just a day before.

After what was only a few seconds but seemed much longer, Rodgers heard Private Honda call for Colonel August.

"Sir," Honda said quickly, "the Tomahawk may strike the ROC or abort in the cave in approximately forty seconds. We're advised to seek cover—"

"Strikers assemble on the double!" August yelled.

Rodgers ran toward them. "Colonel, this way!"

August looked at him. Rodgers was already running down the other fork.

"Follow the general!" August cried. "Ishi, radio B-team to get down the slope with the prisoners!"

"Yes, sir!"

Rodgers reached the prison section even as they heard the bass horn roar of the Tomahawk racing toward the cave. The general ordered the men to throw open the grates and jump into the pits. He opened Colonel Seden's prison himself, making sure that no one hurt him as they climbed in.

Private Honda was the last Striker into a pit. As soon as he was crouched down, his arms over his head, Rodgers stepped back. He stood in the end of the cave, listening to the bellowing as it grew louder. He felt proud of his countrymen as he thought of the Tomahawk, the result of applied American intellect, skill, spirit, and purpose. He felt that way about the ROC as well. Both machines had worked exactly as they were designed to. They did their jobs. So had the Strikers and he was deeply proud of them as well. As for himself, he would have wished for the blast to consume him, whatever form it took, were it not for the fact that his own job was not yet finished.

The walls and floor of the cavern shook. Particles of rock fell from the cave ceiling. The low thrum of the rocket engine grew deafening as the missile entered the cave.

No sooner had the walls of the main cavern begun to glow with the missile's exhaust than the Tomahawk exploded. The glow became an instant of white light, then a fierce red glow as the roar shook down rocks and dirt. Rodgers clapped his hands over his ears in a failed effort to block out the sound. He watched as flame rolled down the main corridor and fragments of the Tomahawk bounced, skidded, and flew along the cavern. Large and small pieces struck the mouth of the fork and ricocheted off the walls. Some were knife-edged sheets spinning edge-over-edge. Others were clumsy, smoking slag. Most fell to the ground before they reached the pits. One popped the light bulb, throwing the tunnel into darkness. Rodgers was forced to duck and turn his face to the wall, not to escape the shrapnel but to protect his face from a massive fist of heat which pounded him. From the time the intense temperatures surrounded him, it hurt to move and especially to breathe.

The sound died first, followed by the flames. A short time later the stifling heat released him. Rodgers heard coughing from the pits. He stood slowly and walked over.

"Is anyone hurt?"

There were a flurry of negatives. Rodgers reached down and pulled up the first soldier whose hand he could find. It was Sergeant Grey.

"Help the others," Rodgers said, "then put a detail together to find and secure the warhead. I'm going to see about the ROC."

"I think Colonel August already did that, sir," Grey said.

"What do you mean?" Rodgers asked. "Where is he?"

"He didn't come with us," Grey said. "He wanted to move the ROC farther away. He thought it'd give us a better chance if the Tomahawk hit it."

Rodgers told him to help the others out, then jogged toward the main corridor. He took the gun from his belt so he wouldn't lose it.

The cave had resisted the United States Navy's efforts to shut it down. There were chunks of still-burning missile embedded in the walls and strewn on the floor. It reminded Rodgers of Gustave Dore's etchings of Dante's Inferno. But the cavern was still whole and still navigable. He turned left, toward the gorge, drawing on the last reserves of stamina to reach his friend.

Rodgers saw the west-side mouth of the cave. He didn't see the ROC. As he came closer he looked out at the thick trees, the surrounding hills, flaming pieces of the missile, and long, late afternoon shadows. He didn't see the ROC. Then he noticed the dirt path which led to the road-cut. The ROC was parked about two hundred yards away. August was running back.

"General!" he yelled. "Is everyone all right?"

"A little scorched," Rodgers replied, "but otherwise okay."

"What about the warhead?"

"I sent Sergeant Grey and a small detachment to look for it."

August reached Rodgers's side. He grabbed his wrists and drew him gently toward the wall beneath the ledge. "There are still some armed Kurds in the hills," he said. He pulled his radio from his belt. "Private Honda?"

"Sir?"

"Let me have Corporal Prementine."

The NCO was on the radio a moment later.

"Corporal," said August, "is B-Team all right?"

"I'm with them now," he said. "They evacuated themselves and the surviving Kurds before the Tomahawk arrived. There were no injuries."

"Very good," August said. "I want you and three other men out here with the ROC on the double."

"What about an HP to find the rest of the enemy force?" Prementine asked.

"Negative on the hunting party," August said. "I want to get the ROC back on the road with everyone onboard as soon as possible. We're getting out of here."

"Yes, sir."

August replaced the radio. He looked at Rodgers. "Let's get you some medical attention, food, and rest, General."

"Why?" Rodgers asked. "Do I look that burned out?"

"Frankly, sir, yes. You do. Literally."

It took a moment for Rodgers to realize what August had said. When he did, he didn't smile. He couldn't. A piece of the process was missing. Rodgers could *feel* the hole, a void where his pride had been. You couldn't laugh at yourself if your self-worth wasn't strong enough to take the blow. The men walked to the cave in silence.

Inside the main tunnel, Sergeant Grey and his team had found the warhead. It had been slammed into the ground when the missile aborted. Remarkably, the warhead—which was located just forward of the fuel section, behind the TERCOM system and DSMAC Camera—was relatively intact. The detonation works were in a modular compartment atop the explosives. By following printed instructions inside the casing, the detonator could easily be reprogrammed or removed. August told Sergeant Grey to input a countdown, but not to start it until he gave the order.

Upon reaching the front of the cave, Colonel August and General Rodgers made their way down the road to the bottom of the slope. As they walked, August told Rodgers how Katzen had saved the Israeli's life by tackling his would-be murderers. By rescuing Falah, Katzen had made it possible for the Strikers to get inside as quickly as they did.

Rodgers felt ashamed of himself for having doubted the environmentalist. He should have realized that Katzen's compassion came from strength, not weakness.

At the base of the slope, Private Musicant, Falah, and members of the B-Team were tending to the injured Kurds as best they could. The thumb-cuffed prisoners had recovered from the neo-phosgene attack and were seated beneath a tree, their backs to the trunk. They were bound man-to-man, unable to run. The seven burn victims were spread out on the grass. Following Musicant's instructions, the Strikers used piles of branches to elevate the men's legs and help straighten their air ways. The medic had already given what little plasma he had to the more seriously burned. Now the men who had gone into hypovolemic shock were being given injections of an epinephrine solution. Falah, who had had some medical training in the Mista'aravim, was handling that.

With the exception of Colonel Seden, who was being cared for by Private DeVonne, the rest of the liberated ROC crew was sitting on boulders and leaning against trees close to the main road. They were looking out at the valley and were unaware of Rodgers's arrival. He wanted it that way for now.

"Private," said August, "I'd like you to have a look at General Rodgers as soon as possible."

"Yes, sir."

Rodgers looked over at Colonel Seden. Private DeVonne had removed his tattered shirt and was washing out his gunshot wound with alcohol. "I want him cared for first," Rodgers said.

"General," said August, "those wounds of yours need to be dressed."

"After the colonel," Rodgers said firmly. "That's an order."

August glanced down. Then he looked at Musicant. "See to it, Private."

"Yes, sir," said the medic.

Rodgers turned and stood over the Kurds. He looked down at a man on the far left. He was unconscious, with dark, leathery burns on his chest and arms. His breath came in irregular wheezes. "This man pointed a gun at Colonel Seden's head when he and I were first waylaid. His name is Ibrahim. He held the gun while his companion Hasan burned the colonel with a cigarette."

"Unfortunately," said Musicant, "I don't think Ibrahim is going to be standing trial for what he did. He's got third-degree burns on the anterior and posterior trunk and he has suffered possibly severe inhalation injuries. Circulating blood volume appears to be way down."

Rodgers usually felt bad for fighting men who had been wounded, regardless of their beliefs. But this man was a terrorist, not a soldier. Everything he had done, from blowing up an unfortified dam to ambushing the ROC, had been worked in whole or in part against unarmed civilians. Rodgers felt nothing for him.

August was looking into Rodgers's eyes. "General, come on. Sit down."

"In a minute." Rodgers moved to the next man. He had red, mottled burns on his arms, legs, and upper chest. He was awake and staring at the sky with angry eyes.

Rodgers idly pointed at him with the gun. "What about this one?" he asked.

"He's the healthiest of the bunch," Musicant replied. "Must be their leader. People were protecting him. He's got second-degree burns and mild shock. He'll live."

Rodgers stared at the man for a moment, then squatted beside him. "This is the man who tortured me," he said.

"We'll bring him back to the U.S. with us," August said. "He'll stand trial. He won't get away with what he did."

Rodgers was still looking at Siriner. The man was dazed, but those eyes were unrepentent. "And when he does stand trial," Rodgers said, "Americans working in Turkey will be kidnapped and executed. Or an American plane bound for Turkey will be blasted from the air. Or a corporation which does business with Turkey will be bombed. His trial and even a conviction will become America's ordeal. And do you know what's ironic?" Rodgers asked.

"No, General," August answered warily. "Tell me."

"The Kurds have a legitimate complaint." Rodgers stood. He was still looking down at Siriner. "The problem is, a trial will give them a daily forum. Because

459

they've been oppressed, the world will regard this man's terrorism as understandable or even necessary. Holding a torch to a man's body and threatening a woman with violent abuse become acts of heroism instead of sadism. People will say he was driven to it by the suffering of his people."

"Not all people will say that," said August. "We'll see to it."

"How?" Rodgers asked. "You can't reveal who you are."

"You'll testify," August said. "You'll talk to the press. You're articulate, a war hero."

"They'll say we made things worse by spying on them. That I invited retribution by killing one of them in Turkey. They'll say we destroyed their—what will they call this? A refuge. A bucolic retreat."

The hum of the ROC's eight-cylinder engine reached them as it emerged from the road-cut. August stepped between Siriner and General Rodgers.

"We'll talk about this later, sir," August said. "We accomplished our mission. Let's take pride in that."

Rodgers said nothing.

"Are you okay?"

Rodgers nodded.

August stepped away cautiously and turned on his field radio. "Sergeant Grey," he said, "stand by to initiate countdown."

"Yes, sir!"

August faced the Strikers. "The rest of you prepare to—"

August jumped as Rodgers's pistol fired. The colonel looked over. Rodgers's bare arm was extended almost straight down. Smoke twisted from the barrel and rose into Rodgers's unblinking eyes. He was staring at Siriner as blood oozed slowly from a raw hole in the commander's forehead.

August spun and pushed the gun up. Rodgers didn't resist.

"Your mission was finished, Brett, not mine," Rodgers said.

"Mike, what've you done?"

Rodgers looked at him. "Got my pride back."

When August released his arm, Rodgers walked calmly toward the road. The rest of the ROC crew had stood up at the gunshot and were looking over. Rodgers was able to smile now, and he did. He was looking forward to apologizing to Phil Katzen.

His face ashen, August ordered Musicant to finish with the Kurds and treat Colonel Seden as soon as they were onboard the ROC. Then he handed the gun to Private DeVonne, who had been looking at her fellow Strikers.

"Sir," she said urgently, "we didn't see that. None of us did. The Kurd was killed in a firefight."

August shook his head bitterly. "I've known Mike Rodgers for most of my life. He's never told a lie. I don't think he's planning on starting now."

"But they'll break him for this!" said DeVonne.

"I know!" August snapped. "That's what I was worried about. Mike is going to do exactly what he was afraid the Kurd would do. He's going to use his court-martial as a forum."

"For what?" DeVonne asked.

August took a quick, shaky breath. "For showing America how to deal with terrorists, Private, and for telling the world that America has had it." He headed for the road as the ROC arrived. *"Let's move it out!"* he shouted. "I want to blow this goddamn cave to Hell...."

SIXTY

Tuesday, 6:03 p.m.,
Damascus, Syria

A convoy of presidential security force cars pulled up at the American Embassy in Damascus at 5:45 p.m. Ambassador Haveles was escorted to the gates, where he was met by two United States Marine guards. A hearse took the bodies of the dead DSA operatives around to the back of the embassy. Haveles went directly to his office, composed despite the fright still in his eyes, and telephoned the Turkish Ambassador in Damascus. He explained to him his first-hand knowledge of what had happened in the palace, and also told him that it had been PKK soldiers, not Syrians, who had been behind the theft of the border patrol helicopter, the attack on the Ataturk Dam, and the incident at the Syrian border. He urged the ambassador to brief the military and ask them to stand down. The ambassador said he would pass along the information.

Paul Hood arrived a few minutes later. He, Warner Bicking, and Professor Nasr had been dressed in *kaffiyehs* and sunglasses and escorted to a bus stop. Hood had always found the idea of disguises a theatrical extravagance when they appeared in movies and novels. In real life, he walked the third of a mile as if he were born and raised on Ibn Assaker Street. He had to. If he were recognized by a journalist or foreign official, it would jeopardize the two women who had come with him.

But he wasn't spotted. Though buses were being diverted around the Old City, the three men reached the embassy in just a half hour. Stopped by two Marine guards, Hood felt like Claude Rains in *The Invisible Man* as he unwrapped his disguise to show the sentries that he was who he said he was. Watching the front gate on closed-circuit camera, a DSA agent hurried out to usher the three men inside.

Hood went directly to the nearest office to telephone Bob Herbert. He shut the door of Deputy Ambassador John LeCoz's chambers and stood alone beside the old mahogany desk. The heavy, drawn drapes cloaked the small office in deep dark and muted silence. Hood felt safe. As he punched in the number of Herbert's wheelchair phone, it flashed through his mind that Sharon and the kids might have heard about events in Damascus. They might be worried. He hesitated, then decided he'd call them next. He didn't want to rush them off the phone, but he had to know about the ROC.

Herbert answered on the first ring. He was uncharacteristically subdued as he told Hood the good news. The Tomahawk had been aborted. Striker had gone in, rescued the ROC and its crew, and all were now safely back at Tel Nef. Syrian Army forces had been alerted about the wounded Kurds and had gone to collect them. In a short interview with CNN, the leader of the SAA force had ascribed the explosion at the cave to PKK mishandling of munitions—but only after the U.S. had agreed to allow Syrian security officials to interrogate the survivors while insisting there weren't any. They wanted to know everything about how Syrian security had been breached in Damascus and at Qamishli. Haveles's deputy ambassador had agreed to that after consulting with General Vanzandt.

Hood was elated until Herbert informed him of Mike Rodgers's torture and his execution of the Kurdish leader who ordered it.

Hood was quiet for a moment, then asked, "Who witnessed the killing?"

"That's not going to fly," Herbert said. "Mike wants people to know what he did and why he did it."

"He's been through Hell," Hood said dismissively. "We'll talk to him after he's rested."

"Paul—"

"He'll budge on this," Hood said. "He has to. If Mike is court-martialed, he'll be forced to talk about what he was doing in Turkey and why. He'll have to reveal contacts, methods, talk about other operations we've mounted."

"In situations involving national security, the records of the court-martial can be sealed."

"The press will still cover it," Hood said, "and they'll be all over us. This could literally bring down American intelligence operations in the Middle East. What about Colonel August? He's Mike's oldest friend. Can't he do anything?"

"Don't you think he tried?" Herbert asked. "Mike told him that terrorism is a greater threat than anything else America is facing today. He says it's time we fought fire with fire."

"He's got to be in shock," Hood concluded.

"He was checked at Tel Nef," Herbert replied. "He's sound."

"After what the Kurds did to him?" Hood said.

"Mike's been to Hell a whole lotta times and made it back okay," Herbert replied. "Anyway, the Israeli medics say he's mentally fit and Mike himself says he's thought this through."

Hood reached for a pen and pad. "What's the telephone number at the base? I want to talk to him before he does anything he'll regret."

"You can't talk to him," Herbert said.

"Why not?"

"Because he's already done the 'anything,'" Herbert said.

Hood felt his insides tighten. "What did he do, Bob?"

"He phoned General Thomas Esposito, the Commander in Chief, U.S. Special Operations Command, and confessed to the killing," Herbert said. "Mike's now under armed guard at the infirmary in Tel Nef waiting for military police and legal counsel to arrive from the Incirlik Air Base."

Hood suddenly became aware of the mustiness of the drapes. The room no longer seemed safe. It was suffocating. "All right," Hood said calmly. "Give me some options. There have got to be options."

"Only one that I can think of," Herbert said, "and it's a long shot. We can try to get Mike a Presidential pardon."

Hood perked up. "I like that."

"I thought you would," Herbert said. "I already called General Vanzandt and Steve Burkow and explained the situation to them. They're with us. Especially Steve, which surprised the hell out of me."

"What are our chances?" Hood asked.

"If we can keep the story from breaking for a few hours, we've got a slim chance," said Herbert. "I've got Ann watching out for that. Once the press gets it, the President won't consider acting until after the case has been heard. An American general cold-bloodedly executes a wounded, unarmed Kurd—the political risks at home and abroad are just too great."

"Sure," Hood said disgustedly. "Even though the Kurd took a blowtorch to the general."

"The general was a spy," Herbert reminded him. "World opinion ain't gonna be with us on this one, Paul."

"No, I guess it won't," Hood said. "Who else can we get to try and persuade the President?"

"The Secretary of Defense is with us, and he's meeting with the Vice President in about ten minutes. We'll see what happens. So far, Ann says that reporters haven't been asking much about the seven Kurds who were injured in the Bekaa. They bought the story the SAA commander gave them. As long as the press is fixated on what they're calling the Border Buildup, that story may slip through the cracks. If it does, we may slip through with it."

"Work the pardon, Robert," Hood said. "I want you and Martha to call in every chit you have."

"We will," Herbert promised.

"Christ," Hood said, "I feel completely useless being stuck out here. Is there anything I can do?"

"Just one thing," Herbert said, "something I really don't think I'll have time to do."

"What's that?" asked Hood.

"Pray," Herbert said. "Pray hard."

SIXTY-ONE

Tuesday, 12:38 p.m., Washington, D.C.

Bob Herbert sat in his wheelchair reading an Eyes Only copy of the single-page document. It was addressed to the Attorney General of the United States and printed on White House letterhead.

Behind his desk the President read a copy of the document as well. Scattered around the Oval Office, standing or sitting, were National Security Advisor Burkow, Chairman of the Joint Chiefs of Staff General Vanzandt, White House legal counsel Roland Rizzi, and Martha Mackall. Each was reading a printout of the paper. Herbert, Rizzi, Burkow, and Vanzandt knew the document well. They had spent the last ninety minutes drafting it, after hearing from Rizzi that the President would consider signing a paper which pardoned General Mike Rodgers.

The President cleared his throat. After reading the paper once, he went back to the top to read it aloud. He always did that, to hear how it would sound as a speech—in case he ever had to defend in public what he'd done.

"I hereby grant a full, free, and absolute pardon to General Michael Rodgers of the United States Army. This pardon is for confessed actions which he has or may have committed while loyally serving his country in a joint intelligence effort with the Republic of Turkey.

"The government and people of the United States have benefited immeasurably from the courage and leadership of General Rodgers throughout his long and unblemished military career. Neither this nation nor its institutions would be well or responsibly served by a further scrutiny of actions which, from all accounts, were heroic, selfless, and appropriate."

The President nodded and tapped his index fingers absently on the paper. He looked to his left. The stout, balding Roland Rizzi was standing beside the desk.

"This is good, Rollo."

"Thank you, Mr. President."

"What's more"—he smiled—"I believe it. I don't often get to say that about documents which I'm asked to sign."

Martha and Vanzandt chuckled.

"The dead man," said the President. "He was a Syrian citizen shot in Lebanon."

"That's correct, sir."

"Should they decide to pressure us, what jurisdiction do Damascus and Beirut have in this matter?"

"Theoretically," said Rizzi, "they could demand General Rodgers's extradition. Even if they did, however, we would not accede to that."

"Syria has given sanctuary to more international criminals than any nation on earth," said Burkow. "I, for one, would love for them to ask just so we could tell them no."

"Could they make things rough for us in the press?" asked the President.

"They'd need proof for that, sir," said Rizzi. "And also to push for General Rodgers's extradition."

"And where is that proof?" the President asked. "Where is the body of the dead Kurdish leader?"

"It's in the cave that used to be their headquarters," said Bob Herbert. "Before they left the area, Striker blew it up with the Tomahawk warhead."

"Our press department put out the story that he was killed in an explosion at his headquarters," Martha said. "No one will question that, and it will satisfy the Kurds who followed him."

"Very good," said the President. He picked up a black fountain pen from his blotter. He hesitated. "Do we know that General Rodgers will toe the mark? I don't have to worry about him writing a book or talking to the press?"

"I'll vouch for General Rodgers," said Vanzandt. "He's a company man."

"I'll hold you to that," the President said as he affixed his signature to the bottom of the document.

Rizzi removed the pardon and the pen from the President's desk. The President rose and the group began moving to the door. As they did, Rizzi walked over to Herbert and handed the pen to him. The intelligence chief held it tightly, triumphantly, before tucking it into his shirt pocket.

"Remind General Rodgers that whatever he does henceforth not only affects him but the lives and careers of the people who believed in him," Rizzi said.

"Mike won't have to be told," Herbert said.

"He went through quite an ordeal in Lebanon," Rizzi said. "Make sure he gets some rest."

Martha walked over. "We'll see to it, of course," she said. "And thank you, Roland, for everything you've done."

Martha and Herbert left, Herbert waving playfully at Deputy Chief of Staff Klaw, who had come to escort them out.

As the group made their way in silence through the carpeted corridor, Herbert had confidence in what General Vanzandt had said. Mike Rodgers would never do anything to compromise or embarrass those who had fought for him today. But Rizzi was also right: Rodgers had been through a lot. Not just the torture. When Rodgers returned with Striker the next day, what was going to bother him more was the fact that the ROC had been captured on his watch. Rightly or wrongly, he would blame himself for the near-loss of the facility and the physical suffering and psychological wounds endured by the ROC crew and Colonel Seden. He would have to live with the knowledge that Striker was nearly wiped out by friendly fire because of what he hadn't anticipated. According to psychologist Liz Gordon, who had bumped into Herbert as he left Op-Center to come to the White House, those were going to be the toughest crosses to bear.

"And there's no sure way of treating that guilt," she'd told him. "With some people you can reason it out. You can convince them that there was nothing they could have done to prevent the situation. Or at least you can make them feel good about other things they've accomplished, their positive body of work. With Mike, there's black and there's white. Either he screwed up or he didn't. Either the terrorist deserved to die or he didn't. Add to that the loss of dignity he and his people suffered—and their suffering was his suffering, you can be very sure of that—and you've got a potentially very knotty psychosis."

Herbert understood only too well. He was intelligence point man for the CIA in Beirut when the embassy was bombed in 1983. Among the scores of dead was his wife. Not a day passed when he wasn't troubled by guilt and what-ifs. But he couldn't let them stop him. He had to use what he'd learned to try and prevent future Beiruts.

Herbert and Martha made their way from the White House entrance to the specially equipped van in which Herbert traveled around Washington. As he rolled up the ramp into the back, he had just one hope. That a little time, a lot of distance, and a great deal of camaraderie would get Rodgers through this. As Herbert had put it to Liz, "I learned the hard way that not only is life a school, but the classes get damned difficult and more expensive as you move through it."

Liz had agreed. Then she'd added, "Still, Bob—it does beat the hell out of matriculation."

That was true, Herbert thought as Martha's driver maneuvered from the tight parking lot toward Pennsylvania Avenue. And over the next few days or weeks or however long it took, he would make it his mission to convince Mike Rodgers of that.

SIXTY-TWO

Wednesday, 11:34 p.m., Damascus, Syria

Ibrahim al-Rashid opened his eyes and peered through the dirty window of the prison hospital ward. His nostrils filled with the smell of disinfectant.

Ibrahim knew that he was in Damascus in the custody of Syrian security forces. He also knew that he was seriously injured, though he didn't know how seriously. He knew these things because when he drifted out of sleep he heard the male nurses and guards talking about him. He heard them distant and muffled through the bandages which covered his ears.

During the short periods when he was awake, Ibrahim was dimly aware of other things. He was aware of being talked to by a man in a uniform but being unable to answer. His mouth seemed frozen, incapable of being moved. He was aware of being carried to a bath where parts of his body were stripped and scrubbed. His skin seemed to come off in pieces, like hardened candle wax. Then he was bandaged and brought back here again.

When he slept, the young Kurd had much clearer visions. He had memories of being with Commander Siriner at Base Deir. Ibrahim could still hear the leader shouting, "They will not fire a shot in these headquarters!" He remembered standing shoulder to shoulder with the commander and shooting at the enemy to keep them from entering. He remembered shouting defiance, waiting for the attack—and then there was the fire. A lake of it pouring down on them. He remembered fighting the flames with his arms, helping Field Commander Arkin beat a path with their own bodies so that Commander Siriner could get through. He remembered being pulled up, covered with dirt, carried somewhere, seeing the sky, and then hearing a gunshot.

A tear formed in his eye. "Commander—?"

Ibrahim tried to turn and look for his comrades. But he couldn't. The bandages, he realized. Not that it mattered. He sensed that he was alone in this place. And the revolution? If it had succeeded, he would not be here with the enemy.

So many people counting on us and we failed, he thought.

Yet did they fail? Is it failure if you plant a seed which others nurture? Is it failure to have begun a thing which had daunted the best and the bravest for decades? Is it failure to have called the attention of all humanity to the plight of his people?

Ibrahim closed his eyes. He saw Commander Siriner and Walid, Hasan and the others. And he saw his brother Mahmoud. They were alive and watching him and they seemed to be content.

Is it failure if you are united in Paradise with your brothers-in-arms?

With a quiet moan, Ibrahim joined them.

SIXTY-THREE

Wednesday, 9:37 p.m., London, England

Paul Hood spoke to Mike Rodgers while Hood was in London en route to Washington. Rodgers was about to leave the infirmary at Tel Nef to join the Strikers for the flight back to Washington.

The men had a short, uncommonly strained conversation. Whether he was afraid of releasing rage, frustration, sadness, or whatever else he was feeling, Rodgers wasn't letting go of anything. Getting the general to answer questions about his health and the accomodations at Tel Nef took very specific questions. And even then his answers were terse, his voice flat. Hood ascribed it to exhaustion and the depression that Liz had warned them about.

When he'd placed the call, Hood hadn't intended to tell Rodgers about the pardon. He'd felt that that was something best done when Rodgers was rested and surrounded by the people who had orchestrated the amnesty. People whose judgment he respected. People who could explain that it had been done to protect the national interest and not to bail Rodgers out.

Ultimately, however, Hood felt that Rodgers had a right to know what had transpired. He wanted him to use the flight to plan for his future in Op-Center and not an imagined future in court.

Rodgers took the news quietly. He asked Hood to thank Herbert and Martha for their efforts. But as he spoke, Hood had an even stronger sense that there was something else taking place, something unspoken that had come between them. It wasn't bitterness or rancor. It was something almost melancholy, as if he'd been doomed rather than saved.

It was almost like he was saying good-bye.

After hanging up with Rodgers, Hood called Colonel August. Rodgers and the Striker commander had grown up together in Hartford, Connecticut. Hood asked him to use whatever stories or jokes or reminiscences it took to keep Rodgers diverted and amused. August promised that he would.

Hood and Bicking bid a warm farewell to Professor Nasr at Heathrow, and promised to come and hear his wife play Liszt and Chopin. However, Bicking did ask him to have the pianist consider replacing the *Revolutionary Etude* with something less politically charged. Nasr did not disagree.

The State Department flight from London had been relaxed and filled with uncustomarily sincere compliments for Hood. They were nothing like the surface-deep congratulations which he sometimes received at meetings and receptions in Washington. Officials on the plane seemed delighted with rumors that Striker had broken a slew of secular laws in the Bekaa Valley. They were almost as happy with that as they were that the Ataturk terrorists had been found and neutralized and that Turkish and Syrian troops had withdrawn from their common border. As Deputy Assistant Secretary of State

Tom Andrea put it, "You get tired of playing by the rules when everyone else isn't."

Andrea also pressed for details on who had helped Hood, Bicking, and Nasr escape the palace assault in Damascus. But Hood only sipped the Tab Clear he'd picked up in London and said nothing.

The plane landed at 10:30 p.m. on Wednesday. An honor guard was waiting for the fallen DSA operatives, and Hood stayed with them on the tarmac until the coffins had been unloaded and driven away. Then he got in the limousine which was waiting to take him and Warner Bicking home. The car had been sent by Stephanie Klaw at the White House, who had also sent along a note.

"Paul," it read, "welcome home. I was afraid you might take a cab."

The car took Hood home first. He held Bicking's hand between his before climbing out.

"How does it feel to have been the pawn of two Presidents?" Hood asked.

The young Bicking smiled and replied, "Invigorating, Paul."

Hood spent an hour lying in bed with his kids. After that, he spent two hours making love to his wife.

And after that, with his wife curled beside him, her hand in his, he lay awake wondering if he'd made the mistake of his life telling Mike Rodgers about the pardon.

SIXTY-FOUR

Thursday, 1:01 a.m.,
Over the Mediterranean Sea

When Mike Rodgers had first enlisted in the Army, he had a drill sergeant named Messy Boyd. He never found out what Messy was short for, but it had to be short for something. Because Messy Boyd was the neatest, most punctilious, most disciplined man that Rodgers had ever met.

Unfailingly, Sergeant Boyd drilled two things into his men. One was that bravery was the most important quality a soldier could have. And the other, that honor was even more important than bravery. "The honorable man," he had said, paraphrasing Woodrow Wilson, "is one who has squared his conduct by ideals of duty."

Rodgers took that to heart. He also borrowed the copy of Bartlett's *Familiar Quotations* Boyd kept on his desk. That started him on his twenty-five-year love affair with the wisdom of the great statesmen, soldiers, scholars, and others. It turned him into a rapacious reader, devouring everyone from Epictetus to St. Augustine, from Homer to Hemingway. It made him think.

Maybe too much, he told himself.

Rodgers sat on the wooden bench in the bumpy fuselage of the C-141B. He was absently listening to Colonel August tell Lowell Coffey and Phil Katzen about their Little League home-run rivalry with each other.

Rodgers knew that he had never acted in a cowardly way, nor had he ever behaved with dishonor. Yet Rodgers also knew that because of what had happened in the Middle East, his career as a soldier was over. He had thought it ended when he failed to retake the ROC from the Kurds at the Syrian border. That had been clumsy and stupid, the kind of mistake a man in his position could not afford to make. But with the death of the PKK leader he had found new life. Not as a soldier in the field, but as a soldier in the fight against terrorism. What would have begun in the courtroom would have become a brave and honorable battle against a terrible scourge.

Now, he thought, there's nothing.

"General," August asked, "what was the name of that catcher who ended up beating us both out in fifth grade?"

"Laurette," Rodgers replied. "I forget her last name."

"Right," said August. "Laurette. The kind of girl you wanted to sop up with a biscuit. She was that lovely, even behind her catcher's mask, glove, and a wad of Bazooka bubble gum."

Rodgers smiled. She *was* cute. And that home-run showdown had been quite a race. But races ended with one winner and several losers.

Like the race we just ran in the Middle East.

The winner there had been Striker. Their performance had been exemplary. The losers? The Kurds, who had been crushed. Turkey and Syria, which still had millions of restless citizens within their borders. And Mike Rodgers, who had bungled security, escape, judging the character of a loyal coworker, and handling a prisoner of war.

America had lost too. It had lost by tucking Mike Rodgers back in his Op-Center cubicle instead of supporting him in the war against terrorism.

And it is a war—or at least it needs to be.

As he'd lain there in the infirmary, Rodgers had sharpened his thinking about that. He'd planned to use the podium of his court-martial to declare that any nation which attacked our people anywhere, in any way, had effectively declared war on us. He'd further planned to urge the President to declare war on any nation which kidnapped our citizens or blew up our aircraft or bombed our buildings. Declaring war did not necessarily mean we'd attack the people and soldiers of those nations. But it would leave us free to blockade their ports and sink any ships that tried to get in or out. To shut down their airports and roadways with missiles. To halt commerce, destroy their economy, and topple the regime which had backed terrorists.

When the terrorism ended, the war would end.

That was what Rodgers had planned. If executing the Kurd could have been the first shot across the prow of terrorism, he would have regained his honor. As it was, having killed the unarmed man who had tortured him was just revenge. There was no honor or bravery in that. As Charlotte Brontë had once written, vengeance was "as aromatic wine it seemed, on swallowing, warm and racy; its after-flavour, metallic and corroding."

Rodgers looked down. He didn't wish he could take the bullet back. Killing the Kurdish leader had spared the nation the agonies of the trial, of Op-Ed justice and handwringing. It had also given the Kurds a martyr instead of a loser. But God, how he wished the bullet had taken them both. He had been trained to serve his country and to protect its integrity and its flag at all costs. The pardon was a blot on both. By showing him charity, his nation had lost sight of a more important quality: Justice.

The error was made by well-meaning people. But for the sake of his country's honor, it was an error which had to be undone.

Rodgers stood stiffly, constricted by the bandages around his arms and torso. He steadied himself on the rope which ran shoulder-high along the fuselage.

August looked up. "You okay?"

"Yes." He smiled. "Just going to the bathroom."

He looked down at the uncharacteristically effervescent Colonel August. He was proud of him and glad he'd won the race. Rodgers turned and headed to the back.

The bathroom was a cold room with a hanging lightbulb and a toilet. There was no door, one of those small touches designed to keep the weight of the aircraft down.

On the way back, Rodgers passed aluminum shelves which carried Striker's equipment. He stopped. His own gear was in a duffel bag he'd had in the ROC. There was still one way to regain his honor.

"It's not there," said a voice from behind him.

Rodgers turned. He looked into Colonel August's long, apostolic face.

"The gun you used to execute the terrorist," August went on. "I took it."

Rodgers squared his shoulders. "You had no right to go into another officer's grip, Colonel."

"Actually, sir, I did. As the ranking officer not a party to a confessed crime, it was my duty to confiscate evidence for the court-martial."

"I've been pardoned," Rodgers said.

"I know that now," August replied. "I didn't know it then. Would you like the gun back, sir?"

Their eyes remained locked. "Yes," Rodgers said. "I would."

"Is that an order?"

"Yes, Colonel. It is."

August turned and squatted beside the lowest of the three shelves. He opened the first of the five cases which contained Striker's handguns. He handed the pistol to Rodgers. "There you are, sir."

"Thank you, Colonel."

"You're welcome, sir. Is the general planning to use it?"

"That's the general's business, I think."

"It's a debatable point," August said. "You're seriously overwrought. You're also threatening my superior officer, a general of the United States Army. I'm sworn to defend my fellow soldiers."

"And to follow orders," Rodgers said. "Please return to your seat."

"No, sir," August said.

Rodgers stood with the gun at his side. Half a plane away, Private DeVonne and Sergeant Grey had gotten off the bench. They looked like they were ready to rush over.

"Colonel," Rodgers said, "the nation made a grave mistake today. It forgave a man who neither deserved nor wanted forgiveness. In so doing it endangered the security of its people and institutions."

"What you're planning won't change that," August said.

"It will for me."

"That's damned selfish, sir," August said. "Permit me to remind the general that when he came in second to Laurette What's-Her-Name, he didn't think he could live with that either. As she rounded the bases he swung an angry bat so hard that had he not been stopped by

481

his frightened best friend, he would have struck himself in the back of the head and probably suffered a serious concussion. But life went on and the former first baseman saved countless lives in Southeast Asia, Desert Storm, and more recently in North Korea. If the general intends to hit himself in the head again, be advised that the former second baseman will stop him again. This nation needs him alive."

Rodgers looked at Colonel August. "Does it need that more than it needs honor?"

"A nation's honor is in the hearts of its people," August said. "If you still your heart, you rob the nation of what you claim you want to preserve. Life hurts, but we've both seen enough death. We all have."

Rodgers's gaze returned to the Strikers. There was something alive in their faces, in their posture. Despite everything they'd endured in Lebanon, despite the death of Private Moore in North Korea and Lieutenant Colonel Squires in Russia, they were still fresh and enthusiastic and hopeful. They had faith in themselves and in the system.

Slowly, Rodgers put the gun on the shelf. He didn't know if he agreed with August about the rest of it. But what he'd been about to do would have killed their enthusiasm stone-cold dead. That in itself was enough to give him pause.

"Her name was Delguercio," Rodgers said. "Laurette Delguercio."

August smiled. "I know. Mike Rodgers doesn't forget anything. I'd just wanted to see if you were paying attention to the story. You weren't. That's why I followed you back here."

"Thanks, Brett," he said quietly.

August pursed his lips and nodded.

"So," Rodgers said softly. "Did you tell them how

I clutch-hit in the last inning of the last game to beat yours and Laurette's home-run butts the following season?''

''I was about to,'' August said.

Rodgers patted the colonel on the shoulder. ''Let's go,'' he said, edging around him. He winced as the bandages chafed.

With a nod to DeVonne and Grey, Mike Rodgers returned to the hard bench to listen to Brett August talk about a time when Little League was the world and a shot at another season was a damn good reason enough to live.

SIXTY-FIVE

Friday, 8:30 a.m.,
Washington, D.C.

The Homecoming, as Southern-bred Bob Herbert had
dubbed it, was as low-keyed as always.

Whenever Op-Center's officers came back from dangerous or difficult assignments, fellow staffers made sure
that business went on as usual. It was a way of easing
people quickly back into an efficient routine.

The first day back for Paul Hood began with a meeting in Hood's office. While flying in from London, he'd
reviewed material modemed up to him by his assistant
Bugs Benet. Some of it required immediate attention,
and he'd E-mailed Herbert, Martha, Darrell McCaskey,
and Liz Gordon to inform them about the morning meeting. Hood did not believe in easing in and out of jet lag.
He believed in waking up when the alarm went off, local
time, and getting to the business at hand.

Mike Rodgers was the same. Hood had phoned him
at home at 6:30 a.m. to welcome him back, expecting
to find the ringer off and the answering machine on.
Instead, he got the wide-awake general. Hood told him
about the meeting, and Rodgers arrived shortly after

Herbert and McCaskey. There were handshakes, welcome backs, and one "You look like shit" from Herbert to Rodgers. Martha and Liz arrived a minute later. Rodgers took a moment to give terse thanks to Herbert and Martha for their help in getting him his pardon. Sensing his discomfort, Hood got right to the matters at hand.

"First," he said, "Liz—have you had a chance to talk to our local heroes?"

"I spoke with Lowell and Phil last night," she said. "They're taking today off but they're all right. Phil's got a pair of broken ribs, and Lowell's got a bashed-up ego and the 'I'm forty' blues, but they'll survive."

"I was looking forward to ragging on the birthday boy," Herbert said.

"Monday," the thirty-two-year-old Ph.D. replied. "I'm sure the target will be just as sensitive."

"What about Mary Rose?" Hood asked.

"I stopped by to see her last night," the psychologist said. "She's going to need some time off, but she'll be okay."

"The bastards used her pain to try and control us," Rodgers said darkly, "over and over."

"Believe it or not," Liz said, "there can be something positive in what she suffered. People who survive one incident like that tend to attribute it to fate. If they get through two or more, they start thinking that maybe they have some steel in them."

"She does," said Rodgers.

"Exactly. And if we nurture that, she's going to be able to apply it to her daily life."

"I always thought she had butt-kick potential behind those soft Irish eyes," Herbert said.

Hood thanked Liz, then looked at Herbert. "Bob," he said, "I also want to thank you for the support you gave me, Mike, and Striker. If it weren't for the timely arrival of your people over there, myself, Warner Bicking, Dr. Nasr, and Ambassador Haveles would have been coming home in boxes."

"Your Druze soldier was also exceptional," Rodgers said. "Without him, Striker wouldn't have found the ROC in time."

"Those people over there are the best," Herbert said. "I hope you'll remind Congress of that at budget time."

"Senator Fox will get a full and confidential report," Hood said. "I'll keep after her."

"While you're at it," Herbert said, "Stephen Viens is going to need our help. A Special Prosecutor is going to be appointed to look into the NRO's black budget. He feels that he's going to take the brunt of the scapegoating, and I agree. For the record, he and Matt Stoll and their teams worked through the night to get our satellites back on-line."

"I know he's a friend, Bob," Hood said, "and we'll do what we can. Mike, who's overseeing the return of the ROC?"

"I'm going to work with the Tel Nef commander and Colonel August on that," he said. "It's safe at the base right now. As soon as things finish quieting down in the region, the colonel and I will go back and get it."

"Fine," said Hood. "Then if you can spare some time today—you too, Bob—I'd like to sit down and put together a file of the money and lives Viens has saved thanks to his work at the NRO. Maybe we can even pull in the accounting department to satisfy the number-crunchers on the Hill."

Rodgers nodded.

"I'll have our bean-counters start pulling together the figures," Herbert said.

Hood turned to Martha and Darrell McCaskey, who were sitting together on the leather sofa. Darrell was his usual stoic, FBI self, but Martha was shaking a crossed leg impatiently.

"You two," he said, "will not be able to help with any of this. You're going to Spain tomorrow."

Martha perked up.

"Bugs sent me a report on the flight back from London," Hood said. "The police in Madrid have been arresting Basque nationals and picking up hints of something big about to happen. Something with serious international consequences."

McCaskey's expression didn't change, but Martha was beaming. She relished any chance to test her diplomatic skills and flex her international muscles.

"The national security chief over there has asked for diplomatic and intelligence help," Hood went on, "and you're both elected. Bugs and the State Department are putting together materials for you. They'll be ready before you leave."

"And I'll lend you my Berlitz tapes, Darrell," Herbert said.

"We'll be fine," Martha said. "I speak the language."

Hood's eyes were on Herbert, and Herbert must have felt them. He squirmed a little in his wheelchair and said nothing. Bugs had E-mailed him about the tension between the two, and Hood knew he'd have to do something about that while Martha was away. Just what, he didn't know. He had a feeling that preventing a war between Bob Herbert and Martha Mackall was going to prove a whole lot more difficult than averting war between Turkey and Syria.

The meeting was adjourned, and Hood asked Rodgers to stay behind. As Bob Herbert exited and shut the door, Hood came from around his desk. He sat in an armchair across from the general.

"It was pretty rough, wasn't it?" Hood asked.

"You want to know what's funny?" Rodgers asked. "I've been through rougher. It was more than just what happened over there that got to me."

"Care to tell me about it?"

"Yes," said Rodgers, "because it has to do with my resignation."

Hood stared with open surprise as Rodgers pulled a business envelope from inside his jacket. He leaned forward stiffly and placed it on the desk. "I was working on that when you called this morning," he said. "It'll be effective as soon as you find a replacement."

"What makes you think I'll accept it?" Hood asked.

"Because I won't be any good to you here," Rodgers said. "No, scratch that. I just think I'll be more good to the country somewhere else."

"Where?" Hood demanded.

"I don't want to sound apocalyptic, Paul," Rodgers said, "but the Middle East really brought this home for me. Amercia's facing a streetwise and very dangerous enemy."

"Terrorism."

"Terrorism," he said, "and the unpreparedness it preys on. The government is bound by treaties and economical concerns. Groups like Op-Center and the CIA are spread too thin. Airlines and companies doing business abroad and armed forces stationed in foreign nations can also only do so much to protect their people. We need more human intelligence instead of electronic and satellite surveillance, and we need a more effective way of acting on it—preventatively. I spoke with Falah, the Israeli Druze who assisted us in the Bekaa. He was semi-retired from reconnaissance work and didn't realize how much he missed it. He's ready to go back into action. I'll talk to allies in other countries, to some of Bob's contacts. Paul, I believe this more strongly than I've ever believed anything. We need a streetwise and equally dangerous force to fight terrorism.''

Hood looked at him intently. "I'm going to try and talk you out of doing this."

"Don't bother," Rodgers said. "I'm determined."

"I know," Hood said, "and I know how you get. What I mean is, I'm going to try and talk you out of resigning. Why not set up this unit of yours at Op-Center?"

Now it was Rodgers who seemed taken aback. It was several seconds before he could answer. "Paul, do you realize what you're saying? I'm not talking about different uses for Striker. I'm talking about a dedicated unit."

"I understand," Hood said.

"But we could never get that into an amended charter."

"Then we don't."

"How would you get the financing?"

"We can learn from some of the mistakes Stephen Viens made," Hood said. "I'll find a way to finance it through here. Ed Colahan can be trusted with that. Hell, I think he'd enjoy it. The CFO's jealous of all your cloak-and-dagger stuff. We've also learned from our mistakes in Turkey. We can review the data, figure out how to use the ROC more efficiently. Keep it in the field permanently instead of only where it's needed."

"A mobile stealth operation," Rodgers said.

"With stealth warriors," Hood said. "It's got possibilities. And you've got the passion to pull it off."

Rodgers shook his head. "What about the actions themselves? I executed a terrorist in Lebanon. It was *imperium in imperio,* jackboot law. I judged him and I shot him. I'm not going to sit here and tell you for certain that I wouldn't do it again. The lives of innocent Americans come first.''

"I know," Hood replied. "And I won't say that I disagree.''

Rodgers snickered. "Really? That isn't you, Paul. You're not even for the death penalty.''

"You're right, Mike, " Hood said. "But that's the thing you learn about managing a team like ours or a city like Los Angeles or even a family. It isn't about what you're for or against. It's a question of what's best. Mike, you're going to do this anyway. I've already half got a picture in mind of you in desert patriarch robes with a staff in one hand and an Uzi in the other, hunting down terrorists. That wouldn't be the best thing for either of us. I trust you and I want to help you.''

Hood reached over to the desk and removed the envelope. He held it out. Rodgers looked at it, but did not reach for it.

"Take it," Hood said.

Rodgers looked at him. "Are you sure this offer isn't about keeping an eye on me so that I don't go off and become the Moses who smiteth?''

"The way you move around," Hood said, "I couldn't watch you even if I wanted to. Actually, what this is about is how to keep Bob away from Martha. He'd love to work on a project like this.''

Rodgers smiled. "I'll think about it. I've got a lot to think about. A few hours ago I wanted to drop out of this whole damned race. I had people running to my rescue, not letting me get out of the trouble I created or face the music myself.''

"Which is what you've always done," Hood said.

"That's right," Rodgers said. "And proudly so." He fell quiet for a long moment as he sat staring into space. "But then this very old teammate of mine reminded me that even though you run the race alone, it doesn't mean you are alone."

"He was right," Hood said. "Didn't Benjamin Franklin have something to say about that?"

"He told the Continental Congress, 'We must indeed all hang together, or, most assuredly, we shall all hang separately.' "

"Right," Hood said. "Who are you to argue with Benjamin Franklin? Besides, didn't he and John Adams and the Sons of Liberty do something not unlike what we're talking about?" He was still holding out the envelope. "I don't want to pressure you, but my arm's getting tired and I don't want to lose you. What do you say? Do we hang together?"

Rodgers looked at the envelope. With a suddenness which surprised Hood, he snatched it back and put it in his pocket. "All right," Rodgers agreed. "Together."

"Good," Hood said. "Now let's see if we can help find a way to save our friend Viens from the vultures."

Hood called Herbert back in, and they sat down to work with a level of enthusiasm and cooperation he'd never before encountered in his group. Hood was not about to thank the PKK for that. However, as they waited for Chief Financial Officer Ed Colahan to arrive with his data, words from a different time and a different enemy flashed through Hood's mind. They were the words of Japanese Admiral Yamamoto. After having led the attack on Pearl Harbor, an attack which was supposed to crush American resistance in the Pacific, Yamamoto was moved to comment, "I fear all we have done is to awaken a sleeping giant and fill him with a terrible resolve.''

After authorizing Rodgers to discuss his idea with Herbert, Hood could not remember a time when any of them were more awake . . . or more resolved.

Tom Clancy's
Op-Centre

Created by
Tom Clancy and Steve Pieczenik

THE INTERNATIONAL BESTSELLER

Situated in Washington, Op-Centre is a beating heart of defence, intelligence and crisis-management technology, run by a crack team of operatives both within its own walls and out in the field. When a job is too dirty, or too dangerous, it is the only place the US government can turn.

But nothing can prepare Director Paul Hood and his Op-Centre crisis-management team for what they are about to uncover – a very real, very frightening power play that could unleash new players in a new world order . . .

A powerful profile of America's defence, intelligence and crisis-management technology, *Tom Clancy's Op-Centre* is the creation of Tom Clancy and Steve Pieczenik – inspiring this novel, as well as the special NBC Television presentation.

ISBN 0 00 649658 X

Tom Clancy's
Op-Centre

Mirror Image

Created by
Tom Clancy and Steve Pieczenik

THE INTERNATIONAL BESTSELLER

The Cold War is over. And chaos is setting in. The new President of Russia is trying to create a new democratic regime. But there are strong elements within the country that are trying to stop him: the ruthless Russian Mafia, the right-wing nationalists and those nefarious forces that will do whatever it takes to return Russia back to the days of the Czar.

Op-Centre, the newly founded but highly successful crisis management team, begins a race against the clock and against the hardliners. Their task is made even more difficult by the discovery of a Russian counterpart . . . but this one's controlled by those same repressive hardliners.

Two rival Op-Centres, virtual mirror images of each other. But if this mirror cracks, it'll be much more than seven years' bad luck.

A powerful profile of America's defence, intelligence and crisis management technology, Tom Clancy's Op-Centre *is the creation of Tom Clancy and Steve Pieczenik – inspiring this and other gripping novels.*

ISBN 0 00 649659 8

Tom Clancy's
Op-Centre

Games of State

Created by
Tom Clancy and Steve Pieczenik

THE INTERNATIONAL BESTSELLER

In the newly unified Germany, old horrors are reborn. It is the beginning of Chaos Days, a time when neo-Nazi groups gather to spread violence and resurrect dead dreams. But this year Germany isn't the only target. Plans are afoot to destabilize Europe and cause turmoil throughout the United States.

Paul Hood and his team, already in Germany to buy technology for the new Regional Op-Centre, become entangled in the crisis. They uncover a shocking force behind the chaos – a group that uses cutting-edge technology to promote hate and influence world events.

A powerful profile of America's defence, intelligence and crisis management technology, Tom Clancy's Op-Centre *is the creation of Tom Clancy and Steve Pieczenik – inspiring this and other gripping novels.*

ISBN 0 00 649844 2

Tom Clancy's
Op-Centre

Balance of Power

Created by
Tom Clancy and Steve Pieczenik

THE INTERNATIONAL BESTSELLER

Spain is a nation poised to suffer its worst internal strife in a thousand years. Certain well-placed Spanish diplomats sense it. Op-Centre's intelligence corroborates it. All the United States and Spain have to do is find a way to avert it.

Before they can, an Op-Centre representative is assassinated in Madrid on her way to a top-secret diplomatic meeting. Now all fears are confirmed. Someone very powerful wants another Spanish civil war – no matter what the cost.

A powerful profile of America's defence, intelligence and crisis management technology, Tom Clancy's Op-Centre *is the creation of Tom Clancy and Steve Pieczenik – inspiring this and other gripping novels.*

ISBN 0 00 651087 6

Without Remorse
Tom Clancy

THE *SUNDAY TIMES* NO. 1 BESTSELLER

It is 1970. Back in the US after serving as a Navy SEAL in Vietnam, John Kelly meets a woman who will change his life forever. She has recently escaped from a nightmare world of unimaginable suffering, yet before they can plan a future together, the horrors of her past reach out to snatch her from him. Kelly vows to gain revenge – but finds there are others who have need of his deadly skills.

In Washington a high-risk operation is being planned to rescue a key group of prisoners from a POW camp deep within North Vietnam. Kelly has his own mission; the Pentagon want him for theirs. As he attempts to juggle the two, he must step into a netherworld as perilous as any he has ever known – from which he may never return. . .

'Clancy's latest action thriller is certain to join his unbroken string of bestsellers . . . a master storyteller.'

New York Times

'Sure to thrill . . . outstanding suspense. Satisfying, engrossing, chock-full of meticulous knowledge of the military, war heroics and nail-biting action.'   *Boston Herald*

'The reader becomes enthralled . . . politically fascinating. Great fun.'   *Observer*

'Heart-stopping . . . the product of a master.'

Washington Post

ISBN 0 00 647641 4

Executive Orders
Tom Clancy

THE NO 1 BESTSELLING SEQUEL TO
DEBT OF HONOUR

The US President is dead – and the weight of the world falls on Jack Ryan's shoulders, in Clancy's most extraordinary novel.

At the dramatic climax of *Debt of Honour*, a Jumbo Jet crashes into the Capitol Building in Washington, leaving the President dead, along with most of the Cabinet and Congress. Dazed and confused, the man who only minutes before had been confirmed as the new caretaker Vice-President is told that he is now President of the United States: President John Patrick Ryan.

And that is where *Executive Orders* begins – as Ryan's new responsibilities crush in upon him with stunning force. But how do you run a government without a government? Where do you even begin? He knows that the eyes of the world are on him now – and many of them are unfriendly. In Beijing, in Tehran and even in Washington, there are those eager to take advantage. Soon they will begin to make their moves; soon they will present Jack Ryan with a crisis so great even he could not imagine it.

'Clancy is the supreme exponent of the technothriller . . . excellent, unsurpassed . . . another gripping read.'

Sunday Times

HIS NEW *SUNDAY TIMES* NO 1 BESTSELLER
AVAILABLE NOW FROM HARPERCOLLINS

Debt of Honour
Tom Clancy

It begins with the murder of an American woman in the back streets of Tokyo. It ends in war . . . Tom Clancy's record-breaking international #1 bestseller.

Called out of retirement to serve as the new President's National Security Adviser, Jack Ryan quickly realizes that the problems of peace are fully as complex as those of war. Enemies have become friends, friends enemies, and even the form of conflict has changed. When one of those new enemies readies a strike not only at America's territory, but at the heart of her economy, it is Ryan who must somehow prepare an untested President to meet the challenge. For there is a debt of honour to be paid – and the price will be terrifyingly high . . .

'Spectacular, scary and very thrilling. His sense of cliff-hanging is state of the art . . . breathtaking.'
Los Angeles Times

'Tom Clancy's mammoth new thriller is a convoluted cracker.'
Daily Mail

'With the grip of a born storyteller, Clancy casts a potent spell.'
Guardian

'Another blockbuster.'
The Times

ISBN 0 00 647974 X

Clear and Present Danger
Tom Clancy

America's secret war against South American drug cartels spirals out of control, in Tom Clancy's highly acclaimed #1 bestseller – which became a major Hollywood film.

Colombian drug lords, tired of being harassed by US law enforcement agents, have assassinated the American Ambassador and the visiting head of the FBI. Their message is clear: leave us alone.

But they have pushed too far. The decision is made to send undercover teams into Colombia. Back in the USA, men armed with the most sophisticated tools their country can devise prepare to take the fight to the enemy. But does anyone know who the real enemy is?

Jack Ryan and CIA field officer John Clark must find the answer. They expect danger from without – yet the greatest danger of all may come from within . . .

'Clancy's most politically sophisticated and philosophically complex thriller.'   *Time*

'A jump ahead of the headlines . . . moves with the speed of light.'   *New York Times*

'A rousing performance . . . a crackling good yarn.'
Washington Post

'The excitement is tremendous.'   *Sunday Telegraph*

ISBN 0 00 617730 1